THE KNIGHTS OF MELLORA

1

THE KNIGHT OF THE TROVE

HOLLY ROSE

Sign up for Holly Rose's Newsletter
at https://linktr.ee/writerhollyrose

To myself, for never giving up

And to Luke and Jack—never give up on your dreams.
(And I love you always, forever, and no matter what.)

Author's Note

While this fantasy romance novel is meant to be hopeful, steamy, fun, and (hopefully, at times) funny, it does touch on some potentially sensitive themes and topics. If you'd like to know more, you can find a full list at https://linktr.ee/writerhollyrose.

CONTENTS

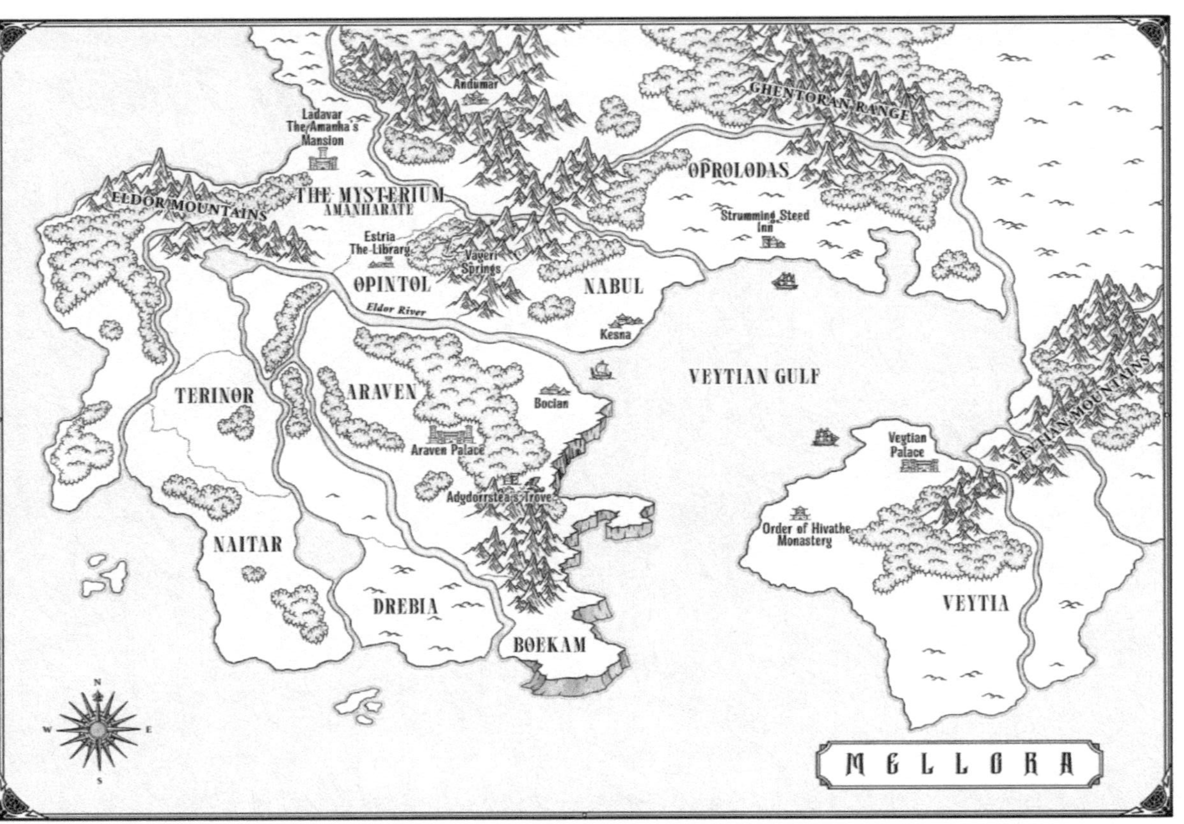

Andumar
Ladavar
The Amanha's Mansion
GHENTORAN RANGE
OPROLODAS
ELDOR MOUNTAINS
THE MYSTERIUM
AMANHARATE
Strumming Steed Inn
Estria
The Library
Vaveri Springs
OPINTOL
NABUL
Eldor River
Kesna
TERINOR
ARAVEN
Bocian
VEYTIAN GULF
Araven Palace
Veytian Palace
Adydorrstea's Trove
VEYTIAN MOUNTAINS
NAITAR
Order of Hivathe Monastery
DREBIA
BOEKAM
VEYTIA
N
W
E
S
MELLORA

CHAPTER ONE

PRINCE FORTH COMES TO CALL

I was sacrificed in the usual way: bound to a pole and left for a dragon I was told would eat me alive. I'll always be grateful that the Dread Dragon Adydorrstea offered me a place in her trove instead of a long, excruciating death. But with every feckless prince and hero who arrived trying to "save" me, I wondered if death would've been a mercy.

"Nesrin! Someone at the gate!" Ady called. Her deep voice pealed through the Great Hall as she flew past the doorway to the treasury, the downdraft from her wings fluttering pages in my record book and littering the worktable with an assortment of her feathers. I climbed the ladder against a sandstone bookcase overflowing with gold coins and knickknacks and tried to ignore the pit in my stomach that churned each time we had a *guest*.

The top shelf was a jumble of armor, crowns, and baubles. A crude wooden box under a bronze shield looked as good as any other place to start. I pulled it out, blew the top layer of dust off, and popped it open: dozens of rings. Hooking my arm on the ladder, I tucked the box close to my breast and dragged my fingers through the top layer. Dust motes swarmed in the light streaming through the stained-glass window overhead. Most of the rings were golden and gaudy, encrusted with precious gems and centuries of neglect.

Nes-reeen! Ady called out to me mind to mind, drawing out the last syllable of my name. *We're waiting!*

Can't you deal with him this time? I answered, taking advantage of her dragonian telepathy to steal a few more minutes at my task. I slipped a dragon-shaped ring onto my finger and rubbed off the dust with my thumb. Its miniature golden scales shimmered, undulating around the shank. Maybe Veytian, from the style of it.

Ady's voice popped into my head. *No. It's your job now: I'm the welcomer, you're the defeater.*

Fine, I huffed. I climbed down and tossed the box on my worktable, the rings popping out and *tinking* as they scattered. My leather boots clomped a quick pattern on the stone floor of the treasury and echoed among the columns of the Great Hall as I jogged toward the armory. Once there, I strapped on basic armor, tightened my bandolier, and grabbed my sword. By the time I got to the stables, Ady's magic had my dappled mare tacked, a lance attached to her saddle.

I urged Pistachio gently out of the stables, creeping her one hoof at a time beneath the low canopy as a brisk autumn breeze stirred a mini whirlwind of red and gold leafmeal on the forest floor.

"How dare you disturb the Dread Dragon Adydorrstea?" Ady's professional, man-eating dragon voice resonated through the forest, deep as bronze windchimes.

Stop riling him up! I grouched. As I came around the base of the steep monolith to approach him from behind, the prince's baritone voice carried through the forest.

"I'm Prince Forth of Oprolodas, and I'm here to rescue the fair maiden, Nesrin of Araven!"

He already sounded like a prick—young and privileged, as if he'd come of age, was gifted a fine horse from King Daddy, and immediately set off to abduct me. I peered up through a hole in the pied canopy. Ady held court on the open landing balcony chiseled high into the nearly vertical front face of her mountain, massive, feathered wings tucked in and front legs resting on a balustrade twice my height. She was swift and fiery death on black feathered wings, and she was flickering out a quiet laugh at my expense.

Her voice in my head shimmered with loving mockery. *Should I tell him you're neither fair nor a maiden?*

I approached the line of poplar trees encircling the glade before Ady's front gate. *Since you can't see me, shall I describe the ugly face and hand gesture I'm making at you? You overgrown lizard bird.*

Her appreciative laugh echoed in my head like a pattering of muted bells as she turned her attention back to the imbecile on the muddy clearing. "Welcome to your doom, Prince Fifth!"

"It's Prince *Forth*," he asserted.

"That's what I *said*," Ady replied, setting a small, already-charred tree ablaze with her sibilance. Her intonation was not unlike that of an heiress with sophisticated manners and a questionable past.

I smirked and peered through the trees, close enough to see but not be seen by Prince What's-His-Name to get a read on him before I engaged. He sat tall and dressed in full metal armor atop the requisite majestic black stallion, which was large enough to bear his weight another time over.

"No, you didn't," he argued back.

Actually, that *was* a nice horse. He tossed his mane, and the feathering around his feet fluttered as he stepped high and proud around the clearing.

"Doom awaits you, Prince Third! You have to fight to bring Princess Nesrin away with you."

The prince whipped his horse, coercing it closer to the cave, and my nostrils flared. That stallion was definitely going to be mine.

"I'm ready," he called up to Ady, unsheathing his sword. "Come down and fight me!"

Ady glanced behind herself as if she wasn't sure to whom he was speaking. "Me?" She raised an obsidian talon to her feathered breast. "Oh dear. You thought you had to fight *me*?" She tutted. "You've been misinformed. How embarrassing for you." Her eyes flickered to where I emerged on the ground, twenty feet behind the armored git.

I nodded to her once. I was in position and ready.

"You see, Prince Second, the princess may occasionally take a lover, but she doesn't wish to leave. To make her leave, you'll have to fight her yourself." Ady tilted her slender head toward me, her black and burgundy head feathers dancing around two gently curved horns. The prince turned quickly, startling at the sight of me.

"Princess Nesrin?"

I wiggled my fingers at him in a bored wave. His head bobbled down then up, no doubt taking in the horse clad in armor and the lance captained by a very unprincess-y woman dressed in fighting leathers instead of a flowing gown.

"Can we get this over with?" I tossed my long braid behind my back. "I'm very busy."

As much as I resented this intrusion into my carefully scheduled day cataloging the treasury, I had to admit this was my favorite part. Every man had the same reaction. I didn't have to see this one's face to know what passed across it: confusion, disbelief, then irritation. Hopefully this one wouldn't balk at having to fight a woman.

Prince Forth's eyes darted between Ady and me. "Surely you don't expect me to fight the princess?"

I grimaced. "Look out, Forth!" Urging Pistachio into a trot, I steadied the lance for impact.

Ady's disappointed voice echoed low into the clearing. "Oh, she's got the *lance*."

Pistachio and I bore down on the prince, and he wheeled his horse around. Despite my perfectly-poised lance, he drove the stallion forward and skillfully turned away at the last minute, rushing past me in the opposite direction.

Damn. This one was significantly better than the last one I'd used the lance on. I reset the weapon into its vertical position and wheeled Pistachio around.

"Are you really trying to kill me?" he shouted from across the clearing.

"Ha!" I barked out an unladylike laugh. "It's a jousting lance, metal-for-brains. If I wanted to kill you, I'd have brought the real one."

He brandished his sword, leaning low and spurring his horse into a gallop toward me. What did he expect to do against a lance? He tried pulling his horse aside again, but my blunted lance slammed into his chest, knocking him backwards off the stallion. He clanged to the ground into a bright pile of fallen leaves, and I circled Pistachio around to enjoy the results. The mouth of his visor was twisted open in a lopsided smile, his metal chest dented with the impression of my lance. He rolled almost to his side, but fell back down, unmoving. I was just about to feel bad for him when he got to his feet.

"What's wrong with you?" He pulled off his dented helmet and tossed it aside.

I cocked my head, appraising. This one was rather good-looking—tall, muscular, kind of dashing. His thick dirty blond hair was a curly, sweaty mess, but he had suntanned, chiseled features under an attractive beard, and his blue eyes were—oh dear. Flashing in outrage. Maybe another tactic would work better.

"I don't want to go with you," I said, "and I don't want to hurt you. But this is my home. Tell your comrades: you all need to stop coming here."

Forth stood and picked up his sword from the ground. "You must be under some sort of fey dragon spell." He held his head at an odd angle, his eyes roving all around me as if trying to see the aura of an enchantment. Which wasn't even possible. "I won't give up!"

To his credit, he was brave, running full at me with a battle cry. But I urged Pistachio straight at him, daring him to back down or be trampled.

At the last possible moment, he yelled "Bloody hell!" and threw himself aside into a low part of the clearing that had taken on rainwater, landing with a clanking splash that sent mud spraying all over him and his horse. He righted himself, pulled off both gauntlets with jerky movements, and threw them hard across the clearing in my general direction. He stood and wiped the mud from his tightly trimmed beard, eyes flashing. A vein bulged on his forehead, and his fists clenched at his sides.

I hated when they stayed to fight instead of just leaving. More than that, I missed the good ol' days when Ady used to fight them off for me. She was up there tossing apples into her mouth like a human would eat popped corn, her eyes tracking the fight. She gave me an enthusiastic talon's up.

"Please." I reset the lance to its upright position. "Just go away. Thank you for trying, thank you for your *concern*, but I don't want to be rescued. Today or any other day."

"What have you done to her?" he shouted, looking up at Ady then back to me.

"Oh, for gods' sake." I dismounted and advanced on him with a sword, planning to drive him farther back down the path from whence he came. I punctuated my words with the clanging of my weapon against his. "Go! The! Hell! Away!"

But he was in his element on the ground. Instead of me backing him down the path, he backed me toward the sheer side of Ady's monolith. I parried blow after blow, but he kept coming, his sword meeting mine at every turn. I was strong, but he was taller and stronger. He backed me up against the mountain, our swords straining together.

His eyes were bright and intense, and his strength was crushing me. I pushed harder, determined not to break, but I was folding.

Unless.

I blinked and shook my head, breaking eye contact and letting up *just a little* on my sword. I looked at him and around the clearing, as if seeing it all for the first time. "What's happening? Who are you? Please don't hurt me!"

His face changed from fury to concern, and he loosened his pressed sword.

Ignoring Ady's snorting laughter in my head, I let him take my weapon. I cowered away from him with my back against the rock. "Please sir, don't hurt me!"

"I won't, Princess! I won't." He threw our swords aside and held his palms out, backing away from me a little. "See? No weapons. You're safe now."

He glanced up at Ady, and I chambered my thigh, delivering a front kick to his face just as he turned back to me. His head spun sideways, and he wobbled off balance as I followed up with a rear-legged kick. He dropped to the ground. I raced to Pistachio, grabbing my secret weapon from a scabbard on her side: Steelbane the Sword Slayer—Baney for short. Forged in dragon fire, Baney lived to break lesser swords.

I whirled around to see him recovered, holding both our swords and advancing on me.

His face was red and twisted. "That was a dirty trick! I came here to help you."

But that was a lie. No one ever came to help me. I learned that lesson at a very young age.

"No, you didn't," I spat at him. "You came here to kill my friend and take me against my will. You'll get what you get!"

I advanced, a battle cry erupting from my lungs. My first hard strike broke his sword off at the hilt. He cursed and flung it away, drawing my sword up to fight with wide eyes.

I pulled Baney back but hesitated. "You're going to make me break my own sword?"

"I didn't come here wanting to kill anyone!" he shouted back. "I thought you were in danger!"

That only pissed me off more. Where were his people when I was *actually* vulnerable and alone, when I was held against my will in my own home? No-fucking-where.

I growled and struck with enough force that Baney broke my sword he carried off at the hilt. I'd liked that one, too. He threw himself sideways, slipping in a patch of mud and falling to his back, floundering. His eyes were wide, and he held one hand up in supplication. Baney had that effect on people.

"I yield!" Forth struggled to his feet and held his mud-streaked palms toward me. "I'll leave you alone. Stormbreaker." He stretched one hand toward his stallion.

"Stormbreaker's mine now." I shrugged. "Spoils of battle and all."

"But it's," he huffed, "a very long way back to Oprolodas."

"You should've thought about that before you came to abduct me. Now go before I change my mind and slice off your head." I whirled Baney around in a flourish for emphasis, its notches catching the sunlight.

His face blanched, and he glanced up at Ady. She drew a talon across her neck and waggled her feathery eyebrows at him. "Oh, no, Nesrin," she deadpanned, just loud enough for us to hear. "Don't do *that* again."

"I'll go." He stepped toward his horse then stopped to look at me. "At least let me get my things."

I nodded once, slowly, like a queen granting a boon.

He bowed then unfastened three saddle bags, arranging them on his shoulders. A couple of times, he took a quick breath and looked at me, as if he had something to say. But both times he closed his mouth and returned his attention to his bags.

Most men took their defeat and left without a fuss. It'd been a long time since I'd cared about what people from the outside world could tell me or thought of me. But for some reason, whatever this was bothered me.

"It's a shame you're so eager to get rid of me." He shouldered his last bag. "We would've made a hell of a team on the battlefield." He pressed his nose and forehead to Stormbreaker's long nose, patting his cheek.

"What battlefield?" I demanded, trying to ignore his kindness to the horse and maintain my anger. But a cold wind snuck down the back of my tunic and chilled a dripping bead of sweat, sending shivers across my skin.

He pulled away and met my eyes, his face softening. "Oprolodas and other nations are joining forces. We're marching against Galter Velius."

I recoiled. That name was a punch in the gut. Frowning more deeply at him, anything I could have said died on my lips.

He shifted his burdens and spoke gently. "I thought you'd want to know." He bowed to both of us. "Dread Dragon, my lady, I'll spread the word that you're happy here and not in need of rescue." He gave me a pained look—was that *pity?* Then Prince Forth of Oprolodas turned toward the forest and walked away.

Dropped that on me and walked casually away, the back of his armor glinting in the nearly-setting sun. An old anger edged with panic rose in my gut. I ceased to see the golden trees, Forth's retreating back. Instead, I saw my uncle's army breaking like a wave against the palace. Saw my eldest brother, Talon, through the iron bars of a dungeon cell, bruised and bloodied on the filthy floor, barely clinging to life. Galter stood beside me. His cruel hand, fresh with my brother's blood, gripped my arm like a vice. *That's what'll happen to you if you don't comply.*

Nesrin. Ady's voice called me back, and the spell of his words broke. A cold breeze careered through the clearing, chilling my sweaty skin and the tears tracking down my face.

I whistled to Pistachio and collected Stormbreaker's reins. I patted the stallion's nose, thinking of how Prince Forth had put his head against him and trying not to feel like an asshole for taking the man's horse.

"C'mon Stormbreaker. You don't have to live with that mean ol' man anymore. Let's find you some fresh apples, hmmm?"

After I'd settled the horses in the stables and put my weapons and armor away, I found Ady sitting in the dragon-sized settee in the treasury. Her tail was curled around its carved feet, and she was painting her talons by the cheerful fire roaring in the hearth.

Her black eyes assessed me from beneath raised eyebrows, a black talon half-painted blood red poised in front of her. "You're no fun anymore," she said, gesticulating with the foreclaw that held her nail brush. "When I first brought you here, I used to at least entertain you when I defeated your suitors. I passed that torch to you because you're capable of defending yourself now, but would it kill you to learn a little showmanship?"

I flapped the hem of my tunic to cool off from the exertion of the fight, but little air reached up into my corset. "I don't enjoy it anymore."

Ady raised her eyebrows and resumed her manicure.

"I've got so much to do in here, not to mention in the library, that I don't feel like kicking the ass of every arrogant prince who comes along to 'save me.' It's getting old, that's all." I poured a goblet of water from the cold pitcher on the sideboard.

Ady glanced at me sidelong, blowing a warm draft of air onto finished nails. "You know, Nes," she said softly. "That one was very handsome. Brave, too. You could've brought him in to play or to see if you were a good match. You've certainly had worse options, and you've been here nearly eight years. All my knights eventually move on, and you're already in the middle of your twenties."

"I've told you." I picked up an apple and tossed it in the air to catch again. "You're not getting rid of me as easily." I scooped up my goblet and crunched the apple at her for emphasis. "I'm staying," I mumbled.

"They're marching on Galter."

"Anh!" I pointed a sharp finger at her, and she rolled her eyes above an unnecessarily condescending smile. I glowered at her a beat longer, then went back to sorting the rings on my worktable, trying to ignore her and not think about the outside world.

The calming flow of cataloging them in my record book had just barely consumed me when Ady let out a soft *oh!* She reached behind her, pulled forth a burlap bag the size of a thirty-pound sack of potatoes, and dropped it in the middle of my work with a clanking thud. The rings scattered in every direction.

I jumped back from the table. "Ady, why?"

She only shrugged. "I found more treasure for you to catalog. I must've forgotten it in my bathing chamber when I came back from the last hunt."

"What is all this?" I loosened the drawstring on the bag.

She avoided my eyes, casting her regal gaze around the treasury walls. "Just some things I picked up. You know how it is."

"Picked up?" I peered into the bag. Seals from at least three different royal houses on more ridiculous gold ornaments. I snapped the drawstring shut, shaking my head. "You know what? I don't even want to know. Can you at least move it over there?" I gestured to the corner of the room I'd managed to clear just yesterday.

Ady shrugged again, her feathers nodding with the gesture, and scooped the bag up with one talon. She dropped it with a clang in the corner, and a golden circle crown came rolling out on its side, emitting a tiny, metallic drumroll as it went across the tiles, out the doorway, and into the Great Hall.

I stared into her glittering black eyes as I listened to it roll...and roll...and roll. It hit a column and spun out quickly, then slower and slower like a coin coming to rest.

Ady smiled, showing all her sharp teeth. "Good afternoon, Nesrin. I'm turning in early to pamper myself with a luxurious bath. May you have happy dreams tonight of counting rings and making small marks in little bound books." She stood and sauntered out of the room.

How she lived with herself in this quixotic state of chaos before I came here was beyond me. I scooped up all the stray rings I could find on the floor and dropped them on a pile on the table, clapping the dust off of my hands. Leaning my hands against my worktable, I surveyed the wreckage of my neat piles. My stomach growled, deciding for me to break for supper now that most of my work was ruined.

Forth's words pushed themselves back into my notice as I walked among the columns toward the dining hall. When Ady first brought me here, I was a child with nothing to offer against my uncle and no will to try. But I was all grown up, and so much stronger. Ady had brought in masterful trainers over the years to teach me how to fight, just as my older brothers had been trained when I was little.

Last I'd heard, Talon and Pendor were just across the gulf in Veytia, but that was three years ago. They had to be involved in the plans against Galter. If Talon was leading this attack to take his rightful place on the throne of Araven, he was long overdue.

My foot kicked against the crown that had rolled out of Ady's treasure bag. It twinkled and skittered away from me, stopping small and still at the base of a massive column. I could pick it up, but no. I was still too aggravated with her. That crown could rot where it lay.

The moment my boot touched the gleaming white tile of the dining hall floor, our front bell clanged again, and Ady's call for me echoed through the columns and sang in my head.

"*Nes-reeen!* There's another contender at the gate. Twice in one day! How exciting. Bring the mace this time, will you?"

CHAPTER TWO

THE BOOKISH PRINCE

Within minutes, I stood with my arms crossed before the weapons rack, glaring at all my choices. My stomach growled, louder this time, and I pulled a sword down hard from the wall.

Does this one have a horse?

Let me peek...no horse. In fact, no armor. Holy Hivathe, he's only got a mule and two large sacks full of books. I don't know, Nes, maybe he plans to throw them at me?

I chuckled despite my irritation, grabbing my sword belt and strapping a bandolier stocked with throwing knives across my chest. If this one was unprepared, that was on him.

I went on foot, creeping to my usual spot under the darkening twilight shadows. No wonder Ady was confused. From behind, this man had an unusual presentation, to put it mildly. The deep brown monk's cloak he wore over tan linen robes covered him from head to toe. He'd light up like a bonfire at the first stream of dragon fire. No armor or weapons, at least none I could see from behind. All he held were the reins of what had to be the oldest mule alive.

"Who dares disturb the Dread Dragon Adydorrstea?" Ady hissed, staring down at the man through haughty dragon eyes.

"Hello...good evening, Lady Adydorrstea." His clear, deep voice lilted with a Veytian accent and only trembled a little as he bowed to her. "My name is Kasper. May I trouble you for a moment of your time?"

This was a new...tactic? *No armor under the robes?* I squinted my eyes in the diminishing light.

"You're a pathetic claimant to battle for the hand of Princess Nesrin of Araven," Ady assessed aloud. "No armor, no weapons, from the look of it." She placed a delicate, blood-red talon beneath her long, pointed chin and leaned farther out, peering intently at him.

"No, no, I'm not—" He dropped to one knee, shaking his head vehemently and putting his hands up, empty palms forward. "That's not why I'm here. I'm a monk. A vestal monk. And I only want to talk to you and your knight. Please," he added, as if aware that politeness went a long way when facing a top-tier predator who held manners in high regard.

Ady cocked her head and dropped her act. "I'm sorry. What did you say?" A beat of silence in which one feathery eyebrow rose.

"I was hoping you'd speak to me about—"

"Young man," Ady laughed, black smoke puffing from her nostrils. "I haven't had a human on my doorstep with the audacity to ask to *speak* to me and my knight in over three hundred years. Who do you think you are?"

He stayed on his knee, removing his cowl to reveal a dark, moppy head of loose curls.

Mmm, mmm, Ady said to me appreciatively. *What a good-looking human to waste in a vow of chastity.*

I closed my eyes and shook my head in irritation. *Not. Interested.*

He took a deep breath. "Pardon my poor manners. I'm Kasper, from the Order of Hivathe. In Veytia. My father, Velarch Oh, sent me to find an artifact, or information about it."

"So, you didn't come to kill me and take the princess as your reward?" Ady's ascertaining tone was edged with a note of disappointment.

"No," he said, as if the idea horrified him. "I would never."

That's refreshing! I spoke to Ady, my voice dripping with sarcasm. *Shall I run him off, or would you like to invite him in for tea?*

I cracked my neck and unsheathed Baney. Interacting with one prince today was more than enough for me, but this one ought to scare off easily.

But Ady sat staring at the man, rings of smoke drifting from her delicate nostrils, each one roughly the size of my head.

"Why don't you come in for tea?" She grinned, showing all her teeth.

My mouth dropped open. *Ady! I know dragons get sarcasm.*

She ignored me. "You're not a thief, are you, little man?"

"No Lady Adydorrstea," he said, putting his palms up again. "Even if I were the sort of man who'd steal, and I'm not, I'd be far too afraid to steal from you."

Stroking her ego with her dread magnificence. He was clever, this one.

"Very well. If you're lying, my knight will slice you limb from limb. She'll see you in."

To me, she snickered, *If nothing else, you might enjoy teaching this one to forsake his vows.* She turned and went in.

Shut up, Ady. I sheathed Baney and walked up behind him. "Kasper, is it?"

He swung around at my voice, catching his feet in his cloak as he tried to stand and falling on his hands and knees. He laughed at himself and dusted off his hands, bringing up one leg to rest his forearms on. Definitely not the bearing of a warrior, and I couldn't see any weapons.

Damn. Ady wasn't wrong, though. Kasper was far more handsome than even Prince Forth. He was quintessentially Veytian: golden tan skin and almost-black hair. But his eyes were a surprise. They shone like bright blue lamps in the relative darkness of his face, studying me without guile.

"Blessings of Hivathe to you, Knight of the Trove," he said quietly. Like he meant it.

My eyes stayed on his as he stood and studied me with polite interest. Tall and broad-shouldered, Kasper carried himself with a slight hunch as if apologizing for being built like a prince when he should've been built like a monk. His warm, unrestrained smile crinkled his light, curious eyes and lit his whole face with charm. He bowed, his loose dark curls falling forward, then stood again.

I shook back the wisps of hair around my face, studying his bearing, his mule, and his bags. "You promise you're not trying to win my hand in marriage by destroying my guardian?"

His smile dropped as he laid a hand over his heart. "I give you my word as a disciple of Hivathe." He reached his other hand out as if he wanted a handshake.

I shifted back, looking down at his outstretched hand. I hadn't seen this gesture of honesty and agreement offered from a man to a woman since my childhood. Since before my father died and everything went to shit.

I slowly reached for his hand and shook it, granting him a small, begrudging smile. As Ady's knight, part of my responsibility was to play hostess. Thank Hivathe it wasn't a role I played often, in fact, hardly ever. But if I had to, this monk was the best sort of guest to have: polite, respectful, and not interested in killing Ady or abducting me. I really couldn't ask for more.

"Follow me. Your beast is welcome too."

"Thank you. Narmer's an elderly gentleman." He picked up the two large canvas satchels of books from the ground and hefted them both onto his right shoulder. "I'm sure he'll be glad to rest. I've been worried about him." Gathering Narmer's reins, he clicked his tongue to him and followed me, favoring his left leg and limping a little as he walked.

I dragged my eyes from his leg to Narmer. "Is he ill?"

"I don't think so." He smiled weakly. "He just didn't like traveling by boat. Well, he doesn't like traveling over land much better."

Despite whatever injury or weakness Kasper had in his leg, Narmer was only loaded with a couple of small saddle bags, presumably with food and necessities. At least this one was kind to his beast.

"Give me these." I pried both book sacks from Kasper's shoulder.

"Thank you! That's very kind." The moment he was freed of his own burdens, Kasper took Narmer's bags from him. I turned away so he wouldn't see my smile.

The firelit stables were a welcome contrast to the cold, gathering dark in the forest. A bucket and brushes appeared out of nowhere and waited in the air, poised to take care of Narmer. Kasper gawked.

"Ady's magic automates the household, even when she's not here, so we don't need grooms or servants. Narmer's in good hands."

He shook the wonder from his eyes and set one bag down before running a hand lovingly along the mule's neck. "Thank you, Narmer. Fill your belly and get some rest. You deserve it." He pulled a small, waxed fabric packet from one of his bags, sprinkled a few dried dates into his palm, and held them to Narmer's mouth. The mule's nostrils widened, snuffling around Kasper's hand until he found the treats.

Kasper's face lit up. "Good boy." He petted Narmer's mane with delight and was met with breathy braying. "Who's the best mule in all of Mellora? You are."

Hiding a bigger smile, I walked toward the wide, winding stairs that led to the Great Hall. "Give him a share of the best grains—or whatever mules eat," I said out loud to the stable, turning back to look at Kasper.

He scratched Narmer behind his ears one last time, then followed me toward the stairs, limping all the way.

I glanced back at him a couple of times on the way up. He looked all around as he followed, tipping his head back and around, eyes wide and mouth slightly open. It's probably what I looked like when I first saw the trove. The stair walls and risers, much like nearly every available bit of wall and floor in the trove, were tiled in intricate, lively mandala and flower designs. Once he reached out to a wall, running his fingers down the smooth yellow glaze of a lotus blossom.

As we stepped from the stairwell into the Great Hall, Kasper gasped softly. The sun's last light flooded through stained glass windows that spanned the whole wall, lighting up the glossy black floor tiles with rainbows. The forest of sandstone columns, tall and wide as giant redpines, were widely spaced to accommodate Ady's wingspan. Capped in blossoming lotus capitals, they supported a variegated field of domes undulating in a stylized pattern of roses and inverted tulips.

The Great Hall's quiet cool, imbued with a faint, holy blend of incense, always made my heart feel closer to the gods and often lulled me into a meditative state of blissful belonging. It was a refuge I'd desperately needed when I left Galter's palace. Ady's trove was, to me, the grandest, most beautiful place in the world, and I would never, ever leave it.

"Beautiful," Kasper said in a reverent whisper. He stepped slowly toward one of the massive columns and dragged his middle three fingers through the valley of a swirling ridge of sandstone. "This is the most..." He faltered for a word. "The most *transcendent* dragon trove I've ever seen."

"How many troves have you seen?"

"Only two others. They were beautiful too, in their own ways. But *this* one..." He turned in a slow half-circle, his head turning to accommodate his wide eyes. "I'm at a loss for words."

I told you that you were lucky I took you in, Ady purred, watching from the dining hall we were approaching. *The trove reflects the refinement of the dragon, and mine is as flawless as twenty-four karat gold.*

I paused to drop Kasper's book sacks near the entrance of the dining hall. I'd been cross with her today, but every day I thanked Hivathe that Ady took me in. It was no exaggeration to say that she'd saved my life.

Ady blew a sleek stream of fire, igniting the fireplace with black flames that popped and crackled with burgundy sparks. As I sat in my accustomed seat at the table, our supper appeared, and Pooka arrived from out of nowhere attracted by the intoxicating smell of pork. He meowed loudly at Kasper, his tiny pink nostrils flaring as he sniffed him and rubbed against his legs.

Kasper's face was a study in delighted surprise. "*Meow* to you too, sir." He set down his bags by the others and stooped, scratching Pooka's cheeks and setting off the loud "give me food and love" purr.

"Good mercy, Pooka," I said. "You're not getting any scraps from him either. Have a seat, Kasper." I gestured to the only other human seat. Pooka rubbed his nose a few more times against the monk's hand, then sauntered off to his own bowls.

If he thought it strange that a fifteen-foot dragon sat like a giant cat beside the gadrooned mahogany table, Kasper had no outward tell as he sat. He was far more polished than I was when I met Ady at the tender age of sixteen—I'd screamed so long and loud I lost my voice for three days.

"Help yourself." I poured my tea and replaced the porcelain teapot onto its warmer. Maybe the only two things Ady's magic didn't do was plate our food and catalog her treasury. She relished judging guests' reactions to not being served, and regarding the treasury, she explained that her magic, as an extension of her, lacked the depth of emotion and sympathetic understanding that, she conceded, might be the only qualities in which humans were superior to dragons.

"Thank you for your hospitality." Kasper closed his eyes and bowed his head for a short moment, apparently in prayer, then helped himself to a plate full of food. He filled his cup with tea, five sugar cubes, and a shot of cream. "Cream?" He poised the porcelain creamer in my direction, as if he would actually pour it for me.

"No, thank you." I exchanged a pleased glance with Ady. "And don't let Pooka coerce you into giving him any, either. It's not good for him."

Ady hooked a talon into the handle of her bowl-sized teacup and brought it to her mouth, lapping her tongue into the vessel with the royal mien of a cat who'd already caught all the mice. "Kasper of Veytia, hmmm? How does a prince end up in a monastery?" The tone of a queen who already knew the answer but was testing him out for the truth.

He finished his sip of tea before answering. "Tradition. The fourth son of the royal house is always promised to the Order of Hivathe Monastery. They sent me when I was young."

"When you were *young*?" Ady chuckled. "Of course, all humans seem like drakelings to me. But even by human standards, you must be young. Certainly no more than Nesrin's age."

He nodded. "I'll be twenty-five this winter. I've lived and studied at the order since I was eleven."

I stole far too many glances at him, looking for the evil in his fair form. I'd never met a man without a selfish agenda, and that especially included holy men. Hivathe was the mother of all, the goddess of wisdom and especially love. The fierce protector of anyone being mistreated. But there were evil men in other nations who perverted what she stood for, called her a bloody goddess of war and used lies about her to further their own gains.

What did Kasper's order worship, the truth or the lie?

"Tell me, Kasper, what did you want to talk about?" Ady's feathered eyebrows rose.

His smile faltered, and his eyes grew darker as he looked between us.

Now we come to it, I said to Ady, raising my eyebrows briefly in an I-told-you-so look. *He's up to no good.*

"I'm sure you've heard," he began, his bright eyes fixing on me, "that the allied gulf nations will be marching soon to stop the Emperor of Araven."

My fork and stomach dropped, and adrenaline shot through my body. I glared at Ady and shoved my hands to my lap. *This again?* She and Kasper were quiet, watching me. Not content to simply steal my brother's rightful title of king, Galter now styled himself an emperor?

Fine. We'd have this discussion. "Who all stands against him?" I asked quietly.

Kasper clasped his hands on his lap and spoke gently. "Veytia, Opintol, Nabul, the Mysterium Amanharate, Oprolodas, and Panir. Boekam too, of course. Talon and Pendor are sponsored by Boekam."

I hadn't heard my brothers' names spoken aloud since I was thirteen, that night my mother and I huddled together in a dungeon cell, right before—gods, right before Galter killed her in front of me because someone loyal to our family tried to help us escape.

And after she was gone, no one came for me. No humans, anyway.

I bit the inside of my mouth, trying to stop my eyes from filling with tears. "Your quest better be *gravely* important to bring my brothers' names to me."

Kasper bowed his head, his own eyes glassy when I dared to meet them. "I'm truly sorry, Princess Nesrin. I can't imagine how painful this must be to hear, but I promise I wouldn't be here if we weren't so desperate. So, before you throw me out, please hear me out.

"Two weeks ago, while I was visiting my father, one of his spies returned. She said Galter knows war is coming for him, and someone put into his head that there's a magical artifact that can make his armies stronger. I've researched the artifact, and I'm afraid that it's very real."

Ady's ears perked up. "*What artifact?*" she asked, enunciating each syllable.

"Both legends and histories talk about caskets"—Ady hissed at the word, and Kasper quailed a little—"containing powerful curses or blessings. Galter—"

"Do we have to say his name so many times?" A poisonous knot had already formed in my chest. As if he could sense my hurt, Pooka jumped into my lap, paws over my heart, rubbing his wet nose persistently against my nose and purring loudly. I rewarded him with scratches and head kisses, and he settled down on my lap like a freshly baked loaf of purring bread.

Kas bit his lip, then softly went on. "He's looking for one of them."

"I've never heard of any caskets, and I've been studying treasures and artifacts for eight years."

Ady said nothing, only closed her eyes.

Kasper continued. "I couldn't find many references to them in my research. Few historians wrote about them, and those that did wrote so little. Like they were whispering in the ink. No one explains what's actually *inside* them."

"*Which casket?*" Ady hissed.

I startled, her vehemence stealing my attention from my own anxiety.

"I painted what the spy described to me and embellished it with what I could find in books." Kasper reached into a pocket of his cloak and pulled out a small leather-bound journal. He unwrapped its cords and flipped through smooth reed paper pages covered in the calligraphic pictographs of his homeland, laying the book on the table and pressing the pages open to a fine painting of a golden box.

Ady leaned forward, peered intently at the drawing, then leaned back again, lapping her tea and gazing at the fireplace. Dark smoke curled from her nostrils.

I pulled the book to me. The painting itself was magical, the casket's details finely wrought by a steady hand. A lion's head was etched on the lid, and crossed arrows and shields on all sides pointed to an ornate lock on the front. Beside it was painted a golden, arrow-shaped key formed with molded curlicues on its fletching in place of feathers.

Kasper leaned forward and pointed a long finger to the book. "The spy said his attention is split right now, looking for the box and its key, that they were hidden apart to prevent the casket from being opened." He frowned, shaking his head. "I'm not convinced it even has a key. There were no references to it in any of the historical records I found in Veytia. But I barely know anything about them. Not who made them, nor when they were made." Kasper fell back in his seat, looking deflated.

"They were wrought by dragons," Ady said, a smug turn to her voice as if surely everyone should know this. "Forged in dragon fire when the age of men was in its infancy." She stopped talking as if that was the end of that.

I ran my finger along the smooth fibers of the page and read the Veytian pictographs with only a little difficulty from disuse of the skill: *The golden casket. One hand high, two hands long, one hand deep. Heavier than natural for the reputed materials.* Veytian was my favorite of the regional languages I'd learned as a child. To me, the pictographs told richer stories than languages written in simple letters.

And this particular story filled me with dread. "And he wants this to make his army stronger?"

Kasper nodded. "Supposedly, what's inside is so powerful it can guarantee an army victory over any enemy."

Panic twisted in my chest at the thought of Galter with that power.

Kasper's bright eyes darted between me and Ady as he leaned forward again. "If this item's in your trove, my father authorized me to bargain for it, or at least beg for your assistance in keeping it away from Galter."

I'd never seen anything like this in the treasury or the library, but it seemed best to let Ady respond about the contents of her own trove. But her eyes were glazed over, still trained on the fire as if it helped her see back over the millennia.

Are you just not interested, I asked, *or do you know more than you're letting on?*

"Caskets don't have keys," she said aloud, leaving my questions echoing unanswered in my head. "That's an old rumor meant to deter anyone seeking them. Galter's a ridiculous old fool with bad information, praise Hivathe. Your lovely drawing is a threat to no one."

I scoffed at the back of my throat. "But how can you be sure?" I'd gleaned long ago that dragons considered themselves part of an ancient aristocracy, superior to creatures of all kinds—humans, manticores, griffons, even undines, if they still existed somewhere in the deep waters of Mellora—and usually treated us like children who shouldn't worry their pretty heads over matters of any import.

It irritated the piss out of me, but still she said nothing.

"How many caskets are there?" Kasper rubbed his beard as he leaned forward, his eyes curious, his deep voice and masculine energy at the table unfamiliar. Gentle, but strong and steady.

Ady continued to ignore him, but he wouldn't let up. "I'm not trying to argue with you at your own table, but I assure you Galter's taking this very seriously. I think we should too."

He went silent, apparently waiting for her reply, and I studied the slight furrow of his brow, the only betrayal of emotion on his otherwise neutral face. Ady leveled appraising black eyes on him, but—credit where credit is due—he didn't flinch or look away.

"This I will say," she finally conceded. "Caskets of any kind should *not* be meddled with. They are best left to rot in whatever secret places they may still curse with their existence. I would advise against anyone trying to seek them."

He blinked and sat back. "Interesting. Can you help me understand? Because I thought golden caskets held blessings, and iron caskets held evil."

"That was the original intention, yes."

Holy damn, he was getting her to answer questions. Maybe I should take notes. *Don't scowl, don't raise your voice, appeal to her vanity...*

"The iron caskets were prisons for evil beings that should never return to the earth. Galter's a nasty little fool, but I suppose you're right. If he's seeking a casket, even a golden one, it should make us all uneasy."

"I agree," I said. "You know he's not looking to bless anything other than his own despicable ass."

Kasper's bright eyes turned to me. "I wonder about that too. Maybe it's a blessing for whoever opens it?"

We both turned to Ady, but her loose tongue seemed to have rolled back up tighter than before, because his question hung in the deepening shadows and the hum of Pooka's purring. We continued to eat in silence, humans waiting for our dragon hostess to grace us with her voice and wisdom.

The fire crackled while my stomach churned, dredging old wounds. Galter had to be stopped. After he took control of Araven, he marched through the highlands of Songy and decimated the kingdom of Crokar, seizing their gold and diamond mines. Before I left the palace, I knew he'd enslaved Drebians living on the border of Araven to work in those mines. He believed in the manifest destiny of the ancient Aravenian Empire to conquer all the known world, and he cared nothing about how he got it.

Damn it all, I wasn't as patient as Kasper. *Ady, what beings are in the caskets?* My mind-voice spoke into her silence, shivering a little at my own question.

Her answer was surprisingly swift. *They are unspeakable.*

"Galter has the support of three powerful kingdoms at his back," Kasper said, an edge to his voice, "and he's working the enslaved peoples of the conquered highlands night and day to forge weapons for him. Last month he snuffed out the Crokar rebellion by torching their wheat fields and arresting all their men." Kasper took a deep breath, eyes wet but hard. "He sent women and children to the mines."

I wanted to go straight to my training room to murder straw dummies until this tightness in my chest abated. Gods above, I wanted to hack my sword through Galter. I looked at Ady, but she wouldn't look at me.

I couldn't bring myself to tell you about Crokar.

"His armies are already formidable and stuffed with mercenaries," he continued. "But with this? The last thing we need is for him to have some kind of occult power. Rumor is he already has witches working for him."

"And you thought *I* would have this horrendous item—this *artifact*, as you call it—in *my* trove?" Ady asked.

He dropped his shoulders, looking weary. "I didn't mean to offend you. I'm honestly grateful you're even talking to me. I visited two other troves on my way here. Chonnenth reluctantly let me go with my life, but without any information. Airrydrim was sympathetic, but he didn't remember anything about caskets."

"That old dragon's been retired from the world even longer than me," Ady said. "I'm surprised he still speaks any languages known to humans."

"He actually has a knight of the trove himself. A woman from Boekam."

Ady's eyebrow raised as I let out an exasperated huff. "Why does everyone else in the world seem to know about knights of the trove except us ignorant Aravenians?" I asked her, not for the first time. I turned to Kasper. "I thought she was going to eat me alive when Galter sacrificed me to her."

"Don't be dramatic, Nesrin. 'Sacrifice' was *his* word, not mine. I never asked him to tie you to a pole."

"*Sacrificed*," I repeated in a vehement, low voice, pointing my fork at her for emphasis.

Kasper wore an appropriately horrified expression. "That sounds traumatic."

"*It was*," I said darkly, stabbing the hunk of meat on my plate that I was no longer hungry for.

"I'm not surprised Chonnenth wouldn't help you," Ady continued smoothly. "She's a vulture who swoops onto battlefields and burrows into the hoards of broken men. She'd happily watch mankind destroy itself."

The waning sunlight had long since ceased filtering in through the high windows, and Ady's enchanted lights twinkled on near the ceiling like early evening stars.

Kasper looked up at Ady, his eyes bright in the gathering shadows. "Does that mean *you'll* help me?"

"I told you I don't have it. What else would you ask of me?"

"Tell me everything you know. Let me use your library, if you have one. Any scrap of information would be more than I have."

She didn't answer for a moment, didn't speak, not even to me. Every moment of silence pressed a weight down on my shoulders, and my thoughts ran far from the safety of the trove. We needed to help Kasper with this quest, with everything we had. We had to help anyone standing against Galter, no matter the cost.

He was my father's brother. My responsibility, and my brothers'. That detestable association made my hands feel like they were covered in the blood of all the people he'd hurt. And if Ady wouldn't help Kasper, I would.

CHAPTER THREE

THE GUEST WING

"I will go find it." My voice pierced the silence with a courage I didn't know I possessed, and Ady and Kasper both turned their eyes to me.

"If Galter has people looking for it, Kasper's quest is dangerous. I'm better suited to protect myself on a journey than a monk."

Kasper bit his lip. "I would welcome your company and your help, but I'm not stepping aside."

I glared at Ady. *I'm going alone.*

You're taking him with you.

He'll be a liability, I balked.

We both turned to him, but he only looked between us as if he was politely waiting for our private conversation to end.

You could go with me.

She blinked once, slowly. *His information raises other concerns I need to investigate. We can trust Kasper,* she assured me. *And despite his lineage, he's more a librarian than a warrior and will need your protection. But he'll be helpful in ways you wouldn't expect.*

When Ady's mind was made up, it was harder to defeat than Baney. I took a deep, irritated breath. *Fine. You win, as always.* Even though it was the last thing I wanted.

Ady lowered her head closer to Kasper. "What do you intend to do with the casket if you find it?"

"My father and Father Ramdar, the head of my order, plan to destroy it."

"Caskets cannot be destroyed," she said dismissively. "What about your father's allies? Do any of them want to open it themselves and use what's inside against Galter?"

Kasper nodded, rubbing his short beard and glancing at me before continuing. "Not knowing what's inside it? Yes, a few. Talon among them."

"Then I will allow you to go with my knight on this quest on one condition: assure me that neither your father nor your order will attempt to open *any* casket you may find. If you find what Galter seeks, I'll let your order temporarily protect it until I've devised a long-term solution. At that point, it must be turned over to me. Humans clearly haven't been equal to the task of safeguarding them."

"You have my word." He turned to me. "Narmer and I appreciate your protection on the road," he said quietly, tucking an errant curl behind his ear.

"I'm not going only to protect you."

His cheeks reddened. "Of course. I only meant—"

"He will need your protection, Nesrin. If Galter's minions are out looking for the casket, that horrible prince from Naitar he had you betrothed to might be out there, too."

And there went my appetite for good. I put down my knife and fork.

"You remember, the nasty little man he sent over and over when you first arrived. What was his name? Regardless, I was hesitant to mention it to you earlier, Nesrin, but I saw a scout in my forest this morning wearing Naitarian livery." She licked chocolate sauce from her foreclaw, looking supremely unconcerned. "But he accidentally impaled himself on my foreclaw, and I couldn't get a thing out of him."

Kasper's eyes and mouth went wide. "You killed him?"

I looked from his horror-stricken face to Ady's careless one.

"No, no. Nesrin was too soft-hearted to let me kill him. She never let me kill any of the princes who came—"

"No, the scout. You killed the scout? How could you just..."

Ady curled her claw. "A simple flick of the foreclaw. I'd teach you if you were a dragon. Nes, what *was* the name of that disgusting little toad from Naitar?"

Kasper swallowed hard. "Do you mean Prince Ash—"

I cut him off. "I don't need to hear it spoken, but yes."

"He's the main reason I trained Nesrin to fight in the first place."

The monk rubbed his beard, looking wholly uncomfortable. "Naitar is famed for fighters." He withdrew a bit from the table, shoulders slumped, as if he'd just realized how dangerous a business it was, being out in the world with a war on.

My last fight with that nasty thug was at least a year back. If he hadn't been scared off by Ady, I may not have lived through it. But Kasper, if he was telling the truth, had risked a lot to come here, much less go on this quest, and he was neither a fighter nor a dragon.

"You said your father sent you on this quest?" I asked.

"I volunteered," he said quietly, shifting his leg down and crossing the other on his knee.

"Why? It sounds pretty thankless to me. For Veytia, and especially your order. Dangerous, too, with people like Naitar's finest thugs on the road, much less unfriendly dragons and regular bandits."

He paused a moment before he spoke. "Several reasons. My father knows he can trust me. I want to do my part in the war, but I can't do anything of value from the monastery." His light eyes met mine with gravity. "And Galter's a bully. I abhor bullies."

Ady watched him out of the corner of her eye. *He's telling the truth.*

I glared at her. *Is lie detection part of your magic now?*

He bit his lip and lowered his brows before continuing. "Also, my parents considered yours friends, and they were deeply saddened at their deaths. We heard the rumors. How you were treated...."

I bit my lip, unwilling to show emotion.

"I'm so sorry for everything you went through. And a big part of why I volunteered for the quest was because..." His eyes grew hard. "Because aside from your brothers, no one alive has as much right as you to take down Galter. And if it were me, I'd want the chance."

And this from a monk. Is that what I wanted? Revenge? More like an assurance that Galter couldn't reach me, even through others. That he couldn't hurt *anyone* anymore. I thought of Forth's words, of my brothers, of the people suffering under his slavery, and a cold determination steeled my veins.

As my eyes focused on Kas's again, he returned my gaze steadily as if he could read the hurt in my soul. "And," he suggested softly, "maybe acting against Galter might bring you some peace."

I nodded and turned away. "Maybe." I needed to leave before I cried or hit something and irrevocably embarrassed myself. "Then I'd better go pack. Which direction will we head?"

"I've already been south, so I planned to head into Nabul next. They—"

Ady snorted.

"Do we have to go through Nabul?" I asked. "I...um...defeated a prince from there the year before last, and I'd rather not see him again."

Is that what the humans are calling it these days? Ady smirked.

Kas frowned as he nodded. "We have to. The king-consort is an expert in ancient artifacts. Do you think they'll be unfriendly because you fought his son?"

Ady winked over her tea bowl. *I don't recall you putting up much of a fight.*

I glared at her. "No, he was friendly, and he left on good terms."

"Good. Then Narmer and I are ready whenever you are."

"No, I have a stallion you can ride. Narmer deserves a retirement of ease, don't you think? And your sacks of books will remain here. No one's carrying that all over Mellora."

"Yes. I agree. Thank you."

Ady stood, and Kasper rushed to his feet, immediately grimacing and switching his weight to his right foot.

"Nesrin, settle Kasper into the guest wing. I have an errand to run, but I'll be back in the morning. Promise not to leave before I'm back."

"I promise."

"Thank you, Lady Adydorrstea." Kasper bowed.

Ady took several feline steps away from the table before pouncing into a low flight. She careened through the columns and disappeared high above into her own chambers.

Kasper sat heavily. He took a deep breath, dropped his shoulders, and leaned back into his chair rubbing his hands over his eyes.

"Relieved that the man-eating dragon's gone?" I gently scratched Pooka's pointed little chin and rubbed my finger on the velvety fur of his long nose, trying to dispel my unease.

"No. Just tired. And thinking you're right." He pulled his hands through his floppy curls and sat up straighter, easing one foot to the side. "Of course, you're right." He took the linen napkin off of his lap and carefully folded it, sitting it beside his plate. A small smile. "The only thing I'm violent with is a tall platter of honey cakes." He stared into the candle flame on the table.

"And you carry no weapons." Less of a question and more of a statement.

He breathed out slowly. "No. Weapons have no place for those who come in peace." He finished the last of his tea and replaced the cup on the table.

"Spoken like a man who'll die on a sword with his morals intact." I scooped Pooka up in my arms like a baby and stood to push my chair in. My teacup and plates, silverware and napkin disappeared, as did the little drop of tea I'd spilled.

His eyes wide, Kasper stood with difficulty and leaned heavily on his chair as he pushed it in. His items disappeared as well. "Can I bring this magic back to the monastery with me?" He waved a hand across the now-empty space where his plate and cup were. "Sanitation duty comes for every man."

I smirked, kissed Pooka's fuzzy head, and poured him out of my arms and gently onto the floor so I could pick up Kasper's book sacks. Pooka sauntered around his legs, sniffing at the left, then trotted up to me with his tail high and happy to have a new person in the trove to worship him.

"Thank you for sharing my burden, Princess Nesrin."

"Call me Nesrin," I offered over my shoulder.

"Thank you, Nesrin. Everyone calls me Kas."

I didn't respond. I needed the meditative beauty of the evening-lit Great Hall to distract me, just for the walk to the guest wing. Ady's lights, small, nebulous spheres of luminous magic, floated among the vaults like stars moving in the heavens. Their reflections twinkling on the floor made it feel like we walked through the sky.

"I don't mean to complain." Kas's voice drifted from behind me, still polite and upbeat. "But is it much farther?"

"Why, what are you morally opposed to this time?" I rolled my eyes and turned to look at him.

"Nothing! It's just—Airrydrim may not've roasted me on sight, but he had traps all around his mountain." He lifted his pants leg and held his left foot forward. The faint tinge of blood seeped through layers of a makeshift linen bandage. "I stepped into one trying to get Narmer out of a patch of sucking mud."

"And *still* you didn't ride the mule?"

"No." He ducked his head, his tone sheepish as he slowly closed the distance between us. "It wasn't *his* fault. And Narmer's...really old."

I took both of his other bags from him, ignoring his protests. "We're nearly there." Walking slowly, I let him catch up. "Why did your father send you on a quest with an ancient mule, too many books, and no weapons?"

He smiled, his eyes twinkling in the torchlight. "What will it take for you to trust me, Nesrin?"

"Being acquainted for longer than an hour would help. You can also drop the pious monk act." I smiled, raising my eyebrows expectantly.

He chuckled. "How does the old Aravenian saying go? 'What you see is what you get?' I'm an open book. I'll answer anything you ask, and honestly."

"Then answer my question, honest Kas."

"I'm only a monk. I'm not worthy of special treatment just because my father's the velarch. My order subsists on charitable donations, and they sent me with the best they had. I've been grateful for it."

"Hmm," was all I said. I wanted to be impressed by him, but he was too pure-hearted, too generous to not be a lying piece of crap, no matter what Ady saw in him. I stole a glance at him again, and he smiled brightly back at me. I rolled my eyes, not caring if he saw.

When I reached the first of the wide, winding steps to the guest wing, I looked back to see him leaning against the nearest column, his skin looking a little too pale.

"I think you have an infection." I left his bags at the base of the stairs and went back for him. "Come on." I pulled his arm up by the wrist and around my shoulder.

"Thank you. It feels so much worse after letting it rest for a while."

The warmth of his body leaning into me brought with it the scent of frankincense, myrrh, and some saintly, woodsy smell I couldn't identify. He felt inordinately warm, and no way was he giving me enough of his weight.

"I know I'm short, but you can lean on me. I won't break."

He replied with a tight, pained smile, and leaned on me more heavily.

Despite the wing not being used in at least the past four years, the wide hallway with rooms branching off was clean and freshly swept. Water splashed in the bathing chamber on the left, so I led him there first, where bright white sails of tiled boats skimmed across the deep blue tiled walls. This bathing pool, like my own, was wide and deep, raised in the middle of the room and scaled with smooth coin-tiles in a smattering of blues. I sat him on the edge of it, and he slumped against a column, his eyes unfocused as he furrowed his brows and looked at the water.

"Is this a bathtub or a swimming pool?"

"Both. When's the last time you had a proper bath?"

"Are you suggesting that I smell bad?" A slightly flirtatious smile lit up his face, and his brilliant eyes locked on mine.

He surprised a half-smile from me. Holy Hivathe. He really was too attractive to be a vestal monk. Maybe he was a faithless womanizer. Maybe that's what was off about him.

"You're the one who said it, *Brother Kas*. You need to clean that wound." I placed my hands on either side of his face to gauge his temperature; he felt like a clay pot left in the sun.

I spoke aloud to the trove magic: "Kas needs medicine for fever, pain, and infection."

A goblet of water and a cobalt blue vial appeared on a silver tray on the ledge of the bathing pool.

I picked up the vial. "Here. Drink this. Ady's medicines are laced with magic. It'll heal you from the inside and take down your fever.

After you're in the bath, ask the trove magic to clean your clothes. They'll be returned to you quickly."

Kas drank the vial down and followed it with water. "Thank you. But I'd rather lie down than take a bath right now. Everything looks kind of..." His pupils were wide, and a bead of sweat trailed down his face. "Covered in gray lace." He looked around and blinked a few times, raising one eyebrow as he focused on my face. "Do you see that too?"

"No, that's just you." I knelt before him and unlaced the leather traveling boot that he'd tied wide over his bandage. Boot removed, I unwound his bandage, and he hissed and clenched his eyes as the wound hit the air. The claw marks left by the trap were small, but an angry, swollen red.

"If you want to come with me on the quest—in fact, if you want to keep this foot—you'll bathe it right now. It doesn't matter to me," I added, unlacing the other boot. "But I assume it matters to you?"

He nodded yes but didn't otherwise move toward the bath. He didn't look so good.

"Maybe I'll wait outside the door in case you need something."

"Wait!" he said, before I could stand. He pulled his book out of his cloak and held it toward me. "Here. Read everything I've gathered about the caskets."

I looked down at it, then back at him. "You trust me with all your research?"

"You can read Veytian, can't you?"

I nodded.

"We're on the same side, Nesrin. I hope you'll trust me." His face softened, and he placed his hand briefly on my shoulder. He opened his mouth to say more, but hesitated, looking at me somberly.

I looked down at his hand on my shoulder, which he removed, took his book sharply, and left the room.

That look again, from the second prince today. I'd heard from several contenders that the story of what I'd endured in Galter's palace had traveled far. But I still struggled to differentiate pity from genuine compassion, so both received my ire.

Standing with one foot against the outer wall of the room, I tucked his book into my folded arms and listened to be sure he was following directions. The water slowed to a lazy trickle and stopped, and fabric rustled.

Kas's voice echoed quietly into the hallway: "Please, wash and dry these clothes. Thank you." A soft splashing, a swift intake of hissed breath and a muttered prayer. More soft splashes reassured me that he was indeed bathing.

I unwrapped the leather cords of his book. Not that I wished him ill, but he may not be well enough to leave in the morning. It would be *such* a shame if I had to go without him. On the other hand, Ady's stupid medicine worked so quickly he'd probably be fine before the moon was high.

I opened his book and nearly gasped aloud. An exquisite painting of Hivathe and her god-consort, Onsorbal, graced one of the first pages. The goddess, dressed in her traditional red and orange robes embroidered with swirls of golden light, was illuminated from behind by her the life-giving sun in the blue sky and bright flowers blooming in a riot of colors. Warmth and joy lit her face as she gazed at her husband. He sat facing her in his traditional robes of blue and silver, surrounded by the dark, mysterious night sky sprinkled with stars and hung with a glowing moon. At his back, a deep dark forest and a lake reflected the stars. The lovers' palms were pressed together in perfect unity, eyes focused on the other.

I almost stroked a finger down the page, but I didn't want to mar the painting. If this was Kas's work, he was supremely talented. On the next page was a beautifully realistic painting of what could only be his family. His parents embraced in the center, and four tall young men stood around them, none of them Kas. A happy family with the fourth son conspicuously absent. Why that should pull at my heartstrings, I didn't know.

I flipped further, coming to the golden casket again, reading all his notes. It was rumored to be about the size of a small loaf of bread and unnaturally warm to the touch, and the last historical record Kas found reported it'd been stolen from an underground crypt in Opintol during the Phoenix Wars, around twelve hundred years ago. Some historians posited that it had been carried by various conquering armies over the ages. Because it'd passed out of human history, Kas surmised that it may be sitting in the trove of a dragon, in another kingdom's treasury, or buried deep within the earth or sea, ensnared in the tendrils of time.

I popped my head up as I flipped the page. It was too quiet.

Closing the book on my thumb to hold my spot, I called out to him. "Kas?"

No response.

"Kas?" I called again, a little louder and closer to the open doorway. Still no response, and a ball of dread curled up in my chest.

I poked my head into the doorway. His eyes were closed, his body was limp, and he was sinking beneath the surface of the water.

CHAPTER FOUR

THE WHITE DRAGON

"**S**hit!" I flung his book onto a chair and sprinted for the pool. I jumped in, boots and all, scooping him under the arms before his head went under. He didn't react at all.

"Kas!" I patted his face, pushed my fingers to his long neck. His pulse was strong, thank Hivathe, but he was unconscious. I realized then that I was straddling a very handsome, very naked stranger in his bath, my own clothes now soaked through. My eyes automatically skimmed down the dark hair of his surprisingly muscular chest to where his lower stomach disappeared into thick, frothy bubbles...and snapped back up, my face heating.

Now what?

I pulled him up to sit on the second step in the water, propped his long arms over the pool's ledge, and grabbed a golden bar of soap flecked with herbs. First I washed his face and hands. That always made me feel better. Then I leveraged his injured foot carefully so he wouldn't sink and removed every fleck of caked blood and all the filth of the infection.

I replaced his leg into the water—too quickly. His feet rose to the surface, and his body started to float out and sink again. I lunged and grabbed under his arms, pulling him back up, stifling an inappropriate laugh. I must've looked like Kas pulling his mule out of the sucking mud.

"Come on, Narmer," I teased, propping him up again. I stepped out and squeezed water from my clothes and thick braid, appraising the unconscious man submerged to the chest in the bathing pool.

I'd gotten stronger since I came here, watching with pride as my body grew lithe and muscled. But I wasn't foolish enough to think I could lift this wet, slippery, dead-weighted, tall man from the tub without dropping him, and a head injury was the last thing he needed. I looked up as Kas's clean, neatly pressed clothes soared into the room on the soft winds of the trove magic and landed on a chair.

Trove magic it is. While I wrung my dripping clothes over the floor drain, I had it lift him from his bath, dry him with plush towels, dress him back in his pants and tunic, and deposit him safely under the covers in the guest bed across the hall. I followed after, calling for ointments and bandages.

"Well done, trove." I rolled up my wet sleeves as sheets billowed down on him and a golden tray materialized on his bedside table

As I doctored up Kas's leg, Pooka trotted in and jumped onto the bed purring. He stuck his pointed nose by Kas's mouth, stayed long enough for Kas to breathe in and out once, then curled up right beside his head.

"Don't get attached," I muttered. Ointments applied, bandages wrapped, so now all I had to do was—a soft *thunky-plink* sounded from the tray beside me. A lavender vial of oil appeared that hadn't been there before. I picked it up and read its label softly aloud. *"Anoint forehead, lips, and chest of the afflicted."*

Despite having fixed myself up many times—illnesses, burns, sword slices, bruises—I'd never seen this vial before. But then I'd never had a wound get infected. Shrugging to myself, I popped out the cork.

Kas's loose curls were nearly dry, and he laid there looking very much like the son of a velarch. His golden skin had lost its pallor, and he seemed to almost be smiling in his sleep. Beautiful enough to paint, if I had the talent. Not a bad choice to invite in as a companion, if he hadn't been a vestal monk.

I poured a little oil onto the pads of my fingers and rubbed them together. A rich scent came alive in the air—frankincense, myrrh, and that same woodsy note I smelled on Kas. It sent shivers across my skin, especially as I looked down at his sleeping face. Long, dark lashes fluttered against his high cheekbones, and even through his short, black beard I could tell his face was nearly symmetrical. He looked like an ancient Veytian statue of Onsorbal, the ideal of male beauty.

I gently smoothed my fingertips across his forehead, traced more oil gently across his full lips. Finally, I pulled the sheets down and his tunic open a little to expose his chest. I poured a small pool of oil on his breastbone and rubbed it over his chest. It was an intimate gesture, and although I used the touch of a healer and not a lover, the hard planes of his warm skin intensified the oil's scent and flooded my body with heat.

I removed my hands and shook off the feeling, covering him back up. As I watched him sleep a moment more, I rubbed the remainder of the oil on my elbows and upper arms. He seemed peaceful and safe now.

"Keep him comfortable," I said quietly to the magic, "not too warm if he's still running fever. And wake me if he's in trouble."

I made soft kissing noises at Pooka. "Are you coming?" I whispered. He opened amber-green eyes, gave me a silent meow, then stretched and rearranged himself in a circle, flopping against Kas's side, his striped brown and black back to me.

I stuck my tongue out. "Fine, then."

I woke before dawn. Rain pattered the stained-glass window of the moon among the stars above my bed. If I started early and worked hard, I might be able to get through that box of rings...

But no. The weight of yesterday and the journey I dreaded to take pressed into me again. I asked the trove for a satchel and started packing in the candlelight, completely unsure of what I'd actually need.

Ady, are you home?

I waited a few moments in vain for a reply, so I dressed in my training clothes and knelt before my altar as I did every morning, then I trekked to Kas's room to check on him.

Still fast asleep on his stomach, he had one arm thrown over his head and the other hanging off the side of the bed. He'd thrown off most of his blankets during the night except for the bit around his legs where my lazy little fluff was curled up in the bent crook of his knee, sound asleep despite the thunder.

So that's where my Pooka had been all night instead of snuggling with me.

I moved to the side of the bed, and Pooka stirred, rolling onto his back with all his glorious belly fur on display. He stretched his legs, yawned, and gave me an upside-down, high-pitched meow.

I rubbed Pooka's lamb-like belly floof before turning my attention to Kas's relaxed, peaceful breathing. Pressing my hand gently to his cheek then forehead. His temperature seemed normal. Good for him, but condolences to my hopes for a solo quest.

Satisfied that my patient was recovering, I left for my training room to throw axes and practice swordplay and the mechanics of hand-to-hand combat, as I did every day. Not for the first time, my imagination superimposed Galter's face on all my straw dummies, and I tore through them with Baney until the whole lot lay in hacked-up pieces at my feet.

I didn't practice doka last night, and my morning training suffered for it. My muscles were still sore, and my emotional cup was turbulent, overflowing with dark memories. I stretched my arms high above my head and brought them down to my sides, promising myself I would do my stretching and meditation ritual tonight come hell or high water, no matter where in the world I found myself. I should pack my doka beads. It would be nice to pray with them while I was away from home.

I cleaned up and dressed for the road, with my leather corset over my tunic and my sturdiest pair of boots over my sturdiest moleskin pants. Three steps into the Great Hall, and the lack of Ady's presence was still palpable. No sign of Kas being up, either. I grabbed an apple on my way to the treasury to resume my cataloging. No reason to disrupt my routine until I had to.

An hour or more passed in the calm, quiet way that days in the trove usually did. Enjoying the sound of the rain, I sorted the rest of the rings into my best estimations of origin and history, cataloging them in my record book.

Making small marks in little bound books, indeed. If Ady's previous knights had been more thorough, I could've checked the records and more quickly sent Kas on his way, or anyone else inquiring about lost artifacts. I would never have known more about the quest.

"No caskets here today, sorry," I mumbled to myself, before answering myself in a deeper mumble: "I'll be on my way then. Thank you for checking your extremely accurate records."

"Who are you talking to?"

My heart sank to my feet, and I made a stray dark line on the page. Heart pounding and cheeks as hot as when I'd finished training, I looked up to see Kas on the threshold of the open door, his hand resting on the edge of the closed one. He peered around the large room lined with shelves of treasure and boxes, his bright eyes wide.

"Nobody," I said quickly.

"Ady asked me to tell you she's back and ready to send us on our way. She's ready for us in the stables." He brought his hidden hand up, holding the circular crown that rolled across the floor yesterday. "I found this in the Great Hall. Were you missing it?"

"No. You can put it there." I pointed at the edge of the worktable closest to the door. "I'll be there in a moment." I chewed on my lower lip, staring at him until he'd placed the crown on the table and left. I waited a moment more to be sure he was gone.

Cursing under my breath and shaking my head, I grabbed my pumice eraser and scrubbed at the stray mark in my book with exaggerated harshness, nearly making a hole in the page. I marked my place and set my table to order. Hivathe knew when I'd be back. I availed myself of my bathroom's amenities, collected my bag from my room, filled my bandolier up with my throwing knives, chose a medium-warmth wool coat, and went to the stables to find Ady and Kas talking together. Pooka was on his lap receiving a ridiculous amount of petting.

"Good afternoon, Nesrin, did you sleep well?" Ady asked

"I did, thank you. How are you feeling today, Kas? Well enough to be alienating the affections of my cat?"

"Much better, thank you. Pooka's great company. He stayed with me all night, didn't you?" He scratched Pooka's mane affectionately, and I could hear the purr from where I was sitting. His eyes alighted on me, his whole face brightening into a smile. "And thank you for taking care of me last night. Ady told me how I—"

"Don't mention it," I interrupted, narrowing my eyes at my favorite dragon as I slipped my coat on. *You're going by nicknames now?*

She didn't look at me or change expression. *I call him Sexy Eyes, but not to his face.*

I brought forward the stallion I'd taken from Prince Forth, which the trove magic already had ready to go. "Here's the stallion I was telling you about."

Kas patted the horse's long nose. "What's his name?"

"You choose." I shrugged, attaching my bag to Pistachio's saddle.

"How about...Balembar, after the horse of our Lady of Wisdom?"

"Hivathe herself would approve of it." I rifled through the bag that already hung from Pistachio's saddle. "Did you pack us medicine, Ady?"

"Of course, including that special oil the trove gave you to use on Kas last night."

"I meant to ask you about that. What was it? It smelled amazing."

"A truly powerful healing oil." Ady chuckled softly, puffs of smoke languorously curling toward the ceiling. *It also functions as a potent aphrodisiac.*

Ady! I scolded, blushing furiously. *That's not okay! I thought it had medicinal benefits! I rubbed it all over him! Now I feel like I violated the poor man.*

Her black eyes gleamed. *Pssh, you did no such thing. Besides. Sensual massage is a healing art in itself.* "Now remember," she said aloud as we mounted our horses, "if you find an iron casket, *do not disturb* it, and don't call attention to it. If you find the gold casket, hide it and bring it straight back to Velarch Oh. If you find either, send me a magpie right away. Take care of each other. Kas, give me a moment alone with Nesrin."

"Of course. Thank you for your hospitality and kindness. Until we meet again." Kas clicked gently to Balembar and left the stable.

Ady watched him go. "So very wasted in a religious order. You should reconsider not seducing him. How are you feeling about the quest?"

"Nervous," I admitted. "Are you sure we can trust the monk?"

She placed a mighty claw gently upon the top of my head. "You are my knight and my friend, and I've trained you well. And when I tell you to go with Kas, know it's for the best."

I fiddled with Pistachio's reins. I'd spent the last eight years cocooning myself in the trove, spinning layers of emotional armor, assuring myself that I would never have to go farther than the forest. It was a frequent prayer to Hivathe that I never have to leave. The trove was my haven. Anywhere else was hell.

"What are you not telling me about these caskets?"

She shut her eyes tightly, looking wearier than I'd maybe ever seen her. "This is why I held you back. I do not know what beings are in three of the iron caskets, but I know about the fourth. And that one I would *still* fear above all others, no matter what they contain. When the world was much younger, a mighty white dragon flew the skies."

Four iron caskets. Four horrific evils. The hairs on the back of my neck rose.

"He had been so kind. Honorable. A protector of early humanity. But as time went by, humans began to populate all the continents of the world and develop a taste for gold. They mined it and fashioned it to their own arts, and the white dragon began to listen to other malcontents. And he changed his mind. He came to view humans like locusts in the wheat, destroying entire nations in his wrath. The proud human kingdoms of Plyscia, Korillen, Ofiera, famed across the world...he and his comrades burned them all."

I blinked at her in horror. "I've never heard of any of those."

"We tried to stop him." Her voice shivered with uncharacteristic emotion. "But he was too powerful, in body and in magic. He killed many of his own kind in the long, drawn-out war. Even his own drakelings had to be hidden from him. We couldn't defeat him, so we contained him. He was the first to be imprisoned in an iron casket."

Shivers had taken up what might be permanent residence along my skin, but if she was providing information, I was going to keep asking. *Solid tone*, I reminded myself, *don't raise your voice. Maybe sound disinterested.* "So...what are in the gold caskets?"

"Blessings from Hivathe's Golden Spirits to help counteract the beings in the iron caskets, should they escape."

"Blessings from Hivathe's *actual* Golden Spirits?" I'd seen Hivathe's influence in my own life, but for an aspect of my religion to become corporeal enough to place a blessing in a physical object was unheard of. A miracle.

Ady smiled indulgently at me, as if I was a child. To her, I was. "Yes, little one, I saw them arrive at the temple the day the white dragon was imprisoned."

"Where are they now? Why can't the Golden Spirits come help us?"

She chuckled softly. "You can't expect them to stay on this plane of existence, can you? Silly human girl."

A dozen questions popped into my head, but none escaped my lips before she continued.

"I voted with the other dragons to let humans keep the casket safe and hidden away. After all, they had the most to lose if he were set free." She closed her eyes and breathed out slowly. "I regret that now. Perhaps relying on creatures with such short lifespans and trusting that their future generations would respect what came before—well, I suppose none of that matters now. But know, Nesrin, that if you succeed in this quest, you'll not only protect my trove, but also the lives of all creatures of Mellora. I know you won't fail us."

No pressure. "What will *you* do, while I'm on this quest with the monk? Stay behind and paint your talons at the fireside?" I teased.

"A quest of my own. Without some other, powerful magic on his side, I can't imagine how Galter could twist something in a gold casket to his uses. And that's what concerns me most: the possibility that Galter has formidable, secret friends. And if any casket is opened, we will need formidable friends of our own to help us. Be careful, Nesrin, and may Hivathe go with you and Kas."

CHAPTER FIVE

THE KAVHAVJI VINE

Kas and I left the stable to find that the morning storm had left us a crisp, clear afternoon. We directed our horses through the glade before Ady's front gate and down the same narrow forest path that every suitor had come and left by.

I rode ahead, mainly to discourage conversation but increasingly to enjoy the afternoon. A woodpecker in a tall oak laid down a rapid-beat percussion to the symphony of birdsong, chittering squirrels, and shifting winds that scattered red and gold leaves onto the mulchy path as it widened and sloped up toward the cliffs against the Veytian Gulf.

But after nearly two hours of blissful solitude, we approached a fork in the road. Several feet down the lower northwest path, a man sat hunched against a tree and wrapped in tattered clothing. An over-patched satchel slouched at his feet.

I kept my eyes on his floppy hat, grateful that Ady directed me to take the high path along the cliffs instead. If we passed him quickly, we could leave him in the dust if something should—

"Hello, friend!" Kas called, cantering Balembar right up to the stranger.

"Don't!" I pulled up on Pistachio's reins, letting my indecision dance her in the neutral space between the two forks.

"Hello, Brother," the man said, struggling to his feet. Beneath his hat, his dark eyes twinkled in the sun in a face smudged with dirt. "Do you have any food to share with a man who's down on his luck?"

"We don't have time for this," I said sternly.

"We always have time to help someone in need." Kas dismounted and rummaged through his bag, coming out with a lovely hunk of bread the trove baked fresh this morning.

"You're too kind." The man took the bread with his right hand—that seemed good to know—and tore a chunk off, bringing it eagerly to his mouth.

The wind threatened to pull the man's hat from his head, but he clamped his hand down over it as he heartily chewed, talking with his mouth full. "Where are you and the young lady headed to on this glorious day, blessed by Hivathe herself?"

"Oh." An invisible string pulled Kas's eyebrows down at the center as he clearly struggled with a lie. "We're...on a humanitarian mission through Araven."

I rolled my eyes. "Okay. That's enough. Let's go."

"But—"

"That's enough." My voice echoed through the trees around me, surprising Kas into turning to look at me. "It's time to go."

"It's alright, young lady. I don't mean any harm, and I don't want to hold you and the kind brother from your journey." A stronger wind pulled at his hat, revealing neatly shaved hair above his ratty beard before he could pull it down.

Apprehension tingled through all my limbs. I brought Pistachio closer and dismounted, reaching inside my coat.

"What a beautiful head of red hair you have, my lady. I haven't seen the like of it—"

I crossed to him in three quick strides and laid my knife against his throat, grasping his right wrist. "Who are you really?"

"Nesrin!" Kas exclaimed, pulling at my arm.

Panic flooded me. Why would Kas say my name? I angled my body away from him so I could keep both men in my sight, but the phony indigent man took advantage, snaking his arm out and knocking mine aside. The bread fell to the dirt, and Kas yelled beside me. I butted my elbow into the man's nose, knocking off his hat. As his blood spurted everywhere, I caught sight of the boar tattoo on his shorn blond head revealing him as a servant of Naitar. His sword was out in a flash, slicing toward me.

But the smooth, metallic slip of pulling Baney from her scabbard didn't reassure me. I didn't know where Kas was, and I barely blocked the man's advances, not even getting the angle right to cleave his weapon. Grunting, he met the arc of my sword with his own, the bone-shuddering clang reverberating up my arm. I grasped the hilt with both hands, backing down from the towering man bearing down on me. Without the ferocious, looming presence of Ady to back me up, all my training fled from my brain. What was Kas doing? Would he come after me too? Every beat of my pounding heart brought another swing of death-edged steel past my vital organs.

And Ady wasn't coming to save me.

A stone sailed inches past my head from behind and hit the man square on the jaw, knocking him back a few paces and probably saving my life. I moved in, breaking his sword off at the hilt, wrenching the steel from his hands. He cried out and stumbled back.

Now this bastard would retreat from *me*.

"On your knees!" I shouted, my hoarse voice laced with more fear than ferocity. But the man stumbled back, easily evading my clumsy swipes.

I pushed him too far. He fell backwards off a high rocky spot along the road, tumbling down and out of my reach. It was too steep to go down without risking falling myself, and with him waiting at the bottom. I stood a second too long in indecision.

The Naitarian scrambled to his feet and sprinted for the northwest path where it meandered to his elevation. I pulled an axe from my belt, throwing it overhand toward him, failing to account for his running. Cursing the straw men in my training room who couldn't run from me, I darted down the path after him, letting loose one throwing knife after another.

But he reached a copse of trees and emerged seconds later on a horse. My knife tumbled harmlessly into the grass as his horse galloped away.

"Nesrin, come back!"

The monk.

I whirled around, taking murderous strides toward Kas. His eyes widened, hands up, but he stood his ground as I waved my sword in his face.

"What the *hell* are you playing at? Are you working for Galter? Stopping for that *poor, starving man*, saying my name out in the open?"

His Adam's apple bobbed as he panted and shook his head, his wide eyes miserably remorseful. He fell to his knees with his hands up in supplication.

"I'm sorry. That was so stupid of me! I swear, everything I said to you was true." His gaze held mine, and his eyebrows pulled to center. "I swear to Hivathe I thought the man was in need. I shouldn't have said your name, and I'll never do it again when someone can hear me say it."

I watched him for long seconds, his eyes steadily returning my gaze, making no movements. He had feathers for brains, but I believed him. I lowered my sword and stumbled back, turning to catch the dust rising in the road from the man in the distance. On his way to tell Galter exactly where I was. Sheathing Baney, I held out my hand to help Kas up.

"Godsdamnit, Kas, if you ever pull anything like that again—"

"I won't!" He grasped my hand and stood. "You could've died, and it would've been my fault. I'm so sorry."

"Help me gather my knives." My voice was harsh, even to my own ears. I turned on shaking legs and walked to where my axe was stuck in the ground. When I leaned over to grasp the handle, my eyes fell on the man's blood still dripping down my sleeve, and nausea roiled in my stomach.

I vomited, wiping my shaking arm and hand against the tall grasses and grabbing my axe's cold handle for comfort. Two hours from the trove, and I was a worthless mess. Just a weakling playing at being a knight.

"Are you okay?"

With a fool nearly getting me killed, then throwing a stone so close to hitting me instead. I worked the handle back and forth in the earth to free the blade—I'd thrown it with some force, at least—and stood to face Kas. He stood between our horses, their reins in one hand and all my little knives held uncomfortably in the other.

"I'm fine." I put my weapons away, staring at him the whole time.

He bit his lip, probably holding back another useless *I'm sorry*.

"My father always tells me I'm too trusting. I'll be more suspicious next time. I promise."

My fingers didn't want to work. I slipped the first two knives back into my bandolier but fumbled the third. It *thunked* cleanly into the earth between us. I finished with the others before picking it up. "That man knew who I was. Stupid red hair. I should've dyed it black with licorice weed before we left."

He frowned. "Don't say that. It's your legacy. Didn't your mother have red hair?"

"You're on thin ice, Kas." I was at the point of tears already.

He pulled both lips into his mouth, looking past me down the road with a frown. "Do you think he'll try to ambush us when we pass?"

"We're not going that way." I swung up into Pistachio's saddle, clicking at her and turning her toward the narrower, rougher fork that led due north along the gulf cliffs.

Balembar whinnied behind me. "But...we have to go that way." Kas rode up beside me, pointing down the gently sloping road meandering through plains of wheat rolling golden in the soft afternoon wind.

"Only if you want to visit the emperor. I don't, so I'm going this way." I nodded to the other path. It was rockier and gloomier, sure, but according to Ady it was also emperor-free.

"No, look." He flipped through the pages of his book and held out a map of Araven marked with the main roads leading to the Eldor River, the boundary between Araven and Nabul. He dragged his finger along the page. "The cliffs are harder to traverse, and they're full of all kinds of nasty creatures. Maybe even manticores. It'll take us longer and be much more dangerous."

"Congratulations on your beautifully drawn map, but I'm not listening to anything you say after the stunt you just pulled."

He bit his lip and held the map closer to me, as if that would change my mind. "I said I was sorry. The west fork will bring us through farming country, mostly. We can skirt the palace when we get closer, but it's a much safer road, overall."

I pulled Pistachio to a stop. "Ady's told me before where Galter's garrisons are, and I'm telling you, at least three contingents of soldiers wait down your sunshine path. And that's before we even get *near* the palace."

"Really?" He looked at his map, crestfallen, then closed his book. "Alright, then. My book knowledge bows to your experience. And Ady's," he added, bowing to me from the horse and putting his book away.

I shook my head and spurred Pistachio onward. The ragged beating of my heart was calming down, but my anger wasn't cooling.

Kas the pest approached me again. "And you're sure there aren't manticores this way?"

"I don't know, but they're nocturnal. We should have enough daylight to get past the cliffs. It's only a few hours to the river."

He looked back the way we came. "Have you ever fought a manticore?" He was probably thinking that we'd both be dead before sunset if we had to rely on my fighting skills.

"No, but I watched my father's soldiers kill one that came too far west. I'll take a manticore over Galter any day."

"Brave words from someone who's never fought a manticore," he said softly.

"Piss off, Kas."

We rode in silence as the path narrowed and became harder for our horses to traverse. Every now and then I glanced back, my anger cooling, begrudgingly impressed to see how well he rode the massive war stallion. Comfortable, relaxed. Gazing eagerly all around the rocky terrain as if he were on an exciting holiday and smiling at me as if I hadn't just had a sword to his throat.

I bit my lip. It would be an even longer road if I couldn't get past what happened at the crossroads. Maybe Hivathe preferred his open-hearted nature, but my distrust kept me alive.

Still. He probably wasn't used to being hunted any more than I was. He saw the beggar by the road, and his first impulse had been to help. That was a good quality, not a bad one. And Ady trusted him, which was high praise. Somehow, I'd have to learn to trust him too.

The sparse grass skimming along the rocks and up to the pitted cliff along the gulf coast had turned a burnished red in the oncoming cold. To the west, woodlands condensed into a thick forest as the land sloped into a valley. But before we could reach the cliffs, we faced a narrow pass pitted with hundreds of caves. The land grew sandier and rockier after the fork, the path pockmarked with holes full of rainwater. Scraggly vines clung desperately to the rock that steadily grew taller on either side of us.

Kas dismounted and led Balembar ahead of me, going around the holes in the path and peering into the caves he passed. I opened my mouth to tease him about manticores, but he suddenly sank in the sand and yelled out.

My heart went to my feet. Kas whirled around and pushed against Balembar to keep the stallion from following him in, only sinking himself further in.

I jumped off Pistachio and played a real-life game of "the floor is quicksand," making rushed decisions about my own footing as I lunged forward to grab Balembar's reins. Kas thrashed wildly and sank deeper.

"Stop moving!" I yelled. "Stop! You're making it worse."

He froze at my command, holding his long arms straight out from his shoulders as if he couldn't rely on them to stop otherwise. His eyes were wide, but he didn't sink any further.

I pulled Balembar to safety, just beyond Kas's reach. "If you stop moving, you'll stop sinking." No branches were near us, and I stupidly didn't pack rope. "Shimmy one leg back and forth to make room in the sand, and then pull that leg up higher. Trade legs and keep going. Got it? I'll be right back."

He didn't reply but immediately did as I asked. I ran back along the ravine to the vines. They were as thick as sword hilts, and I grabbed the longest pieces with the fewest leaves and pulled on them. No thorns, but the vines' broad, serrated leaves were stiff and sharp. I pulled several lengths down, hacking them off the stony wall.

"Nesrin! This isn't working!" Kas's voice echoed through the cliffs.

"Shut up!" I hissed back. If there were manticores here, they knew where we were, now. I scooped up the length of vine I'd cut and bounded back to the quicksand. Kas was thrashing around again, the sand up to his thighs.

"Stop moving!" I ran up as close as I dared.

He froze, his wide eyes looking all around the ground.

"What happened to the careful shimmy I taught you?" I coiled the vine up in my arms so I could toss it to him. "When I throw you the vine, keep shimmying—"

"I can't!" Terror made his voice tremble.

"Yes, yes you can." I repeated my instructions. "If you do that, you'll get far enough out to reach the dry ground. Here. Catch!" I tossed the vine out toward him.

Kas looked up, but he shouted out and threw his body away from the vine as if I'd thrown him a venomous snake. Now his back was in the sand too.

"What's wrong with you? Grab the vine!"

"That's a kavhavji vine!" He shouted. "It's poisonous! Put it down!"

I threw the vine away from me and looked at my hands. Thin red lines crisscrossed my palms where the leaves' sharp points had scratched me.

"They're just scratches. I'm all right." I reached for the vine again.

"No! Don't!" He yelled, frantically shimmying his right leg. "Stop!" He pulled his right leg out a little and began to shimmy the left as I coiled the vine up for another throw.

"Just catch it this time, and I'll pull you out."

One second, I was leaning over reaching for more of the vine, and the next I was belly down in the sand. No in between. Kas's yelling echoed in my head from far away. I moved my head to the side to breathe, and then I couldn't move at all. My hands felt like they were both on fire and made of lead, and an unbearable, creeping itch started at the crown of my head spreading rapidly to my toes.

A hard lump formed in my throat. I could barely swallow. I couldn't speak. Rising panic corked securely in my chest. I'd never survive this.

Kas was suddenly beside me, kicking the vine away. He turned me onto my side and pillowed his cloak quickly under my head, wedging my back against a rock. His mouth moved, but my ears rang so loudly I didn't know what he said.

Help me. I took too-small, desperate breaths. The center of my vision went white, and the blankness spread outwards, stealing my sight. I fought for consciousness as tears tracked like ice across my nose and cheek into the sand. In my dimming peripheral vision, I saw Kas mount Balembar at a run and gallop away.

Leaving me to die.

CHAPTER SIX

BOCIAN

A damp breeze lifted my hair, bringing with it the homey smell of woodsmoke and the crackling of a campfire. A man's deep voice hummed against the shushing of distant, crashing waves, and I opened my eyes. Bright embers flittered past golden-leaved trees into the black sky, dying against the stars. A cold breeze blew in from the gulf, and I shivered where it stole beneath the blanket covering me.

I sat up gingerly, testing the heaviness I found in my limbs, elated that moving was even possible. That my heart was still beating. My coat was neatly folded on the ground near me, and my hands were wrapped in a plaster of leaves and a scent that brought a clear memory of walking with my mother through the herb garden when I was a child.

Kas was across the fire with his back to me. Behind me, a rocky outcropping protected us from the worst of the gulf wind battering the high branches of trees gathered thinly around us. Before me, the land fell quickly away, gathering density in an ash forest. Kas's little book sat open-faced on the ground, a few small stones weighting the pages open to a drawing of the kavhavji vine with Kas's careful handwriting beside it: "The kavhavji vine is deadly to anyone who cuts their skin upon its jagged leaves..."

"You're a smartass." My voice was hoarse, but thank Hivathe it worked.

"It's a blessing and a curse." He offered me a water skin and sat cross-legged beside his book. "Drink this."

"But I was right about the quicksand," I rasped, snatching the water skin from him with both leaf-wrapped hands and drinking deeply. Nothing had ever tasted so good, bursting down my scratchy throat and coursing through the dry valley of my body.

"You were, thank you."

I came up for air and wiped my mouth against the back of my sleeve. "The last thing I remember is you taking off on Balembar." I nearly added, *I thought you were leaving me*, but it sounded like a pathetic thing to say, even if it was true.

His small smile suggested that he guessed my unspoken words. "I saw alobelia growing back under the trees, and I needed it to activate the plantain leaves in my bag. Thank Hivathe it all came together. I don't know of another treatment for kavhavji." He reached his hands toward mine. "May I?"

I sat the water skin down as he scooted closer on the soft grass and unwrapped the leaves from my hands. Close enough that I inhaled his scent on every breath. The lavender wafting from his curls reminded me of my soap at the trove and brought with it a pang of homesickness, even this early in the journey.

"Ady packed medicine infused with her magic in our bags, remember? You could've used that."

"Yes, and I'm sure I'll be glad of it later. But dragon magic has no effect on kavhavji."

"There can't be anything Ady's magic can't heal."

He shook his head and began on my other hand. "Not kavhavji. It's one of the oldest plants in existence. It adapted alongside dragons for millennia, and it's developed an immunity to their magic."

The white dragon. "Could it kill one?"

He raised his eyebrows and nodded. "If it scratches them and goes untreated. But most dragons keep the cure for it with them.

So I've read." He took my unwrapped hands in his and held them up, examining them in the firelight.

For such a gentle man, he had an alluring presence. Having him so near made me a little flustered. He ran a finger alongside one of the healing scratches on my right palm.

"They're looking much better." He smiled and released my hands. "Are you hungry?"

"Starving." A shiver skittered through me as the breeze reached me again.

He tutted and stood, draping another blanket around my shoulders and returning to the fire. Standing over a pot suspended from an iron hook, he knotted a leather strap and tied his hair back as he plated something for me to eat.

All my previous anger at him had evaporated, leaving behind the beginnings of...friendship? Huddled inside the warmth he provided for me, I could be nothing other than grateful. Grateful and amazed at how he was looking after me, caring for me in a human way and not in a *man wanting something from a woman* way. Maybe—and gods, I hated to admit this, even to myself—maybe having a friend wouldn't be a bad thing.

Especially one who saves my life then feeds me. He passed me a plate piled with a fluffy, aromatic rice with a crispy bread crust. The mingling of cinnamon and cardamom wafting up with the steam made my stomach growl audibly.

"I wish I could take Ady's packaged, magical food back to the monastery with me." He wriggled, settling into his bedroll. "And this is far more comfortable than my cot back home. More magic?"

"Yes. Ady is a creature of comfort."

We ate, both observing our surroundings in companionable silence. To my left, the land inclined steeply to the rocky pass where we'd both nearly died, its peaks dark and jagged against the night sky. To my right, the rocky outcropping declined into rolling hills of thick ash. The untacked horses grazed on tall grasses just beyond our campsite. Kas had taken care of everything while I'd been out.

I finished up my last bites. Had I even thanked him for saving me? I cleared my throat. "Thank you. You must have had to carry me a long way."

He shrugged, looking back the way we came. "Of course. But Pistachio did most of the work. I had to get us away from those caves."

I looked that way too and shivered despite the warm blankets and fire. "Did you see any?" Surely my voice was only low and raspy because of the vine, and not because I couldn't bring myself to voice the word *manticore*. Apparently I was less brave at night and after nearly dying twice in one day.

He sucked his lips in, looking between me and the high pass. "Only shadows at the backs of the caves." He swallowed hard. "Probably just my eyes playing tricks on me. Right?"

"Oh, probably," I agreed too quickly. "Are we camped far enough away, though? Just in case?"

He nodded, pulling his blanket tighter. "They won't venture this far from their caves. Not this near a forest."

"You're a manticore expert too, then?"

His eyes darted to me, snagging on the upward turn of the corner of my mouth. He smiled. "I came prepared."

I grimaced, setting my eaten-clean plate before the fire. "Not for quicksand."

That surprised a small laugh from him. "No, not for quicksand." He cleaned up our plates, poked at the fire again, then curled up on his bedroll. "Try to get some sleep. Your body needs more time to recover."

Now that I had food in my belly, my eyelids felt heavy and my limbs, sluggish. I curled up on the sinfully soft bedroll, and the laundry soap scent of the trove on my blanket lulled me into sleep.

I awoke to see the sun quite advanced in the sky. Kas already had us packed and the horses ready to go, but he still bustled around the campfire checking bags and fussing around the horses' tacks.

"Anxious to get on the road?" I struggled to my feet, my body still stiff from the vine's poison.

He glanced back toward the caves, dark circles under his eyes. "You slept like the dead." His accusatory tone sounded more afraid than anything. "They brayed almost all night."

A chill went through me mid-stretch. I was completely awake now, balling my blanket into a hasty bundle. "Manticores?"

He ran a hand through disheveled curls. "I don't know what else it could've been. Braying. Harsh echoing laughs. They sounded far away, but it still took far too long for the sun to come up."

I scrambled to get myself together, and in no time at all, we sat on horseback at the top of a hill leading down and away from the cliffs. Bocian, a major Aravenian port city, sat in the angle between the gulf coast and the Eldor River. Made visible with my spyglass, army tents gathered along the river like a flock of seagulls.

My shoulders slumped as I handed it to Kas. "We're not getting across the river here."

"We never were." He raised it to his eyes with a smile and looked down toward the city.

"What do you mean?"

"The ferries stopped crossing the Eldor a few years ago, but there's still one illegal ferry. It changes position every few days, but I know where it is today. We just have to get to it. Should we wait till nightfall?"

I studied him and the city below for a moment. After he saved my life last night, I woke up with a far more trusting heart. But him springing the illegal ferry on me at the last minute brought some walls back up. "Um...no, Galter requires a curfew in big cities like Bocian. I think we should go through while more people are out."

I coiled my braid around my head and tied a black silk scarf over it, fitting my open-crown helmet on top. For good measure, I pulled the green scarf attached to the helmet across the lower half of my face and hooked it on the other side. It'd been a long time since I'd been seen by any Aravenian soldiers, but I didn't want to risk it, especially not knowing if that phony beggar had Galter's dogs sweeping the streets for me.

"Think our friend will cause us any trouble?" Kas asked, practically plucking the question from my brain.

"I'd be shocked if he didn't. Here." I took a sheathed dagger from my belt and held it out toward him. "Take this. I don't know what we're going into down there, and you shouldn't be unarmed."

He waved me off, shaking his head. "I don't want it. I worship a goddess of peace and wisdom, and I don't believe in bloodshed."

"But throwing rocks is okay?"

Half his face pulled up in a smile, but he didn't reach for the dagger.

Although nothing about his face or demeanor was judgmental, hot shame burned in my cheeks. I pulled the dagger back, hastily snapping it onto my belt again and grateful the scarf covered the lower half of my face. "Then I'm a shameless heathen, because I'm not giving up my knives, and I'll use them if I need to."

His face dropped at the bite in my words. "I'm sorry, Nesrin. I meant no offense."

But I was already urging Pistachio down the hill road, and I didn't bother to respond. After a moment, Balembar's hoofbeats sounded softly in the mud behind me, but Kas said nothing more.

Before our horses' hooves even touched cobblestone, the crowded, noisy, dirty denizens of Bocian dragged us along into the nois-

ier, dirtier, thickly packed warren of streets and mud brick buildings of the city. Along with the crowds of pedestrians and horse
traffic, dozens of beggars lined the city streets, inadequately dressed
against the oncoming cold and thin from lack of food.

"Get out of the way!" A well-dressed man on a horse with gold-
en-edged tacking kicked his shiny boot out as he nearly trampled a
group of women soliciting food from passers-by. The older women
screamed and wrapped their arms around each other, scrambling
higher on the choked sidewalk.

"Hey!" Kas yelled after him, his face uncharacteristically angry
and shoulders tense as he geared up to spur Balembar after the
man.

"Shut up!" I hissed, edging Pistachio slightly in front of his
stallion to stop him from making *another* stupid mistake. The
man, thank Hivathe, didn't seem to hear Kas above the cacophony,
and he continued around a corner.

"What are you doing?" I whispered fiercely, grabbing Kas's arm.
"Don't bring attention to us!"

Kas looked past me, his muscles tense beneath my hand. "But he
just..."

"And what are you or I going to do about it?"

His flashing eyes slid past me, but he didn't move. Several horse-
men pushed past, shooting us dirty looks as I tried to shift us
back into the slow flow of traffic. I followed his eyes to the trio of
women who now moved along the sidewalk just ahead of us. "But
he could've killed them."

I leaned in close. "Anybody prospering under Galter's rule isn't
someone who'd care about basic human decency." I released his
arm, looking around to be sure no one was watching us. At that
moment, a fight broke out on the other side of the street, snarling
the crowds of soldiers and civilians even further. The only people
getting through this wretched city unscathed were those who kept
their heads down.

The women who'd nearly been trampled stood close to the street, their backs to me as they comforted each other. I covertly drew fifty kalpers from my saddlebag and dropped them into one of their baskets as we passed, in small enough coins not to arouse suspicion at the market.

A few minutes later, I caught Kas grinning at me.

"What?"

"Nicely done." He nudged Balembar ahead of me and led us down a narrow street sloping toward the docks. "Follow me and act like you know where you're going."

He turned into a tight alley, crowded with leaning drunks and reeking of ale, unwashed bodies, and refuse. After several turns across smaller streets and narrower alleys, we ended up around the backside of a tavern. Between its crumbling wall and the thick birch forest behind it, over a dozen flea bitten horses stood at hitching rails in a small yard. Two women with glassy eyes, flushed cheeks, and low bodices laughed carelessly with a group of men, leading them toward the door of the tavern.

Kas tossed his head to me in a "come on" gesture, dismounted, and led Balembar around the back of the yard. I followed suit, and when the group had gone inside, Kas pulled Balembar into a thin gap in the trees.

CHAPTER SEVEN

THE FERRYMAN

As I entered the forest, Kas put his index finger to his lips and pointed with it over his left shoulder. About ten yards away through the thick line of trees, two guards sat with their backs to us on a high tree stand. The further I went into the forest, the more their carousing separated from the fiddles and drunken chatter of the tavern. They each had one hand on their crossbows, one hand on their bottles, and at least one foot in the grave, judging by the thick cloud of tobacco smoke and the hacking coughs punctuating their laughter. I hurried past them after Kas.

Even though the ground growth wasn't dense, the birch trees grew so closely packed that making our way through without a path was slow and difficult. Just as I started to doubt that Kas knew where he was going, the mighty roar of the Eldor River reached my ears.

Kas put his hand up, palm out toward me. He whistled a high-pitched birdsong—*fee-bee, fee bay*. Immediately the answering call came back. Once more he called out, and the song came back.

Kas sighed, looking all kinds of relieved. "Okay," he said softly. "It's safe to go."

He gestured me on, and there in the middle of the press of white tree trunks, an overgrown path appeared, just wide enough for one horse to make it through at a time. He turned and spoke softly. "Our contact is just around the bend of the river."

"How do you know about this ferry?"

He looked at me sideways. "Ady told me about it."

That meddling dragon did that on purpose, splitting information between the two of us.

His smile grew sad at whatever he saw on my face. "I'm sorry to be the one to tell you, but there's a lot she doesn't tell you about Galter's crimes."

When I got back, I was going to have to have a very frank discussion with a certain overprotective dragon. "What else don't I know?"

"She helps pay the expenses for a man named Rav and his crew who take refugees into Nabul to keep them from being enslaved in the mines."

I held my breath a moment, betrayed in maybe the best way. My eyes filled with tears. People were so desperate to leave my kingdom for such a basic thing as safety. I was glad Kas rode ahead and that I still had my face scarf latched to catch my tears.

Soon the path opened onto the rocky shore of the wide, muddy Eldor. Just a few yards away, a couple of men looked up from where they stood beside a plank set on the shore from a wooden pole boat. Half a dozen people huddled on benches on its deck.

"Welcome!" one of the men said, his young, deep voice quiet but carrying. "You're just in time. A few more minutes, and I would've had to leave you behind." Despite his words, the slightly drooping corners of his mouth behind his beard made him seem almost disappointed at our arrival. But then his big brown eyes smiled at us, and the moment, whatever it was, passed.

Tall like Kas but even broader-shouldered and a little older, the man seemed far too handsome to be running an illegal ferry. His partner merely frowned at us, checking his sword and measuring Kas and me with his bright blue eyes over a long, bushy beard.

"Thank you for waiting." Kas shook the friendly one's hand and turned to include me. "My fellow traveler and I are in somewhat of a hurry."

"Of course. I'm Rav, by the way." His remarkably beautiful eyes slid to me, and he smiled brighter, reaching out his hand.

I gulped, shaking it and managing to squeak out a small *hello*. Was it strictly necessary for him to be so attractive?

Handsome Rav kept my hand a moment in his larger one, dropping his other hand on top of it and raising his eyebrows. His eyes dropped to my sword belt and back up. "I appreciate having a fierce warrior aboard. You never know when you'll need one in this line of business."

My face burned as he winked and dropped my hand. After they helped us get our horses on board, Handsome Rav directed one of the crew to weigh anchor. Then he picked up a bow and pulled a painted red arrow from a quiver tied to the side of the ship.

"I'll get that," the bearded man said gruffly.

But Rav pulled it out of his reach, shaking out the thin rope tied at the end. "Don't be ridiculous, Grumpy. You're a terrible shot." He flashed me a grin while Grumpy sat beside the arrows. "He'd never hit the far shore."

Kas looked between us, and a crease formed between his eyebrows. He leaned closer. "Something's not right here," he murmured. "Ady said—"

"Everything looks fine to me," I murmured back, watching Rav's muscled back through his thin shirt as he notched the arrow, drew the bowstring, aimed, and skillfully shot it in a clean arc across the wide river, the rope silking out behind. Gods, that was attractive. It sank into a trunk on the far shore where someone pulled it free and wrapped the rope around a crank.

"Hey, man the pole, will ya?" Rav called to a man leaning against the rails who took his post, and the boat moved across the current of the ancient river, guided both by the rope and the poleman.

Grumpy moved toward us, but Rav stepped in front of him, stopping his progress with a hand on his shoulder. "It's a short trip across the river, but let's have some fun. What else is an illegal ferry for?" He pointed to a man on the bench with a violin at his feet among the baggage. "You sir, will you play something sprightly for us? And you," he pointed at me. "Will you dance with a lonely man who spends all his time on the water?"

My heart launched into nervous pounding. "Me?"

Grumpy glared at us, shifting from foot to foot, but Rav stepped close.

Kas stepped closer. "The lady doesn't want to dance."

Rav ignored him. "Of course she does. My lady?"

My cheeks were about to catch fire. "Oh, um, I don't know how to…"

Rav placed one hand on my waist and took my hand in the other, turned me around. Somewhere behind me, the violinist's first notes slipped into the air, and my feet felt like lead.

"Is it a good idea to play such a loud instrument right now?" Kas's voice was tight, a little peeved.

But the violinist played on. A handful of men stepped up from their places on the bench as Rav held my gaze. "Ady says you like to *dance*," he said softly.

I frowned. "No, I don't."

"Follow my *lead*, okay?" His eyebrows went up as if was trying to convey something I was absolutely not catching.

His hand on my waist slid lower. Maybe Kas was right. Maybe—

Rav grabbed the hilt of my dagger at my hip, unsheathed it, and whirled me aside, releasing the weapon in a bright arc to sink into Grumpy's chest.

Grumpy recoiled, his raised sword dropping in a clank. Bright blood spread across his shirt as he fell. Then everything happened at once.

The travelers huddled, screaming. The men who'd stood up started fighting amongst themselves, and one headed for me. I registered Rav pulling a sword from a barrel as I grabbed throwing knives from my bandolier, moving on instinct to fight on the side of the man who knew Ady's name.

I didn't have time to process Kas being thrown roughly against the side of the boat, just threw my knives at the thick man advancing on me who only batted them away. But it bought me time to unsheathe Baney and block his next blow, cracking his sword and pissing him off. The meaty man charged, swinging hard in an arc that would've claimed my head if I hadn't had Baney to block it. Meaty's sword cracked off at the hilt, the force of the blow windmilling the blade. It slashed both our arms on its track as the momentum of his swing barreled him into me, slamming me to the deck with him on top. I nearly lost Baney, but I grasped her with my left hand and brought her hilt down hard on his head, slipping out of reach before he could pin me. I stood and swung Baney back. Just one smooth swing. Just like the straw dummies in the trove.

But I'd never killed before. I hesitated.

Meaty's fist grabbed my ankle and pulled hard. I crashed to the deck on my back, and Baney clattered away along with my helmet and scarf. The man wrapped his hand around my throat and squeezed.

But a bloody sword broke through Meaty's neck. I screamed as his blood spattered across me, and he collapsed to the deck at my side.

Rav pulled me to stand on my shaking legs. "I'm so sorry. That was the best I could do. They arrived about twenty minutes before you and threatened to kill everyone on deck if I didn't lure you onto the boat." He held Baney out to me and put his hand gently on my upper arm, looking me over. "Are you okay?"

I grabbed Baney with shaking hands. "Where's Kas?"

"The monk? He's fine." As Rav answered, I spotted Kas across the boat saying a prayer over the crumpled form of a man. All around us, it was business as usual. The violinist and three others I'd taken to be refugees bustled around the deck.

Rav pulled off his shirt and used it to gently wiped the man's blood from my face. "You're trembling."

"How did you learn to do that?" I asked in a hushed tone. Even Rav's rippling, tattooed chest was extraneous information to my fumbling brain. "To take a man's life?"

He closed his eyes and sighed. "Sometimes it's kill or be killed. And I'm morally opposed to it being the latter, for you, for me, for my men. For anyone I can help protect."

The violinist, a tall, dark-haired man with pale brown eyes and a kind smile approached us with my dagger offered to me hilt-first. None of Grumpy's blood remained, but I could only stare at my weapon.

Rav took it from him and gently slid it back into the sheath at my waist. My cheeks burned at his closeness, but I wasn't certain my legs would hold me if I tried to step away.

"Let's see what we can get from the last one standing." Rav clapped his hand on the violinist's shoulder. "Dax, send the all-clear."

As Rav strode across the deck toward where Grumpy was tied against the sidewall of the boat, Dax grabbed a ropeless green arrow from the quiver and expertly shot it into the target on the shore we were rapidly approaching.

"Are you alright? That isn't your blood, is it?"

Kas's voice close to my ear made my body turn toward him. We grasped each other at the elbows.

I bit my lip. "No. Some of it, but I'm okay." I scanned his panicked face. A bruise had started to bloom across his cheek. "Are you okay?"

He shook his head. "Furious at how I walked us right into this."

"No, you were right. Something was wrong, and I didn't see it. I'm beginning to see why Ady insisted we go together. We keep trading the roles of dumbass and smartass."

He smiled. "At least one of us is always right."

I pulled in a shaky breath, letting the pools of his crinkling eyes calm me enough to smile weakly back.

"My lady? Brother?" Rav beckoned from across the deck where he crouched before Grumpy, who was still alive despite his knife wound, his hands tied above his head. "I think you'll want to hear what he has to say."

I let Kas grasp my hand, and we went together toward where Grumpy's cold eyes followed me with pure hatred. I twisted the end of my braid around my free hand for comfort.

Rav casually sliced the air with his dagger. "I told Grumpy here—"

"That's not my name!"

Rav slapped him hard across the face. "Hush. I told Grumpy I'd spare his life if he told me why he wanted you two on the ferry." He flicked Grumpy's nose. "That's your cue, asshole. Spill your guts, or I will."

Grumpy scowled. "Prince Ashur hired us to follow the monk to see what he knows about some treasure the Emperor's looking for. Bringing the dragon whore—"

Rav grasped the man's beard and hacked it off, nearly skinning the man's chin and sending blood dribbling down a crossed arrow tattoo on his neck. A mercenary.

I pulled Kas closer. Rav may've been handsome, but his brutality was not.

"Don't call her that again, or I'll slice off something else that protrudes from your body. And neither of us wants that. What were you saying about this fierce, admirable woman?"

"Ashur hired us to capture them and torture them into telling us what they know." Grumpy smiled wide, teeth missing. "Then the bitch would go to Ashur for his *personal* use."

Kas stepped in front of me, and Rav neatly sliced a finger from Grumpy's tied hands. He yowled, blood dripping down his arm. I focused on the back of Kas's robe, willing myself not to look. Not to get sick.

"You *will* learn your manners," Rav said darkly.

Kas's grip on my hand stayed strong, but gentle. "What treasure is Galter looking for?"

"I don't know," the man howled.

I risked a look around Kas to see Rav glance at the side of the ship where his crew was about to drop anchor.

"You only have a few moments to tell us everything you know." He pressed the edge of his dagger to the man's neck.

Grumpy's throat bobbed, and he flattened himself against the side of the ship. "That's all I know! I swear!"

"Where is Ashur now?" Kas demanded.

"How should I know?"

Rav pushed his dagger deeper into Grumpy's neck, and he winced, shutting his eyes and murmuring a prayer. "I swear. I don't know!"

"I think I actually believe him." Rav raised his dark eyes to me. "Do you believe him?"

Kas nodded.

"Yes," I said.

"Good." Rav withdrew his blade and grinned, patting Grumpy on the arm. "See? That was easy, wasn't it? And just before we reached the shore." Rav slashed his dagger across Grumpy's throat, and Kas and I cried out as his blood rushed down his chest.

I clamped my hand against my stomach and buried my face in Kas's sleeve, breathing in the trove's laundry scent, biting back tears. His hand came to my back.

"I hate doing that," Rav said quietly.

"Then why did you do it?" I cried, not opening my eyes to see the carnage I could already smell.

"A few reasons," Rav said, a terse calm in his voice. "I have no place to keep prisoners. If we set him free, he'd have gone straight to Ashur. And you weren't here earlier when he bragged about violating women he'd helped enslave in Crokar. He didn't deserve my mercy, and he doesn't deserve your pity." Rav dispassionately gave instructions to his crew to carry off the dead men and disembark the passengers.

Finally on Nabullian ground, Kas and I watched Dax and the rest of the crew load the refugees with as much food and other supplies as they could carry.

Rav gestured toward them as he approached us. "Do you need any food? Water? Gold? Other supplies?"

"No, thank you." Kas reached out his hand. "We're provided for."

Rav shook Kas's hand and smiled. "Remember me in your prayers, Brother. I'm sure I need it."

Kas smiled back. "May Hivathe bless you for the generosity and protection you've offered us and so many others."

Rav laughed. "Very diplomatically spoken." He turned to me. "It's been an honor to fight beside you, Your Highness." He leaned over and kissed my hand. "Ah, if only I were a prince." But his broad, handsome smile no longer held charm for me.

"I don't know how you live like this," is all I said back.

His smile dropped, eyes turning sad and thoughtful. "You may have to do the same before all this is over. May Hivathe be with you on your quest." He clapped his hand to his chest, his dark eyes solemn. "I pledge my life in service to you and your people, who love you and await the return of the true king."

He graciously accepted my awkward *thank yous*, and Kas and I headed into the woods toward Kesna.

CHAPTER EIGHT

KESNA, THE CAPITAL OF NABUL

With the sun sinking at our backs, Kas and I emerged from the woods beside the Eldor River and into a huge press of people on the road into Kesna. The traffic only increased as we approached the bottleneck of the city gates.

"Why are there so many people?" The stupid drunk men in the group behind us jostled me and Pistachio for the third time, and I was already done with Kesna. Excepting Bocian earlier today, I hadn't been in a crowd this size in years and my anxiety flared like flames drenched with alcohol. Especially after the ferry.

Kas peered with interest into the crates of oranges in the back of the cart rumbling beside us, moving faster in the carts-and-carriages-only lane. "Probably headed to the market."

Ah, the famed market at Kesna. I'd been ruminating over Rav's words and hadn't remembered. The last time I'd been here was with my family. I looked more carefully at the crowd. People hailed each other excitedly, their voices mingling and rising with laughter and singing, random violins and pipes twittering up and dying suddenly.

At least I liked the intentions of this crowd—revelry, not desperation and dominance. A far cry from Bocian. Even the many Nabullian guards watching the people on the road seemed more like mature house cats watching kittens gambol. Still. Between the ferry and my long disuse of socializing, I was an exposed nerve desperate to divine the mood and intentions of every human taking up space within thirty feet of me.

Kas turned every which way in his saddle. "I wonder how much he wants for those lamps." A pause. "Look at all those books! Do you suppose he sells charcoal, too? I'm running a little low." A few minutes later, through laughter, "Did you hear that woman's joke about her potato crop?"

Meanwhile I was trying to ignore the blood of two dead men caked on my pants. I stared at him for several long moments before he turned my way, his excitement shifting to concern.

"What?"

"Enjoying our holiday, are we?"

He gave me a small smile, his eyes growing darker. "If I didn't find something to be interested in or excited about, what happened this morning would completely drown me." He swallowed hard, and when he looked back at me, his eyes were glassy. "You might try to do the same." He looked ahead to the gates, lit with braziers blazing against the oncoming sunset. "I hope Queen Carusa's willing to speak with us," he said quietly.

The prospect of presenting ourselves before foreign royalty made my stomach turn. Or maybe it was still the crowd? Maybe it just didn't feel right to see her without my parents.

"Are we expected?"

"My father sent magpies, but don't you know the prince?"

Another wave of panic roiled through my stomach as a raucous laugh bubbled out of the group behind us, and they pushed us forward. "Yeah, we're, ahm, acquainted. But maybe it's best if you do the talking?"

"Sure. If you want me to."

Inside the wide gates, we moved with the bulk of the crowd down a wide main street lined with gardens and tall sandstone buildings decorated with pennants and festoons. Everyone's faces were lit with excitement as if we were all heading to a festival instead of a market. And maybe we were. The market was held only once a month over a long weekend, and everyone came to it who could.

As much as I didn't like being in the middle of the crowd, being a stranger on horseback allowed me the distance to admit the city was beautiful. If I'd encountered it as a painting in a book instead of in person, I would've pored over it, noticing the beautiful diversity of the crowd dressed in styles from all over the gulf nations, their skin tones ranging from palest pink to darkest brown, conversing and doing business in peace. How the lit windows of shops and upper apartments twinkled like luminous gold in the darkening evening. I'd run my finger along that road ahead that sloped up toward the palace.

Within the mile, the street opened onto a roundabout encircling a vast central coliseum sunken into the ground, the stage in the center at street level. Through the encircling columns, I spied an acrobatics troupe performing for hundreds of spectators whose cheering made the air electric. Billowing patterned silks like sails, resplendent in a myriad of bright colors, stretched high from the columns down to the tops of the booths lining the streets, a cheerful, intimate cocoon in the darkening night, and no doubt protection from the sun by day.

The noisy babble of a thousand people talking was punctuated by the occasional baby crying, friend calling to friend, haggling patrons, and barking dogs. Somewhere in the distance, a band played, the drum beats low and rumbling up through Pistachio's hooves into my body. The higher notes of intertwining koras and flutes slipped around us like ribbons in the air.

Not one spot of the booths packed side by side was empty. Kas and I pointed the wonders out to each other as we passed them—a dozen bins of colorful spices piled high like fragile pyramids in jeweled yellows, reds, and greens. Hanging metal lanterns with candlelight sparkling through cut-outs of stars. Baskets overflowing with crystals and geodes in all the luminous colors of the rainbow, and nifesta leaves wrapped in twine for smoke cleansing beside divination cards and velvet bags of runes from the far northern seas.

The savory smell of roasting meats pervaded the air, and on the upper fringe of each inhaled breath I caught spices from my childhood. It carried on the breeze with the blooming sweet olive trees that lined the streets, mingling into a delicious tapestry of scent and color and joy I hadn't experienced in far too long. I unhooked my scarf to take it all in, my anxiety quelling with happier memories of being here with my family.

But we didn't have time to linger over any of the market's delights. Despite Kas's longing looks at the booth of art supplies, we made the half-circuit around the coliseum and left the hubbub of the market behind to navigate a thinner crowd approaching the palace, a multi-towered edifice clad in smooth limestone. Guards flanked its massive ironwork gate at the top of wide marble steps.

We dismounted and joined the short queue waiting to speak to two guards who, judging by their sashes and position at the center, were of a higher rank than the lines on either side of them. The taller one with a beard and a bald, dark head seemed to be deputized with the decision-making. He allowed one man through the gates and sent a page to the palace for a couple with a message, but everyone else ahead of us in line was turned away, and quickly.

"Good evening," Kas said brightly when it was our turn.

The guards looked us both over, and the one in charge addressed him. "Good evening, Brother. What's your business?"

Kas leaned in, speaking softly. "I'm Brother Kas, son of Velarch Oh of Veytia"—the guard exchanged a doubtful, bemused expression with the guard beside him—"and my companion is the Knight of the Dread Dragon Adydorrstea's Trove. My father sent me to speak to Queen Carusa on an important, urgent matter."

"The royal family has retired for the evening," he recited, "and is not available for visitors. Come back in the morning when they're handling the business of the realm, and you can add your petition to the day's agenda. Next!"

But Kas stood firm. "My father sent a magpie to inform Her Majesty we'd be coming soon. We're sorry for the lateness of the hour, but we've traveled a long way to speak with her, and we couldn't help our timing."

The guard raised his eyebrows at the younger one, who pulled a rolled parchment from his belt and looked it over. "Nothing here about expecting a foreign dignitary. Do you have any proof that you are who you say you are? A signet ring, perhaps?"

Kas bit both lips into his mouth and turned to me.

As if Galter hadn't stripped me of all my jewelry along with my rights. I shook my head and leaned toward Kas. "Don't you have anything?"

He shook his head, his brow furrowing. "Not since I was sent to the Order."

I cocked my head. Was he no longer considered part of his own family? The faces of his parents and brothers from his drawing came to mind, and my heart twinged for him. But I pushed that aside for later, turning to the guard in charge.

"Look. You let those other people send a message to the palace. Can you at least send word to Queen Carusa"—gods, I hated to do this—"and to Prince Javid that Prince Kasper of Veytia and Nesrin, Knight of the Trove, are here to see them?"

"Fine." He rolled his eyes and turned to a page standing just inside the iron bars of the gate. "Go ahead. Bring word to the palace as she says." He turned back to us as the boy hurried away. "It might be a while. Enjoy the market and come back when you hear the bell. Next!"

The group behind us pushed forward, and we went back down the steps into the street.

"At least we get to go to the market." Kas's voice matched his wide-eyed smile.

I mounted Pistachio. The delicious smells from down the street called me onward even as the thickening crowds repelled me. "I guess so, but you lead."

Kas stayed on foot, hurrying Balembar and Pistachio back toward the busy circle of booths as if afraid the bell would sound for us at any moment. Completely in his element, Kas stopped to converse with shop owners about their friendly dog, intricately woven baskets, adorable baby, or clever toys.

The kaleidoscope of things for sale, people, scents, and sounds was nothing like the old daily market outside Araven's palace that sold food, fabrics, and other staples. Maybe spending some time and money here wouldn't be the worst thing ever. Mother used to say the marketspace was owned and operated by a woman's group, and that the majority of profits from the entertainment and renting the stands went to helping the indigent people of Nabul.

People laughed here, broke bread together, haggled good-naturedly, and lived peacefully. It was everything Araven used to be and might never be again.

A booth in the arc of the road was hung with embroidered silk robes in deep jewel tones. My mother would have headed there first, crooning with admiration over the artist's handwork. Talon and Pendor would have eaten all the kabobs they could fit, and then they'd be begging my parents for a glamorous new sword or shield. My father would talk to the man on the right whose stand held clever stone board games and a bronze mechanism with gears that predicted the movements of the moon and stars. But what did I want to do?

Ultimately, it was the stomach-ensorceling aroma of rosemary grilled pork that lured me off Pistachio's saddle. While Kas talked to the bookseller next door about charcoal and leather-bound journals, I bought us each a kebab. Then we continued walking the market with Pistachio and Balembar at our backs. A portion of the obscene amount of gold and silver Ady sent with me was burning a hole in the bag at my belt. Beside me, Kas followed my gaze toward that stand of colorful robes.

"Do you want to look at those?"

I took too long to answer, clinging close to Pistachio. The stand was across the street, and the press of the crowd was overwhelming.

"C'mon. I'll go with you." He placed his arm around my shoulder and walked us over there with the horses at our backs. I let him. It was comforting to be protected on at least two sides from the jostling of the crowd.

A young man with a toddler on his hip held a burgundy robe up with his free hand. "How about three silvers for this robe?"

"Three silvers?" The shop owner scratched his graying beard. "My friend." He patted the man heartily on the back. "The fairest woman in Nabul embroidered this robe." He gestured to the silver-haired woman sitting behind the stand who smiled but didn't look up from her embroidery.

"So you understand why I can't take any less than five silvers for it."

Kas grinned, his eyes flicking between the players in the tableau.

"Four silvers then, and it's my finest offer."

The owner clapped his hand to his chest in pretend agony and caught the eye of his wife, who gave her husband a nearly imperceptible approval with her eyebrows. "It kills me to let it go for that price, but four silvers it is."

I sidled to the edge of the booth away from where the shop owner still chatted with his customer as he wrapped up the robe. Kas followed. I softly pinched the fine plum silk of a robe embroidered with vines, but the rough skin of my fingers caught on it. I pulled my hand away, grateful I hadn't torn anything. Beautiful clothes like that weren't for me anymore, I guess.

"Do you like it?" Kas asked softly.

"It's lovely." I'd spoken quietly, but the woman of the shop glanced up at my words and put her sewing aside, approaching me.

"Thank you for your kindness, my lady." Her eyes searched my face. "You remind me so strongly of a fine lady who bought my robes many times, so many years ago. The same hair like fire…"

I hurriedly poked a loose strand of my hair back under my scarf.

"The same pale skin and big brown eyes." The warm smile that spread across her smooth brown face barely carried a wrinkle, despite her age.

I smiled back. She was probably only guessing a swift avenue to an easy sale in a market with thousands of intergenerational customers, but I still ate her words up like sugar. Because I did have my mother's hair and eyes. And I missed her. I blinked against the tears forming in my eyes. "Your skill is unmatched."

"I have something I think you'll like. It's something like she might have purchased." She turned and lifted the hinged top of a wooden trunk full of more robes and returned with one. "I think this one would suit you best, as it did her."

I gasped. The deep moss green silk robe was embroidered with wild roses in shades of cerise down the lapels and circling the cuffs of the sleeves and hem. It looked so much like one my mother had when I was a child.

The woman's husband approached us as his previous customer walked off with his package. "Ah, you have excellent taste. The *nesrin* pattern is a top seller."

Kas looked at me in surprise, but I only smiled and dug money from my bag.

"*Nesrin* is a type of wild rose," I explained to Kas, pulling ten silvers from my bag and holding them in my hand, palm down, until the man placed his hand beneath mine. "I'll buy it, please."

The coins clinked into his palm, and his eyes went wide. "This is far too much. We're only asking six silvers for the robe. Do you wish to buy two?" His wife looked at his palm and eyed me anxiously.

"No, just the one." My eyes were growing dangerously watery, and I needed to move on.

The couple exchanged worried looks. "Are you sure you don't want something else, too?" the man said.

Truthfully, I didn't know what a fair price was. Handling dragon gold for years had apparently degraded any frugality I may've started life with. I scanned the table with swimming eyes and spotted a mulberry scarf. I handed the beautifully soft item to the man to wrap up. "This too, please."

"But that's not even half a silv—"

"The lady knows what she wants." Kas laughed, bringing lightness to the conversation. "And she seems happy to pay you handsomely for it. Why not call it a blessing?"

The owners thanked us profusely as the husband wrapped up my purchases and his wife pocketed the sum. Kas chatted with them, giving me a chance to turn away and dry my eyes. I both wanted to ask the woman a million questions about my mother, but I couldn't bring myself to say another word. I fiddled unnecessarily with Pistachio's tack.

"Lady Knight of the Trove?" A deep voice I'd hoped not to hear rose above the crowd.

CHAPTER NINE

THE STAINED-GLASS WINDOW

I plastered on a smile before turning to face Prince Javid of Nabul. He stood in a little pool of cleared space just behind me, his personal guards in tow.

"Prince Javid! Hello."

"It's so good to see you!" He stretched his arms toward me, but my palms went up and my eyes went wide. He withdrew his arms and bowed awkwardly instead. He was just as tall and glamorous as the last time I'd seen him, handsome and elegant with dark brown skin and rich eyes like fallen brown leaves. Impeccable in a stylish off-white suit with gold trimmings. I twisted the hem of the worn purple tunic under my coat. Javid and I had very little in common but our history, and seeing him brought back vivid memories of the days and nights he'd stayed with me.

"In my own mother's kingdom. I didn't believe it at first when they told me." He narrowed his eyes and spoke kindly. "But if you've come to call in my offer, I'm afraid you're too late. I'm to be married in a few months to the love of my life."

The genuine joy in his smile when he spoke of her relaxed me, and I finally smiled back. "You're looking well, Javid. This is Prince Kasper of Veytia," I indicated to Kas, who waited politely at my side. "We've been trying to see your mother. It's very important."

"Of course." Javid offered his hand to Kas, who shook it graciously. "Any friend of Nesrin's is a friend of mine."

"Likewise," Kas said, smiling broadly.

With me on his arm, Javid escorted us back to the palace and through its gates, incessantly asking me questions about how I'd been and what I'd been up to. After calling over groomsmen for our horses, he brought us through another gate and through a quiet courtyard that blocked the noise of the city beyond. Here, servants scurried in quiet shadows under deep balconies overflowing with bright pink flowers, a splashing fountain tumbled into a pool tiled in lively colors, and cherry trees dripped with a late harvest.

"You're just in time to join my family for our evening meal."

My cheeks burned. "Oh, no, that's...we don't want to impose."

"No imposition. My parents insist."

Inside a dining hall lined with large windows, a bevy of servers refilled cups, removed dirty dishes, and offered platters of steaming foods to only two seated diners, the queen and her husband.

Javid spoke as a graceful young woman in blue robes led us to empty chairs across from the queen. "Princess Nesrin, Prince Kasper, allow me to introduce you to Queen Carusa, my mother, and Prince-Consort Hirach, my father."

"Thank you for welcoming us to your table." Kas bowed before sitting.

"Hello," I murmured. Servers placed spiced meats on our plates, and my stomach growled. The kabob on the streets, while one of the most delicious things I'd ever eaten, hadn't been enough.

"Welcome to Kesna, Your Highnesses." Queen Carusa's voice and charisma easily filled the room. "It's a pleasure to see you again, Princess Nesrin. My how you've grown. When Javid returned from your guardian's trove a few years ago, he was quite impressed with you and the Great Adydorrstea." Despite the gray curls peeking out at the crown of her braids, Carusa's clear, brown skin fairly glowed, and her eyes were vibrant and sharp, lit by the magenta of her dressing gown. Her impeccable posture made me sit up straighter, and her mention of Javid sent heat creeping up my neck. Blessedly, Javid's bride-to-be was apparently elsewhere.

Hirach, who Javid favored most, nodded. "We thank Hivathe that you survived the coup and were rescued from your uncle."

Carusa harrumphed. "Galter's existence is a stain on the world, and no one will miss him when someone finally ends his miserable life."

"No offense," Hirach said, smiling weakly.

I smiled. Carusa was my kind of queen. "Absolutely none taken, Your Majesty. I couldn't agree more, and I'd be pleased to be the one to do it." Big words from someone who still hadn't recovered from the deaths on the ferry wrought by others.

Like me, Nabul had every reason to hate Galter. It'd only been about a hundred years since they'd won back their border-lands, just north of the Eldor Mountains, from my power-hungry great-grandfather, and Galter coveted them. Hell, Galter coveted the entire queendom of Nabul, which had been part of the old Aravenian Empire.

I waited briefly for Kas to begin the conversation, as we'd discussed, but he was pink-cheeked and encumbered by the attention of three lovely servers who'd flocked to him.

"Your Highness, would you like some strawberries? They're very sweet," one said, flashing her long lashes at him as she leaned toward him with a tray. She smelled of jasmine and may have been the most beautiful woman I'd ever seen.

Kas blushed and barely looked at her, just raised a palm toward her tray. "No, thank you."

"Some coffee then, Your Highness?" asked another beauty with a husky voice and skin as clear and pale as a winter morning.

"Thank you, yes." He held a ceramic mug up to her to be filled but didn't meet her eyes.

Kas's discomfort with this female attention contrasted so sharply with my earlier suspicions of him that I held back a smile and found the courage to speak up. "Your Majesties, Galter's the reason we've come to you tonight."

Kas carefully disentangled his mug from the long fingers of the server. "Did you receive a magpie from my father?"

Carusa exchanged glances with Hirach, and both shook their heads. She placed her fork down and turned all of her attention to us. "No, no word from Veytia. How can we help you and the velarch?"

"One of my father's spies learned that Galter's looking for a powerful magical artifact to use against the allied armies. We're trying to find it before he does."

"An excellent plan. What's he looking for?" Carusa waved to the servers, and they all left the room, closing the doors behind them until only the five of us remained.

"A golden casket from ages past. We were hoping to take advantage of your expertise, Prince Hirach." Kas pulled out his book, opened it to the right page, and passed it to Javid's outstretched hand, who reviewed it briefly then passed it to Hirach.

Hirach's dark eyes widened, and he let his glasses fall to the tip of his nose as he peered at the drawing. "A casket? Those are better left undisturbed."

"The iron ones, you mean?" Kas asked, glancing briefly at me.

Hirach shook his head and looked at us each in turn. "Most assuredly both. Are you sure this is what he seeks?"

Kas nodded politely. "Our sources tell us that Galter thinks carrying this casket before an army in battle will make it invincible."

Hirach placed a hand on his stomach, looking like he might be ill. "That's definitely not a story I've heard."

"Will you tell us what you know about caskets?" Kas asked.

Hirach's shoulders hunched forward. "I can't say I know much. Hivathe herself knows which of the many stories are true, if any." He pressed his lips together and swallowed hard, Kas's book going slack in his hands. "The prevailing legend says half were iron, trapping evil beings so they couldn't harm anyone anymore. The other half were golden and supposedly held spells or blessings to balance out the evil of the iron."

"But," he continued even more quietly, "some legends mix up the contents of the iron and the gold, saying it's the gold ones that contain evil, and the iron ones that contain good things. I don't know much, but I'd never go looking for one."

"We don't have a choice," I said. "We have to find it before he does."

Carusa shook her head, catching us with her intense, shrewd eyes. "Legends aren't fact, and Galter's a gullible fool. He'll grab at anything shiny if he thinks it'll help him. I doubt such a thing even exists."

"Adydorrstea says the caskets are real, and that the beings inside are all very dangerous," I said.

"Have you ever learned anything about this particular casket, with the lions engraved?" Kas pressed.

Hirach brought the book back up closer to his face and laid a finger on the page. "I don't think they have keys. At least, I've never seen anything about keys. The lion engraving might mean the casket's from somewhere up northwest or east?" He shrugged. "Lions are typically found in a swath from Mysterium through Opintol, Oprolodas, and Ghente—really everywhere the old Ghentere Empire used to encompass."

I glanced at Kas. "So, the caskets are decorated according to where they were made? Were they made in different parts of the world?"

"I believe so." Hirach adjusted his glasses again. "But I don't remember where I heard or read that. Have you thought about going to the Mysterium Amanharate? These little stylized fern fronds scattered around the sides...I feel like they might have some Mysterium influences."

I looked excitedly at Kas, but he deflated. "Thank you, but those are meant to be feathers."

"Ah, my mistake." Hirach politely handed back the book.

"We're traveling to Mysterium after we visit the Library." Kas took a sharp piece of charcoal from a back pocket in the book and wrote dark pictographs on a blank page.

Hirach nodded, pushing his glasses back up his nose. "I'm sorry I don't know more, but the Library is a good place to learn more. Mysterium, too." He sighed and studied Kas and me for a moment. "As much as I'd love for you to deprive Galter of something he wants, I don't think it's safe for you to go looking for this."

"We'll do our best to be safe, and thank you. This is more than we knew before." Kas rubbed the charcoal from his fingers onto his robe, then put his book and charcoal away.

"Galter will already be hard to defeat with the support of Naitar and Terinor at his back." Carusa looked at her son.

Hirach followed her gaze, and his eyes softened. No doubt Javid would be among those going to fight in the coming war. Hirach probably, too. It made my heart ache to think of all the people putting their lives on the line to stop my uncle.

Hirach cleared his throat and raised a glass. "Let's finish our meal. Too much talk of war makes for poor digestion. Princess Nesrin, thank you and your guardian for your hospitality to our foolish son." He threw a glance at Javid who smiled and looked down. "Did you know that when he petitioned us to let him try to rescue you, we forbade him from going?"

I looked pointedly at Javid, who was staring down into his coffee cup. "No. He never told me that."

"Not that we didn't want you to be rescued, if you were in distress," Carusa picked up a small bell from the table and rang it. The servers entered the room and began to tend to glasses and empty plates. "But you have to understand our concern as parents. A lot of princes don't return home from quests like that. But he

left without telling us, and then he was gone so long we started to
really worry. In fact, he met the troop we sent after him on the way
back."

The blush creeping up my face was almost painful. In the corner
of my eye, I saw Kas turn toward me. Surely everyone in this room
knew what happened between me and Javid.

"It's just like I said," Javid swooped in to my rescue. "Once we
sorted out that no one wanted to kill anybody, or forcibly remove
a knight from her trove, Adydorrstea and Nesrin were generous
hosts."

Carusa turned toward a server who approached her with a
carafe, seeming to talk without paying much attention. "I'd never
even heard of a knight of the trove."

Hirach's brown eyes were wistful. "I've always wanted to see
inside a dragon's trove."

"Adydorrstea's is the most exquisite I've ever seen," Kas gushed,
perfectly happy to fill in the conversation. "The walls are covered
in intricate Drebian tile mosaics, and oh! The stained-glass windows!"

I wrapped my hands around the warmth of my coffee mug and
took a sip, so thankful for Kas deflecting attention off of me.

"They're everywhere," Kas continued, "and so beautiful. In the
high corners of the Great Hall, in the guest chambers…"

"The stained glass!" Javid recalled with obvious fondness. "So
beautiful. My favorite one was the moon in the night sky over—"

I started coughing, and his eyes widened at his error. "Oh, um…"
He made several stalling noises, feigning trying to remember where
it was when we both knew it was directly over my bed. "In, well,
I'm not sure where it was, to be honest," he said, looking everywhere except at me.

Kas leaned forward with an academic's interest in architecture.
"The night sky? I don't remember seeing that one."

"It wasn't on the tour." I took another sip to hide my face behind the cup.

Kas's eyes on me were pure innocence. "Will you show it to me if I'm able to visit again?"

I nearly choked on my coffee, coughing in a very unladylike manner. "Sure," I squeaked. "Sounds fun." Unbidden, my mind conjured an image of Kas in my bed, his bare body pressed to mine. My face flushed harder. The thought wasn't unwelcome, but it wasn't right.

I forced my naughty brain to attend to the turn in conversation, about the market and performers, which lasted until the meal was finished and petered out as the plates began to be cleared from the table.

"It's getting late. Let me get some rooms together for you. Milanda?" Carusa waved a server over.

"No thank you," I said quickly. "I don't want to get caught in the traffic leaving the market in the morning."

Carusa nodded. "Understandable. But please at least take advantage of the Qinas Campgrounds just northwest, along your route to Opintol. It'll give you a much faster start than staying in the palace, but it's heavily guarded and inside Kesna's last ring of walls."

We parted warmly from the royal family, with hugs and handshakes and promises to stay safe, some from them, and some from us to Javid and Hirach. I studied their faces and prayed it wouldn't be the last time I saw them alive.

CHAPTER TEN

SWEETDROPS AND SORROW

On the gently rolling hills just inside the northwesternmost gates of Kesna, the fires and tents of dozens of campsites speckled across the low grasses. The night was clear and lovely, so we took advantage of the well-guarded camping grounds and found a sheltered spot against the slope of a hill to stay overnight, a little away from the dozens of other campers. I watched Kas writing notes in his book, the swift black strokes of his charcoal artfully marking the sand-colored page.

I'd never watched a native speaker write Veytian until today. Aravenian, which was used as the common tongue throughout the gulf nations, was based on a letter system, straightforward and unadorned. But watching Kas's words bloom across the page was like watching a story come to life. Stylized birds, feathers, snakes, and hands were born and danced across the page, accented by upward and downward strokes. It was a joy to watch him.

"Have you always been an artist?"

He grinned and looked up at me from his page. "An artist? I don't think I've ever been called one before. That's generous."

"But those are your paintings in your book, aren't they? Hivathe and Onsorbal, the casket, the maps, your family?"

He nodded, continuing to dance his charcoal across the page. I watched him silently a minute more, thinking about Kas giving up his signet ring, basically being kicked out of his family just because he was born the fourth son.

"If you hadn't been forced into the monastery, what would you have done instead?"

His eyebrows shrugged as he finished up his writing and put everything away. "I don't know. I didn't have much time to dream about that before I went in."

Galter stole away my dreams too, but he was my enemy. What was it like to have your parents, who were supposed to support your dreams, do that to you? Just because of something as impersonal as tradition. "And since you went in?"

He shrugged, his smile gone. "It really doesn't matter, now." He swallowed hard and poked at the fire with a long stick. "I appreciate Prince Hirach's information." He broke the stick up and tossed it into the fire. "But every place I go, I wonder if they know more than they're letting on."

I pulled my coat tighter and let him change the subject. The hill's slope at our back helped cut down on the wind, but it was still chilly. "I don't think anyone in Kesna was withholding information. Do you?"

"No, you're probably right." He rolled his bedroll out not too far from mine and sat cross-legged beside me. "Because if my country's about to go to war beside Nabul, I have to believe they're loyal."

Even though I'd eaten my fill from Queen Carusa's generous table, the savory smoke from the cooking fires and the murmur of conversations all around us brought the festival feel of the market onto the hills and nudged my stomach.

"I have a surprise for you." I pulled two small paper packets from my saddle bag and handed one to him.

His whole face lit up. "For me? What's this?" Opening it, he pulled out a round, fried ball of dough drizzled with honey and powdered sugar. "*Sweetdrops,*" he groaned, popping the honeyed sphere into his mouth.

"I bought them while you were talking to the man with the lamps." I opened my own packet and soon we were both smacking our lips and licking sugared honey off our fingers.

The campgrounds contrasted sharply with my last several years of eating in a grand dragon dining hall. The wind rippled the sparse trees, voices hummed and sparked with occasional peals of laughter, crickets chirped in the grass, and stars lit the clear, cold sky.

Kas was nice to share silence with. His hair pulled back in a hasty ponytail, he finished off his last sweetdrop and curiously watched the people around us. I'd never known a man quite like him, a gentler soul and kinder presence, and yet he somehow made me feel protected. It had taken me a couple of days to admit it even to myself, but I was glad I hadn't taken off on this quest all alone like a fool.

He caught me looking at him, smiled, and swallowed the bite he'd been chewing. "I've read historical accounts about knights of the trove, but I don't see you leading an army for Ady or acting as ambassador to Araven. Not that anyone would do that these days. And unless I missed it, nobody else lives there with you. What's your role in Ady's principality, exactly?"

I took a swig of my water. "Just what you saw. Live-in archivist. Occasional butt of brutal dragon humor." Kas chuckled, and I smiled. "And I'm supposed to help her protect the trove if it's under attack. But let's be honest: Ady doesn't need my help. She used to even defeat the men who came for me, but now that I'm trained to fight, I do it for myself."

He licked the last of the honey from his fingers and slipped the paper packet into the fire. "What's so interesting to me about that is that knights of the trove, historically always women, tradition-ally chose their mates in a contest of swords."

"Really?" There was so much that tight-lipped lizard didn't find important enough to share with me.

"Really!" His blue eyes lit up in the firelight, his face transformed at the chance to talk about something he'd studied. "Dragon troves used to house entire communities of people, very tight knit. When the knight of the trove was ready to marry, the call would go out, and eligible royalty and nobles and heroes from all over the world would come to take part in a series of trials."

"That sounds barbaric!" I imagined being on the stage in Kesna's coliseum with a full city of people ringed around watching me fight suitors. "None of the suitors were killed, were they?"

"No, no. The point was for the knight to get to know them. Spar with them, see who was a good fit for the knight and trove leadership. You have to remember what a position of honor it was to be a knight of the trove. The entire trove community, not to mention the kingdom the dragonian principality was located in, was *heavily* invested in who the knight would marry. They held festivals and feasts, and the celebrations almost always ended in a wedding."

The entire time he spoke, I could feel my mouth getting wider. "Thank the gods that isn't done today. I would have to host all those people?"

Kas leaned forward, a smile playing about his lips. "All of them."

"And then pick a husband, in front of the gods and everyone?"

"Or a wife, according to your interest. In front of *hundreds* if not thousands of people."

"That's horrifying. So why did it all die out? All Ady'll say is,"—I stuck my nose in the air and did a horribly lacking impression of her—"'You know, Nesrin, you're lucky I took you in at all. I've declined to take a knight for centuries.'"

Kas laughed, leaning back on his bedroll, and it was adorably infectious. "She's not very forthcoming, is she?"

"No! She *hates* explaining things to me. Were the other dragons you met that secretive and condescending?"

He threw his head back, groaning. "They were *so much worse*."

"Hard to imagine. So why doesn't anyone know about knights of the trove these days?"

"It fell out of practice when the big empires started falling apart. Fewer and fewer rulers could afford to send their royal daughters away because they needed them for treaties and heirs. A lot of dragons pushed back, too, demanding them. Burning fields, pillaging livestock, the usual. That's how people started thinking of princesses as being sacrificed to dragons. Unfortunately, women had become bargaining chips in their own homes, so it was a great sacrifice to let them go to a trove.

"But the thing is, royal daughters *wanted* to go. Knights were highly respected and allowed an independence they increasingly wouldn't get back home or as the wives of treaty marriages. They were so much better off in a trove. A lot of women ran off to join them, and once they were there, they didn't want to leave."

"Now that, I understand." I raised a toast with my water skin before drinking again.

He tucked a flyaway curl behind his ear as he poked at the fire. "So, say a princess runs off to a trove. Her kingdom would offer huge rewards to whoever could bring her back. Marriages, land, gold, treaties." He shrugged. "I guess that's how you get where you are today, defending the trove from a bunch of miscreant princes. How many have actually come for you?"

"So many, I've stopped counting. As soon as Galter realized I'd been rescued and not eaten, he sent droves of men to forcibly bring me back."

Kas's light eyes narrowed. "Like the prince out of Naitar?"

"Who, my dear betrothed?" I pretended to gag. "*Especially* him. For the record, I never agreed to that. Obviously." I popped my last sweetdrop into my mouth, chewed it thoughtfully. "After a while, my uncle either ran out of people to send, or he was too busy, or maybe he thought I was no longer worth his attention. Must take up a lot of your time, being a heartless emperor." I dropped my packet into the campfire, watching it grow bright with flames and send crackling embers into the sky.

"So, you've been with Ady...eight years now?"

I nodded.

"Don't you ever get lonely?"

I leaned forward and put my hand on his arm as if imparting a secret. "Between you and me, I don't enjoy being around a lot of people."

He smiled, glancing down at my hand as I pulled it away. "I've noticed. But you don't seem shy. Are you shy, Nesrin?" He leaned forward, eyes gently watching me as if I was the most interesting woman in the world.

It's probably why I continued answering his questions. Besides, it was exhilarating to have a conversation with a man *this* attractive, even if he was a monk. "I wouldn't say I'm shy, so much as that being around too many people at one time makes me want to stab them."

He laughed.

"I'm not joking!" I laughed a little, too, despite being very serious. "There are far too many people in the world."

He chuckled and unfastened the fresh brown boots Ady had sent him with before lying all the way down on his bedroll, pulling up his blanket, and letting out a long, contented sigh. "Aren't you going to ask any questions about me?"

"I don't like to be rude by asking a lot of questions." Sort of teasing, but also not. I didn't think *he* was being rude, but I always felt intrusive asking someone questions about themselves. I plucked a reddening blade of watermelon grass and laid back on my own bedroll, crushing the leaf in my fingers to release the sweet scent.

He breathed a soft laugh out through his nose. "It's not rude to want to know about other people, especially when you're traveling with them."

"Okay. What do you want to tell me about yourself?"

He turned to me, eyebrows raising. "What do you want to know?" His bright eyes twinkled mischievously as they held mine—a look I would've expected him to turn on those lovely serving girls at dinner, but he hadn't.

It honestly sped my heart a little. "Are all monks this flirtatious?"

He stopped smiling. "I'm not flirting. I just like people. I like you."

"Oh," I laughed wickedly, "Kas *likes* me!"

"You know what I mean." He flopped down with his back facing me. "I was just trying to make conversation."

I hadn't meant to hit a sore spot. And I didn't expect his sore spot to make me feel a little sore, too. "I'm only teasing, Kas. Hmm. Let me think of a question...I know. Did you grow up wanting to be in the order?"

He rolled onto his back, eyes on the trees above. A brisk wind fluttered the treetops, and a shower of golden leaves drifted down across our camp. "No. But I was *supposed* to, so what I wanted didn't make a difference. I was raised to be obedient."

"You didn't want to go into the order, but you were completely compliant when they sent you?"

He chuckled. "I ran away a lot at first, but they always found me and brought me back. My parents are good people, but very traditional. It's a rare honor to be the fourth son of the velarch and be taken into the order. Supposedly. The whole kingdom expected it of me."

"But are *you* happy?" I asked gently.

For several minutes, the campfire and our fellow campers settling down for the night were the only sounds. "Sometimes," he said finally, in a wavering, unconvincing way.

My heart insisted that he was as miserable in the monastery as I'd been in the palace with Galter. Why were there so many different ways to be controlled by your family?

I covertly watched him as he fell asleep, his eyes closed, long lashes fluttering against his cheeks. He'd probably never tell me what he really wanted out of life, and it hurt my heart.

He must've been such a precious, sad little boy. With those bright eyes shining in the dark, wandering through the wide, gray halls of an ancient stone monastery. Missing his mother. Frowning, wringing his hands, and looking through every barren window for a way out.

CHAPTER ELEVEN

THE ROAD TO OPINTOL

After turning our horses for the northwest road toward Opintol, we spent two long, uneventful days traveling. Tonight, we hunkered under a quiet rain on a road overhung with a thick forest on either side, our breaths fogging the darkening air.

A man approached us from behind on horse. I turned around several times to gauge his purpose, but he really did seem like just another traveler, although we hadn't seen anyone else in the hours since we'd passed a small village. Kas nodded and said good evening as the man passed us, but he only grunted in reply. But he did eye me and our horses from head to toe as if checking my body or our weapons. Didn't like that. I was immediately on edge, and my hand strayed to my dagger. But so little seemed to bother Kas.

"You've never been to the library before?" he asked me, paying no further mind to the man who'd passed us.

"No." Raindrops pattered in the forest around us, and thunder grumbled from somewhere to the west. "I've always wanted to go." Turning in my saddle, I caught movement behind us in the dark. Far back, another man followed. A coincidence?

"You have such a treat ahead of you. When my uncle brought me and my brothers there when we were little, I begged him to convince my father to let me study there instead of going into the monastery."

"Uh-huh," I replied, barely listening.

The man in front glanced back past us to the man behind us, and my heart sped up.

"Kas," I interrupted quietly, leaning toward him.

"Because...yes?"

"Don't react. I think we're being cased." A bolt of lightning streaked to our right, illuminating the dark forest for just a moment. Its quick, attendant thunder warned the storm was intensifying.

"What do you mean?" He stiffened but didn't turn around.

"One ahead, and one behind. Bandits maybe?"

Kas shrugged. "Or it could be nothing. Do you think we should talk to them?" He slowed his horse.

"Don't stop!" I hissed. Not that I knew what to do either. I pulled out the sheathed dagger I'd offered him a few days before and thrust it at him. "Take this."

He hesitated, reached out his hand, then pulled it back. "No." He glanced at the man ahead of him. "I won't use it."

"Please just take it." Hoofbeats behind, heavier rain from above. The man ahead quickened his horse and disappeared over the hill.

Kas's bright blue eyes were wide in the gathering dark. "I'm not going to fight." He looked behind us.

"Okay, but surely you want to—"

"He's lining up an arrow!" Kas shouted.

"*Shit*!" I whirled around, aimed my dagger, and threw it. Lightning illuminated its arc as Kas yelled out, charging Balembar past me up the road.

The man behind me cried out. Miraculously, I must've hit my mark. I turned Pistachio in a tight circle, charging him while I might have an advantage. He'd dropped his bow in the muddy road, but now he tore my dagger from his thigh and launched it back at me.

I knocked it aside with a vambrace and scrambled along my sword belt for something to meet whatever was at the end of the hilt he grabbed. His sword stuck in its scabbard, but my long Pendoran dagger caught the next flash of lightning and sliced across his middle. The sickening *squelch* traveled up my arm. He shouted, and I spun Pistachio around in time to see him fall off his horse into the mud.

Kas was nowhere in sight, but shouting echoed from the road ahead. Dismounting Pistachio before she'd fully stopped, I raced to the fallen man with my dagger pointing at his neck. "Why are you shooting at me?" I shouted above the storm.

But blood bubbled out of his mouth. Lightning illuminated a flood of it from the gash I'd cut across his belly, his insides...

No. I averted my eyes and stumbled backwards, looking up into his face in time to catch his eyes going blank. He was gone. My stomach heaved as a strangled cry escaped my lips, doom settling on my shoulders.

I took his life. He'd been trying to kill me, right? Yes. I hadn't imagined the arrow, the knife thrown back at me. The mis-pull of his sword that probably spared me. A crossed-arrows tattoo on his neck caught my attention, pulling Rav's face starkly into my mind.

Shouting and raucous laughter rang from the road ahead.

Kas! I whirled around toward Pistachio but stopped short when I looked up the road.

Two mounted men, one of whom had passed us on the road, led Balembar and another horse between them. A third man, short, stocky, and dressed in black and red like some devilish imp, pushed a bloody, disheveled Kas ahead of him down the road on foot, a sword at his back.

Shock ricocheted through my body as if lightning had struck me.

I'd know him anywhere. In Galter's palace, outside Ady's gate, here in the dark and the rain. Recognized the pale brown hair streaked with gray. Recognized my body's innate revulsion to the nasty little man Galter betrothed me to.

Prince Ashur stopped twenty feet away from me and the man I'd killed, close enough for me to see Kas was clutching his stomach, blood down his face from lacerations. Even though my stomach twisted and my heart pounded in my ears, I swallowed the bile rising at the back of my throat and armored myself with bravado, hoping Ashur would talk and give me time to think.

"Ashur," I said with a swagger I absolutely wasn't pulling off. "Time continues to be a bitch to you, doesn't it?"

"If anyone's a bitch here, it's you." His two flunkeys laughed with him, completely ignoring their dead man on the ground. One of them dismounted and started going through Kas's saddlebags.

Gods I hoped Kas had his book well-hidden. I caught his eyes. His golden skin was pallid, and he stood still as a statue except for his eyes, which rapidly blinked against the rain, holding my gaze and oceans of fear.

"I left Araven to hunt down the discarded son of the velarch." Ashur pressed a dagger against Kas's throat, and a bright drop of his blood trickled down the blade. Kas gulped and clenched his eyes shut.

Blood rushed in my ears, and I flexed my grip on my dagger. My fingers itched for violence: all of Ashur's blood for that one drop of Kas's.

"And as a happy surprise, I learned he's traveling with my property. *My betrothed.*" Ashur bowed slightly in my direction. "Who I'm sure will be the shining star in my harem."

Old fear clutched my belly. "You hold a special place in my esteem too. You know, I've never met *anyone* more naturally repulsive than you."

Ashur chuckled as the man ransacking Kas's bags emptied one of them into the mud. "He doesn't have it," he said to Ashur.

"Why don't you two check out what my nubile young bride has in her...*saddlebags.*"

"That's the quickest way to get yourself killed," I snarled, scanning the armor of the men stalking toward me.

"You may still be as stubborn as you were as a child, but you're certainly all grown up now," Ashur drawled, fucking me with his eyes. "How about you save us all some trouble and surrender to me now? That way, I won't have to kill a holy man, and I can"—he thrust his hips in a revolting, sexual rhythm—"ride behind you the whole way to the Emperor's palace where we can finally consummate our union."

Fury and fear burned hot and cold through my body, leaving my hands trembling. Hivathe forgive me, but I wanted to kill him. I wanted to see all his blood outside his body.

I backed up cautiously toward Pistachio, calculating what weapons I could draw quickly as the men came closer, their faces bruised and covered with cuts. One with a broken nose. I glanced at Kas. Did he do that?

One of the men stepped faster toward me. I plucked a knife from my bandolier and threw it, but he batted it aside with his sword and lunged for me.

My Pendoran dagger was formidable, but it was a paltry weapon against a sword, especially when both hands clutching its hilt were numb from cold and fear. Our blades met again and again, and he made me retreat past the reach of my other weapons. Why had I attached Baney to my saddle instead of my belt?

The other man reached Pistachio, but the adversary thrusting his steel toward my stomach commanded all my attention. I jumped back, caving at the middle to avoid getting sliced across the navel. My awkward movement allowed him to kick my feet out from under me, and I hit the ground hard, smacking my head against the mud. The air whooshed from my lungs, and stars sparked behind my eyes, but it only made me madder. I rolled to my feet and twisted quickly, sweeping his legs and knocking him into the mud. He landed on his back, his arms spread wide, and I didn't think. I landed on top of him with my dagger in his chest like he was a straw dummy back home.

His sword hilt slipped from his opened hand, eyes blanking and panicked as he clutched at the dagger, but he was too late. A river of red rushed out into the mud with the rain. I stumbled back and away from what I'd done, almost shocked to see blood and not straw.

"She doesn't have it either, Your Highness." The other man's voice coming nearer pivoted my attention. I scrambled to my feet, belatedly yanking the dagger from the dead man, cringing as the blade scraped bone on its way out. I was going to throw up or pass out. I didn't know which would win, but either would mean my death and maybe even Kas's.

Pistachio whinnied, coming closer to me, and the man paused ten feet away, his sword out and eyes aimed on me. "Should I kill her?"

"Not yet. Keep your sword on her, though. I don't want to waste money on your replacement." With no warning, Ashur punched Kas square in the jaw, dropping him to the ground with a grunt. My scream mingled with thunder as he kicked Kas in the ribs, once, twice. Kas coughed on the ground, curled into himself.

"Stop it!" I screamed, wanting to go to Kas, but cowed by the man pointing his sword at me.

"Get her under control," Ashur shouted.

I edged toward Pistachio as Ashur kicked Kas again. "What do you know, holy man?" he sneered.

His last man took another step toward me, but only one. His eyes darted to his two dead comrades.

"Don't touch her!" Kas choked out. "We don't know anything!"

A sob escaped my lips, my heart aching in its terrible, pounding beat. The life of my only real, human friend in eight years was in danger, and his first impulse was to protect me.

Ashur threw his head back in a laugh. "You have guts, I'll give you that. But she's not worth your life, *Brother*." Ashur twisted the word. "Tell me what you know."

"You're looking for an iron goblet," Kas gasped out, curling tighter into himself in the mud, "with your ugly face on it."

Ashur kicked him again, harder, and Kas half-groaned, half-shouted in pain. "Your goddess abhors a liar. Are you sure you checked every bag?" he asked his man.

I took advantage of the man's split attention. Darting to Pistachio, I let my brain slip into the groove of muscle memory. Sheathed my dagger, grabbed my armed crossbow, disengaged safety, aimed. The coiled, barbed bolo shot across and wrapped around the man's neck and torso, impaling him like a hundred little knives. Limbs trapped, he fell to the ground fighting against it.

Ashur shouted and sprinted toward me. I deployed another knife from my bandolier, but it pinged uselessly off of what I thought was a gap in his armor. I threw my crossbow aside and unsheathed Baney from Pistachio's tack just as Ashur lunged at me with his own blade. Baney cracked a fat splinter from his sword at my parry.

Snarling, he drew back, eyes darting for an opening. I slashed Baney at him but undercut, narrowly missing his thigh. He neatly dodged me and swung back around, hitting my calf with the flat, dull edge of his backsword.

My world went black with pain. He'd hit an old wound inflicted by Galter that not even Ady's magic could fully heal. He laughed at my shrill scream, and it galvanized my pain into cold, sharp fury as my vision cleared.

I snaked a barbed whip from my belt and snapped it at him. It wrapped around his sword hand, and I pulled hard. The barbs cut deep into his gloved hand, and he dropped his weapon, crying out, his face twisted. Blood dripped with the rain from where the barbs dug deep through leather and skin, and I pulled harder against him. I needed more of his blood to spill.

"Do you yield?" I yelled, more of a statement of *you'd better yield* than a question. I tugged at the whip. One hard pull, and his hand would be torn to shreds.

"Never!" he yelled, the rain pouring off his tiny nose. He grabbed the whip with his free hand and pulled back hard, throwing me off balance and tumbling me forward to the ground. Baney skittered away as I fell hard in the mud, rolling away seconds before he kicked the ground where my head had been.

I pulled both Pendoran daggers from my thigh sheaths, crossing them in time to trap his sword at his next blow. The rain pinged on our crossed blades as I pushed his sword back toward his face, kicking in to sweep his legs before he could pull back for another swing. He fell hard to the mud. I thrust my daggers back home and whipped three knives at him in quick succession, following his movements as he got to his feet. But each plunged into the wet ground a second too late, leaving a trial of metal that glinted in the next lightning flash. I pulled my daggers out again and circled him.

He plunged his sword at me, and as I turned to throw it off course, he surprised me, punching my lower back. I cried out at the sharp pain ricocheting deep into my body, stealing my breath. He grabbed my braid, and a halo of pain erupted around the edges of my vision. I fell back hard to the ground, gasping for air in the driving rain. I rolled over out of sheer instinct, and Ashur's heavy boot slammed into the mud where my back had been. As he lunged for me, I slammed the hard outsole of my boot underneath his armor into his crotch. He wailed like a dying manticore and crumpled to the ground.

I jumped up, pushing my knee hard into his spine, pinning his face to the ground. I grabbed a knife from the mud and seized a fistful of his hair, pulling his head sharply back, pressing my knife against his throat. His other man had nearly disentangled himself from my bolo, and he started to move toward us.

"Not a step!" I yelled, spitting rain and hardly recognizing my own voice beneath the rage. I pulled Ashur's head back harder. "Yield or I'll slice your throat!"

His hands reached toward me in vain. One jerk of my arm, and he would be gone.

"Yield, godsdamnit!" Why couldn't I do it? *Just kill him.*

He choked out an unintelligible noise, but all I could focus on was the bead of blood breaking from his neck under my blade, how badly I wanted to spill all of it. But should I keep the asshole alive long enough to get information?

I pushed my knee harder against his spine and pulled his head back more, taunting him in a cruel singsong above the driving rain. "I can't *hear* you!"

"I yield!" he rasped. With an effort, I took my knife away from his throat and smashed his face down into the mud.

I grabbed one arm and yanked it behind his back, but he darted his other arm out and around me, pulling me hard to the ground before I knew what was happening. He pushed my face into the mud and dug his knee into my back where he'd punched me—a violent spasm of pain momentarily paralyzed me. I screamed and sucked in a panicked breath, coughed out mud. My own warm blood now registered in my senses, trickling into the insides of my clothes, staining the air with copper. The bastard hadn't punched me. He'd stabbed me.

Ashur and his man mounted their horses, and Kas still lay motionless on the ground. Thunder grumbled and the rain lessened.

Ashur pulled a handkerchief from his coat, pristine white against the darkness, and wiped the blood and mud from his face and neck. His cold blue eyes sought me out. "If you weren't so filthy and bloody, I'd take my fill of your body right now. But you disgust me, Nesrin. I'd say you haven't seen the last of me, but

I don't think you'll be seeing much of anything after your heart stops."

"Go to hell," I shouted, my voice a raging, splintered thing. "If I ever see you again, *in that moment* you'll be dead."

Ashur and his man rode away, and I stared after them, panting with unshed tears, gasping with pain. I pressed my fingers to the epicenter of the throbbing spasms at my back, and came back with my own blood, bright and red on my pale, shaking fingers.

CHAPTER TWELVE

A REVELATION

I shut my eyes against a wave of nausea. "Why didn't I kill that son of a bitch when I had the chance?"

"Nesrin! Are you alright?"

"Kas!" Thank Hivathe he was alive. Staggering to his feet, clutching his hand to his ribs and stumbling toward me, but alive. I took a deep breath, bracing myself against the pain to speak again. "He stabbed me."

Kas was muddy from head to toe and covered in gashes, and his face pulled into a grimace with each step. He needed me. I pushed my hands against the cold, squelching mud and pulled my knees to my chest, willing myself to get up, but at the movement a heavier flood of warmth seeped down my backside. I was too afraid to move again.

"I'm coming," he gasped. "Stay there."

Thunder grumbled, farther away. They'd emptied all my things in the mud. My beautiful new robe and scarf, my weapons, a scattering of gold, the medicine vials from Ady.

"Blue bottles!" I pointed them out with an effort. "Two of them!"

Kas held his hand against his side, grunting, but he nodded and changed course. A moment later he settled gingerly into the mud beside me, wiping a cobalt blue glass vial on the inside of his robe, uncorking it, and passing it to me. With a shaking hand, I tipped the bottle to my mouth. The sweet, tart grape taste woke up my tongue and slipped down my throat. I braced myself for the metallic aftertaste as the elixir moved sinuously through my body as if sentient and hunting for something to heal.

Kas took half a breath and grunted, holding the second vial toward me.

I pushed it back. "Drink it."

"You need it worse than I do," he wheezed.

"Does it hurt when you breathe in?"

"Yes, but—"

I settled into the mud as the acute pain lessened. "*Drink it.* You might have a broken rib. Or worse. It'll heal you."

Uncorking it, he sniffed the vial before draining it in one big gulp. He coughed and immediately stifled it, crying out in pain and clutching his ribs. He turned his head and exhaled loudly with his mouth open.

"It's got a kick, doesn't it?"

He suppressed another cough. "Yeah," he rasped. He reached out and pulled one of our satchels through the mud, digging in it and coming out with a water skin and a roll of cloth-strip bandage that miraculously hadn't gotten muddy. "I don't think I'd marry Ashur, if I were you."

"Really? I was hoping you'd officiate." I uncurled just enough to let him pour water over my wound, press a wad of bandage against it, and tie it around my middle.

We sat for a moment in stunned silence. I turned more toward Kas to block the sight of the dead men.

"They didn't even want your money."

I followed his blank gaze toward the dull coins in the mud. "No, they don't care about that." My breath hitched as I pulled my legs around in front of me.

Kas patted my knee gently. "Stay here. I'll gather our things."

As I watched him slowly collect our horses from the fringe of the forest and pack everything haphazardly back into our bags, sleep pulled at my eyelids and weighed my limbs deeper into the gushy mud. But I forced myself to watch Kas's every movement, to stay present. To not let the darkness win. To not let Ashur win.

Still, no one had passed on the dark road when Kas came to help me to my feet. He wrapped an arm around me and led me and the horses off the road.

We may only have walked about fifty feet into the woods, but it felt like a mile. I stumbled down a gradual hill with him holding me up, and we were rewarded with a grassy clearing near a wide stream.

Ady's elixir dulled the pain, but my injury made me heavy-limbed and weak. Kas used a piece of Ady's ever-dry kindling to get a small fire going as I threw our bedrolls open directly side by side on the ground, throwing a prayer up in thanksgiving for the gift of Ady's plush camping extravagances that repelled mud and water.

I settled onto my mat, needing the comfort and softness. The drying mud on my face and scalp pulled my skin taut and itchy, except where my tears tracked. Kas came back from the stream and sat beside me, sloshing a basin of water. His teeth chattered, and his whole head was wet and cleaned of mud. The cuts and bruises forming on his face were stark against his skin, some still trickling bright red blood. I deeply inhaled the familiar soap scent emanating from him, longing for the clean, healing comforts of my bathing chamber.

"We didn't survive that for you to die from sticking your head in an icy stream," I teased.

"Needed it," he shivered. The inconstant light from the smoking, spitting fire cast shadows across Kas's face as he tied back his wet hair, making him look gaunt and far older.

"Lay down and pull your robes up," I ordered.

He looked at me quickly. "What?"

"I'm worried about your ribs and lungs, and I want to see if you need more of Ady's elixir."

He shook his head and kept digging for salvageable food. "I'm fine."

"Except you're not. You might need more medicine, or I may need to supplement with other ointments." I spread my hands out in front of me, my fingers caked with mud and blood. The scrape of that man's bone against my sword shivered like a ghost through my hands. Did the blood on my hands belong to me or the men I'd killed?

Rav's words came back to me. *You may have to do the same before all this is over.*

"I'm just going to wash up a little first." I eased my coat and bandolier off, dug out my cleanest tunic, and scooped up the bar of soap on my way to the stream.

I carefully rolled my sleeves up and kneeled with a crunch into the pebbles lining the water. For a moment, I closed my eyes with the bar of soap slack in my hand and listened to the night, the splashing water, the wind. *Thank you, Hivathe, for Ady's magic and medicine, for sending Kas with me.*

A swift wind sent shivers through me. I didn't want to sleep coated in the blood of those men, but I didn't know if I had the strength tonight to do any better. Hivathe willing, the sun would be up in the morning, and I could take a partial bath at the stream before we moved on. Plunging my hands into the icy water, I built up a froth with the fragrant soap, deeply inhaling its comforting scent.

I held back a sob. My hands shook. I'd taken two lives. *Please forgive me, Hivathe.* Without Ady's medicine, we would've been lying dead in the road next to those men I killed. Tears slipped down my face, making the mud sting more as I scrubbed up to my elbows. I took out my braid and wove it back in again. With trembling hands, I washed my face, removed my corset, and changed into the fresher tunic.

When I returned, Kas was lying down on his bedroll in a cleaner robe and pants. He wiped his face when I walked up and slipped my coat back on.

I held my hands over the fire and pretended not to notice. "Pull your robe up and let me check your ribs."

He complied, lifting his robe to expose his stomach and chest above his pants. The chill speckled his skin with goosebumps. I knelt beside him and gently pulled his arm up over his head, and he fixed his gaze on the treetops swaying above. The firelight cast dark shadows over his ribs and muscles. That and his black chest hair made it hard to tell if he was bruising. I ran my fingers lightly along each rib.

"When did you learn how to check for broken bones?" His voice was quiet, his long lashes fluttering as he studied my face. His poor lips and cheek were swollen, and a gash cut right across his eyebrow.

"When I was a child, one of my older girl friends was training to be a doctor, and I loved helping her in the infirmary. I wanted to be a doctor, too." An irregular shadow darkened his bottom right rib—probably a bruise forming. But his chest didn't look or feel swollen. "Did you hear anything snap when..." I took a breath. I firmly brought the door down between my brain and the emotions swirling in my chest. "It happened? And does it hurt worse when you breathe?"

"No, and no."

"Good. Twist a little, if it doesn't hurt too much." I pressed my ear against his chest to listen, and his warm body tensed under my cheek. His heart beat hard and strong, and nothing popped inside when he moved. I sat back up. "I wouldn't be surprised if they broke your ribs and punctured your lung, but I think Ady's elixir did its job. It seems only bruised now."

"Her medicine can fix such a serious injury?"

I nodded. "Ady says it binds veins and bones and stops internal bleeding. "

He started to pull his robe down, but I kept my hand on his chest. "Not yet. Let me put ointment on your cuts and bruises. You'll still turn all kinds of colors tomorrow, but this should ease your pain and speed the healing."

He gingerly patted his fingertips against his left cheek as I dipped my fingers in the ointment and smoothed it across his ribs. I'd told him in the trove that I wasn't going on the quest to protect him, but my unkind words haunted me now. I was cold, inside and out, with hatred for Ashur. Kas didn't deserve any of this. And he deserved better than me to protect him. Apparently, I could only *barely* protect myself against one fighter at a time, and only with a giant dragon at my back. I blinked away the tears blurring my vision, and they ran down my cheeks as I finished tending to the last of the bruises on his torso.

"You have a soft touch," he said.

I chuckled and narrowed my eyes at him as I pulled his robe down, amazed that I could feel amusement after the night we'd had. "Are you flirting with me again, Brother Kas?"

He sat up and made a soft sound at the back of his throat. "I wouldn't know how to." He studied me with those bright eyes, his face a little sad.

Noticed that wasn't a *no*. I felt a small smile pull at my lips. "Complimenting the way a woman touches your body is certainly one way."

His eyebrows came together as if he was pained. "Nesrin, I can't..."

"I was just playing." I rushed out.

His voice was soft and deep. "I've never wanted to more."

With a pang in my chest that wasn't from my injuries, I shook my head and looked everywhere else—the bruise spreading across his jaw and cheek, the split of his lip—but not into his eyes. "It's fine, Kas." Better to douse these confusing feelings I was having for him. It wasn't like we could do anything about them.

"You would've made a wonderful doctor," he said gently.

"Thank you." I took his hand to rub ointment on his knuckles. Both hands were cut and bruised. The holy man had fought back. "And I think you would've made a great warrior. You must've gotten some good hits in before..." I swallowed hard. "Those men were pretty beat up."

He sighed. "When I was young, the captain of the guard trained me in jabal-zie hand-to-hand combat." He took a breath as if he'd say more but closed his mouth instead.

Another reason I wanted to stay sequestered in the trove. Out in the world, violence came for even the most peaceful. Child or monk, evil people didn't care about your principles and were eager to subvert your innocence. And there was nothing I could do about it.

But maybe I could lighten our hurting, be like Kas and focus on being light-hearted when everything felt so heavy.

"I thought maybe there was a secret fight club in the basement of your cult." I snorted at my own bad joke, settling back onto my mat and scooping some ointment for my own bruises.

He chuckled. "It's a religious order," he said mock-reproachfully, "not a cult." He took the ointment from me. "Your turn. Let me help you. I found a cleaner bandage for your wound."

"Thank you." I lifted my tunic and coat to expose my lower back and laid on my belly, pillowing my head on the arm opposite the wound. I allowed heaviness to settle in my limbs and eyelids because I finally, truly believed that Kas had my back.

He hissed. "So much blood."

"If it's too much for you, you don't have to clean it. I can take care of it later."

"The sight of blood doesn't bother me. The sight of *your* blood spilled by that monster bothers me." His voice was tight. Angry.

I appreciated his loyalty, but I vehemently didn't want to talk about Ashur. I was vaguely aware of the small noises he made digging in saddle bags and dipping cloth into water he'd warmed for me by the fire, but the babbling of the stream, the crackle and hiss of the flames, and his tender ministrations were all seducing me into sleep.

Before long he finished, left for the stream, and came back with clean hands. "Let me make something to eat."

Extreme sleepiness warred with my grumbling belly, two insistent desires forcing me to choose. I nodded and sat up, stretching my back a little, testing it. Only a sharp ache where the knife had gone in. But I had another wound to attend to.

As Kas dug in our bags for food, I pulled my boots off and rolled up my pants leg up to get at the old wound Ashur had pummeled. I didn't want to be the kind of person that prayed for another's death, but still I found myself biting back that horrific prayer as I rubbed Ady's ointment into my calf.

Kas sat beside me and handed me a plate with bread and cheese, looking pointedly at my calf, but not asking questions. Maybe he wanted to distance himself from what just happened, too.

I ate quickly and without joy in between trying multiple ointments to get at the right combination for my calf. The fight on the roadside kept replaying in my mind, and it brought me back to my father's palace under Galter's rule, those dark days before Ady came to save me.

Kas cleared his throat. "We're really not going to talk about nearly being killed in the road?"

"I can't stop thinking about it," I said, wiping tears from my face. "Do we have to talk about it too?"

He took my empty plate from me. "I think it would help us both to talk about it." He went off toward the stream, giving me a moment alone to put the ointments away and curl up in my bedroll under a blanket, shivering from more than the cold.

He returned a moment later with both plates clean, and he settled down in his own bedroll. I was glad I'd placed them so close together. I needed him near me. Ady's medicine was taking away my body's pain and making my brain light, but not light enough.

He pulled off his boots and looked my way. "Are you alright?"

My tears came faster, spurred on by his unfailing kindness. "I'll be okay. It just stirred up…" I sniffled. "He stirred up bad memories." I remembered my manners. "Are you alright?"

"I'll be fine." His hand landed on my arm. "I'm worried about you." He was silent a moment longer, and I tried to get my crying under control. "I can't believe your uncle tried to marry you to him."

"My father would rise from his grave if he knew how Galter treated me like his property. I went from learning medicine and sciences in my father's peaceful kingdom to being trained, even as a young girl, to live only to please whoever Galter sold me off to."

Sharing these painful memories with Kas felt natural. Safe. And thank Hivathe, because I couldn't hold them in anymore. Tonight had broken my dam. "And I'm not talking only about how to be subservient, but to please my future husband in all matters, as if nothing I felt or wanted was important, from handling his household to pleasing him in bed."

Kas turned bright red and started coughing unaccountably, groaning and taking his hand back to clutch his chest. "They taught you *what*?"

"Starting when I was thirteen."

"Nesrin," he said softly but firmly, grunting as he pushed up on his elbow to look at me. "He didn't—"

"No. If you're asking if he personally abused me, no, thank Hivathe. No one ever laid a hand on me. Well," I clarified, with a dark laugh, "besides when he drove an arrow into my leg and when he tied me to a pole to be sacrificed to a dragon."

"He did *what*?" Kas sat up fully, his words quiet but fierce.

I sat up too. "After I tried to run away. To keep me from running away again, he drove an arrow into my calf with his bare hands. The wound was too old for Ady to do much for it after she took me in."

Kas moved closer, pulling an unspoiled cloth from his bag. He slipped his hand along my jaw and dried my tears. "I'm so sorry you went through all of that, and all alone." He shook his head and removed his hand, seemingly at a loss for words. "I can't even imagine. But I'm here now. Do you want to talk about it?"

His brows were together, his eyes darkened. Kas was the first human I'd ever talked to about this. The first to ask. No one had spoken to me so gently, and with such concern, since I lost my family. Ady had tried, but dragon sympathy wasn't the same as human compassion. I'd spent years hardening myself against being vulnerable, but I hadn't worked hard enough, or the task itself was impossible. Or tonight was *just too much*. My tears flowed faster, and I ducked my head down.

He sighed and wrapped his arms around me, a human kindness that only made me cry harder. I was equally grateful and embarrassed by how easily and quickly his concern had broken the vessel of pain I'd been carrying, and I clutched him, sobbing against his chest as he held me and gently rocked me back and forth. I thought I'd grown past this pain, but it still hurt so badly.

"It must be so hard for you to talk about," he murmured. "Thank you for trusting me with it. I'm so sorry we couldn't help you sooner."

I pulled back to look at him. "What do you mean?"

He sighed, and his eyes were bright in the darkness as he gently wiped my face again. "I'd only been in the monastery for a few months when your brothers escaped. They took refuge with my parents for a time, and my mother would tell me about it when she visited." He smoothed hair away from my face, searching my eyes. "My brothers and yours tried over a dozen times to rescue you and your mother, but all of their attempts failed before they got near the palace. My father was angry, but my mother was beside herself. For you most of all. You were just a child like me, and she was so scared about what Galter would do to you."

I blinked at him, at a loss for words. My brothers had tried *that* many times to save me?

"She was determined to get you out. She convinced my father to offer a betrothal treaty between you and my older brother Berem, but Galter wouldn't see our emissaries. Then...I think we were about thirteen? *She* organized a mission to rescue you." He looked down, anger and sorrow sparking in his eyes. "No one returned from it, but Galter sent us a magpie, threatening war if we tried it again. He told us..." Kas hesitated, his eyes glossy in the firelight.

When I was thirteen. "About my mother." My tears fell faster.

He nodded, a tear slipping down his own face. "My mother blamed herself for Queen Melida's death. She was afraid to try again for fear he'd kill you, too."

I shut my eyes tightly. My mother's name. *Melida*. It sounded so strange in his Veytian lilt, and so beautiful. I took a shuddering breath and tried to calm my tears.

"Thank her for me. What happened to my mother wasn't her fault." My breath hadn't worked, and I was crying again. "It was *his*. I almost can't believe your parents and my brothers were trying to help me." I let out an unfunny laugh. "I didn't know anyone was trying. I was so alone, so sure that no one gave a shit about me."

Kas pulled me into his arms again, squeezing me tight, hugging my soul back into my body after the night we'd had, after my long years of solitude. "I'm just so grateful my plan worked."

"*Your* plan? What do you mean?"

"My mother and I talked about you all the time when she visited me in the monastery." He huffed a small laugh. "Well, in between the times I ran away. As hard as it was for me being sent away from my family, I knew what you were going through had to be so much worse. So, I did the only thing in my power to do: research. I learned about knights of the trove and knew there was still a dragon in Araven—and a peaceful one at that."

I pulled back and stared at him. Certainly he wasn't saying...

He shrugged and tucked hair behind his ear. "My mother thought it was far too risky. It took me months to wear her down. But I pestered her until she sent a message to the dragon to see if she would take a knight."

CHAPTER THIRTEEN

A CONFESSION

My heart hammered, and nothing existed in the world but Kas's soft smile. I whispered, "What?"

He nodded. "She finally sent a man to Ady, telling her about your situation and offering her gold if she'd take you in as her knight. Ady sent our messenger away without a reply, but about a month later we heard that a dragon had terrorized Galter into giving you up. And my mother," he snorted a laugh. "My poor mother thought she'd gotten you eaten."

A small laugh escaped my mouth.

"It's not funny," Kas said, rubbing his eyes and trying to stop. "I think Ady's medicine is making me delirious. Mother sent Berem to check on you and was so relieved to find out you were safe and uneaten. Ady even refused our gold."

It's hard to describe the moment when your whole universe shifts. The world didn't physically change around me—the fire crackled, an owl called, *whoo-doo,* from somewhere in the dark trees, and the wind was cold and sharp against my skin as if nothing had changed.

But *everything* had changed, and the wheels in my head couldn't spin fast enough to process it.

"You saved me?" I whispered.

Kas cocked his head to the side, raising his eyebrows.

My heart was in my throat, and I could hardly speak. I searched his eyes as if something in them would help me comprehend. "*You* did this for me? *You're* the reason Ady came for me?"

He blushed and looked down. "I think I may have given her the idea."

"Thank you!" I whispered ardently, wrapping my arms around his neck and hugging him as hard as I could as tears streamed down my face. His arms came around me, just as tightly. "You saved my life," I sobbed. "All this time I've been thanking Hivathe for Ady, but I should've been thanking her for you, too."

He said nothing, but he returned my fierce hug, patting my back. He rested his chin on my shoulder and sighed, and for a few minutes, I held onto him as if he were the only solid land in a turbulent sea. In so many ways, he was. We'd only just met, but he'd been protecting me for years. He was the kindest, best man I knew.

And being in his arms felt right. Safe. Like home. Like I could finally be content. What would it be like between us if he wasn't...

No. I couldn't think that, and maybe hugging him was making him uncomfortable. I pulled away and saw his hand offering me a handkerchief. I took it and started drying my tears. "Kas, I owe you my life. You don't even understand."

"No." He ducked his head and brushed the idea away with his hand. "Don't you remember? You bought me sweetdrops. We're even."

The humor twinkling in his bright eyes was contagious, and I started to laugh, the medicine, the relief of surviving the night, having Kas—it all combined to lighten my heart.

"Yes, Kas, those two things are completely equal." I dabbed at my eyes, which still leaked from tears of sadness, shock, or happiness, I didn't know which anymore. I took his hands in mine. "You're literally the reason I was plucked out of hell and brought to my heaven on earth. I'll never get over this. You just became my favorite human in the entire world." I pressed a kiss against the whiskers on his cheek, then squeezed him one more time.

His face was bright red when I pulled away. "That's a high honor."

I took a shaky breath and blew my nose. "Why didn't you tell me when we first met? Gods above, Kas, I held a sword to your throat because I thought you might be working for *him*."

He shrugged. "I didn't know if you knew already. And when you didn't seem to know, I didn't think you'd believe me. You didn't seem to like me much when we first met." His rueful smile made me laugh again.

I nodded, my tears finally slowing. "I probably wouldn't have believed you. But I do now." We smiled at each other for a moment while I got myself under control. Kas was a beautiful man, maybe the most beautiful I'd ever known. But his true beauty wasn't just the fairness of his face and form, but the goodness of his heart. It shone through his smile now, and with a pang it hit me: he'd saved me, but I had no hope of saving him from the monastic life he didn't seem to want. The life I was selfishly wishing more and more he wasn't bound to.

He frowned and looked down. "There's something else I've been keeping from you. I have to tell you, but I'm afraid you might be angry with me."

My heart sped. Was it about the way he smiled at me? "What is it?"

He sighed heavily. "I'm not exactly the peaceful monk I presented myself to be."

I sat back, waiting for him to go on. Now I was getting whiplash. "What do you mean?"

"I'm a...fairly well-trained fighter. I didn't stop training when I went into the monastery, even though I was supposed to. After my father ordered his captain to stop training me, the captain's son kept training me in secret. Ari was my best friend. A few years older than me. And at a time when I had no control over my life, learning how to fight gave me the chance to move my body when I spent all day kneeling in prayer or hunched over a book. And deliberately disobeying my father behind his back was almost the best part."

The muscular physique, the cuts and bruises on those men's faces. I studied his contrite face, pieces of Kas fitting into place but still not quite making sense. "Why didn't you say something?"

"I didn't mean to lie to you. I went through a lot to be the non-violent man you see before you, but our shadows always follow us, no matter how hard we try to stay in the light." His face crumpled, and he shut his eyes. "I'm just so angry with myself. If I'd taken that dagger you offered me, I might've been able to stop them before they hurt you."

I hated that this bothered him. I hated that it bothered me. "I'm sure you did your best, but I doubt you could've taken them both on, and Ashur too."

He rubbed his beard and shook his head. "They must've thought I wouldn't fight back, because they didn't even use weapons against me. I had them both on the ground until Ashur's whip caught my leg and took me down from behind."

This was so hard to wrap my mind around. "So that stone on our first day out wasn't a lucky throw. And on the ferry?"

He ducked his head again. "I thought for sure you saw me fighting, but you didn't say anything, so..."

I wanted to be angry, but it wasn't like he'd backed down when I needed him. If anything, I felt safer than I had in days. He'd had my back. "Why didn't you tell me?" I asked again. "I thought I was fighting for two, that I was all alone."

"I've always had your back, Nesrin, and I always will." He spoke with the same gentle vehemence as he had at the trove explaining his reasons for undertaking the quest. "At every step, even without weapons. But you have to understand. After what I did when I was seventeen..." He sighed heavily and closed his eyes, shaking his head. "I vowed to myself and Hivathe that I'd never fight again. And that's all well and good in a monastery, but not in the real world." He tossed a stick onto the fire. "Not on a quest like this."

I swallowed hard. "What happened when you were seventeen?"

"Our city guards found Ari beaten and left for dead in an alley. And it was my fault. He was attacked at night on his way back to the palace after training me. I didn't know until the next morning when they sent for me to tell him goodbye. I got there in time to watch him die." His voice cracked. "His death wrecked me. He was the only person who treated me the same before and after I was forced into the order."

Tears stole down his face, and he didn't bother wiping them away. Just stared into the fire as his voice grew harder. "And there was no question in my mind who'd killed him. These older men—bullies with criminal records. They always hassled Ari when we were out together, but they never did anything with me there." He pulled at his tunic. "My stupid robes are like a little oasis of holiness back home. They only jumped him because I wasn't with him.

"Nesrin, I can't explain what came over me." He rubbed his whole face with his hands. "The night he died, I stole black clothes from the monks doing their vows of silence, covered my face with a mask, and found them on the street. I picked a fight. Two to one, and I left them in the alley the way they'd left Ari. I was back before anyone knew I was gone."

If I'd known how to fight, how many times would I have tried to take Galter's life? Over and over until one of us was dead. I took his hand. "I'm sorry you've carried this for so long. But you were grieving and angry, and you only wanted justice for your friend."

"You don't have to make excuses. What I did was wrong." His body was stiff. He wouldn't squeeze my hand back or accept any comfort. "I don't *think* I was trying to kill them. But I can't say for sure that I wasn't. It was dark, and I was angry. One died in the alley, and the other died a few days later."

I rubbed his hand, my own tears falling now, understanding all too well. That first man on the road. I was angry. My sword went across his middle, and the next thing his blood was all over me and the road. "I'm sorry, Kas."

"You shouldn't be. A few days later, an eyewitness came forward. Ari was killed by an opium dealer, who'd since been killed by somebody else. Not even one of the two men I'd gone after. We had no idea he was mixed up with that. I went to my father and told him everything. I offered myself up for arrest. But he and Ari's father praised me for taking criminals off the streets and trying to avenge Ari. They told me to go back to the monastery and pray to my goddess.

"And I thought, 'if they won't punish me, I will.' I stopped taking care of myself. I took vows of silence. I fasted to the point of illness until an elder took me under his wing and helped me grow through it." He pulled his hand from me and took his hair down. Wrapped the leather string around his fingers as if he didn't know what to do with them.

"You were young. You're still young. You made a mistake, and you tried to make up for it. Honestly, I think that's all any of us can do."

His pained eyes met mine. "Why aren't you angry with me? I'm angry with myself."

"Kas! After what you did for me? I could never be angry with you."

He wiped his face on the sleeve of his robe. "Well. You deserved to know the truth. And I wanted you to understand why I don't believe in violence. I'm not trying to be sanctimonious, and it's not that I'm not capable. I'm just trying to choose peace."

I took his hands in mine. "You broke your vow of nonviolence and risked your life to protect me. You kept our quest alive, and that's not nothing. You're a good person, Kas, and if—"

"No, I'm a faithless monk, and a terrible fighter." He ducked his head. "Somebody like *Rav* could've protected you from Ashur."

Was Kas…jealous of the ferryman? Was it because of Rav's free lifestyle or his seeming interest in me? And why did that make my heart speed up? I pulled out one of my Pendoran daggers and handed it to him, sheath and all. He took it from me without a word.

"Maybe, maybe not. But Rav would've protected me out of duty. You've been protecting me because your heart is full of love for other people. And love's far more important than duty. Honestly, I'm glad you told me about everything. It helps me understand you so much better."

A small smile played around his lips, and his eyes met mine. Soft. A little sad. "Do you want to understand me, Nesrin?"

Butterflies stirred in entire body. "More than anything," I said softly.

He sighed, and his smile grew sadder as he looked away and sequestered himself back inside his bedroll. "We should get some rest. We have a lot of ground to cover if we're going to make it to the library tomorrow."

"Absolutely. I was thinking the same thing." I was thinking I wanted to hug him again, but okay. I burrowed into my bedroll and let the quiet forest unwind between us. I turned on my uninjured side toward him. Thank the gods for Kas. Today had been a nightmare, but having him here was a blessing. His very existence was a blessing.

We didn't speak for a long time, but I craved more connection. "Kas?"

His voice came back soft and near sleep. "Yes?"

"Can I hold your hand?"

His hand poked out of his blanket toward me. I grasped it between both of my hands, beneath my blanket, and tucked it under my chin. He squeezed my hand, and calmness spread through me.

The quiet night lengthened for some time. Just when I thought he'd fallen asleep, he murmured very quietly, "Good night, Nesrin."

CHAPTER FOURTEEN

A STEAMY INTERLUDE

The morning dawned promising and bright, until the events of last night rushed back into my consciousness. Kas consoled me while I cried over the men I'd killed, and then he insisted on warming water for me to bathe with while he went back to the road to be sure we hadn't left anything behind and say prayers over the dead, which he felt would make the guilt I was carrying lighter. After a quick meal, we were on the move again.

Skirting the road to avoid the scene from the night before, we traveled through a blissfully uneventful day of following his map northwest toward Opintol while staying off the main road as much as we could. The next morning, our progress steadily rose in altitude as we wended through a mountain pass, and the temperature dropped despite the sunny day.

Kas veered us off the path we were onto a smaller path through an even thicker forest filled with rushing waterfalls and strange calls of birds I couldn't identify.

"Are you sure we're going the right way?"

"We're taking a short detour."

"To where?"

"The Vayeri Springs. They're not far off the road, and I think they'll help your leg."

I'd heard of those. I had a small statuette dedicated to Vayeri, goddess of healing and water, on my altar in the trove. "Are you sure we can spare the time? We'll be lucky to make it to the library before dinnertime as it is, but—"

"We shouldn't stay long, but I think it'll be worth it to make you feel better." He smiled and took a slight lead.

Along the narrow path, hand-hewn sticks of different heights had been driven into the earth, some short and others nearly reaching up to Pistachio's back. Some were whittled smooth, others were left with crooks and offshoots, and many others had dulled, splintered, or fallen over with time.

"What are those?" I asked.

"Grace staves. Each commemorates a healing from the springs."

A woodsy, citrus scent grew heavy in the air, and as we took a turn in the path, hundreds more grace staves came into sight. "That's a lot of healing."

He nodded and sniffed the air. "And that must be the smell of the springs. We're getting close, I think."

We turned into a flat, rocky clearing with rough-hewn benches and firepits, blessedly free of other humans. Before us to the left stretched a series of small pools naturally terraced high up into the side of a cliff. From the top, a stream poured into the array, a dozen waterfalls filling the pools one to one. Steam from the water curled sinuously in the chill autumn air, drifting up into the trees.

We dismounted and laid the horses' reins across a rustic hitching post near a marble shrine decorated with swans, which were sacred to Vayeri. I approached the edge of the lowest pool. The milky turquoise water inside churned and steamed like a frothy bubble bath, both from the waterfall splashing into it and bubbles rising from a bottom I couldn't see. And the scent, peculiar but lovely, was almost a combination of citrus and cinnamon. The trees soaking in the rising steam added their own holy aroma—that was the woodsy smell on Kas I hadn't recognized before. He walked up beside me now.

"What are these trees?"

"Silva trees. Their fallen branches are harvested for oils. We use them a lot at the monastery." He dipped his hand into the pool. "The temperature's perfect, like a hot bath."

"Are you sure it's safe to go in?"

"Definitely." His hand emerged whole from the water, not burned and nothing bitten off, so I slowly immersed my hand, ready to pull it out if anything went wrong. But he was right: it was perfect.

I pulled off my coat. "I'm going in. Do you think it's safe for us to stop here for a little while?"

"I think so." He sat on a boulder and removed his boots. "We haven't seen anyone traveling near us all day." He set them carefully aside, laid his cloak and robe on the boulder, and walked toward the pool.

"Wait," I called, sitting on a bench to take off my boots. "You're going in with all your clothes on?"

He turned and looked at me with his brows as low as they could go. "What else would I do?"

"You're not going to get the full effect of the minerals that way."

He looked at me, considering. "You have a fair point." He pulled his tunic off over his head, draped it across the rock, and climbed the steps to the pool in his pants and bare feet.

My bench was coated with moss and something that looked like bird crap, so I carefully folded my coat up and laid it across Pistachio. I grabbed the satchel containing my clothes and brought it back to the bench closest to the pool.

Kas already stood on the ledge, his arms wrapped around his bare chest and muscular arms, sticking his toes in the water. Now that I was looking for the body of a fighter, I could see it. My gaze traveled down his sinewy back from his broad shoulders to his narrow waist, and hovered around his hips and bottom. He wasn't thickly muscled, but he definitely didn't have the body of a man who spent all his time reading books and praying. No, Kas was very finely made.

And I shouldn't be having such thoughts about a monk.

"Are you going in or not?" I teased.

He slipped his feet into the water, sinking to his waist and groaning appreciatively. "It's amazing!"

I was almost jealous that he'd gotten in first. I quickly unloaded all my weapons, pulled off my socks and pendant. I glanced at Kas. He seemed to be sitting on a shelf inside the pool, only his head visible above the water. With his eyes closed, he leaned back against the rock with a blissful smile on his face. I turned my back to him and removed my corset and tunic, folding everything and putting them back into my bag. I full-bodied shivered, my nipples pebbling from the scandalous sensation of free, cold air. I was unbuttoning my pants when I heard Kas shouting behind me.

"Nesrin! Stop! What are you doing?"

I looked over my shoulder at him, my braid whipping across my bare back. He stood in the middle of the pool with his back to me and his hands over his eyes. Steam rose off his wet shoulders.

I definitely should stop noticing his body. "I'm getting ready to go into the hot springs." I removed my pants and folded them into the bag too.

"But you don't have to take all your clothes off," he argued.

"What do you care? You're a monk." I wrapped my braid up on top of my head and secured it with some pins I'd brought, then scurried up the steps and into the pool.

The fragrant water enveloped my body like nothing I'd ever felt before. It was hot in a sublime, transcendent way, and as my shoulders slipped under the water, I let out an audible moan.

Kas took a step away at the sound, eyes still covered and the frothy water churning at his waist. "What's wrong?"

"Nothing in the world is wrong when I'm in this water." I spread my hands through the bubbles at the top, marveling at how they disappeared immediately below the surface into the milky green-blue water. "You can open your eyes now."

"Are you sure?"

"Lady of the Waters, Kas, don't be such a prude. I'm in the water and fully covered."

He turned his head to the side and looked down at me through his dark curls, bright eyes narrowed and his lips upturned. Maybe it was the sensuous embrace of the glorious water encompassing my body contrasting with the chill in the air, or maybe it was the sheen of water on his beautiful body. But he looked so masculine and unbearably handsome that it sent a shiver through me.

He waded to the rocks on the other side of the pool, turned to face me, and sunk down to his chin in the froth. "Maybe we should stay here all day instead of traveling on."

"Fine by me." I leaned my head back to look at the silva trees. All my muscles relaxed in the enveloping waters, even my old-injured calf. Birdsong and falling, rushing, bubbling water filled my ears, and the green needles of the evergreen trees contrasted exquisitely against the bright blue late-morning sky. It was a holy requiescence, a deeply centering calm to simply exist here in the water.

Kas was laying back against the rock wall, his eyes closed. I took the opportunity to move around the small pool.

His hands went over his eyes again. "What are you doing?"

"Just exploring." I swam across the pool and stood beneath the falls. The cold air was a shock, but I let the water tumble down my shoulders and chest, moving around in it to keep as covered by the bliss as possible. It was meditative and acutely pleasurable, but it wasn't enough to keep me warm. I plunged down into the water to meet an even toastier embrace than before.

I swam to sit beside him. "You can open your eyes now."

He turned, eyes guarded when they focused on me so close. But his face quickly broke into a grin when his eyes went up to my hair.

"What?"

"Your face is almost as red as your hair." His smile was amused but not mocking.

I put my hands to my face in dismay. "Really? It's my fair skin. Ady says I look like a lobster when I get overheated."

He looked away, a muscle in his jaw hardening. "I don't think lobsters are nearly so lovely as you."

Warmth that had nothing to do with the springs flooded my body. I resisted the impulse to move closer, to touch him. "Thank you," I said softly.

A flush that hadn't been there with the heat crept across his cheeks, and he rubbed his forehead, looking suddenly very embarrassed. Then cold shame shivered through me. All he'd done was compare me to a lobster, and somehow I'd come out on top.

"I'm sure it's a tight competition for loveliness between me and a lobster." I laughed nervously.

He shook his head and glanced at me, every part of his body above the water tensing. "That's not what I meant at all," he murmured.

The flooding warmth was back. Beneath the cover of the opaque water, I ran my hands down my breasts, stomach, skirting the place between my legs that ached. I pressed my hands between my thighs, trying not to touch myself with him so near. Trying not to admit to myself how badly I wanted to touch him and myself at the same time.

His eyes were closed again. Gods, he was beautiful. And so good-hearted. Could he possibly feel something for me like I was feeling for him? And what would be the point of it?

"Thank you for listening last night," he said quietly, eyes still closed. "I'm relieved you weren't angry with me."

I crossed my arms over my chest. "Of course. Thank *you* for listening. It really helped to talk about what I went through. I mean, I talked to Ady, and she tried to console me, but...well, you met her."

The brights of his eyes appear through narrowly opened lids. "You really haven't talked to *any* humans for eight years, except the men you've defeated? What about Javid? You seemed to know him pretty well."

Gods, I did not want to answer that question. "Kas," I said miserably. "You still haven't put that together?"

"What do you mean?"

"Like I told you, ever since Ady rescued me, Galter sent man after man trying to get back his princess-shaped bargaining chip. He promised rewards to anyone who could defeat Ady and collect his *property* for him. And in the beginning, they were all looking..." I took and let out a heavy breath. "They were looking specifically for a maiden. So, a few years ago, I decided they might stop coming if I was no longer..." He cocked his head at me. "Mother of wisdom, Kas! You're going to make me say it? I took Javid in as a lover, okay?"

"Oh!" His eyes went wide as the full idea of what I was telling him sunk in, but then he crunched them shut and shifted away from me. "I'm so stupid." He swallowed hard, and his voice was hard as he went on. "Of course, that's not something I would know about. I mean I understand the mechanics, but I've never experi—"

"Javid was near my age," I rushed out, wanting him to stop talking. "Handsome, and kind. Best of all, he hadn't come to curry favor with Galter, so I invited him in."

That muscle in his jaw worked again as he seemed to force himself to look at me. "Was he the only..." He shook his head suddenly. "I'm sorry. I don't know why I asked that." He looked utterly miserable. Red-faced and refusing to meet my eyes. Like all his anger was directed inward. "You don't have to..."

"Two," I said gently. "The second one turned out to be an asshole. I haven't invited anyone else in for a long time."

"Why not?"

I chose my answer carefully. "I love my solitude. Any man I bring into the trove has to make my life better, not worse." *Like you*, I wanted to add.

"I see." He stared up into the trees chewing his lip, his eyes seeming to follow the movement of the leaves.

"My turn for an intrusive question."

He looked at me, his expression guarded.

"You told Ady you were a vestal monk. In your order, does everyone make a vow of chastity?"

He nodded, his eyes returning to the tree. "Every man does."

"But not the women? They're free to sleep around?"

His laugh immediately died in a grimace and a hand pressed to his chest. "Don't make me laugh, Nesrin. My bruises are still sore." He cleared his throat. "There aren't any women in the order."

"So, you and your brothers aren't allowed to be intimate, but your counterparts in Hersia, who worship the *same goddess* as you, are rumored to express *their* devotion by living in a commune of free and rampant lovemaking. Orgies twice a year, more, some say. I just think it's a little odd, that's all."

He looked back up into the trees, a slight smile on his face, and we were both silent for a minute.

"We've lost a lot of monks to Hersia," he said quietly.

His bright eyes slid to mine with a smile, and we broke into guffawing laughter.

A chattering caught my ear and turned my head. I pressed my hand to Kas's shoulder. "Hush!" A monkey curiously watched us from a nearby branch. "Look at him!"

We both went silent, watching the little guy. He was adorable, nearly all white with rust-tinged fur around his face.

I'd never seen a monkey in person before, and I was rapt. He swung down through the branches and stopped on one at the bottom of the canopy, gently swinging from side to side from one long arm, watching us watch him. Kas's soft breathing beside me proved that he too was enchanted.

"He's so *cute*," I whispered in breathless wonder as the monkey hung there, his little dark eyes flitting around, observing us and the whole area around the pool.

Suddenly he chattered and swung back up into the tree as if something scared him. Kas and I both instinctively looked behind us just in time to see another monkey running away with Kas's robe in his arms.

"Stop!" he shouted. I devolved into breathless laughter as Kas shot out of the pool, rivulets of steaming water running off of him, his wet pants sagging low and exposing the rounded tops of his buttocks. I was laughing almost too hard to watch him run around the clearing after the monkey, shouting the whole time. The monkey jumped from rock to rock, and just when Kas was close enough to nearly snatch him, it scuttled high into the trees. I cackled as Kas jumped up after it, just missing its tail. The monkey chattered at Kas in angry, shrill staccatos.

"Stupid monkey!" Kas shouted at it, hiking his pants back all the way up.

The monkey plucked a cone off the tree and threw it at Kas, who ducked it, his hair flinging droplets of water everywhere. I laughed even harder.

Kas jumped and grabbed hold of his cloak with his long arm outstretched. The monkey let it go and scampered off as Kas whirled around and shouted, pointing to where I'd left my clothes bag. The first monkey was sitting on the boulder reaching for the strap.

My laughter died abruptly. "No!" I shouted.

I stood up to run after it, and Kas dropped his robe, whirling away from me with his hands over his eyes. He thrust his open palm back at me, shouting in a commanding tone, "*Don't* get out!"

I squealed as the monkey grabbed my bag and took off toward the line of trees. I sank down screaming. "Stop him!"

Kas hesitated.

"I'm in the pool! I'm in the pool!" I screeched. "Stop him!"

He sprang into action, chasing the furry bastard as it swung from tree to tree into the forest.

Cursing, I scrambled out of the water, the cold air a million tiny arrows on my skin. I ran across the campsite on tiptoes and picked up Kas's discarded tunic, pulling it on over my head. It warmed me down to my thighs, at least, and I dug his packet of dates from his satchel, grabbed his robe, and ran toward his shouting.

Not ten feet in, the prickly forest floor ceased to bother my numb legs and feet, which felt like ice blocks and moved about as well. I found Kas stopped beside a wide, rushing stream, the monkey on a high branch over it with my bag.

I pushed Kas's robe at him, and he murmured his thanks and slipped it on. But then he cast a second glance at me and pulled it back off, pushing it at me.

"Hey, you nasty, wretched little thief," I said in my sweetest voice as I gratefully wrapped up in Kas's robe. "Come back down and give me my clothes, or I'll come up and wring your furry neck."

The monkey leaned down and chattered vehemently at me. I cringed backwards and handed Kas the dates.

"I don't think he likes you."

"It's mutual," I said darkly, backing away where I wouldn't spook the stupid beast.

Kas sprinkled some dates into his palm and made kissing noises at the filthy thing. "Here, little guy, look! These are delicious! Don't you want some?"

The monkey cocked his head and looked carefully at him, his nose sniffing toward Kas's outstretched hand.

"That's right! Delicious dates." Kas shivered but moved slowly, reaching his hand up toward the monkey. It stretched its face down toward Kas's hand, sniffing. "Come on. Free dates! A bargain in this forest." Kas slowly stretched his other hand up toward my bag.

The monkey grabbed a date, nibbled it experimentally, then tossed my bag away to use both hands to scoop them all up from Kas's hand.

I lunged forward but helplessly watched my bag fall directly into the stream.

Kas ran in after it, stumbling a few feet downstream to where my bag was lodged in the rushing foam against a boulder. Mercifully, it didn't spill open as he grabbed the strap and threw it across his body.

"Thank you!" I held my hand out to Kas, who bit both lips as if trying not to laugh.

He sighed, his wet curls swaying. "Your face is still red, but now your lips are blue." He threw his arm around me. "Come on. I'll start a fire."

A few minutes later, I finished laying my wet clothes out on makeshift clotheslines and sat miserably huddled on a bench. Kas's fire, made with fallen silva wood, released a holy smell like incense as its embers twinkled into the air. I reached my hands and icy feet toward its warmth.

Kas knelt before me and tugged one of my feet out. "Furry miscreants." He smiled at me and slipped an extra pair of his warm socks on one foot then the other.

I gave him my best can-you-believe-this smile. "Stupid, cute little monkey thieves."

The socks were a warm blessing, and when Kas wrapped a blanket around both of our backs, pulling it closed around the front of us, I sighed and leaned into his warmth, scooting to sit pressed up against him. He slipped his arm around my shoulder and rested it chastely on my upper arm as I leaned my head against him.

"So much better." I tucked my hands in my armpits, still shivering. "You really have a way with monkeys."

"They're a lot like little kids," he said. "If they have something they shouldn't, just distract them with something new."

"When are you ever around children?"

"One of my favorite missions is going to the orphanage." His voice was soft and low, so close to my ear. "The kids are so much fun. They know the best games and have the best stories."

Before my father died, I'd wanted kids. But after what happened to me, I was afraid of not being able to protect them from the horrors of this world, the way my parents weren't able to protect me.

Kas and I both had the lives we wanted taken from us. But I could imagine him in the middle of a tumble of kids, laughing. "You'd be a wonderful father. Is having kids something you want from life, for yourself?" I asked gently.

I felt him shrug beside me. "No point in dwelling on something that's not on my path."

"You're pretty young to have already decided what your path is, especially when you seem so unhappy about it. You must know," I continued, bumping playfully against him, "that you're very handsome."

He laughed and turned his head away from me.

"Really! You saw the way the Kesna serving women were fawning all over you. 'Don't you want strawberries, Prince Kasper? More coffee, Prince Kasper? Let me have your babies, Prince Kasper?'" I asked in an exaggerated, overly feminine voice. "You can't tell me you've *never* dreamt of leaving the monastery to have a family."

His smile had a blush, but he wouldn't look at me, wouldn't answer me.

"No woman's ever caught your eye?"

He hesitated. "No." But he said it as if he wasn't convinced himself.

"Any man?"

"No." He was silent for a moment, then a smile crossed his face. "When I was ten, I thought I was in love with the stablemaster's daughter. She was smart and brave. Beautiful, too."

"But?" I asked dramatically, willing him to go on.

"But I'm a...vestal monk, now." His tone was soft, but sad, as if he was trying to convince himself it was for the best.

"You're a human, Kas," I said gently, "with a human body and a human heart. You're not an awful person if you want human things. Being the fourth son of the velarch sounds like a traditional sacrifice."

When he finally answered, it was diplomatic, befitting a prince. "My life *is* my own, but I've made promises to Hivathe." But then he met my eyes with pain and uncertainty I'm not sure I expected to see. "What kind of faithless man would I be if I abandoned my duty?"

I opened my mouth but found I had no answer for his very serious question, especially posed with his eyes looking at me like *that*.

He cleared his throat. "What about you? You sound like you want a family, but I thought you had everything you needed at the trove."

"Don't try to turn this around on me. I *do* have everything I need there."

"You didn't choose to go to the trove any more than I chose to go into the monastery."

"That's completely different. I left a horrible life for a much better one, but your family pushed you into a life you hate."

He looked at me sharply, as if surprised. "You think I hate the monastery?"

"I do. I almost can't get it out of my mind. Someone could do you a big favor by burning it to the ground, couldn't they?"

He laughed, cleared his throat, then said very seriously, "That's not funny."

But I was laughing too hard to stop, and he devolved into laughter too. It took a while for it to peter out.

"We should leave as soon as you have something dry to wear."

"Probably. But first I'd like to make a grace stave and pray to Vayeri."

"Is your leg feeling better?"

I stretched the muscle out, testing it, and I smiled. "You know, I think it is."

CHAPTER FIFTEEN

THE LIBRARY

Estria, the capital of Opintol, was nestled in a valley of rolling foothills that gently cascaded down from the snow-capped mountains to the north. As we approached from the southeast road just before nightfall, the city appeared white and gleaming out of the mist that settled low over the autumn grasses.

"The famed Columned City," I marveled, jostling with Kas and dozens of other travelers down the wide, cobblestoned street that led into the city's heart.

Entering Estria was a graceful distraction. Nearly every building was constructed of white marble or whitewashed stone, their rounded arches supported by wide columns and adorned with the careful geometric script of Opintolian. Little green gardens were tucked into the skirts of every building, still blooming with lark's bells and sundancers in the warmth of the valley despite the advancing autumn. Fountain waters trickled and slipped down marble obelisks and finely carved statues of Hivathe's Golden Spirits, especially Aringiel, the spirit of peace. Nowhere was the statuary finer than in the city square before The Library.

Founded during the reign of Emperor Opintol over a thousand years ago, the Library had grown into the hills like a living thing, sprouting new, columned buildings connected to each other with white bridges and breezeways like the reaching tendrils of a melon vine. The entire complex was bookmarked with ancient trees and trailing flowers, making it difficult to tell where the library ended and the adjacent university began, especially in the waning light.

We left our horses and bags at an inn's stable across the busy city square and began up the wide marble steps of the main building, a beehive of activity. After the short marble foyer, hundreds of people moved in different directions in a massive, vaulted atrium. Children pulled their parents along by the hand, scholars debated philosophy, students laughed and chatted with their peers, and a trio of older women walked past us discussing a romance novel.

The atrium itself was so large at its center that trees grew in large, wide pots, their branches reaching to the sunset streaming in through the glass ceiling overhead. Kas pulled me along to the center where he hailed a concierge at the desk.

"Good morning. I'm here to see Izdu. Can you tell him his cousin's friend is here from the Order of Hivathe in Veytia?"

"Of course." The gray-haired woman directed us to a waiting area where we sat beside a wall tapestry titled "The Halcyon Peace," depicting soldiers laying down their arms on either side of a battlefield.

"Look." Kas pointed to a small collection of buildings on the tapestry. "That's the original library. They say that during the Phoenix Wars, General Opintol of Ghentere and General Tilius of the Archipelago halted the battle before the library and began to negotiate peace. And that was the last war that touched Estria."

"That's really true? Estria hasn't been attacked in over a thousand years?"

Kas nodded.

"What made them stop fighting?"

"Battle weary? Too many deaths on both sides? I'm not sure anyone knows for sure. But the people here are very proud of the legacy of peace the generals left in Estria. And so they especially revere Aringiel in honor of it."

Just then, a short man in flowing white robes approached us while adjusting his glasses. "Hello. Can I help you?" He looked more closely at Kas, and his face opened in amazement. "Prince Kasper!" he exclaimed, bowing down before him.

Kas reached out his hands and gently pulled him back up. "Just Kas. And that's not necessary. You must be Izdu?"

"Yes, Your Highness." Izdu bowed lower than before. "And I'm from Veytia, so I can only call you, My Prince. But how do you know my name?"

Kas and I exchanged glances. "Your cousin, Okesli, sent a magpie to let you know I was coming?"

Izdu shook his head, eyes wide. "I never received it, but I'm happy to help, Your Highness."

We exchanged glances. That was two magpies suspiciously gone astray.

"It's just Kas." He lowered his voice. "Can we speak somewhere privately?"

"Of course." Izdu's white teeth shone in a smile, bright against his dark skin. "I'll bring you to a private consultation room."

Once we were seated around an ebony table in a stained glass-walled chamber, Izdu leaned forward, hands clasped and shaved head shining under the lamplight. "Tell me, Prince Kasper, how can I help you?"

"This is Nesrin, the Knight of the Dread Dragon Adydorrstea's Trove." Kas brought out his book. "And we're looking—"

"A knight of a dragon's trove!" Izdu crooned, studying me with his wide eyes. "Fascinating! I would love to learn all about you."

"Another time, maybe," I said diplomatically. "Right now, we're looking for this." I tapped the page Kas had open.

"My father sent me to find this golden casket. We need to find it first and keep it out of Galter Velius's hands. He thinks it'll make his army invincible."

Izdu adjusted his glasses and took the book from Kas. "A golden casket." His sonorous voice and rapt posture revealed a keen interest.

"Yes, I think you can ignore the keys. We're pretty sure now that caskets don't have them."

"You're correct, Your Highness. They do not."

"You've heard of them?"

"Of course. Eight caskets were made ages ago. Four in iron and four in gold. In fact," he lowered his voice and glanced up as someone passed outside the room. "We have an iron casket here in the Library."

A chill skittered through my bones.

"Really?" Kas's bright eyes lit up. "Can we see it?"

"Absolutely! But you should know it's been opened, and it's empty."

"That's...comforting?" Cold sweat slipped down my back.

Kas looked at me quizzically.

"Somebody opened it, and the world didn't end. That has to be a good thing, right?"

"Our magical scholars say there's no magic remaining. But of course, it's made of iron, so it can't be the one you're looking for."

"Still," Kas said, "this is the closest we've come. Can we see it?"

"Of course." Izdu handed Kas's book back and led us from the consultation room, taking us through a dizzying labyrinth of rooms and breezeways. My eyes couldn't take in enough of it. Some rooms had multiple balconies with winding stone staircases, while others had deep shadows behind locked iron gates. Even at this hour, we passed classrooms, laboratories, and a boisterous group of children in an interior garden happily planting seeds. One room we walked through had six deep balconies circling around the room overhead, with winding staircases at each corner and middle point. We walked past the cavernous pull of another room that was built into the ground like a stepwell.

On a busy upper-floor hallway, Izdu led us into a solid stone room lit with torches. Three other people lingered there, looking over the dozens of artifacts, pots and casks, jewelry, tools, and weapons that hung on the walls and were divided among the room's cases and tables.

"This is our gallery of...*eccentric* items procured from the old Ghentere Empire, which dissolved eight hundred years ago into four of the twenty-seven nations."

I glanced at the other people and looked at Kas.

"Do you think we could have the room to ourselves?" he asked Izdu.

"Of course. Ladies and gentlemen, can we have the room, please? We have special guests with private questions."

The others smiled and nodded, and Izdu closed the door behind them after they left.

"Everyone's so nice here," I noted, leaning to inspect a sparkling necklace of cascading sapphires laid out upon black velvet in a glass case.

Izdu put his hand gently on my shoulder. "That necklace was crafted by a deadly, ancient secret society, the Archē Cruor. It's enchanted to poison its wearer."

I stepped quickly away from the necklace and joined Kas and Izdu in the middle of the room where a small, unassuming iron box sat with its lid open on a wooden table. It looked like a worn jewelry box, and not a very fine one at that.

"Here it is: the Ghentere Casket." Izdu pulled a pair of white cotton gloves from his apron and slipped them on before gently lifting the casket and bringing it closer for us to see.

No rust for something so old, but bits of paint survived in spots all over the box, brown here, yellow there, some blue at the deepest points of the engraving. I squinted. The animals etched across it sort of looked like weasels or maskless raccoons. Red pandas?

Without scale or context, I couldn't tell what they were, but they postured as if being attacked by unseen assailants.

"Are they...bears?" Kas asked.

"Yes, we think so."

"But why are their tails so frizzy and un-bear-like?" I asked.

"They're Vardu bears, from the Vardu Mountains in Oprolodas," Izdu said. "They have longer tails than their western counterparts."

"What does it say?" I asked.

Kas answered before the librarian could. "'If you value the blue sky and not the final sunset, the rolling hills of green and not a burning field of death, if you value life and all who dream to breathe it, leave this casket sealed for all eternity.'"

I gaped. "What fantastic fool would open it?"

"We acquired it already open, but some of our scholars think that's what caused the Ghentere Empire to split, possibly even the eruption of Mount Beyazut. The emperor disappeared, and the city-states started fighting amongst themselves. War tore it apart soon after that."

Kas's light eyes took in every detail of the casket. "Its task is done, then? It's been...neutralized?"

"Our best people say so."

"May I?" Kas gestured to Izdu's gloves.

"Of course, Your Highness."

"Just Kas, thanks," he corrected again, slipping them on. He picked up the casket, weighing it in his hands. "It's heavy, even for iron."

"Yes, that's an unusual characteristic of it."

"As if it's not...quite...empty." Kas's voice trailed off as he lifted and turned the casket, studying it from all sides. He closed the lid nearly all the way, then opened it again. "What's the best theory on how it was locked? And how it was opened?"

Izdu pointed to the smooth junction between the lid and box. "As you can see, there aren't any keyholes or fasteners. But if you study the glyphs on the side, you'll notice that the words can be read backwards as well as forwards. Our experts seem to think it was locked with magic words and opened with them as well."

My brain was still stuck on one question. "Who would've opened such a thing?" I peered at the casket around Kas's arm.

"Somebody either very evil or very desperate, I guess," Kas replaced the casket onto the table slowly and gently, as if he were afraid it might explode. "What else can you tell us about the caskets?"

"Unfortunately, what I've told you is the extent of my personal knowledge. The only person on staff I can think of who would've known more about them passed away a few months ago."

Kas nodded with a frown. "I'm sorry for your loss. If not another expert, do you have any books concerning the caskets that we could see?" He offered the gloves to me, as if I wanted to touch the nasty thing.

I shook my head. "I'd rather marry a manticore."

Kas smirked as Izdu answered.

"Of course. I can bring you to the esoteric section of the museum, where all the books about prophecies, magic, dragons, and other mysterious subjects are kept."

We followed Izdu back the way we'd come and into the room ringed with deep balconies. After placing a fat hunk of amethyst on an empty table to reserve it, he led us up one of the staircases, explained the general layout of the section, and pulled a few books that he suspected might contain references to the caskets.

"One last thing I've just remembered about our iron casket. I remember hearing it was brought to us at a great expense of lives. The archaeologist's team who went after it...well, not everyone in her party returned from wherever they found it."

Kas's eyes lit up. "Could we speak with her?"

Izdu grimaced. "That was over four hundred years ago. You might consider going to her homeland, the Mysterium Amanharate, to read more about her. The Amanha is a lovely man with a fantastic collection—writing originated there, after all. But he's funny about letting our scribes visit to copy them, even worse during an election year. And we haven't gotten to copy that collection yet."

"I see. Thank you for the information," Kas said.

"Thank you, my Prince, for your kindness and your service. Lady Knight." Izdu bowed and excused himself.

We loaded a wide selection of books onto the book flight, a magnificent contraption that lowered books on a pulley system, and brought our haul to our reserved table. Sitting in silence for a while, we skimmed through the books we'd pulled.

"Here's something," Kas said. "A reference to a pair of caskets...nope. Not the ones we're looking for. The iron one is engraved with bats, and its counterpart gold casket has ravens."

"Bats and ravens? Okay, ravens are sacred to the Golden Spirit, Varanor. But what do the bats signify?"

He shrugged. "Something we probably don't want to know about."

"Where were they from?"

"Um..." He turned a page. "Hersia. That's an adventure for another time."

Several fruitless books later, I found something about Hivathe's Golden Spirits placing blessings in the caskets. It did little more than list all seven spirits' names, but...Ady said there were only four golden caskets. So which four contributed blessings? Varanor was a strong contender, if what Kas found could be trusted. I looked around the room, and my eyes fell on yet another statue of Aringiel. Aringiel, the Golden Spirit of peace, with her mythical halcyon alighting on her outstretched hand. In Estria. Where there was an open iron casket.

"Kas, I have a theory." I tapped the book I was holding. "It's all mixed up in an epic poem, but this history makes another reference to the spirits placing blessings in the caskets. There are seven Golden Spirits, right, and each stands guard over one of the seven boons."

"Of course." He counted them on his fingers. "Love, community, protection, charity, justice, prosperity, and peace."

"Exactly. We haven't been thinking—or at least I haven't been thinking—about which spirits placed blessings in the four caskets. Varanor's maybe one. And isn't it awfully miraculous that Estria hasn't been at war in all this time? I'm not sure any place on Mellora can say that, or at least very few can. And peace is Aringiel's boon." I let the book go slack in my hands. "What if, whenever the iron casket upstairs was opened—or if another was opened somewhere—what if someone opened Aringiel's golden casket here to try and counteract whatever came out of it?"

His frown deepened. "That would make sense. So, if someone opened Aringiel's golden casket, they must've believed it could counteract an already-open casket."

I shrugged "Or not. Maybe they were just desperate to stop the war."

"But if they *were* trying to counteract an iron casket, and if it was the one upstairs, why did the archeologist have to hunt down its counterpart somewhere presumably far from Estria?"

"No idea. But if I'm right, the golden casket Galter's looking for might already be empty."

"We can only hope, if that's even the same one. He surely isn't looking for something that can bless the world with peace. But if your theory's correct, that would place those two caskets here about twelve hundred years ago, during the Phoenix Wars, which matches my research. But it still doesn't answer who opened the iron casket, or what happened to the horror inside."

I shook my head. The thought of the iron casket merely existing somewhere nearby made me shiver. "No. It doesn't."

Kas pulled his book out and made notes. "It's something to consider, though."

I went back to our stack. Thunder sounded from outside the library, and a heavy rain settled in. Some time later, in a history of the Northern Empire by Sten the Ulf, I found an engraving of a casket with dolphins on it.

"I found a gold casket! Listen. 'Knud the Trygve thought he had a great bounty of wisdom to share, describing how the dolphin casket was sacred to Sianira and would come to our aid against the hydra he sworn he'd seen in the ocean, although he shared the information over a bottle of whiskey and cannot be trusted to hold his liquor. He thought he was providing me with new information, but he offered nothing not already known by everyone with ears to hear. In fact, my first mate's baby sister is better versed on the caskets than Knud the Buffoon with whom I played dice tonight. Had I not honor, I would have owned his entire fleet of ships at the close of the game.'" I waited until Kas was finished writing in his book. "So there may be a golden dolphin casket associated with the Golden Spirit Sianira, and maybe a hydra is in its paired iron casket—unless Knud just had too much to drink. But why would a little girl know more?"

Kas looked at me for a moment, then pushed away the book he'd been pouring over. "Because the caskets were created before humans started writing."

"So...why would she know more?" I felt stupid.

"The same way all stories were told before people wrote them down: storytelling. The child knew songs and nursery stories, and I bet there's one about the caskets."

He stood and pushed in his chair.

"Where are you going?"

"I'll be right back." He went off in the direction of the information desk. Darkness crept through the high windows, and our room had nearly cleared of patrons. Only two groups sat at tables across the room, and one librarian reshelved books upstairs.

While I waited for him, I went through the remainder of the books we'd pulled, but none of them yielded any new information. I rubbed my eyes. My brain was saturated and begging to do anything else. I picked up the amethyst stone, examining its facets. I should've grilled Ady more about the caskets. I had questions before, but so many *more* now.

Kas slipped suddenly into the seat beside me with an open book. "Sometimes I think I'm brilliant," he said with a self-satisfied smile.

"Tell me something I don't know," I teased.

His cheeks pinkened with the compliment. "Challenge accepted. Look what I found in this children's book of verses." He removed the amethyst from my hand and slid the book in front of me. I glanced up—we were the only ones in this room now—and softly read the part of the verse he pointed out:

Sing for me, the song of old,
Iron and gold, eternal foes.
Wolverine meets halcyon gold,
The shark against the dolphin goes.
The hell dog fights the bees in flight,
The bats of hell 'gainst the raven's flight.
Hivathe with her spirits bright
Defeats the wicked, brings the world to light.

I looked up to him with excitement. "These are all the pairs! And there's a halcyon for Aringiel!"

He nodded, grinning. "Exactly. But notice the absence of lions and Vardu bears?" Kas pulled his book and charcoal out, leaning close to me to peer at the nursery rhyme while writing the animals in neat columns, along with the Golden Spirits associated with halcyons, dolphins, bees, and ravens. "It didn't occur to me before, but in old Ghentere, the words for *halcyon* and *lion* are very similar. If someone came across the word *halcyon* with no context, and say the *C* wasn't clear or was missing and maybe it's a bad copy—old parchment is notoriously difficult to read—you might think it said 'hal lyon,' or, *the lion*."

"So Galter's looking for a lion casket, when he should be looking for the halcyon casket. But that doesn't explain why he'd want a casket blessed with the peace of Aringiel, which is probably empty anyway. Wouldn't he be looking for the—" I looked back at the poem, the hair on my arms standing up. "Kas, what's a wolverine look like?"

Kas raised his eyebrows and looked directly into my eyes. "Like a little Vardu bear."

I leaned against the back of my chair, dread sinking in my stomach. "But the one upstairs is empty. The golden casket with the halcyon peace blessing must be empty, too. What are the other golden caskets again?" I pulled the book to me. "A dolphin, bees, and a raven. Do you think he could be looking for a different pair?"

Kas rubbed his beard, looking very tired. "I don't know. I'm still stuck on what Izdu said about how they think the iron casket caused the downfall of the Ghentere Empire. But what happened to its prisoner? The spy was very clear that we're looking for a casket, not for a monster."

I ran my finger down the page. "I don't know what a hell dog is, and I'd be happy to never learn. But bats and sharks and wolverines, those are just animals. Not one-of-a-kind or special in any way. What could they contain?"

"Well." Kas bit both of his lips. "Bats are usually pretty gentle. In Veytia they're seen more as helpers. They eat mosquitoes; their dung is used for fuel. They symbolize a long life, or rebirth."

"In Araven they're associated with witchcraft and dark deeds."

"So maybe something that seems fair but is really foul? And then wolverines are notoriously unfriendly and vicious."

"Sounds like your garden variety monster."

"Sorry to bother you, but the library's about to close." The librarian's voice from the doorway startled both of us. "We welcome you back in the morning."

"It's ridiculous," I said, stacking the last book up. "Everyone seems to agree that they're horrifying, but no one will explain why."

"I guess people don't write down things they think everyone knows."

I bit my lip and watched him stack books back on the lift with guilt eating at my heart. I knew one thing, and it was past time I shared it with him.

CHAPTER SIXTEEN

A NIGHTMARE

We stood under the library's portico surveying the evening lights of the city around us, which were dimmed and dripping with the thunderstorm.

"There's only one place left on my list to check."

Although his eyes were alight with the lamplight and eagerly watching the activity on the street, his expression was sad. I couldn't tell if he was more disappointed because we hadn't found the casket or because his quest out in the world had only one last stop. It was too much to hope that it had something to do with me.

Lightning streaked across the sky, bringing with it the memory of daggers glinting at Ashur's feet. I slipped my arm in Kas's. "Let's stay in an inn tonight. I'll bet whatever they have cooking is better than what we can stir up over a campfire."

He looked at the passing horses and lit-up windows with obvious longing, but he ultimately shook his head. "We should really keep going. Our time's limited."

"Kas, I don't think I can do another night on the road in the rain so soon after..."

He looked sharply at me, his eyebrows lowered. "Alright. Let's stay. But where?"

"We left our horses at The Wild Rose Inn. Like my name. It's practically begging us to stay there." I pulled him into the rain. "My treat."

"Alright. I guess we've earned it."

The Wild Rose lived up to its name in beauty and frivolity. Shaking the worst of the rain from our hair and clothes, we squeezed through the heavy wooden doors among other patrons coming and going to find a packed dining room of people eating delicious-smelling food, laughing, arguing, and trading stories. Kas grinned from ear to ear as I pulled him with me toward the bar. The interior was paneled and floored with rosy oak, and the walls, pillars, and balustrade of the balcony above were carved with wild rose vines.

Behind the counter, an older man with red cheeks and considerable girth was laughing boisterously, busily filling drink orders for servers and the customers sitting along the bar.

"Good evening, sir, who can we speak to about some rooms for the night?" Kas asked.

"Good evening to ya. That'd be me. I'm Dell, the proprietor." He plopped two spilling pints of beer on the counter which were immediately taken away by a server. "We're nearly full tonight, what with the festival beginning soon. But I do have one room left for you and your lady," he said, nodding to me.

"What festival?"

Kas turned to me. "Don't you keep holidays? The autumn equinox is the day after tomorrow."

I'd completely forgotten. "I guess we've only been celebrating the winter solstice."

Kas bit his lip and turned to me. "You take the room. I'll camp outside the city."

I ignored Kas and smiled at Dell. "We'll take it! And who can we talk to about keeping our horses overnight? They're in your stables now."

Kas looked doubtfully at me as Dell dried his hands on a towel of questionable cleanliness. "I'll settle your horses. C'mon. Let me show you the room." He left the counter and started through the thick crowds toward the stairs.

Kas held my arm back. "We can't both stay here."

"Why not? How is a room different from a campsite?"

He grimaced, but he followed me as I wound through the crowd after Dell.

Not long after, Kas had retrieved our bags from our horses and had two meals sent up to what was a very small room. The bed, sized for two, took up most of it, and a tiny table with two chairs was tucked beside the window. But it was clean and cozy, and it had a lovely view of the library.

I sat beside him at the table. "You could've eaten downstairs. Just because I don't want to be around all those people doesn't mean you have to be a hermit too."

He shrugged. "I didn't want to leave you alone. You're always alone."

"I'm never alone. I've got Ady and Pooka."

"A dragon and a cat?"

"They're company. You should know. Pooka's practically your cat too, now that he likes you better."

He smiled. "But they're not *human*. You don't miss being around other humans?"

I chewed thoughtfully for a moment. Truth was, I could do without everyone else we'd met, but Kas had been a joy. "I guess. But Ady and Pooka are more human than lots of other people I've known."

"I think I know what you mean." He nodded sagely. "Pooka really gets me."

"He's my kitten, Kas, and you can't have him."

He chuckled and dug into his food.

"Did Ady tell you anything more about the caskets before we left?"

He shook his head, eyes twinkling as he glanced at me. "No. She told me how you saved me from drowning, and then she spent a lot of time selling me on all your good qualities."

I rolled my eyes, my cheeks heating. "Sometimes I think she's trying to get rid of me. Well, she told *me* something about the caskets when I was alone with her." I recounted everything she'd told me about the fearsome white dragon, and how he'd been trapped in an iron casket.

He listened, rapt, asking questions that I mostly couldn't answer.

"I'm sorry I didn't tell you sooner. I guess I wasn't sure at first if I could trust you."

His hand landed on my arm for just a moment. "That's okay. It's excellent information, but I'm not sure it helps us. We don't know which casket he was placed in. For all we know, his nickname could've been 'hell dog.'"

"Ady said it was a white dragon who definitely didn't play well with others. Kind of like a wolverine, right?"

He pulled out his book and charcoal, marking this new information down. "I'll add it to our mystery, but if a white dragon of that description had been released, he'd surely be wreaking havoc somewhere and not sitting quietly."

After a while, we finished our meals and settled the covers back on the platters. It was late, and I couldn't wait to spend my first night in a while in an actual bed. I took off my boots and worked my hair loose from its braid. "Tomorrow morning I have a date with the big bronze bathtub by the kitchens. I booked twenty minutes for you too, if you want it."

"Thanks! Maybe on the next stop we can spend some time with laundry facilities, too." Kas stoked the fire, turned out the oil lamps, and laid blankets on the floor.

I unhooked my corset and slipped into the bed, pulling the heavy blankets up to my neck and over the back of my head, leaving a tiny place for me to breathe out of. It was such a luxury to be under a roof, and even though the bed wasn't plush, it was warm and not lumpy. Kas shuffled on the floor, and his blankets rustled amid a soft thump.

"You don't have to sleep on the floor. The bed's big enough for both of us."

I could barely hear his reply through my cocoon of blankets. "It's bad enough you won't let me sleep in the stable."

I opened my eyes just to roll them. "For heaven's sake. Look." I unwrapped myself and got up. "Look what I'm doing."

Kas sat up and watched me pull a blanket off the shelf.

I threw the covers back and rolled the blanket up like a low fence down the middle of the bed, gesturing grandly at it. "There. We'll never know the other's there."

He shook his head and laid back down. "I'm fine."

"Fine then." I re-cocooned myself. It was a cold night, especially with the rain. I wouldn't have slept on the floor for any money. Kas tossed and turned for several minutes.

I smiled and turned toward the empty side of the bed. "This bed is so warm, and so comfortable," I said drowsily, taunting him. "So many warm blankets."

He let out a cross between a growl and a sigh, and after several thumping and rustling noises, I felt his weight dip the bed. I opened my eyes in surprise to see him lying next to me with the covers pulled up almost over his head.

"It was freezing down there."

"Good night, Kas," I grinned.

"Good night, Nesrin."

I drifted into sleep, contentedly thinking of the Library and this peaceful place in the middle of busy Estria where I could rest my head. It was the farthest I had ever been away from the trove. For a moment, I let myself think of my father's palace, my first home, and I fell asleep mixing the two together.

Mother and I run down a dark corridor of reflective black tile, our feet splashing, turning corner after corner, but still the wolves close in. Their howling fills my blood, and I cling to her hand. We jump onto an impossibly high cliff, edge across its narrow ledge, and squeeze on our stomachs through a space too small for rats. But the wolves are behind us, closer, closer, snapping at our heels. A light appears ahead. If we reach it, if we swing on that rope across to the torches that line the hall, we can escape. We'll be safe. But an abyss gapes at our feet, and Mother picks me up, throwing me across the gap. She pulls back, mustering the strength to jump to me, to safety, but a wolf catches her arm in its jaws, and she goes down screaming in the dark in a pile of snarling, snapping maws. I fall to the ground, wailing. Large hands pull me roughly from behind "Mother! Mother!" I cry, my hands and bare feet splashing in the water. No, in her blood running across the stones where the abyss was, just a moment before. "Mother!" I scream until my throat is raw and bloody with the wounds of a thousand knives, but no sound comes out, and I can't move. I'm paralyzed with fear. Strong hands pull me away, away from her—

"Nesrin."

I woke up sweating in the dark, not sure where I was. Blankets ensnared me, and I thrashed my arms and legs out of them.

But Kas's warm hands grabbed my arm, his voice louder in my ear. "Nesrin, wake up. You're having a nightmare." His bright eyes reflected the firelight, wide and concerned. I wiped my hand against my damp cheek—tears, not sweat, and they'd streamed down my face, down my neck, into my hair and pillow. I took a shuddering breath and looked around the quiet room, at the whitewashed walls, the steady fire, the long, blue curtains swaying in an unseen draft.

"What were you dreaming about?"

"I don't know," I lied, wiping my face and taking another shaky breath, pulling all my hair into one place from where it had wrapped and tangled around my arms and shoulders. "I'm fine. It was nothing."

He wiped a tear from my face with his thumb. "It didn't seem like nothing."

"It's fine." I laid down and turned away from him, pulling the covers back up.

After a moment, he lay back down too. His hand lightly touched my back and lifted again. "I'm here if you need me, Nesrin."

I shut my eyes tight against the threat of a dream that faded too slowly from my brain. I hadn't had that nightmare in years, not since I'd first come to the trove traumatized and so alone. Ady did everything she could to comfort me, but I was so sad. Just me and a dragon in an empty monolith. To cheer me, she brought me Pooka when he was a tiny, mewling kitten. He'd curl up beside me at night, purring and warm. I'd grab onto him like he was a doll, and the warm, breathing, growing weight of him finally calmed my nightmares.

I missed my Pooka, my warm, purring love. He surely missed his scratchies. I missed his quizzy little face and sweet wet nose. What was I doing so far from the trove? I shivered, wiping away fresh tears. The images from my nightmare kept intruding on my thoughts. A dog barked, and I opened my eyes with a start, my heart pounding again.

Kas took a deep breath, sighing a little in his sleep. Unless I laid beside a warm body right now, I'd never be calm again. Kas had turned away from me. I carefully pulled the rolled blanket out of the sheets from between us, spread it over the bed, and I scooted my back against his. His warmth and the rise and fall of his breath instantly soothed me, and I fell asleep.

CHAPTER SEVENTEEN

THE MYSTERIUM AMANHARATE

Nearly two days later, Kas and I emerged from an oak forest into the bustling stone streets of Ladavar, seat of the democratic Mysterium Amanharate. Where Estria had been all graceful curves and columns of white marble, Ladavar was all straight lines, flat arches, and more trees than gardens. The streets, lined with stone and golden marble buildings, were choked with horses and carriages bedecked in festoons of red, orange, blue, and silver for the Festival of the Sinking Sun. After another hour of traffic, we entrusted our horses to the pages at the Amanha's sprawling mansion just around sunset.

Dropping our fathers' names to the gatekeepers got us quickly into a side hall, and a messenger was dispatched to tell the Amanha we were there. Even though the mansion was gearing up for the celebration, he came quickly and welcomed us with one open arm. The other was holding a small girl of about four years.

"Prince Kasper, welcome to Mysterium."

Amanha Rislan shook Kas's hand. Although lines were beginning to show around his eyes and gray slipped through the waves of his black hair and short-clipped beard, he was still young and handsome. A palpable joy and warmth radiated from his open smile, and I couldn't help but smile back when he turned to me.

"Princess Nesrin, I'm so happy to see you well. My predecessor briefly sponsored your brothers, before they went to Boekam," he said, shaking my hand.

"Thank you, Amanha Rislan," I said, grateful I remembered not to call him *Your Majesty*. Mysterium was the only democracy in the gulf nations, and they were fiercely proud of it.

"Who is this little sprite?" Kas asked, stepping around the Amanha to make a goofy face at the little girl who'd buried her face in the Amanha's shoulder.

"This is my daughter, Aira."

The little girl giggled at Kas as he went around the other side, surprising her with another silly face, her large brown eyes laughing although the rest of her face was hidden, buried in her father's blue suit.

"I'm sorry for intruding on your celebrations," I said, glancing around at the workers setting up tables and decorations in the adjacent ballroom. "But we were hoping to talk to you in private."

"My dear," the Amanha began, placing his wiggling, giggling daughter on the ground so she could play with Kas. "I would be happy to, but tomorrow. It's against Mysterium tradition to discuss business on festival days. I insist that you both be my special guests at the celebration tonight."

I glanced uncertainly at Kas where he paused from spinning in a circle with Aira on his back, her long black hair falling all around Kas's shoulders as she squealed with joy.

"Thank you for your hospitality," Kas said. "It would be an honor to attend."

Aira giggled and lightly kicked her legs to Kas's sides. "Go horsey!" Kas neighed and rode Aira around the hallway to the Amanha's delight.

I smiled, trying to keep the disappointment from my face, and echoed Kas's sentiments.

"Thank you from the bottom of my heart for brightening up my Aira," he said to Kas. The Amanha leaned in toward me. "She's been clinging to me and her mother all day. Excited about the party, I think. Maybe now that my little equestrian found someone to play with her for a minute, she'll be in a better mood." He scooped a giggling Aira off Kas's back, instructed a steward to bring us to guest rooms for the night, then took his leave of us.

After bringing us down a wide stone hallway, the steward pushed open a set of elaborately carved wooden doors that gently curved into a pointed arch. "This suite is for you, Princess Nesrin."

Elaborate tapestries lined the walls of the spacious room depicting historical scenes from Mysterium's history. Granite statues of graceful women dancing posed around the room on plinths, and against one wall sat a massive bed, beautifully draped in colorful falls of pinks and golds.

A young woman walked into the room and bowed to us. "The Amanhara wishes to know if you'll need a gown for the evening's festival, and a suit for the Prince?" She turned to include me but focused all her smile and attention on Kas.

The Festival of the Setting Sun was the holiest of days for most gulf nations. It was customary for women to dress in beautiful gowns in the colors of the sun, and for men to dress in fine suits in colors of the moon and night sky. Certainly nothing I had in my travel bags was going to cut it.

I exchanged glances with Kas. "That's very kind of her, but we don't want to put your household to any trouble on our account, especially on such short notice."

Kas smiled at me and at the woman, as though he approved of my response on his behalf.

"No trouble at all. The Amanhara insists. We'll return with selections for you both." She bowed, smiled extra at Kas, and left the room.

I rolled my eyes. I truly couldn't bring him anywhere.

The steward turned to Kas. "Come with me, Your Highness. Your room is directly across the hall."

Kas nodded to the man and gave me a winning smile before following him back out into the hallway, the heavy wooden doors swinging closed behind them.

I'd barely had time to bathe when I answered a knock at the door to find three women with their arms full of colorful gowns. As they entered, I saw a small troupe of men entering Kas's room with armfuls of clothing too.

The ladies, all of whom were already dressed in a range of sunny hues, seemed excited about getting to dress one last guest. They laughed and chatted with me and each other, offering me one beautiful, embroidered gown after another to try on. But although the colors looked stunning on them, everything clashed with my fair skin and orange hair. Worried I would offend them when I rejected the fourth gown, I explained my worries, and they pulled me away from the mirror, insisting that I trust them to make me gorgeous. I laughed and good-naturedly dared them to try.

Several changes later, they seemed pleased with their decisions. While one altered my gown, the others sat me in a robe to comb and style my hair, paint my face, and dab me with jasmine perfume. Finally dressed, I was proclaimed a vision.

I let them lead me back to the mirror. Framed in the thick, golden frame as if I were a painting, I was surprisingly pleased by what I saw. I was a stranger, almost beautiful. I smiled at the unfamiliar sight of kohl rimming my eyes, and ochre lip paint reddening my lips. They'd styled my thick hair with a crown of braids and left the rest of it down to flow freely in long waves. My strapless coral and gold bustier, laced up with patterned ribbons, exposed my stomach and the tops of my breasts, and an exquisite matching silk skirt sat low on my hips with high slits on the front of either thigh, embroidered all over with golden designs of the sun. A gauzy turquoise wrap with embroidered suns completed the look. I'd never been dressed in anything so beautiful since I'd grown to adulthood.

I wiped away a tear.

"You don't like it?" One of them asked.

"No, it's lovely. Thank you. I just wish my mother could see me."

The ladies patted my arm sympathetically and wished me a happy evening before they left.

I stood before the mirror, imagining myself back home, healthy, happy, content, maybe on my way to a party my parents were throwing to celebrate my engagement to some amazing man. Kas's smile popped into my head. A whole future that could never be mine *or* his spun out in my mind, and I had to turn away from the mirror and think of something else before I ruined the cosmetics the ladies so carefully applied.

Although I'd agreed to go, I would rather have danced alone in my room in this beautiful dress than suffer through a social event. But I promised Kas and the Amanha that I'd be there, and the Amanhara had been so kind in letting me dress in this stunning Mysterium gown. And, if I was honest with myself, I was excited for Kas to see me like this.

By the time someone came through the halls ringing a bell, I could hear the revelry beginning in the ballroom. I hurried into the hallway to find Kas leaning on the wall beside his door, transformed into a virtual stranger.

Gone were his daily beige-and-brown loose robes and pants, and in its place was a black velvet suit generously embroidered with silver designs reminiscent of the moon and stars. My gaze roved down and back up his body. Shockingly well-tailored, considering our late arrival. A midnight blue scarf was casually draped in a loose curve around his neck and over his shoulder, the end of it falling down his chest to his waist with silver beading and tassels decorating the border. His curls were loose, and his blue eyes rimmed with black kohl turned to me. He pushed off from the wall smiling, his habitual hunch nowhere in sight.

My heart hammered as I approached him. "You prince up impressively."

"So do you," he said, a catch in his throat. "I mean...you look very beautiful."

"Thank you." I felt my face flush as I looped my arm through his, and we walked down the hallway. "So here are the rules. You're not allowed to leave me alone at any time, or for any reason," I murmured as we passed a group of women craning to look at Kas.

"Understood," he smiled, only at me.

"No matter how many of these beautiful women ask you to dance, you're stuck with me, okay?"

"As I should be."

The grand ballroom was packed and enlivened with the electricity of a special holiday. After a solemn ceremony honoring Hivathe and Onsorbal, servers wove through the ballroom with trays nearly overflowing with delicious foods and drinks. As the night wore on and the little ones were put to bed, the sacred dancing began.

The festivalgoers broke up into couples all over the dance floor, the colors of blue, black, and silver, and red, orange, and yellow, swirling together as autumn swung toward winter.

A beautiful woman about our age with black hair and clear, brown skin barreled over to Kas. "Will you dance with me, stranger?"

He barely glanced at her as he took and held my hand. "I'm sorry, but I'm spoken for."

I turned my head to him so fast that I didn't even see the woman walk away. His head was down as he studied my hand in his. He looked so sorrowful.

"We can leave, if you're uncomfortable with the dancing," I murmured.

Kas's face was pained. "Nesrin, I wish…"

"Good evening," the Amanha said, suddenly appearing beside us. "May I introduce you to my wife, the Amanhara?"

"Thank you for the warm welcome," I said.

"I'm so pleased you could join us tonight," she said. "Princess Nesrin, you are stunning in that gown." The music began, and couples around us began to sway. The Amanhara looked all around. "Oh! The dancing is starting."

"Excuse us," the Amanha said. "We're expected at the front of the ballroom." The two of them hurried away toward the dais. Couples pressed all around us in the sensual, intimate dance that was intended to be with a romantic partner of their choosing.

Kas watched them go and looked around, frowning. "I think it would be rude to go now, and we need his help tomorrow. Do you…know the dance?"

My insides lit up when his bright eyes met mine. Kas wanted to dance *this* dance with me?

I nodded. "Mostly, I think."

He nodded as Mysterium's celebrants swayed in their established pairs, consecrating the movement of Hivathe's fertile autumn toward the dark, moody winter in a slow, sensual dance. Considered the most romantic night of the year, little ones all over the gulf nations dreamt about attending when they were grown to fall in love. Most people learned the dance as teenagers, but I had lost those years. Kas had, too.

I glanced at the other couples and copied them, taking Kas's hands in mine and placing them on my hips. He swallowed hard as if nervous, but I smiled at him, and he rewarded me with a small smile back. At first Kas seemed to be looking at a point just past my right ear as he mechanically performed the steps, but then he looked into my eyes. Although our bodies weren't pressed close, his face was closer to mine than usual because of the heeled slippers the ladies had given me. His bright blue eyes were soft, pupils wide. I'd never noticed how much green was in his eyes, actually a pale green directly around the pupil, fading out to blue.

All around us, couples completed the first circuit of the dance, and I rushed to study and translate what they were doing. I'd forgotten this part, having only ever practiced a made-up, not-at-all-sensuous version of this dance with girls my own age as a child. I twirled myself under Kas's arm, then we spun slowly in a circle back to back. The other couples spun around into each other's arms and shared a kiss...oh no.

Each circuit of the dance ended in a kiss.

Kas had apparently been in society enough to know the dance. He hadn't missed a step, and when I whirled around to face him, he was flushed, his bright eyes watching me, his eyebrows crinkled in a quick moment of apparent pain.

He definitely knew about the kiss. His competing desires showed so clearly on his face that I was overcome for him.

I placed my hand on his cheek and brushed my thumb across his lips to stand for the kiss, and he leaned his face slightly into it for a moment before breaking away from me.

"I'm sorry," he murmured, his hands leaving my body. "I can't." His face closed over like a mask, and he turned and fled the ballroom.

And left me alone in the middle of hundreds of couples starting another circuit of the dance, including the Amanha and Amanhara, who only had eyes for each other. I caught sight of Kas's back just before he turned off into the hallway that led to our rooms. I was the only unmoored sailboat on the sea, the only unlit candle. All around me couples moved together, immersed in each other, some slipping out of the ballroom at various points around, presumably for secret and not-so secret trysts. I bolted like a scared rabbit.

I walked the mostly-vacant hallways toward my room, mad at Kas, mad at myself. I should've stayed in my room. What was wrong with him? It was only a dance. I never asked him to kiss me. I knew he was a vestal monk. Everyone knew he was a vestal monk. No one expected anything else from him, especially not me. He could've just kissed my hand, or my cheek.

Unless...did he only object to kissing *me*?

I paused with my hand on the elaborate bronze handle to my room and looked at Kas's closed door. He was probably on his knees in there now, enumerating his many sins and begging forgiveness.

I pushed into my room and forcefully locked myself in. He did the one thing I asked him not to do. I pulled off the gauzy wrap in a snit and tossed it on the bed, reached to unbraid my hair.

But I caught myself in the mirror. For a moment I forgot how Galter had jeered at my too-big eyes in my too-long face. The young woman before me was beautiful. All grown. Her hair cascaded in bright, sunny waves all around her shoulders and down her back. The corset top accentuated her womanly body, displaying the tender freckles on her pale breasts that were always hidden under more modest clothes.

She was me. And I looked healthy, proud, and strong. I sat my hands on my own warm hips and felt how lovely they were, how deserving of being held and loved. I was formidable on my own, and I didn't need anyone's judgment or adoration to make me feel whole. My eyes filled with tears. I hadn't known I needed this moment.

Someone knocked at my door. I hurriedly wiped my face and opened it a crack. Kas leaned against the doorway, his scarf removed but still in his fine black suit, a button open at his neck. His smile was sheepish.

"What do you want?" I asked ungraciously.

"May I come in?"

I took and released a deep breath, trying to let go of my frustration toward him and myself. I stood back and held the door wide open.

"I'm sorry I left you in the ballroom," he said as soon as I'd closed the door. "You asked me not to leave you, and it's the first thing I did. I'm very sorry, Nesrin."

I loved the way he said my name. My irritation melted. I couldn't begin to imagine how he felt watching all the couples around him, knowing he could never have what they have. And surely he couldn't understand how overwhelming a dance floor would be to me, or how emotional being dressed this way made me feel.

"You left me, in the middle of *all* those people," I said over-dramatically with a small smile, trying to hold the momentum of being irritated at him and him being repentant.

"I'm *really* sorry," he said, matching my silly tone. He studied me a moment more, then took a step forward. "How can I make it up to you?"

I narrowed my eyes at him a moment, the faint sultry music drifting into my room. "Why don't you fly me to the moon," I laughed, spinning around, "or tell me the secrets of the stars?"

He sighed and cocked his head at me, eyes narrowed but with a smile about his lips. "I don't have any wings, so..." He hesitated, stepping forward. "Maybe I can offer you a dance instead?"

I laughed. "You don't have to if you don't want to, Kas. In this dress I'd be happy to dance with myself all night." I turned toward the mirror, swaying slightly, admiring the way the dress moved and sparkled in the oil lanterns hanging from the ceiling.

"But it's your first Festival of the Sinking Sun, and we got all dressed up." He appeared behind me in the mirror, one corner of his mouth turned up. He took my hand in his, but his other hand hesitated. I could see its reflection hovering beside my bare hip that'd been covered in the ballroom by the wrap I'd since taken off.

The night had cast a spell on me. I laid his hand on my hip, a perfect fit. He gently spun me around, and his hands reversed their placement. He smiled down at me as I placed my hands on his shoulders, and we began the dance to the distant strains of violins, picking up from the beginning, both of us barefoot in the low light of the candles. My loose hair swung around us in long copper waves in a turn, then he took me again in his arms. He placed his hands on my bare waist and lifted me into the air, spinning us around slowly.

His eyes lingered on my breasts as he brought me down, and all the bare surfaces of my skin felt suddenly aglow. His bright eyes seemed to grow darker, more serious. We let the time for the kiss pass us by. He held my hips tightly against his to keep me from falling as I leaned backwards in a deep backbend, then I stood, reaching one hand around his neck and the other at his handsome face, feeling the prickle of his whiskers against my palm. I raised my leg up, breaking through the slit in my skirt, against his side. Without breaking my gaze, he reached down, his hand on my bare thigh, and pulled it up higher, leaning over me, his face close at my breast as I leaned backwards again in the dance. He kept one hand on my back and the other on my leg as he lifted me against his body and spun slowly around, with me pressed against him. His desire for me danced in the light caresses of his fingers across my skin and hardened in a line against my lower belly.

We skipped the kiss again.

He placed me on the ground again and turned my back to him, pulling me close against his body, splaying his fingers wide but gently across my belly, his other hand raising my arm into the air. Our hips gyrated slowly together as our feet moved, his breath at my ear, his arousal against my bottom. My body flooded with warmth, and I held back a whimper.

I faced him in the final part of the dance. He brought my arms up over my head, not breaking our gaze. Desire clutched low in my belly, a sweet ache anticipating the path of his fingers. He traced them softly from the delicate insides of my wrists down the length of my arms, clenching his jaw as he grazed the sides of my breasts and my stomach to place his hands firmly at my hips again, and still we moved together, face to face, chest to chest, stomach to stomach, pelvis to pelvis. The music played on to a dizzying height, the drums beat louder. He glanced down at my lips, pulling me closer until our lips were a finger's breadth apart, and his sweet breath fanned my face. I parted my lips, completely lost in the sea of his eyes.

For a moment, I thought he was going to kiss me.

For a moment, I knew I would let him.

But his hands left my skin abruptly, leaving behind a chill as he backed away.

"Goodnight, Nesrin." He hurried past me and out my door.

I spun around to watch him leave, wrapping my hands around my arms and rubbing them, feeling lightheaded. Wanting more. *So much more.* Everything. Butterflies swarmed in my stomach, and my whole body tingled with desire for him.

What was *this* madness?

Part of Kas's initial appeal was his unavailability. The one man who didn't want anything from me, who would help me on this quest then bring me back home to the trove.

But he *did* want something from me. I sat heavily down on the bed. I wanted it too. So badly and so impossibly. I wanted to know how his skin tasted, and as electrifying as his touch had been on my bare hips, I wanted his hands exploring my nakedness. I wanted him in my bed tonight, moving inside me and forsaking all his vows. His gentle, deep voice rasping my name against my ear.

I laid back on my bed, but it was a long time before I could sleep.

CHAPTER EIGHTEEN

THE LOST CITY

I finally slept deeply near morning and was late to get out of bed and ready. I hugged last night's gown for a moment before dressing in my boring, regular clothes. The Amanha had sent word that he'd already met with Kas this morning, and he was bringing us to the famed Pyramids of Mysterium to help on our errand.

When I reached the hall to meet them, the Amanha and Kas were waiting for me. Kas was back in his familiar robes, the hunch returned to his shoulders and his hair pulled back as he often did as we traveled. Something huge between us had shifted last night, or it'd been shifting all along and had finally slipped into place. I'd never be able to see him as only a monk again, or only as my friend. And I'd never stop wanting more.

Even just approaching him this morning kicked off that flight of butterflies in my stomach. But when I smiled at him, he averted his gaze and inclined his head, returning a shallow echo of my expression. His eyes were completely closed off, a little of Kas lost to me. My heart sank, and all the butterflies alighted in my insides. Mourning, but poised to fly again at the slightest provocation.

Seemingly unaware of our drama, the Amanha took us on camels across the rocky, sandy land west of the mansion. Soon the four pyramidic temples came into view. I'd seen them before in drawings, but in person they took my breath away. Each pentagonal pyramid had a massive limestone statue of one of the Five

Prime Gods carved into one of their five sides: Hivathe; Onsorbal; Vayeri; Arra, goddess of nature; and Etyx, god of the peaceful haven of death. They were exquisite, and although each pyramid had all five gods depicted, as we wove through them toward the smallest structure, I noticed that the entrance of each was on the side of a different god. Hivathe's statue faced the sunrise, the other three statues faced the other cardinal directions, and Onsorbal faced his love.

This temple was our destination. After dismounting, we climbed the wide, front steps and walked between Onsorbal's feet into an inner hallway lined with engraved copper. Sunlight and strategically-placed torches bounced off the walls, lighting the whole passage. When we reached the heart of the structure, we ascended a tight, triangular staircase that spiraled up around a central pillar, leading to a hallway that ended in a few wide steps into a sunken room with a balcony. Outside its windows sat a small city of army tents along the river.

"Are those soldiers..." I didn't know how to phrase my question, being a princess of the nation they were going to war against.

The Amanha joined me by the balcony. "Yes. We're preparing to march on Velius." He patted my shoulder and turned back into the room. "We couldn't find much on your archeologist, but this library details the contents of every tomb and treasure house in Mysterium." The Amanha accepted a reedpaper scroll from a man and unrolled it onto the table. "I had my archivists pull this for you. It's the only reference we know of to the caskets, and my intuition tells me it may be the one you seek. It says..." His voice trailed off as he searched through the scroll. "Here. The halcyon casket was in Mysterium eight hundred years ago, and then it...well, camel dung."

Kas pulled his book out eagerly. "What's wrong?"

"It was sold in the estate of Yarlad the Bold to a private collection in Andumar."

"Andumar, as in the *Lost City* of Andumar?" I asked.

"Yes," Kas sighed, rubbing his beard.

Looking at him in the daylight, he seemed not to have slept well either. Did he have butterflies distracting him this morning? Were they better behaved than mine? Because him calling my attention to his face only reminded me of the near-kiss, and all mine fluttered their wings in warning.

"Andumar was lost beneath the earth not long after this sale." The Amanha frowned at the reedpaper.

Kas already had his charcoal out and poised to write. "That's around the time Mount Beyazut erupted, isn't it?"

"Yes, that's right," the archivist beside the Amanha said. "After a series of violent earthquakes. It swallowed the city and completely transformed the land. The area's still plagued by tremors. No one lives there, and nobody sane will go there."

Kas's eyes slid to me, and all my butterflies took flight. "I know of an archaeologist who probably traveled there."

I nodded. I also knew one knight of the trove and one monk who'd be traveling there in the near future.

Kas had been abnormally quiet and dismal as we'd said our good-byes to the Amanha, the Amanhara, and Aira. We barely spoke the whole morning as we traveled away, not about our quest, and especially not about what happened between us last night. Just after we forded a shallow river, Kas finally spoke.

"I want to keep searching, but I have strict orders to return home to report out in a few days. I guess we should take heart that if we couldn't find it, neither could Galter. As soon as I get home, I'll let my father know where to send his people."

I took a breath to scold him, but no words came out. He would really give up when we were so close? I twisted Pistachio's reins in my hands. "Certainly," I said tightly. At least his not wanting to find Andumar was a reasonable thing for me to be irritated with him about. Unlike my unreasonable hurt over last night.

Up ahead, a barren fork in the road indicated where we needed to turn right to go southwest through Opintol and back the way we'd come. Left led toward the mountains where the Lost City of Andumar was rumored to be. My heart pounded. Would I really dare to go alone? Would I really part with Kas if he wouldn't come with me?

I didn't have a choice. I had to find the casket as soon as possible. So, when we reached the fork, I went left without a word.

It took Kas a few feet to notice I wasn't beside him. "Not that way." He pointed down the right fork. "We have to go back home."

I stopped Pistachio and called to him across the sand and rocks. "You can go home if you want, but the Lost City of Andumar is this way." I pointed to where the left road turned sharply northeast with mountains looming in the distance. "And that's where I'm going."

He shook his head but turned Balembar around on the road. "I'm not authorized to go there. And we only have enough supplies to make it back home."

We? A corner of my mouth tugged up. He was coming with me, wasn't he?

"All right." I clicked at Pistachio and gave Kas my cheekiest smile. "I guess I'll see you when I see you. Be safe on your way home."

"But..."

"Bye, Kas," I sang back to him over my shoulder, smiling. I'd bet Ady's whole trove that he would follow.

In less than a minute, Balembar's soft hoofbeats sounded behind me, and then Kas was beside me. "You're going to get me in so much trouble with my order."

"Oh no! What will they do to you?" I said in mock horror, my hand pressed to my cheek. "Will they say you can't sleep with women?"

He glared at me, and my heart kicked against my ribs. I'd gone too far, especially after last night. But a small smile grew on his face as he looked off to the horizon. "You have a fair point. The order doesn't punish us."

A cutting retort was on the tip of my tongue, but I let it die. Because now thinking of Kas being intimate with some beautiful woman made all the butterflies in my stomach throw up.

We rode on toward the mountains, spending the whole day in a pine forest infested with scorpions, and one short, sleepless night fraught with worlds of tension—and so many scorpions—in the ten feet between our bedrolls.

The next day, the land grew rockier, sparser, and sandier as we traveled deeper into the old Ghentere Empire. When the sun dipped below the horizon and the temperature dropped, we sought shelter in a shallow cave against a mountain, and settled the horses outside with blankets.

The campfire cast grotesque shadows on the rough stone walls as Kas put together something for us to eat. I busied myself with my bedroll, wracking my brain for something safe to say to him. Because every time I opened my mouth to speak, what wanted to barrel out was *I'm sorry for dancing so intimately with you*, or *I'm sorry for almost kissing you.*

But the truth was, I wasn't sorry for either of those things. Not at all.

I was sorry he was trapped in an unhappy life. I was sorry I was making his vows more difficult for him. I was sorry we hadn't met in a totally different life, as potential suitors in some extravagant Veytian ballroom where we could've fallen in love without guilt.

My heart thudded. In love? Was I in love with Kas?

He stepped closer and handed me a plate of meats and cheeses, and I looked up into his small smile. A rush of joy, comfort, and affection surged through my whole body and erupted in a full smile on my face. His smile grew too, but he ducked his head and went back to sit on a rock across the fire.

"Do you think..." he started, taking a bite.

I hung on his pause, wanting the words that followed to be about us.

"Now that we've gone this far east, do you think it'd be better to cross into Oprolodas on our way home?"

My heart sank, and I picked at my food. "Probably. And if we don't find Andumar, maybe they'll know something in Oprolodas. Hopefully Prince Forth isn't too pissed off at me still."

His pained gaze met mine briefly across the fire. "Prince Forth. I hear he's...handsome. Is he the other...um. Like Javid?"

I laughed, and he looked up, startled. "No. He arrived a few hours before you. I kicked his ass, stole his horse," I tossed my head toward the cave entrance, toward Balembar, "and sent him on his way."

Relief softened Kas's features.

"I felt a little bad about it afterwards, especially taking Storm-breaker, em, Balembar. I don't think Forth's a bad guy. He just...doesn't suit me."

He nodded, not meeting my eyes. "What kind of man suits you, then?" he asked quietly.

I finished off my meal and dusted my hands of crumbs. "Kind...intelligent. Tall, dark-haired, and exceedingly handsome."

He nodded as if he understood, and it was better that way. "Like Javid."

"No. Not like Javid."

His blue eyes popped up and caught on mine.

I held his gaze. "Not like Javid at all."

His eyebrows lowered, and his expression of pain cut deeply into my heart. He looked away but said nothing, rolling out his bedroll as far from mine as the smallness of the cave allowed. I curled up under my blankets, Kas-bereft in the dark. I missed his nearness, our easy companionship. Gods, I missed his laugh.

The earth shivered beneath me, and eerie sounds emanated from the darkness. I sat up instantly.

Kas sat too, his eyes wide in the firelight. "An earthquake?"

Denial seemed like a good idea. "Nope. I don't think so." We sat quietly, waiting for something else to happen. The world stayed still for long minutes, then he laid back down.

I couldn't sleep, but it didn't take long for Kas to go out. He turned toward me, sleeping peacefully. And looking unfairly handsome while he did it. Long lashes fluttering with dreams, curls across his forehead. His full lips I nearly kissed. I huffed and burrowed in my blankets with my back to him. The last thing I needed was to moon over a prince of Veytia, a *vestal* monk no less, in the firelight.

It took a while to get comfortable. As I drifted off, I dreamed that the earth trembled beneath me, unearthly sounds echoing around me. Fear stalked me in my semi-sleep.

Focus, my brain fussed. *Sleep.*

The sewers. Howling wolves snap at my heels as I run. Mother screams my name. The word reverberates through me, and I lose my balance and fall, my hands scrabbling over pebbles. Into the abyss, I fall and fall, rocks pelting me from all sides. A man screams my name.

I woke abruptly to chaos. The ground rolled like sea waves. Kas crouched over me yelling my name, rocks and pebbles and dust raining onto his back as he protected me. A great, thunderous cracking slammed again, and again.

I clung to him in terror, ducking under him with my arm over my head. I didn't know which way was up, much less out. Kas pulled me to my feet, but the rolling earth threw us down again. Then everything stopped, and my stomach roiled. We clung together, hiding our faces from the showering of dust that filled the air.

When it was nearly clear, I looked toward the cave entrance. Rays of sunlight broke into the darkness through a wall of fallen rocks. The earthquake had almost completely sealed us in.

One breath free of my sleeve, and I immediately started coughing. Kas took my hand, both of us trembling. Covered in dust and bruises, we stumbled toward the entrance.

"How is it morning already?"

He put his eye to one of the holes of daylight between two boulders. "I don't see Pistachio and Balembar. I hope they only ran away." He released my hand and pulled experimentally at a few small rocks, which crumbled off the cave-in and tumbled across the ground.

He pushed one large boulder out, and daylight spilled into the cave, and with it, blessedly dust-free fresh air. I pulled another rock down and stood aside, watching it roll past me to the back of the cave.

Where there was a gap that hadn't been there before.

"Kas, look!" I whispered, grabbing his arm. "The earthquake opened the back of the cave."

He turned and surveyed the gap I pointed to. It was definitely large enough for us to slip through. I took three steps toward it when an aftershock tremored through the earth.

"Don't!" he whispered fiercely.

I stood still until the earth did too. "But there's a draft coming from the gap." I put my hands on either side of the crevice and peered in. It went deeper than I'd originally thought. "I think it's a passage. What if it leads to Andumar?"

Either Kas hadn't heard me, or he was pretending not to. He worked quickly, uncovering the entrance like a man possessed. Good. He could do that while I packed us up for our adventure through the gap.

He glanced back at me as I pulled our things up out of the rubble, likely mollified by the erroneous assumption that I was getting us ready to leave. Bedrolls wrapped up, foodstuffs packed away. The cave-in had already put out the fire. I grabbed a torch and my matches from my bag.

"What are you doing?" He turned toward me, wiping his dusty, sweaty face on his robe. Behind him, a hole big enough for us to climb through showed a bright blue sky.

"We have to see what's down there."

He made a frustrated sound at the back of his throat and came closer. "No. You can't go down there."

I ignored him and pulled out a second torch, fastened Baney around my waist.

He grabbed my arm. "It's too dangerous. We shouldn't have come."

I grabbed his arm back and looked him in the eyes. "Kas, Galter wouldn't let something like this stop him from sending people down there to look for the casket. I can't stop now. You don't have to come."

I tried to shake his hand off, but he held me firm. "I'm not ready to die today. Are you?"

"No," I p'shawed. "We'll be fine."

His shoulders drooped. "What about our horses?"

I smirked. He was definitely coming with me. "They'll be fine," I whispered, waving off his concerns and walking toward the back of the cave. "Are you coming or not?"

He looked between me and the mouth of the cave where the sun, now pouring in, was wholly unaffected by the massive earthquake.

He sighed dramatically, probably just to make me certain how he felt about this, and he reached out for the second torch.

I smiled as I struck the match and lit them.

"Nesrin," he said quietly, mirth and fear flickering in his eyes in the torchlight, "you're going to be the death of me, aren't you?"

I smiled into his eyes, thrilled that he was looking at me like he used to. "And you'll love every minute of it," I teased, turning into the crevice and slipping into the dark passageway ahead of him. It started rough and cracked and quickly closed into an even smaller passage that we had to double over to get through. But it never grew impassable. Soon we came to a taller, wider crevice with smooth walls leading steeply down.

Old ropes clung to either side of the rock hall like banisters. The idea of disturbing the deep dark with my voice terrified me. I tugged on Kas's arm and pointed them out to him.

Gripping one of them as I walked, my feet slipped more and more as the sharp slope of the passage increased. The rock floor leveled off for another hundred feet or so before sloping more gently down and widening into a gaping black chasm. No sound met my ears but our spitting torches, Kas's quiet movements behind me, and cold air rushing past me from the darkness below.

The rope's fraying strings stuck to my sweaty palm. Small stones skittered past my feet on the gravelly stone, and I lost my footing. The rope broke away from the wall in my hand, and I slid on my bottom down the slippery rock toward the chasm.

"Nesrin!"

Kas's whispered shout hissed and echoed around me as I scrabbled for a handhold on the stone, cutting my hands on the gravel and pebbles. My torch clattered across the stone and sailed like a comet into the dark abyss, and my feet kicked wildly out into nothingness. I desperately grabbed hold of the raised ledge as rocks skittered past me into the dark.

Kas appeared above me. He laid down his torch and flattened onto his belly, reaching for me.

"I've got you!" he whispered. His warm hands wrapped around my arms, and he pulled me up far enough that I was able to throw my leg over the ledge. I clambered up, shaking and cold, and Kas pulled me fiercely into his arms, repeating "you're all right," over and over.

I wrapped my arms around his back and squeezed him, glad for the warm solidness of him. I'd missed him. "That was terrifying," I whispered.

"I can barely hear you over the sound of my heart in my ears," he murmured.

"Is it just...empty?" I looked off the edge into the dark abyss below.

"I don't know, but look. Stairs going down, cut into the rock."

"Stairs?" I whispered incredulously, turning around to see where he was pointing. A narrow, steep set of stairs was indeed cut into the rock, running perpendicularly down away from our ledge. "I guess we go down?"

Kas looked back up the way we came. "I'm not ready to go back that way. I almost fell trying to get to you." He laughed a little, as if so terrified by the thought he couldn't do anything else.

I grabbed his forearm. "Let's try the stairs."

I stood up slowly on one foot, keeping the bulk of my body close to the ground until I got a handhold on the woven vines against the wall. I pulled experimentally on them and got to my feet, stepping down onto the first step.

"Wait. You hold the torch." He passed it to me and wrapped his arm around my waist from behind. "You're not falling again."

So protected and suddenly overheated by his hand across my belly, I continued carefully down the narrow steps. I paused to lean away from the wall a bit, holding the torch aloft and looking down. The cavern was enormous and deep. Not too far away, water rushed in an underground stream or river. The stairs went down until they disappeared into a silent city.

"Ruins!" I said breathlessly.

We crept to the bottom and touched our feet to the broken, tumbled cobblestone of what had once been a wide street. Sandstone buildings in varying stages of tumbledown decay stretched like rows of broken teeth, punctuated by massive stalagmites. Winding roads and deep ravines snaked through the broken city, skeletal staircases without walls wound up into the air like twisted witches' fingers, and broken statues stood guard at intervals like ghosts. Aside from the water, the cavern was quiet as a tomb.

Our broken street met a wider path lined with mostly-broken statues of griffins. Far up and away in two places on other sides of the cavern, faint daylight glowed. Other entrances?

Once off the staircase, Kas kept his arm around me as we walked cautiously across a mostly flat street. "It looks abandoned," I whispered.

But it was not.

CHAPTER NINETEEN

THE FOUND CITY

Hieeeeeeeeeeeeeeee! Hieeeeeeeeeeeeeeeee!

I stopped in my tracks, dread stealing like ice through my veins. Kas shifted his hand around my waist and pulled me flush against him. That chilling bray could only belong to one kind of creature.

Hieeeeeeeeeeeeeeee! Hieeeeeeeeeeeeeeeee!

With numb, trembling fingers, I grabbed Kas's arm, pulling him toward an alleyway and batting the torch against the rocky ground to put it out. We crouched together in the dark, our eyes adjusting.

Hieeeeeeeeeeeeeeee! Hieeeeeeeeeeeeeeeee!

Kas clutched me tighter. The braying was closer now, and my heart thundered. I peered over a wall at the end of the alley. In the lower city, over a dozen fires flared to life at pinpoints in the broken streets below. The chilling, horrible braying, part brass instrument and part human scream, was joined by dozens of other voices, just as terrifying.

One of the fires near us moved in our direction.

"They'll kill us as soon as they see us," Kas whispered fiercely. "We have to go back!"

I looked back the way we'd come, then down into the city. "We can't leave. What if it's down here?"

"Then we have to hide!" He pulled me backwards behind a low wall.

From that vantage point I peered into the lower city, watched the fires moving, and listened to the braying. They gathered more on the left side, approaching where we'd come down the stairs.

"This way," I whispered. We crept to the edge of the next street. I looked both ways, judged it safe, and ran across to the next narrow alley with Kas on my heels. In this fashion, we crossed deeper and deeper into the city, from safe alley to safe alcove, ever mindful of the fires and braying moving all over the city, no doubt searching for us.

We were nearly halfway down the sweeping slant of the broken city. Rough voices were ahead, and a torch wasn't far behind. Kas pulled me sideways and into a broken townhouse with a skeletal winding staircase. It had once been grand, but now it curved up with broken steps into a wide room whose walls were still partly intact. I scampered across the floor with him behind me, every step a prayer that it would hold our weight, to a wooden door half-hanging on hinges. I pulled it open and pushed Kas inside, closing it behind us.

I'd closed us into a roofless crevice—a closet?—blocked off into a wedge by two stalagmites and only large enough for Kas and me to stand face to face, our bodies crushed together.

The pattering footsteps of creatures with feline pads and claws scampered down the street we'd just been on, and we clung to each other in terror. Our hearts pounded against each other in a jagged, trading rhythm.

More braying, and more swift footsteps down the street below.

I closed my eyes and laid my head against Kas's chest, breathing in his comforting scent and listening to the thumping of his heart. He rested his head on mine, his deep, centering breaths inspiring mine.

Several minutes of silence passed. I lifted my head and looked into his eyes. With the immediate terror past, our intimate embrace came to the forefront of my attention. He watched me steadily back, sharing my breath. The barrier he'd kept himself behind over the past few days was gone, and his heart was in his eyes. Beautiful, soft, vulnerable. I tipped my face fully up to his. Even with the danger lurking somewhere in the darkness, my eyes slipped down to his full lips, and I had the sudden urge to taste them. The bottom one—his lips were slightly parted—I'd take the bottom one in the tenderest kiss. He was watching my mouth, too. Pressed against me, his body was starting to respond to our closeness, and my back arched instinctively.

What in heaven's name was I doing?

I fumbled the door open and rushed out, my face heated through. It was bad enough we both felt this way and him unable to do anything about it. Indulging in what could never be was cruel to us both.

I crept slowly down the stairs with Kas a half-second behind me, my heart hammering. Gods, he had felt so good, and smelled so good. My fingers ached to explore all the surfaces of his skin, my core ached for him to fill me.

Stop it.

I pushed all my feelings down as I crept toward the street outside. *Focus.* We had to find the casket, if it was here, and get out alive. Casket, then out alive.

We slipped like ghosts down the broken streets. *Casket, out alive,* I repeated in my brain. *Casket, out alive. Casket, out—*

Hieeeeeeeeeeeeeeee! Hieeeeeeeeeeeeeeeeeee!

It wasn't close, but all the hair on my body stood on end. We crouched behind a stone wall and peered over it. The fires had retreated to a different area of the sprawling, broken city. My stomach sank. How would we possibly find one small, gold artifact in this labyrinth of stone and ruin, if it was even here? We could split up to cover more ground...no, I actually detested that idea.

"Let's search the city," he whispered to me, "carefully and quietly. Together."

I nodded, surveying the ruins and making a basic plan to systematically move through them. "Row by row," I whispered, gesturing down the street with my head. I checked to be sure the area was clear, then moved across to the next building in the row. Once inside, we split up and moved through its rooms. Furniture and belongings, hundreds of years old, were scattered and broken throughout the house, but there was no sign of a casket.

After checking that building, Kas peered left and right into the street with me behind him, then gestured for me to follow him to the next house. This one had either been cleaned out already, or empty when the city fell. I shrugged and made a face at Kas, and he crept to the doorway. I looked with him, double-checking that we were clear to cross the little courtyard.

Halfway across, three figures bounded from nowhere on their hind legs, blocking our path. I screamed and unsheathed Baney, stepping in front of Kas on instinct.

The manticores brayed at us, their sharp-toothed, too-wide animal maws set in near-human faces devoid of emotion. Bright red manes, long and matted, stuck out from their splotchy, orange-tinged faces in all directions, and fat horns grew from their temples, tapering up and lost in their manes. Haunting yellow, feline eyes reflected in the torchlight one of them held as they called for others and fanned around us.

We turned to go back the way we'd come, but more digitigrade manticores bounded in. Their gruesomely clawed toes were set at the bottom of long feet striated with bones and sinews. Their massive legs were like a lion's, coated in chestnut fur which thickened to almost conceal their privates. Their angular, muscular torsos and breasts were lean and similar to humans, but spotted and thin-furred almost like a leopard's. Long, segmented tails like those of scorpions swept back and over their heads and were loaded with projectile stingers. To kill or to incapacitate? Depended on how angry they were.

Kas grabbed my arm and tried to push me behind him, but I stood firm, nearly frozen in terror. I swung Baney in an arc of protection around us, but all it did was make them back up half a step. Which is all they needed. More room to let their stingers fly.

One manticore stepped forward, surveying us with bravado fueled by absolute control over his captives. He brayed again, displaying three rows of spiked teeth, and the three behind him snapped their tails up at attention, stingers quivering and ready for release.

One fired past my face and embedded in the wall behind us. A warning shot.

"We don't want to fight!" Kas put both hands up in supplication. His face was pale, and he'd angled himself in between me and the manticore who'd shot at me. "We'll put away the sword!"

"The hell we will," I said.

The leader spoke to the manticores at his back, spitting hideous words I couldn't understand. The twisted face of the female who'd shot spread in a parody of a human smile. She bristled her stingers and loosed one toward me.

Kas jumped in front of me and took the stinger full in his chest. He fell to the ground grasping at it, his eyes wide in shock, and didn't move.

I screamed and fell to my knees at his side. Another sharp whistle and a keen razor pain jabbed into my neck. My vision blurred and went black.

My head pounded like Prince Forth had forged his armor on it.

How long had I been out? The left side of my body was afire with pins and needles, and my wrists were tied behind my back. Where the stinger had gone into my neck was sore, hot, and swollen. With what felt like sand in my eyes, I blinked into the darkness lit only by one torch. Something warm laid against my legs. Kas's legs.

"Kas!" I whimpered, nudging him with my knee. He was tied beside me to his own tall, wooden stake driven into the ground. His chest rose and fell in the dim light, and relief shot through my body. We'd gotten so lucky.

I leaned my head back against my stake and took a shuddering breath. We were alone. Around us, over a dozen iron bars had been driven into the ground haphazardly, making a hasty but efficient jail. Beyond that, the tumbledown stone building ended at a thatched roof overhead, just beyond the jagged spikes of the bars.

"Kas!" I whispered, nudging him with my knee. "Please wake up! Please be okay."

He opened his eyes slowly, blinked and took in our surroundings before turning to me with bleary eyes. "Nesrin?"

"Oh, thank Hivathe. Are you alright? We have to get out of here."

He sat up more fully, pulling at his tied hands and looking around the room.

I strained against the ropes. With the full return of feeling to my body, panic rose in my chest. "I can't stand being tied up." The sewers that night. The blood on the ground. My arms were trapped then, just like now. And just like the morning I spent tied to a pole, waiting for a dragon I didn't know would spare me.

"Kas, I can't. I just can't." Dark terror threatened the edges of my eyesight. Pulling against the ropes only made my wrists rawer and my heart beat faster.

"Nesrin," Kas murmured calmly into my ear. "Breathe. Stop fighting. We have to think. Take a deep breath and think."

His breath in my ear caused a visceral response that pivoted my attention quickly. I took a deep breath and tried to think. They'd taken my bandolier, the knife in my boot, Baney, my Pendoran dagger, the one I gave Kas too, I'm sure...but they missed something.

I whispered back. "I have a knife they didn't get."

"Great! Where is it?"

I gave him an "I'm sorry" sort of look and purposefully looked down at my chest.

"In your belt?"

I shook my head, and he leaned his head closer so I could whisper in his ear. "My pendant opens into a knife."

He exhaled and rolled his eyes with practically his whole body. "That doesn't do us any good. You can't possibly get to it."

I wrinkled my nose and pulled my shoulders up under my ears. "But you probably can?"

He shook his head, huffing. "Nesrin, this is no time to flirt with me."

"*Me*?" I whisper-balked, scooching my bottom and legs around to face him as well as I could. "This from Prince"—I lowered my voice in a husky interpretation of his— "'*how can I make it up to you?*'"

"What's that supposed to mean?"

"'Look at me,'" I mocked him in whispers, "'I'm Prince Kasper of Veytia. Men want to be me, and women fawn all over me because of my sexy eyes and overwhelming charisma.' Can you get over yourself for a minute and try to get my knife before one of us dies?"

He glanced down to my chest, his cheeks red. "I can't even...get my hands...there."

"I'm not talking about your hands, you prude. This is life or death. Use your teeth."

"I can't even see it."

"You've spent enough time looking at my chest," I scoffed. "You've never noticed the necklace?" I leaned in toward him. "Just get in there. Open up my tunic, and you'll see it. Kas, please, I don't want to die here."

He took a deep breath and scooted his body around to face me more fully. Bending his knee, he pulled his long leg to one side of me. As he leaned in, I pinched my shoulder blades back, puffing out my chest to give him easier access. He put his face down and came closer.

After a few minutes, I'd barely felt a whisper of the collar of my tunic moving. "Just get in there and get it!" I hissed.

"Fine." His warm breath huffed against my neck, and I felt a tug at my collar. Grumbling, he moved his face further down my chest, just below my collarbone. His mouth pulled my tunic away from my skin, his lips against my chest, and his teeth scraped across my skin. I closed my eyes and pressed my lips together, a shiver skittering through my body. His beard softly scratched my chest above my corset as he pushed back my tunic with his face and tried picking up the chain in his teeth.

After a few failed tries, he sucked softly against the skin over my breastbone, his tongue slipping warm along my skin, the chain tugging against the back of my neck. I held in a whimper as my body flooded with warmth, and I reminded myself that we were in a manticore's den. He pulled harder at the necklace with his teeth, but he accidentally dropped it and had to go in again, sucking harder against the swell of my breast, using his tongue and teeth to get the chain back into his mouth and arousing a stabbing pang of desire through my core.

I opened my mouth and turned my head, inhaling hard. "Godsdamn, Kas, do you kiss your mother with that mouth?"

He yanked the chain hard, and it snapped apart at the back of my neck with a sting.

"Ouch!" I hissed. He pulled away with a very grumpy face, the silver chain hanging out of his mouth, the knife-concealing pendant swinging.

I turned around and he dropped the pendant into my hands.

"Hide it! They're coming!" he whispered.

I balled the necklace tightly in my palm as three manticores strutted into the room. Despite our arguing, Kas and I shrank together. Very little differentiated the creatures from each other except scars and the length and shape of their manes. Probably their faces had differences, but I couldn't look into those feral eyes set into human faces for long enough to be sure.

They looked among each other, chattering in their horrible, screeching, spitting language, like trumpets melting or wolves being tortured.

"Tekacolios, brrakka gundoon," the one on the left said to the one in the middle.

"Nah! Nah, Tekacolios, rekeswa tsromas swhatas!"

"Are you Tekacolios?" Kas politely addressed the one in the middle as if we were at tea.

I looked at him sharply. "You speak Manticorian?"

Tekacolios stepped closer to the cell, baring his teeth. "Gah," it said, stroking its mangy beard.

"Great! You understand me."

"Let us go!" I demanded.

Their shrieking laughter proved Kas right.

"Maybe we can try a little tact," Kas muttered to me. He spoke slowly, enunciating each word. "We are sorry we disturbed your great city. We did not know you were here. If you let us go, we will be peaceful and never return."

"Why come here?" Tekacolios sneered out, his broken, guttural words barely intelligible.

"We wanted to find out what happened to the Lost City of Andumar," Kas said, skirting around the truth.

"Nah!" the left manticore growled at Tekacolios. "No talk!" he grunted, pointing at us. "Lies! Like other one."

Before Tekacolios could answer, the manticore on his other side spoke up, pointing up and down at our bodies. "Feast good, Tekacolios?"

I shrank back. Manticores were well-established man-eaters. Like scorpions, they generally only paralyzed their prey to feast on them later.

"Gah, gah," Tekacolios brayed, holding a clawed hand to his companions. "Skkirroticha hrabadok a dirnyda." He pointed at the door and walked out. The remaining two manticores hissed and grumbled at his retreating back, but they opened the rudimentary cell door and cut the ropes that bound us to the poles, but not the ones that bound our hands. A sinewy paw-like hand grabbed my arm, and I cringed. His sharp claws, longer and more feral than my fingernails, dug into my flesh as they pulled us roughly to our feet and propelled us into the street by our bindings.

We were in the lower part of the city now. Across from our prison, our weapons had been dropped unceremoniously into a large pile of other discarded weapons in an alley at the foot of a broken bell tower. I prayed those belonged to humans who were still alive and well out in the world.

Dozens of manticores of all ages gaped and brayed, shaking their tails at us as our captors pushed us down the street and inside a crumbling temple. Lined with cracked columns on either side of a great hall, the temple's upper story and ceiling were partially caved in. An altar rose at the back flanked with burning torches, and five metal poles like our prison bars were driven into the stone before it. To one was tied a man, his back to us, limp and held up only by his bound hands and feet. They tied Kas and me to two of the others.

"Why are we your prisoners?" I demanded.

Kas spoke quietly, his voice barely audible above the posturing of the manticores who tied us. "I think we're being sacrificed to their god."

"No! No no no no no!" I shouted, pulling against my bonds. "I'm not being sacrificed *again*. Once in a lifetime is enough! Let us go!"

Kas grew still. "Nesrin. Nesrin, stop."

Two manticores approached me with their tails rattling, stingers poised to fly, and I shut up. They growled as they passed us toward the entrance, leaving us in the near-dark under sputtering torches.

"Sir." Kas leaned toward the man tied to the pole beside him. "Are you alright?"

I twisted around. The manticores' retreating backs were near the exit. They'd met up with a third and exited the way we'd come in. I flipped open my knife.

"Are you alive?" Kas was still trying to get a response from the other man.

Concentrating on where the blade was positioned behind my back, how best to turn it and gouge away at my ropes, I stared straight ahead. And my eyes landed on the altar—on a golden casket.

"Kas!" I hissed, sawing frantically at my ropes.

He turned to me. "I don't think this man's alive."

"Don't worry about him." I tossed my head toward the altar. "Look!"

Kas's mouth dropped open, and the stranger tied to the pole took a long, gravelly breath. "You can cut your ropes, but you're not getting out of here with just that little knife."

The timbre of his voice made my stomach roil.

CHAPTER TWENTY

THE ENEMY OF MY ENEMY

Ashur pushed his body up so he was no longer hanging from his wrists. "I've been here a few days, I think."

As if either of us had asked, and as if we hadn't both gasped in outrage at recognizing him.

Covered in dust and grime, he tossed his head toward the altar, his voice raspy. "After I left you on the road, I got intelligence that what the Emperor seeks, is here." His icy eyes met mine. "If you want to get out alive, you'll set me free."

The ropes on my hands snapped. The manticores still weren't watching. I leaned over and began sawing the ropes on my feet. "Why on Hivathe's green earth should I not come straight over and slit your throat?"

"Because I know their weaknesses. I nearly escaped last time, and I know the way out. It's your choice, of course, but they're planning to eat us at their next sacrifice to the casket."

Kas looked at the casket with wide eyes. "They worship it?"

"If you know the way out, why are you still here? How did the great and mighty Ashur get caught?" I cut the last rope on my feet. Still, no one was coming. I bounded over softly to Kas and sawed at the ropes on his hands.

"Testing exit theories, collecting weapons, and gathering materials for firebombs. I'll share them with you if you cut me loose."

"I don't trust you as far as I could drop-kick you," I said, nearly through Kas's hand ropes. "No deal. I hope they find you delicious."

"Nesrin," Kas whispered to me. "If we grab that casket and run, we'll have the whole nest behind us. Yeah, he deserves to be eaten, but we'll make a better deal with him than the manticores."

"Screw that!" I hissed into his ear.

"But think of it, dragon whore," Ashur continued, "our interests align, for now. We all want to escape this infernal mountain, and we all want the casket. If we help each other with the first, we can fight over the second later. Two against dozens? Terrible odds. Three with weapons and firebombs? Now that has potential."

I snapped through Kas's hand ropes and passed the knife to him, walking to Ashur and punching him hard in the gut. He doubled over gasping. "I hope you're alive when they start eating you."

I went back to Kas. "Almost free?" I glanced around him at the entrance, but I didn't see anyone. Their braying wasn't far, though, just outside the structure.

Kas pulled the last of the cut ropes from his feet and passed my knife back into my hand. He pulled me to the side, turning me away from Ashur.

"I don't like it either, but—"

The manticores' twisted laughter floated into the temple, echoing off the stones. Kas ducked and put his hands on my shoulders, looking into my eyes. "You know I'll fight alongside you, but as much as it pains me to agree with him, we need him."

"They're coming," Ashur sang softly to us.

I glared at him as Kas went on.

"We know he can fight."

"Kas," I whispered lower, "he left us for dead. He'll just kill us and take the casket to Galter."

"We won't let him. I promise."

He held my eyes, and I searched them. He was right. I knew he was, but I didn't want him to be. I cursed and crossed the room to Ashur, flipping open my knife and holding it to his throat.

"Do you see that man?" I tossed my head toward Kas. "He's the only reason I'm not slicing your neck open right now. But that doesn't mean I won't do it later." I went around him and started cutting through ropes on his hands.

Kas came close and glared down at him. "If you hurt her..."

"I know, brother, you'll pray for my sorry soul." Ashur smiled indolently as I knelt to cut the ropes off his feet, because no way was I giving him my one knife.

"No." Kas scowled, voice low and threatening. "I'll be the one who cuts your throat." Kas stared him down a second longer with hard eyes, then ran for the altar.

Everything hurt at the thought of Kas killing someone for me. "What's your plan, asshole?" I cut through the last of the ropes on his feet and pocketed my knife.

Ashur rubbed his wrists and tried his weight on either foot. I followed his eyes to where Kas carefully took the golden casket off of the altar, handling it like it might bite him at any moment.

"The second time I tried to escape, I stashed weapons up there"—he pointed to a narrow upper balcony—"where they're too big to go. Did you notice they don't use weapons? They don't have the manual dexterity, and why bother when their stingers are fatal? So the trick is to get them in close quarters. If you can avoid being shot with a stinger or disemboweled with their claws, you can slice off their tails or their heads with a sword."

My shoulders slumped. "So, your plan is to get closer to the deadly manticores?"

He shook his head at me and scowled as he strode to the side wall. On the altar, Kas was knotting his robe into a makeshift satchel. Satisfied that he wasn't in immediate danger, I followed Ashur up the narrow stone stairwell. Dodging missing and broken steps, I reached the upper balcony as Ashur jumped across a missing slab of floor to get to his stash. He tossed a sword, a busted-up shield, and a few daggers to me, one of them a beautiful, twisty one I was definitely keeping. As I finished securing them to my belts the best I could, a commotion on the floor of the temple grabbed my attention.

"Grakbifas irouhg!" A manticore stood by our abandoned poles, calling back toward the entrance, pointing at the altar Kas crouched behind. *Shit.* Kas was a sacrificial lamb alone and unarmed as he tied the makeshift satchel to his body. I raced silently down the steps and hid behind a column as five more creatures entered the temple and fanned out, braying and growling. They advanced toward Kas with their stingers bristling, and one set of animal-like eyes swung up toward Ashur. She called out orders to the others.

They split up, and I took my shot. Running up behind the three heading to the altar, I sank daggers into two of their backs and took off after the one running to Kas. But stingers zinged past my head. I whirled around, barely knocking more deadly missiles aside with my dented shield. Two of Ashur's manticores were after me, now.

Vaguely I was aware that Kas held his own with the one that'd reached the altar, so I ran at the two before me, slashing my sword across the unprotected torso of the manticore on my right and slamming my shield into the hands of the one on the left who grabbed for me. Thank Hivathe the rusty old sword was sharp enough to open his chest and send him to the ground, bleeding out.

As the dying manticore on the ground howled like Ashur being slammed in the crotch with my boot, I ducked behind the shield and ran full out at the other one, rushing past her and hacking off her tail. She screeched in pain and whirled around, grabbing me hard by the shield arm. I swung my sword around and slashed her across the neck, her bright red blood streaming out with a gurgle. She released my arm to bring her hand to her own dying throat.

Up on the altar, Kas stood over the dead body of a manticore, looking more like a warrior than a monk.

That really shouldn't have excited me.

Ashur ran past me. "Exit behind the altar!"

I glanced back. His manticore was dead on the ground, but three more entered at a run from the doors of the temple. I snatched up the daggers from the backs of the dead manticores and ran after him.

Ashur rushed past Kas through a narrow doorway, and Kas waited for me before following us out. We ran through the priestess's antechambers, meeting Ashur at the back wooden door.

"Get ready," he said, his hand on the doorknob.

I sidled past Kas who'd gotten between me and Ashur. "Dagger?" I asked him.

He glanced with disgust at the dagger dripping with manticore blood, and hefted a tall, bronze candlestick from a pile of rubble, nearly as tall as me. "I'm good." He brandished it skillfully like a staff, taking practice hits against the air.

Ashur eyed him. "The holy man contains multitudes." He opened the door, surprising the two manticores who seemed unaware of the battle inside the temple. In just a moment, Ashur and I had them dead on the ground.

Kas and I raced after Ashur through the dark city streets, the smell of smoke thickening the air. Behind us, drums beat in a tense, alarming rhythm, *boom, boom-boom boom*. Ashur cursed at a crossroads, looking around wildly, then ran purposefully to the left.

Several streets later, we dove into an abandoned building after him and followed him up narrow stairs to a room at the end of the hall. He pushed the door open and ran to the far wall, pulling a filthy, moth-eaten blanket off of a pile of items on the floor: old clay pots, tangles of ancient cotton fabric, and a couple of oil lamps nearly full to the brim. And a miniature barrel of magnificent sulfur.

Shouting and braying echoed up from the street outside, and we crouched low, catching our breaths, watching each other with wide eyes as the tromping and braying passed underneath the window of our hiding place.

When the sounds moved farther away, Ashur crouched beside his cache and began fashioning firebombs with his contraband. Kas and I kneeled down to help. We worked quietly with pointing and whispers to get our job done.

My brain skipped ahead. Even if we could find the stairwell we came in through, how would we get *to* it much less *up* it without them picking us off the stone staircase with their stingers? They were definitely shooting to kill, now.

"The stairwell I came in through closed up after the last earthquake," Ashur whispered, his eyes fixed on me. "Which way did you come in?"

"We approached from Mysterium," I answered, thinking about the direction that would be.

"Northwest of here," Kas said. "There's a staircase up the inside of the cavern."

"Good," Ashur whispered. "We'll go back out that way, too. These"—he gestured to the firebombs—"are mostly distractions, but we'll save a couple for throwing at them if we need to."

"It's awfully quiet out there," I whispered, thinking of the stairwell I passed in the house's hall that led up to another level. "I'll try to get to the roof and see where they've all gone."

Ashur simply nodded and continued working.

I started to get up, but sank down beside Kas again, my hand on his arm. "Which way is northwest?" I whispered.

He pulled out a small compass from his robes and let it adjust.

I nodded and crept low to the ground, across the room, and out into the hallway. The stairs that led up looked solid enough. I went up slowly, avoiding cracked steps that might give out under my weight. On the third floor of the structure, I spotted a ladder leading to a hatch in the roof. *Perfect.*

I laid flat on my belly on the broken tiles to survey the cavern. Smoke from a large fire billowed from the west, and over a dozen torches moved rapidly through the city. Most of the search parties had progressed to the other side of the vast cavern, but a small scraping noise from the ground below made me pause. I crept to the edge and looked down. One manticore without a torch walked slowly through the ruins.

My heart pounding, I pressed myself to the tiles. After a few minutes, the creature continued down the street to another area. I spotted the bell tower where our weapons were. The ancient weapons were greatly inferior to what I came in with. And besides the hordes of manticores, Ashur would be another fight once we got out of here. I needed Baney. I plotted a route across the rooftops that I hoped would get us to the belltower safely, then I tracked the path across the cavern to where dim daylight barely leaked into the darkness. That was our exit.

Back inside the house, the men packed the bombs in old satchels, and I told them my plan.

"My sword was my grandfather's," Ashur rasped. "I'm not leaving it with this nest of monsters."

"Good," I whispered. "We're agreed. First to the bell tower, then to the exit. They're lurking the streets with and without torches, so they won't be easy to spot."

Ashur and I each took a satchel of bombs, and we all climbed to the rooftop. For the next several minutes, we crept from broken rooftop to broken rooftop, ducking down flat against the walls and shattered chimneys to hide from manticores passing in the streets below. We stopped on a rooftop across the street from the bell tower.

I sat my satchel onto the roof beside Kas. "Come on, Ashur. Let's go get our things."

He nodded and dropped his satchel too as Kas gripped my arm. "Let me come. I can fight."

I gripped him back. "I know you can, but you have to guard the casket. I'll be back. I promise." My gaze hung on his for a moment, then Ashur and I left him grumbling on the rooftop.

Down on the street below, we went down a block or so and ducked behind a stone wall to peer through its cracks. Between us and our weapons were a dozen creatures milling about in the street. Ashur cursed softly. Probably all he could think to do. He followed as I went to the back of the house we were beside. In the alley, a decrepit wooden awning barely supported the weight of a pile of broken stones. I got my bearings...it was as far away from Kas as I could wish for.

"We're going to knock that down and run like hell, that way," I whispered, pointing. "Follow my lead."

Ashur nodded. We ran to the awning and braced our legs to hit and run. On my count of three, we kicked the wooden supports and tore off the long way to the bell tower as the rubble crashed to the ground.

Howls and braying arose, and clawed footsteps pounded toward the noise. We hit the street before the belltower with shields and ancient weapons out, such as they were. Only five manticores remained in the street.

Ashur and I each took one down with flying daggers to the throat and chest, and as he ran toward the other three, I detoured to grab Baney, shining and dear near the top of the pile. I snatched her up just as one of the creatures dashed toward me. His stingers pinged off my shield and the bell tower behind me, until I decapitated him in one stroke.

Ashur fought another, leaving the last for me, which succumbed to Baney across his gut. After loading up all my weapons in a rush, I pulled a lit torch from its sconce and tore off around a corner and down another street with Ashur at my heels. I had to lead the creatures away from Kas.

I tossed my torch into a precarious pile of stone and desiccated rubble after we passed it. It crashed into flames and blocked the paths of the manticores chasing us. We dashed down the street and straight into two more creatures, but we took off their heads before they could sound an alarm. With no more in sight, I led Ashur in a circle back to the building Kas waited on top of.

We ran up the stairs and to the roof. Kas was crouched where we'd left him, face pale, candlestick poised to strike. He looked up at our soft noises with wide eyes then visibly relaxed. Ashur and I sank down beside him, panting. Kas gave me a small, brief smile of relief and wrapped his arm around my waist, squeezing. I entangled my fingers in his and laid my head against his shoulder. Ashur watched our affection, but he only sneered and kept quiet.

We waited in the dark. Chilling braying and shouting echoed through the city while the pounding of clawed feet chased our ghosts. I discarded all of the weapons I took from the temple except the shield and that fantastic twisty dagger and rearmed myself properly. Kas took my Pendoran dagger back in a sheath at his waist, but he kept his candlestick.

We three exchanged glances, nodding. It was time to leave.

Ashur set two firebombs aside and looped the bag around his shoulder. "Get ready. When I throw these, we'll run for the exit."

Kas and I got to our feet, crouching. Ashur lit the old fabric fuses and tossed both firebombs as far as he could in the opposite direction from our planned path. Explosions rocked buildings on the next street over as we tore across rooftops.

Braying screeched and echoed as their scraping footsteps ran toward the conflagration. We ran on unimpeded, but a few houses down, the rooftops and our luck ran out: a barrier of stalagmites halted our progress. The nearest way through was down the street.

Drums pounded again as we ran down an outside staircase and into the street below, directly into a group of manticores running toward our diversion. They skidded in the streets and shot stings at us. Kas had gotten in front of me with those long legs. I lunged with my shield to block three stingers that almost hit him square in the chest.

The three of us barreled toward the creatures, hacking at them with weapons, the ringing bronze of Kas's makeshift staff singing as he fought. We ran on, slipping on their blood on the cobblestones. We were so close to our exit, but footsteps and braying were ahead. I pushed Kas up another outside staircase to a rooftop with Ashur close behind. We ran from rooftop to rooftop again, and soon we were across a wide street from the stairway and our freedom.

But it was guarded by a big group of manticores. I counted them in dismay—fifteen.

Ashur pulled out his last firebomb. "Give me your bombs."

I threw off the strap of my satchel and carefully pulled them out. We only had four remaining.

"Two as diversions," he whispered, "and we'll throw the others at any creatures in our way."

Kas and I nodded and crouched to run as Ashur tucked two in his satchel then lit the other two, throwing them in toward the city we'd left behind. They exploded, and only five of the manticores blocking our exit ran toward the commotion.

Nothing for it. We took off down an outside staircase and into the wide street they patrolled. Ashur lit a third bomb and threw it directly at the crowd of them. The resulting explosion lit over half on fire. They fell into hysterics, some running and some dropping to the ground. We ran toward the last creatures blocking the stairs.

Two advanced on me at the same time. One got my shield to its head, and the other got Baney slashed across his tail. Just as I sliced the head off the second one, a manticore lying half-burnt and dying on the ground grabbed my leg, sending me sprawling to the stone. Baney clattered away. I lunged for her, but another braying sounded just behind me and a stinger whizzed past my cheek. Before I could react, a loud, metallic *bong* rang through my bones. Twisty dagger in hand, I whirled around to see Kas holding his metal candlestick over the unconscious body of a manticore.

"Thanks!" I grabbed his hand and pulled him toward the staircase, pushing him up first so I could better protect him with my shield as stings pelted all around us. Ashur followed, manticores on his tail. He lit the last firebomb and threw it into their midst.

With a bang, fire and death exploded through the group, causing enough confusion that the rain of stings ceased long enough for us to get to the wide passage I'd slipped down on the way in.

We ran flat out up the slope, our hands lightly skimming the rope handrail along the wall. The braying grew louder. They weren't far behind. I prayed the staircase and slippery passage would be hard for them to navigate, heavier and taller as they were.

But just before we got into the tighter, twisting passages, stings pattered all around us on the stones, narrowly missing us. Daylight bloomed up ahead, and screeching echoed behind me. I turned to see Ashur slashing and kicking one back into the others that followed him.

Finally we were in the cave where Kas and I had spent the night, Hivathe knew which day before. I silently thanked myself for packing up so well. We grabbed our packs as we ran through the cave and tossed them out before us through the holes in the rubble wall that Kas cleared after the earthquake.

After Ashur dove through, the three of us piled rocks back into the hole. Manticore eyes were suited to the dark, and they wouldn't usually venture out during the day. But we'd stolen their god from them, and only Hivathe knew whether that was enough to draw them out under the sun.

Horses neighed behind me. Pistachio and Balembar were only about thirty feet out into the woodlands. I grabbed Kas's arm, and we took off running for the horses, leaving Ashur behind struggling to fit a heavy boulder into the wall.

His shouting echoed off the side of the mountain while Kas and I jumped a small ravine and splashed through a low stream bed, mounting our horses almost at a run. I couldn't believe our luck, that they were even still here at all, and Ashur was far behind, noisily running after us through the wilderness and shouting obscenities. But the moment I turned Pistachio around to run, Kas shouted. Four men on horses and a riderless horse had us surrounded.

"Holy hell!" I yelled out.

Ashur ran up beside his men, catching his breath and laughing. "Thank you for finding what the Emperor wants and for going to such great personal risk to get it for him."

The men on horses laughed, closing the distance around us. We couldn't fight our way out of this many trained fighters, not after they nearly killed us last time with fewer. Balembar raised and lowered his strong legs, his feathering fluttering, itching to run. One of us might be able to get away, but not both, and the men who'd been outside the mountain wouldn't know which of us had the casket, with all the satchels and bags we had.

I pulled my sword out. "Hold on, Kas," I said quietly. I waited for Balembar to turn and face a wide stretch of land through the wilderness between two hills—excellent places to hide and lose riders—with a path right between two of the smaller men. "Thank you, with all of my heart."

He turned his head to me, confusion and fear on his face.

"Hivathe be with you always." I kicked Balembar hard in the ass and shouted "HEEYA!"

CHAPTER TWENTY-ONE

THE DEATH OF A FRIEND

Balembar whinnied and barreled in between the two men on horseback with Kas yelling "No!" and holding the reins for dear life.

I swung my sword at the closest man and took his arm clean off at the elbow. He screamed, reaching in vain for his arm with his other hand and falling back out of the fray. The two men Kas rode past watched him go, then turned to Ashur for an order.

"Go after him! He has the casket!" Ashur shouted, mounting his own horse.

Balembar easily outstripped the other horses while I drove Pistachio toward Ashur, swinging my sword to buy Kas more time. But Ashur threw himself out of the way, pulling his sword back.

Instead of driving the sword at me, he drove it deep across Pistachio's neck. Pistachio wailed with my screaming and staggered, crumbling to the ground beneath me. I rolled clear of her as she fell, but I scrambled back up to get to her, my heart in my throat. *My Pistachio.*

Ashur circled around for another pass at me, but I couldn't drag myself away from her. Blurred by my swimming tears, her bright red blood pooled on the ground, and her beautiful brown eyes rolled up in her head to look at me as if asking how I could ever let this happen to her. She was dying fast, and the pure and utter rage that now drew me to my feet made me certain that her quick death would be the only mercy this ground would see.

Hate bloomed wild in my chest. I ripped my barbed bolo from Pistachio's saddle and threw it at Ashur, but he expected it this time. He easily blocked it with a shield, and the bolo fell harmlessly to the ground. I threw knife after knife at him, which he easily dodged as he drove his horse directly at me. But I was on foot and harder to catch. And I still had Baney.

Ashur dismounted. "You want a rematch while my friends kill your lover?"

All I saw was red. The red of Pistachio's blood, Kas's bloody face when Ashur beat him on the road to Opintol. The red of my own blood on my fingers after Ashur stabbed me. I yelled a battle cry and went after him.

Every time our swords met, his fractured just a little more. It was a heavier, thicker sword, and it took me several minutes of intense striking to break it in two.

He tossed the pieces away. I drew my sword back to take off his head, but he got low and dove at my middle, knocking me to the ground with him on top of me. Baney flew from my hand across the rocky ground. Ashur's fists rained blow after blow. I blocked and punched and kicked until I threw him off me. I scrambled on my hands and knees toward Baney, but he grabbed my ankle and pulled me backwards. I kicked him in the head over and over, and he let go. I ran for Baney.

My hand closed around Baney's hilt, and a whistling shrieked through the air. A dozen sharp barbs wrapped around my body, knocking me into the ground. The barbs of my own bolo dug into my stomach, my arms, my back, embedding like a circle of thorns. The ones I landed on buried themselves into my back with the impact. The more I pulled to get free, the deeper they dug into my flesh. Blood trickled from my wounds, but I couldn't get Baney up to cut myself free. I couldn't reach a single dagger.

Ashur walked up, panting hard from our fight and laughing at my struggle on the ground. "I can't wait to tell Galter about this. I'll spare him no details of your death."

He thrust his sword toward my chest, but I rolled over, impaling myself on a dozen new barbs as his sword sunk into the ground beside me. I struggled and tried to get to my feet, but a searing agony drove through my thigh, pinning me momentarily to the ground until he pulled his sword out of me.

Seconds passed in shock. I rolled onto my back. He'd stabbed me. The son of a bitch had stabbed my thigh. My blood spurted out onto the dusty ground. Nausea and cold fear roiled through me.

He mounted his horse. "I'm on my way to kill your lover, too. When you meet your goddess, tell her you failed." He spat on me and rode away after Kas.

I had seconds before I bled out. With trembling hands and an eerie calm, I ignored the barbs digging deeper into my flesh at every movement and pulled my belt off, muscle memory from my time in the infirmary taking over. I wrapped it high around my thigh and tightened it, twisting one of my sheathed knives as the windlass of a tourniquet until my wound stopped bleeding. Between death and the excruciating pain of the tourniquet, I calmed my mind and chose the excruciating pain with my whole heart.

Kas needed me.

I delicately disengaged the bolo from my body, and with the last of my strength, I crawled through Pistachio's blood on one knee toward her. Or maybe it was my blood. I couldn't tell anymore.

Gods, the smell...I vomited, and only bile came up. When had I last eaten? My priorities fell into line like the lists I used to make of what to catalog next in the trove. Bag, medicine, move away, eat.

I pulled my saddlebag off of Pistachio and flipped it open, my hands shaking as I reached in and closed my hand around a cold blue glass vial. Ady's last-ditch medicine. I opened it and drank the whole thing down. Bag and medicine, done.

But I couldn't make myself move. I laid on the ground, dazed, my vision getting bright, the sky disappearing into white light.

Kas.

Ashur and his men would kill him and take the casket.

But at this moment, all I could do was pray. *Please, Holy Mother Hivathe, please help me live to help Kas. I can't die. Kas needs me. Please ride with him. Protect him.*

With Hivathe's grace and Ady's medicine coursing through me, I found the strength to loop the satchel around my neck, press my face into Pistachio's forehead, and kiss her goodbye. The smell of her brutal death was sickening me, heart, soul, and body. I dragged myself away.

I woke up what seemed only a few minutes later, farther away from Pistachio than I remembered getting. The pain was agonizing, but my head was clearer and my other limbs felt a little stronger. I might actually live. I opened another glass vial and drank it down. Grabbed a roll from my bag and forced myself to eat every last crumb as I surveyed my surroundings. That branch might work.

I pulled myself to it. After cutting off its side-shoots to fashion a walking staff, I leaned on it, forcing myself to my feet. I struggled in the direction Kas had ridden away, dragging my injured leg because it didn't work anymore, not with the tourniquet still wrapped around my thigh.

Only birdcalls and the wind met my ears as I came upon an ancient, overgrown road. It spun out into the distance with fresh hoofprints, and hopelessness pressed into my heart under the guise of reason. Even with Ady's medicine stitching my veins back together, Kas was too far away, and Hivathe knew in which direction. Had he even taken the road? I twisted my head to get my bearings, but I still wasn't sure which way he'd gone. He'd ridden off on Balembar, and that beautiful stallion was probably in Oprolodas already. What could I possibly do to help him?

No. I wouldn't stop. Those were the hills I pointed Kas between, and this road was the wide path. I kept going, thanking Hivathe for every agonizing step. I pulled my doka beads out of the satchel and threw them around my neck, a prayer for each bead, even though I had no hands free for touching them. Every step was a prayer, a blessing, and a curse.

Please, I begged, *just one more step. Give me one more step back to Kas. Let me get vengeance for Pistachio, for myself.*

Under the gathering clouds, I walked for an unknowable length of time and finally collapsed, pulled myself back up to walk, and collapsed again. My injured leg was numb. Dead weight. I ceased to recognize it as part of my body, and this disowning was the only reason I made any progress. The third time I collapsed I opened up my last bottle of Ady's medicine and poured the precious liquid into my mouth, sucking on the vial to get every drop.

Medicine and magic flowed through my veins, numbing the pain and trying to knit my body back together, but I was damaging myself worse by forcing myself on, especially since I couldn't feel what damage I was causing. But I got back up and kept going.

The trees around me began to move, and not in the natural way of breezes. Walking with my eyes closed didn't help the vertigo, and I began to feel like I was falling asleep on my feet. The bracing numbness that Ady's medicine had gifted me was wearing off, and my strength and tolerance for pain were waning fast.

I tumbled into bushes on the side of the road and pulled my tunic open at the neck to let the cold air hit my hot skin. My hands fumbled for my water skin, and I brought it to my lips with shaking hands to drink the last drops. I dropped my hands and laid back, too weak to move. Clouds shifted across the sinking sun in the too-bright sky, and in my delirium, I saw shafts of golden sunlight streaming through the clouds. It was sacred and glorious, and I knew then that I was dying.

Once, when I was little, I saw a sky like this. Its divine beauty inspired a fit of devotion, and I'd prayed to Hivathe, *please, when I die, let the sky be* just like that *so I'll know you'll come for me and take me home.*

But now that I lay dying in the shafts of heavenly light that I once prayed for, I begged Hivathe to reject that childhood prayer.

Please, I'm not ready to go. Kas needs me.

I prayed and begged and watched the sun through the clouds, the sky golden and blue. Everything was illuminated, bright and holy, my eyes a prism. Its glory was painful, so I closed my eyes and let go.

CHAPTER TWENTY-TWO

AFTER THE LIGHT

The persuasive aroma of freshly baked bread woke me from a dreamless sleep. As awareness came back into my body, so did a dull pain radiating down my leg and at nagging points on my arms and torso. But I was lying somewhere soft, at least, and from nearby came the gentle, percussive noises of spoons and bowls, cups and decanters. I shifted my head, and the comforting smell of lavender soap wafted across me followed by the alluring, mingled scents of frankincense, myrrh, and silva.

As I climbed through layers of sleep, not ready to return to consciousness, a familiar deep voice hummed beside me. Large, smooth hands rubbed warmed oil in circles across my belly and side, and down my thigh where I'd been stabbed.

Mirth bubbled out of my mouth in a soft laugh. Ady's oil smelled like Kas.

I breathed in deeply and turned my head to the other side. "You don't have to do that," I mumbled sleepily. "She's just trying to get you into my bed." My eyes flew open.

Kas broke off his humming and leaned toward me, his dear face radiating joy and confusion. "You're awake! What did you say?"

"Nothing." I cleared my throat. "How long have I been out?"

"Almost a whole day, but you're healing so fast." He poured more oil onto my belly, rubbing it across my skin in soothing, broad strokes.

I closed my eyes and breathed the oil in deeply, relishing the way his fingers made slow, gentle circles beneath my belly button. My toes curled, willing his fingers to go lower.

"Are you hungry?" Kas asked.

Extreme sleepiness warred with my grumbling belly, making that *three* insistent desires to choose from. But one spoke loudest. "Yes, I'm starving."

His warm hands abruptly left my skin, and he pulled my tunic back down over my stomach, rubbing the remainder of the oil into his hands and arms. "I love the smell of that oil. It smells like your lavender soap. Here. Can you sit?"

I smirked. Ady and her magical matchmaking. "I think so."

He helped me sit up, bunching pillows behind my back. The small, wood-paneled room glowed warmly with candles and a fire, but no daylight filtered through the pale green curtains pulled across the window as he leaned over the hearth.

My hair was clean and loose in cascades around me. I pulled my tunic up. Small scars across my belly and arms were nearly healed. I took a deep breath and threw off the covers. I wore a pair of Kas's linen pants with both legs cut short, and a jagged, angry wound slashed across my thigh. But it had healed to the point of not needing a bandage. I sagged with relief and twisted that leg gently from side to side, wiggling my toes. How on Hivathe's green earth had I lived and even kept the leg?

Kas bustled over with a plate piled high with pork, rice, and the most beautiful hunk of steaming bread I've ever seen. "It just got here, so it's still hot. Here." he handed me a cup of water.

My hand shook a little as I took it and drank, cold and delicious.

He held the plate out. "Can you manage it?"

But I could only place my hand against his cheek and look at him. Kas. Alive and here with me, his bright blue eyes looking at me with such caring and concern. I'd never seen anything more beautiful than his face.

"How am I alive?" A tear slipped down my cheek.

"Ady stowed medicine into my bag too." He smiled, laying his hand briefly on mine. "It's healing you, but you have to meet it halfway. Eat." He plucked off a morsel of bread, dipped it into the gravy, and held it to my lips.

I dropped my hand and let him feed me the warm, soft bread, its savory taste making my stomach beg for more.

He watched me, biting his lip as if he wanted to ask me a hundred questions but didn't want to overwhelm me. He let me eat a little more in silence, but when I reached for my water, he clearly couldn't take it anymore.

"Ashur did this to you." Protective male vengeance sparked in his eyes.

I nodded. I wanted to cry, throw my arms around him, and tell him about Pistachio, but I forced the images from my mind. I needed food, or my body would shut down again. I took the plate from him and ate on my own. He sat beside me, attentively holding my cup.

I cleaned my plate and drank the last of my water. "Are you alright?" I asked, handing the cup back to him.

"So much better since you woke up." His eyes were glossy, and his smile was broad.

"What happened after you left?"

He leaned back, placing the plate and glass on the table. "Balembar left Ashur's men in the dust. I went up and around a hill, hoping they'd pass me so I could go right back for you. And that worked for his men, but when I came around the other side and saw Ashur ride past without you…" He scooted his chair closer and took my hand. "I went looking for you. I missed you the first time I passed. And when I got to the cave, all I saw was…"

I nodded, tears welling in my eyes.

He squeezed my hand with both of his. "I said a prayer over her."

"Thank you," I whispered.

"Of course. I came back up the road more slowly and found you in a ditch. I thought you were…" His voice choked, and he wiped tears from his eyes.

"She was gone," I whimpered, my own tears falling. "And I was dying."

His brows furrowed, and he wrapped his arms tightly around me while I sobbed, rubbing my head, then my back. His caring for me was a haven I didn't know I had and didn't know I needed. He'd been saving my life for years before I met him, and I clung to him now, buried my face against his neck. Breathed him in. He was mine. My Kas. And I refused to think about bringing him back to the monastery. I settled into the moment, and after a long time, his breath in my hair and the beating of his heart calmed me, stilled my crying. But with the clearing of my mind came a realization.

We had *it*.

"Where is it?" I whispered.

He glanced over his shoulder toward the makeshift satchel slouched on the floor at the farthest point across the room. "There. I think it helped me evade Ashur's men, but I didn't like carrying it. I don't even like being in the same room with it."

We both looked at the bundled cloth it was concealed in, and I shivered.

"It's the halcyon casket?"

"Yes." He looked quickly to me, and I met his eyes. His beautiful eyes with his whole heart in them.

I put my hands against his cheeks. "Thank you for coming back for me."

"I'll always come back for you." He took my hands in his again and squeezed them. "But you're not allowed to scare me like that ever again."

"Deal," I smiled, looking around the little room. "Where are we?"

"The Strumming Steed Inn in south Oprolodas."

Prince Forth came to mind, and with him thoughts about the armies marching. I sighed, a small groan slipping out.

"What's wrong?" Kas asked quickly.

"I'm so tired." And now that my belly was full, I was getting woozy again.

"Can I get anything for you? More bread?" He released my hands and plumped up my pillows.

I shook my head, grabbing his hand again, making him sit beside me on the bed with his arm around me so I could lean against him.

"Your clothes were soaked with...when I found you. I washed them and everything else in your saddle bags. They'll be dry by the time you feel up to changing into them." He cleared his throat. "I kept you covered while I—"

"I trust you, Kas." I closed my eyes, relaxing against his shoulder.

The soft huff of his chuckle ruffled my hair as he closed me into his arms. "It's getting late, and you need sleep. I'll try to be quiet while I finish cleaning up. Just call out if you need me, even if it's the middle of the night. I'll be right beside you on the floor."

He started to get up, but I grabbed his arm. "Don't start that crap again. You're sleeping with me. We'll have a long day tomorrow traveling back." But that wasn't the reason.

Kas watched me with narrowed eyes. "It's no fair turning your big, brown puppy eyes on me. They're too beautiful and sad to resist."

I kept staring at him, and he set his teeth and cocked his head. "I might jostle you if I sleep in the bed."

"Please lay by me?" As soft as the peaceful light in this little room was, panic still stalked the corners of my heart. "If you're not next to me, I don't know how I'll get through the night."

His face softened. "Okay. I'll be back in a minute."

I relaxed against the comforting sounds of Kas puttering around the room. It wasn't long before I felt his weight slipping beside me on the mattress, taking care not to lay too close to me. I reached out and found his hand, pulling it from where it was curled up beside his face.

"Thank you for saving my life," I said sleepily.

He didn't say anything, just squeezed my hand back. I wrapped both of my hands around his and held it comfortably on my stomach. I was afraid he'd let go, but instead he took me into his arms, our limbs entangling. I clung to him. I'd spent too much of my life without a human who cared for me, and I wouldn't let go of him a minute sooner than I had to.

"Nesrin," Kas called softly, "time to wake up."

My eyes fluttered open. He sat in the chair beside the bed, leaning in and softly patting my arm.

"A big group of travelers is heading to the coast, and I think we'll be safer if we go with them. They're leaving in a few hours. Can you make it? How do you feel?"

I mentally scanned my body. "Like I got stabbed the day before yesterday," I decided. "Is there a wagon I can ride in? I don't think I can manage a horse."

"I'll ask." He stood and set a pair of my pants and a tunic on the chair along with my corset. "There's no bathtub, but I brought you a basin of warm water and soap. Can you get up and dressed on your own? I'm going to get you something to eat."

"Only one way to know." I sat up slowly, threw off the blankets, and carefully swung out my two pale legs, setting my feet on the floor. A huge purple and yellow bruise spread out surrounding the nastier jagged scar on my thigh. But it looked much better today. I held onto Kas's hands and tried to stand, wincing at the pain. It wasn't easy, but it was possible…until the room spun. I sat back down.

"Maybe I should eat first."

"Probably so." He pulled the bedside table closer and moved the basin of water and soap onto it. "Better?"

I nodded. "Thank you."

He smiled and left the room, locking the door behind him.

I was eager to join the land of the living and regain my strength. I pulled my hair back and washed up, giving myself a deeper clean than the one Kas had given me, which hadn't included any of my more sensitive parts. I really liked these short pants, though. I was definitely going to steal this pair and ask the trove's magic to make me more when I got home.

Not long after I was done dressing back in my clothes, including my moleskin pants with the sword hole neatly mended, Kas was back with breakfast and news, both of which I took in greedily.

"I found a family willing to let you ride in their wagon. They wouldn't accept our money, but I thought—not to spend your gold—I thought maybe we could slip them something when we get to the coast."

I nodded and let him go on, my mouth stuffed with bacon and eggs.

"Once the ferry drops us in Veytia. Balembar's sturdy enough for both of us, if you're feeling up to it then." He swallowed, his face betraying nothing of his feelings about going back to the monastery.

"That sounds good," I lied, my gaze soaking up every line of his body as he finished packing us up. The last place I wanted to go was Kas's monastery. Because once I left him there, I would probably never see him again.

CHAPTER TWENTY-THREE

THE MONASTERY

Two days later, we disembarked in Veytia within five miles of the monastery.

Traveling with the others and crossing on the ferry hadn't given Kas and I any time alone to talk. He'd taken charge of the casket, for which I was grateful. I'd looked at it only once before we left the inn in Oprolodas, just to verify with my own eyes that we had the halcyon casket. We did, and like Kas, I didn't like it.

Even now, climbing the massive front steps of the monastery, we exchanged glances with each other and at the satchel containing the nasty thing.

The vast, ancient stone monastery sat at the top of a hill, and I had to lean on Kas to get all the way up the wide, stone steps—nearly a hundred feet—to the main entrance. He'd offered to carry me, but the dozens of monks milling about the terraces were already watching us closely enough. A few approached to clap Kas on the back, but no one spoke to us.

"Vows of silence," Kas explained before I could ask. "I'm supposed to take mine in a few months."

His passive face gave nothing away, but my already-grieving heart squeezed in sorrow, and I hugged his arm closer. I couldn't, didn't want to imagine cheerful, personable Kas isolating himself from others for that long. I hated it, and I hated his parents for making him throw away the life he wanted.

The monastery was much more decorated than I'd expected. Reflecting pools, gardens, and statues of the goddess graced each of the three wide terraces we climbed past, and the back of each terrace was lined with stone columns holding up a roof crowned with terracotta tiles. Finally at the grand entrance on the top terrace, we were greeted by the ostiary who let us in without question.

Inside the wide, stone antechamber, four monks looked up from their conversation and greeted Kas with pats on the back and welcomes home, but even the monks who spoke wouldn't speak to me, though many of them inclined their heads respectfully. I returned the gesture but made a point of speaking to each of them with a "hello" or "how do you do?"

Kas smirked at me and spoke quietly. "It's not personal. They're not allowed to talk to you." He squeezed my arm where he still helped me walk. "If I hadn't gotten special dispensation before I left, I wouldn't have been allowed to talk to you either, much less touch you."

The butterflies in my stomach transformed into angry, swarming bees. When I left him here, I wouldn't even be allowed to hear his voice again? *No*, I decided as we entered a wide chamber in which a large group of monks were practicing doka. I would yell at the head of the order until he gave Kas *permanent* dispensation.

As soon as Kas appeared in the doorway, an older man in white robes that matched his beard jumped up from the ground and approached him. Kas bowed low.

"You're back!" He reached out to shake Kas's hand with both hands, completely ignoring me. "I'm so glad to see you safe and sound, Brother Kas. Were you successful?"

Kas's eyes darted around the room, and he simply nodded.

The priest's face lit up in a smile, until he finally turned his bright green eyes to me. "And who is this?"

"Father Ramdar, this is Princess Nesrin of Araven, Knight of the Dread Dragon Adydorrstea's Trove." Kas's smile at me was fond. "She's the only reason my quest was successful."

"Thank you, Nesrin," Father Ramdar said, inclining his head toward me and ignoring all the honorifics Kas had just given me.

Ass. I supposed if you were "important," you were allowed to talk to women. My returning smile was sour.

"Brother Kas, come with me." As he walked away, Kas raised his eyebrows at me, and we both followed the head priest down a hallway.

At the end of it, Father Ramdar opened a door and held it open for Kas to pass through, but he blocked my way.

"My apologies, but women aren't allowed in this part of the monastery."

"But I wouldn't have found it or even survived if it weren't for Nesrin. She deserves to be here too."

Ramdar's bland smile never left my face. "Rules are rules for a reason, Brother Kas. No offense is meant."

"But—"

"It's fine, Kas." I was probably pushing my luck by being in the monastery at all. "And don't worry at all about me, Ramdar. I'll just hobble back to the terrace."

Kas's sad smile disappeared behind the door, and I walked back into the bigger room, nearly stopping a monk with a touch on his arm before I remembered he'd probably have to spend a year in silence for my transgression. "I need to send a magpie. Can you help me?"

The man nodded and bowed, gesturing at me to follow.

Thankfully, the charm wasn't up any more stairs. I scribbled a quick message to Ady and attached it to the foot of the strongest-looking magpie I saw.

Dearest Lizard Bird. Come get me from the monastery? Love, Your pale, freckled wraith.

Afterwards I sat on the front steps in the shade to wait, plotting ways to break Kas permanently out of this misogynistic prison. What if I talked Ady into terrorizing the monks until they gave Kas up?

No, that wouldn't be right after the kindness his parents showed me all those years ago. But how did they feel about gold? I looked around, noting patches in robes, columns in need of fresh paint. I could buy his freedom with a pile of Ady's treasures. She wouldn't be hard to convince.

I pulled Kas's book from his bag. I could leave a message in it. But what would I say? *I love you Kas, come live with me and be my husband?*

No. I couldn't tell him the truth. Never the truth. He was too honorable and already too conflicted to tempt. I couldn't bear to torture him.

As the evening wore on, and I still didn't see Kas, I started to worry I'd have to knock down some doors for the chance to tell him goodbye. But just then, familiar footsteps came up behind me.

"I was scared you'd left without saying goodbye." Kas sat beside me. "I'm sorry Father Ramdar kept me so long. He wanted to know every detail. Is Ady on her way?"

I returned his sad smile. "Probably by now, if she was home when the magpie came."

He nodded. "I got special permission to give you a tour of the monastery. Maybe we can have one last adventure?" He leaned his shoulder briefly into mine.

"I'd love that." *Anything to spend more time with you.*

So, Kas walked me through the stone corridors of his home. It was lofty and grand, and if I'd never seen Ady's trove, I might've thought it to be beautiful. But for all its architectural beauty, it was cold and gray inside. Few colors, no joy, and little comfort. It was the anti-Kas.

But he seemed excited to share his world with me, even though dread crept through my insides like a kavhavji vine. How could I leave him here?

Eventually we wound around to a music room. I walked past a small organon, dragging my fingers gently across the keys without depressing a single one.

"Do you play?"

"Not anymore." I'd played for my father the day before he died, and never since. I touched a key lightly, and the note rang softly through the room.

"Here." He pulled out the bench, sat, and patted the seat beside him. "Come sit with me."

"You play?" I sat beside him, pleased to be pressed against him again.

"Very poorly," he laughed, "but I think I can play something for you. Sing with me?"

Under Kas's fingers, the small organon's notes rang gently through the room as he launched into a familiar melody, a duet, a song of childhood known across many kingdoms in many tongues. He played the lively intro, then paused.

"Do you know it?"

I nodded, and he repeated the intro while I joined him, tapping out the high part. We sang together.

"The foam on the wave,
And the moon on the sea,
Don't you know my darling,
That's what you are to me?
And if I didn't have you,
My life would be so grim!
I never, ever, ever, would
be happy again!
But when you are with me,
You make my heart smile,

It makes the moments we're apart,
Fully worth the while.
The foam on the wave,
And the moon on the sea,
All the best things in life, my love,
Are what you are to me!"

As the last notes rang out, and we were laughing, a young monk with a very disapproving scowl poked his head into the doorway. "Brother Kas, the Dread Dragon Adydorrstea is here for her knight."

"I guess I have to go now," I said softly.

Kas studied me, his bright eyes thoughtful. Neither of us spoke for a moment. Finally, he picked up my braid, yanked it gently, and tossed it behind my back. "I guess so. Ady's waiting."

We stood slowly. I stopped to push in the bench, and Kas took his time closing the instrument's lid. Near the doorway, his fingers skimmed my hand, but when I reached out to him, I only caught air as he waved to another brother.

From the upper breezeway, I saw Ady sitting grandly beside a reflection pool on the great lawn. Kas gave me a side smile, and my chest tightened.

How could I leave him?

I spoke to Ady, mind to mind. *I missed you. Do me a favor?*

Anything for you, my dear.

I need a minute with Kas. Distract them?

Just before we reached the stairs that led to the lowest terrace, Ady stood on her back legs and flapped her wings. Men shouted and a mighty gust reached us even in the side hall. I spun around and pulled Kas into a dark corner. We stared at each other, my hands on his face and his on my waist.

"I can't leave you," I choked out.

He frowned, his gaze catching on my lips. "You have to."

"Do you *want* me to leave?" I asked softly.

His face crumpled, and he pulled me tightly into his arms. "Of course not," he breathed against my neck.

I squeezed him back as tightly, and he lifted me up, his hand on my thigh as I wrapped my legs around his waist. For a long moment, he held me, our bodies pressed together. He planted a long kiss on my temple, and I gripped him tighter with all my limbs, all my selflessness gone.

I peered into his bright eyes. "Come with me, Kas. Come back with me to the trove."

"To...to visit?"

"No." I pressed my forehead to his. "To stay."

He breathed slowly out, setting me down softly with tears in his eyes. "I want to, with all my heart. But they'll just hunt me down and make me come back. I couldn't bear to part with you a second time." He cupped my face with both hands and smiled softly, even as tears tracked down his face. "Thank you for everything, Nesrin. I'll never forget you, and I'll always care for you."

My heart felt like it was breaking apart inside my chest. I studied him, never wanting to forget a thing. The cool blue green of his eyes fringed with black lashes, the shape of his lips I'd never get to kiss. I cupped my hand on his cheek, and he leaned into it, turning suddenly to kiss the palm of my hand with his eyes closed.

Tears streamed down my cheeks, and I made myself turn away before he opened his eyes. I wiped my face as I walked toward the stairs, and he rushed to help me walk down to where Ady struck fear into the hearts of the brothers gathered in front of the monastery. She stopped and sat primly when she saw me.

"Thank you for retrieving me, Oh Great One," I said to Ady, bowing deeply. My voice trembled with held-back tears.

"It's about time," she replied haughtily. *Do you need more time? I can carry one of them off for a few minutes. It'll cause quite a stir. They won't even remember you're here.*

No. It won't matter.

Kas helped me climb onto her back and asked several times to be sure I was comfortable. He backed away with his hands in his cloak pockets, hood pulled up over his head in the moon and torchlight. Maybe he was trying to hide the tears I saw on his face.

"Thank you, Nesrin, Knight of the Trove." He reached up to me. "May Hivathe keep you and bless your path, which I hope crosses mine again."

It was a customary parting, but I knew he meant every word with his heart. I clasped his hand with both of mine. "Let Hivathe make it so," I smiled. I held his hand probably longer than was appropriate with the monks watching, but I didn't care about them.

I released Kas so he could step back, then Ady sprang into the night sky. The evening wind blew through the stars and my hair, and I watched Kas until he was a speck on the ground, until he disappeared from my sight. I buried my face in her feathers.

Ady beat her wings against the cold gulf wind and was silent until the worst of my crying passed. *Congratulations on your quest, Nesrin. Father Ramdar wouldn't sully himself to speak with me, but his prior reported that the velarch's guards were already on their way to take and hide the casket away until I can arrange a better place for it.*

Good. It's a horrible, horrible thing. Did you see it?

Yes. I used as much of my magic as I dared to divine what was inside, but I still do not know.

I wiped my face against my sleeves and stared into the night sky, picking out the bright constellations of Arra, Varanor, and Marabon against the dark endless field of the universe freckled with celestial bodies and dripping with shooting stars.

Do you want to talk about it? She asked.

Not even a little. I curled up against her feathers and tried to think about making small marks in little bound books.

CHAPTER TWENTY-FOUR

THE HOLLOW TROVE

At some point over the gulf, I told Ady everything. She gasped in all the right places, went silent when I told her about the iron casket in Opintol. She hadn't gotten the magpie I'd sent her, which, coupled with all of Kas's missing magpies, made us both certain they were being intercepted. And she bellowed and shot fire into the air when I sobbed about Pistachio. When I told her about lying on the side of the road expecting to die, she vowed—for the second time in my story—to gobble Ashur up whole if she ever saw him again.

Is it true, I asked her, *that Kas's parents asked you to take me in?*

It is. The whole thing was Kas's idea. Why else would I have brought him in to tea? I'd been absent from my trove and late to find out about your father. After Velarch Oh and Queen Raia alerted me, I investigated for myself and found everything just as they said. So, I harassed Galter until he gave you up.

I remained quiet the rest of the flight home, recalling every detail about Kas before he faded from my memory. Trying to comprehend that my quest was done, and that Kas wouldn't be at my fireside with the flirtatious, easy smile he reserved for me and obscure facts about something random like apricots or hawks.

When we arrived home, Ady flew me to the back of her Great Hall, letting me off at the foot of the stairs to my chambers. The very first thing I did was take a long, much-overdue bath. I sank into the foamy, rose-scented water and tried not to think about Kas. I soaked for a long time, washing off the road, the dust. The blood I couldn't quite scrub away in the Strumming Steed Inn. I sobbed for Pistachio, for Kas, for me. I curled into a ball on the step and cried just like the first time I arrived at the trove.

Pooka trilled, groggily ambling into the room, his nose dark pink as it always was after a nap. He butted his furry head against mine over and over to welcome me home, purring like a thunderstorm and settling on the ledge of my bath.

I should've been happy. We won. We kept the casket out of Galter's hands, and we survived.

But not Pistachio. Not Kas's freedom.

I couldn't stop crying. *We won*, I repeated to myself. *Pull yourself together. You knew the road had risks.*

But I hadn't known what it would do to my heart.

I soaked for hours after most baths would have long since gone cold, and until I'd emptied my heart and washed my hair and skin in my favorite soaps. But their scents were flat, and home didn't feel like home anymore.

Not without him.

Afterwards I dressed in my favorite silk nightdress, and while I dried my hair in the warm downdraft of Ady's trove magic, I forced myself to list in my head all the work I'd left in the treasury. Focus: that's what I needed. Distractions.

Before I slept, I sat at my desk and wrote out my plans for the week. I'd finish the box of rings and start on Ady's burlap bag sitting in that corner I'd been eager to reclaim. Then maybe I'd assess that pile of golden trash—broken chains, smooshed goblets, rings with missing gems—and see if Ady wanted to schedule a melting day.

Who was I kidding? Of course she'd want to schedule a melting day. Dragons liked the smell of molten gold as much as cats liked catnip.

But I wasn't sure when I'd train again. I deserved a break after traveling and nearly being killed so many times. I'd turn an unused room in my suite into a meditation room, with soft wooden floors like that last inn. I'd double my daily doka practice in the pursuit of peace, and maybe as a way of honoring Kas.

That was macabre. He wasn't dead.

Although he almost was, to me. Forever out of my reach like a mountaintop or a sacred cave at the bottom of the sea.

I laid in my bed, tears flowing endlessly, faster when Kas's laugh came to mind. Pooka curled up beside me and let me hug him tightly. I curled into my aching heart and warm cat, and slept dreamlessly, staying in bed until noon. When the sun shone down through the stained-glass window of the moon and the stars, I asked the trove magic to make it into a scene of a campfire instead, the embers dancing into the stars. Then I got up, and life went on.

Ady had errands to run and dragons to see, based on the tale of my journey, and I made good progress on sorting the box of rings. I even visited my soon-to-be meditation room and explained to the trove magic exactly what I wanted. It also produced for me several pairs of short pants.

I pretended to refuse to notice that the day was overly quiet, and that it went on devoid of joy. A suitor rang the bell in the late evening when I was in my bath, and I sank my ears beneath the water until he went away.

This was going to be a long, unhappy lifetime.

Everything was shaking. I sat bolt upright from a sound sleep and looked around my still, quiet room. My heart was racing. Pooka was nowhere about. Was that an earthquake? Araven had never had an earthquake, that I knew of. Maybe it was just a dream of Andumar?

Pooka came tearing into the room and jumped up into bed with me, his fur and tail fluffed out.

"What's wrong, baby cat?" I pulled him against my chest and pet him, wishing Kas was here to comfort me. But of course, he wasn't here. Why would he be? It'd been nearly two weeks since I left him at the monastery, and not a word from him since. Sleep had been my only refuge from missing his voice, his warmth beside me. His scent and smile and laugh.

Ady, are you home?

A tremor ran through the ground, and Pooka jumped from my arms, scratching my stomach in his race under my bed. "Ow, Pooka! It's okay. You can come back."

No response from Ady, and after long minutes of waiting, no more tremors, either.

Outside my windows, the world was still dark, but my sleep was certainly done for the night. Or day. Whatever.

Ady said she'd be out overnight, but hopefully she'd be home soon. The air was heavy with dread and mystery, and I was tired of being alone.

I got dressed, knelt before my altar to Hivathe and said a prayer for Kas and one for me before beginning another empty day. I took a bath, I visited my new meditation room, and I made my way toward the dining room, finally able to walk without the ghost of pain.

Eight newly-placed burlap sacks by the armory door proved Ady had indeed come home. I pulled the drawstring open—a sorry collection of armor oddments.

Ady, are you home? What are these bags by the armory?

No answer, and my heart sank. Had she already gone out again? She was always coming and going since I'd been home. Sometimes she was gone for days at a time. I tried not to let her know how much it bothered me to be so alone all the time. It hadn't bothered me before I met Kas, but since leaving him...

Never mind. That couldn't be helped, and I had to live with it.

I think she did know I was lonely, but in her typical dragon lack of empathy, she didn't seem to know how to help me. But some nights when she was home, she was deliberately jovial. Like the other night when she regaled me with stories of her scavenging from vain kings and far-flung islands. I wanted her to think she was helping. But her stories only scratched the surface of my heart. The rest lay undisturbed beneath the armor I'd been carefully laying down since Kas...

Since Kas.

Today was just another blank day. Training, breakfast, stack of golden bullshit. I pushed the hair from my face and looked around the treasury. Enough work for a lifetime. A long, lonely, joyless lifetime, as if the bookish prince had never appeared on our doorstep.

Ady's wings whooshed through the Great Hall. Judging by the slant of the sun through the windows, it was time for tea. I pushed away from my work and made my way to the dining hall where tea and scones appeared as soon as I sat.

It's piping hot, Ady. Come sit with me. I know you're here. Was there an earthquake this morning? And we have to talk about your collection of golden bridle roundels. They're taking over the west alcove of the treasury, and you can't even ride a horse.

No response for a moment, but then I heard her in my head: *Come to the porch, Nes.*

I snapped my napkin across my lap. *I've already sat down to eat, so if it's another suitor, tell him to kick his own ass and save me the trouble.*

Nesrin, right now.

Her uncharacteristically serious tone stopped me as I reached for the teapot. I ran all the way to the front stairs and up to the balcony porch overlooking the forest. Ady sat still, looking off to the horizon and shading her eyes with a wing, the strong late-autumn wind ruffling her feathers.

I climbed up to the platform that allowed me to look over her balustrade and looked, but all I saw were red and gold treetops starting to go bare. Nothing new. "What is it?"

"Smoke."

I shielded my eyes and looked harder. "Really? Where? What's burning?"

"Even I can't see precisely over the great distance, but..." she glanced at me. "I think it's something in Veytia." She waited a heartbeat. "Near the monastery."

I gripped the stone balustrade and leaned out farther, my heart dropping. "Kas's monastery? Is it burning?" I craned my eyes toward the horizon, the hairs on the back of my neck standing up. "How can you possibly see that, all the way in Veytia?"

"I see it, and I taste familiar dragon smoke in the wind. Go get your weapons. We're leaving in five minutes." Ady turned and dove into the Great Hall.

I ran to the armory, strapped on my bandolier with all my throwing knives, and affixed Baney in her belt around my waist. Grabbed the wicked, twisted knife I'd stolen from the lost city and rehabilitated when I'd returned.

I was back on the balcony in under five minutes, but Ady was already waiting, dressed in armor with what looked like a war saddle strapped around her middle.

"Climb on. I hope we're not too late."

The moment I sat, she took off against the cold autumn wind.

Whose smoke could it be? My pounding heart dreaded her answer. *Chonneth?*

She laughed darkly. *If only.*

Then whose?

But Ady would answer no questions. In less than an hour, I too could see the haze on the horizon, could taste the metallic tang of dragon smoke being pulled into the gulf by the high winds. Ady's smoke had a pleasant taste in the air, like a campfire, but this smoke was foul, like sulfur. I secured my face scarf across my nose and mouth.

As we got closer, other scents mingled in that smoke: burnt wood, charred stone, melted metal, seared flesh.

I willed Ady to fly faster.

Finally, Ady flew within *my* sight of the monastery, or what remained of it. It was on fire, and the top two terraces had collapsed.

Put me on the ground.

Nesrin, he may not have surv—

"You don't know that!" I shouted. "Put me down!"

Brothers and neighbors from the nearby village ran a bucket brigade, clearing rubble and looking for survivors. Nearly everyone ran when Ady came in to land, but once we were on the ground, a few brave souls met us.

"What happened?" Ady asked.

"Where's Kas?" I asked immediately after, my voice breaking as I jumped down.

The monk who'd come to tell me Ady had arrived that day was the first to speak. "The monastery was torn apart by a dragon," he said.

Smoke poured from Ady's nostrils. "*When?*"

"Where's Kas?" I demanded again.

"Last night," he said, and then he turned to me, his eyes hollow. "No one's seen him since evening prayers. He could be inside," he turned around to look at the smoldering ruin, "but we've only found three survivors. Over half of the brothers are missing. We just don't know where they are."

I ran for the broken monastery, distraught that the man was shaken enough to break his vow and talk to me. With Ady's help dropping large amounts of water and moving big pieces of stone and wood to an adjacent field, a team of us worked for over an hour to clear away sections of the rubble and look for survivors. We found over a dozen dead and only five alive, but injured.

Soon Ady had removed the final, largest sections of the rubble, and we could see the bottom floor of the monastery. Where could Kas be? I pushed on in the recovery efforts, my heart in my throat, tears streaming as I worked. So many were still missing, so many were dead.

I combed through the rubble on the back hall of the ground floor, lifting twisted floor tiles and pulling tapestries off caved-in walls. Something about the pattern of destruction was all wrong for a winged attack. If the dragon attacked from the sky, why were the columns all thrown back away from the center hallway, almost in a circle? Why were pieces of stone sticking jaggedly up, like everything busted upwards?

Smoke emanated from beneath a floor tile a few feet from me. I kicked aside a pile of broken ceramic pots...wait. That floor tile wasn't a floor tile. Stones were adhered to a metal door that had molten and twisted in the dragon fire, and beneath it wasn't earth or stone. Only darkness. A trapdoor? I cleared the debris around it, found its edges and a metal handle. I pulled, but it wouldn't budge.

Ady, help me get this open!

After a moment, Ady flew down, gripped the metal door with her claws, and broke it away with a great crack. Revealing a wide stairwell going down into a vast, dark chamber.

"Hello!" I called into the smoky void. It reeked of charred flesh, and only my own voice echoed back. "Is anyone alive?" Something came back that wasn't my echo, and I rushed down into the darkness.

The deep stairwell was eerily cool despite the small fires dotting the wreckage. Massive columns that had previously supported this underground portion of the monastery were toppled over and broken. I crawled over, across, and under huge stone and wood piles of debris.

No one answered, because everyone here was dead. Dozens of bodies charred, trampled, crushed. *Ady, I found them.* Even though I'd know Kas's form anywhere, I still looked into every face as I checked pulses. Over and over, fear then overwhelming relief that made me feel like the most selfish human alive.

Several monks entered the chamber from the stairs, all of them shocked and confused that it was here at all. They helped me look for survivors under my strict instructions to tell me immediately if they found him. But not much later we'd checked every body—only four survivors, and no Kas.

Ady carried the dead and injured away and strategically cleared debris as I went further into the rubble. I stood back so she could pick up a part of the ground floor that had cracked and fallen. Dust filtered down with the daylight into the underground chamber, and something moved in the shifting light and lingering smoke.

"Is someone there?" Yes, someone definitely was moving at the edge of the room. I ran toward the movement, clambering over fallen timbers and broken furniture. Something above me shifted, and a volley of stone and wood came raining down in the hallway. I stumbled against the wall, taking cover under a wide lintel until the dust cleared.

Someone coughed in the darkness ahead of me. I picked my way toward it, my heart pounding in my ears. I couldn't be so lucky, could I?

When I was only a few feet away, a dust- and blood-covered hand reached up through the rubble. A hand I would know anywhere.

CHAPTER TWENTY-FIVE

KAS'S STORY

"Kas!" I clasped his hand, eyeing the crevice between stones where he was trapped.

"Nesrin?" He choked out, his cough echoing.

"Kas! Oh, my gods. Are you hurt?" I pushed away a chunk of rock and pulled off a torn tapestry, and there he was, trapped in a blessed little air pocket.

His bright eyes locked on mine, blood dripping down his charcoal-stained face as he grasped my arm. "Nesrin," he choked out, his voice raspy and pained. "They have it!"

Ady! I found Kas. Come quick before this place collapses!

"Who has what?" I pulled rubble from the pile to clear his way, but his leg was trapped under a wooden column, maybe broken, and wedged so he couldn't get out. I paused as what he said hit me. "Oh gods, did Galter do this for the casket?"

"No. It's worse." His eyes were haunted as I stepped inside his haven and wrapped my arms around him. "It's so much worse, Nesrin," he choked out. He clutched me back, burying his face against my neck as I twisted my hands into his hair. My Kas. Safe and alive.

Ady flew down and pulled first the stone away, then the column off his broken leg. I tucked my shoulder under his arm and helped him stand on the other as Ady hovered back down and grasped him carefully in her claws. I scrambled into the saddle, and she took us away.

Ady placed Kas gently near the relief efforts and landed a few feet away for me to dismount. She gently placed her clawed foot above Kas's leg, using her magic to speed his healing as I pulled out her medicines and handed him a cobalt blue glass vial. He drank it down in two gulps.

Ady fixed her black eyes on him. "They freed him," she said. Not a question, a statement of fact she clearly needed but didn't want verified.

He looked up at her miserably, tears in his eyes. "Yes. They freed him, and he tore everything apart."

Ady shrieked into the sky, shooting a long stream of fire into the air. "I'm such a fool!" She cursed, dragging her talons across the ground, leaving long, muddy gashes in the grass and scaring the shit out of passing monks and rescuers.

"Was it the white dragon?" I pulled out bandages and started wrapping Kas's leg. "What happened?"

"Yes. I..." he breathed out, eyes tortured as if he didn't want to go on. He shut his eyes tight. "I missed...sleeping under the stars. So, I left my room and—" He swallowed hard. "There was this giant *crack*, and the ground shook. A fissure ran through the floor under my feet, and then I heard voices coming from beneath what I thought was the ground floor. Disturbing chants about death and ruin. I thought I was imagining it, but it got so loud...

"I went looking for it. There was this...door behind a tapestry." He shook his head, looking from me to Ady. "There's this...this whole underworld of passages under the monastery, and the stairs just went..." he paused, gesturing down with a shaky hand before running it through his disheveled curls. "So much deeper than where you found me. It was my brothers. Monks. Dozens of them chanting evil psalms. And bowing on the floor toward this hideous altar that looked like it was writhing with white snakes."

A chill raced across my skin, and I looked to Ady as I tied off the bandages. She shook her head, eyes closed.

"Father Ramdar was on the altar, and Ashur was with him. He had a torch lit with..." he looked at Ady. "Well. With a black flame that sparked burgundy."

Ady's eyes narrowed dangerously, and smoke poured from her nostrils. "Ashur had *my flame*?"

He nodded. "It looked like yours, like that night you lit the fireplace. They put it in a brazier, and Ramdar dropped the casket into it." He clutched my arm, his face stricken. "The one *we* gave him thinking we were doing the right thing. He dropped it into the fire, and words appeared in the smoke. He read them, and the casket rose out of the fire and opened. He took something out, said more spells, and then all hell broke loose."

"I'll bet he did," Ady said quietly.

"A massive white dragon."

"They moved him into a gold casket to hide him from us," Ady's voice was edged with anger and regret. She sank onto the grass like a tired old cat.

"He was..." Kas stumbled for the words. "He erupted from the flames like he was born from them. He told the monks that only the strongest would survive their devotion to him, and then he breathed fire over them. Gods, the screaming..."

His hoarse voice quivered as he spoke, and I took his hand in mine and rubbed his back with the other.

"Everyone who wasn't dead or on fire, ran. Trampling each other. Ramdar and Ashur got on the dragon's back, and it flew up through the ceiling like the stones were made of paper. The monastery broke apart, great hunks of it into the brothers running. I ran with the crowd as far as the top of the stairs, but the ground shook, and I fell a long way. I couldn't help myself, much less anyone else. How many of my brothers survived?"

He looked to me, but I looked to Ady.

"Around forty are up and walking," she said softly. "Maybe sixty have mild to grave injuries. The rest are dead or missing."

Kas put his head down and leaned toward me.

"How many were here?" I asked.

"A hundred and eighty-three." Kas covered his face with his hand. "I'm so sorry, Ady. You asked and asked what they'd do with it. I never imagined..."

"Ady, please tell me this is a different white dragon than the one you told me about?"

She shook her head. "It's Seviiranth."

"I can't believe that nightmare has a name," Kas said quietly.

"Seviiranth's a monster. When you first asked about a golden casket, Kas, I was really more curious that Galter would want such a thing. Carrying a casket before you in battle isn't a legend I'd ever heard, gold or iron. Nothing evil's supposed to be in a gold casket, and they were sealed so long ago. Somewhere along the ages, someone must have transferred him into a golden casket."

Realization hit me. "Because dragons gain magical power from gold."

Ady nodded. "Since you returned, I've been trying to figure out this puzzle. Galter's too stupid to orchestrate something like this on his own, but it all makes sense now. I went to the library to see the iron casket for myself. It had to have been Seviiranth's. And you were right, Nesrin. While I was there, it became very clear to me that Aringiel's golden peace had settled on the city."

"So why wasn't the white dragon released *then*?" I asked. "And how was a massive white dragon imprisoned in a little box?"

"Because part of the imprisonment is shrunken inanimation. He was reduced to a small size, and a spell froze him in time. It's one set of spells to open the casket, and another set entirely to free him from his inanimate state."

I searched the clearing skies. "Won't Aringiel's gift come to fight him?"

Ady shook her head. "That's not how it works. The blessing forms a perimeter around where its casket is opened. It was opened in Estria, so the blessing remains there."

"That's a shit blessing," I said, "if putting him in the gold casket let them smuggle him outside its perimeter. Where do you think he's gone?"

"Probably to join Galter," Ady said. "Their interests align, for now. My intuition told me Galter was connected with something older and eviler than himself, but I couldn't put my finger on it." Ady stood and shook out her wings. "Ramdar's his connection. The question is, who is the *pious* father, really? When this battle's won, we'll have to seek the roots of this evil. But that will be a war for another time."

She shook her head and turned her attention back to us as if she'd forgotten we were there. "Get up on my war seat. I'm bringing you both back to my trove. The allied armies have already taken the gulf, and they may be ready to attack Araven as early as tomorrow or the day after. We'll need you both on the battlefield, so you need to rest and gain your strength somewhere safe. Does that suit you, Kas?"

He nodded without hesitation, and with my help, took his place in the saddle behind me. His thighs pressed against my bottom, stirring my blood, but his hands rested chastely on my waist. Selfishly, despite the world falling apart around us, my mind was stuck on one question: what did all this mean for me and Kas?

CHAPTER TWENTY-SIX

VOWS

Ady flew swiftly toward her monolith as the night fell around us over the gulf, and it didn't take long for Kas's weight to shift against me in his sleep. I pulled his arms tighter around me and let his head rest against my shoulder. I smiled. My Kas was coming home with me, and as sorry as I was that it was under these circumstances, my heart was full of gratitude.

Kas had lived, and he was coming home with me.

Soon Ady was depositing us outside my suite while calling out instructions to the trove to place meals for us on the table in my room.

"I have to go," she said, "but I'll send for you."

Her black eyes turned to me. *Take care of him*, she said in my mind. *He will be instrumental in trapping Seviiranth again. I trust Sexy Eyes, but I sense something in his story wasn't true. Suss it out. We cannot afford for him to be distracted.*

My heart resisted her words, but I nodded. She took off flying and left the trove.

Kas let me help him to my table, but my chest tightened thinking over Ady's words. Everything he'd said made sense to me. Kas would never lie to me. Maybe he omitted something he didn't want to say in front of Ady. But what?

Kas took off his robe as he approached the table, crumpled it up, and dropped it to the floor. I wanted more than anything to throw my arms around him and never let go. Instead, I busied myself with filling my plate. Pooka made his appearance with pork in the air, and Kas almost smiled greeting him.

But a perpetual spark of his optimism was dimmed, and in my gut, I felt that it was more than the trauma he'd experienced. We ate in silence, and the butterflies in my stomach were walking on eggshells. I had what I'd been wanting with all my heart: Kas here with me. But he wasn't himself, and I didn't know what the future held or how to help him.

He chewed on a roasted potato, pushing his other food around the plate, and his haunted eyes stared at the fire.

"I'm here if you need to talk about it," I said softly.

He took a deep breath and let it out, finally meeting my eyes. "Nesrin, I didn't think I'd live through it. I didn't think I'd ever see you again." He launched into a more detailed account of the dragon's release, starting from the crack that initially shook the monastery. The more he related details about the night—his friends who had been lying all this time, the head of his order being in league with a cult, seeing Ashur and the golden casket together—the more animated he became and the more he ate. Good. He needed something in his stomach after going nearly a whole day stuck in the rubble.

By the time he'd finished his story and his meal, he looked tired, but calmer.

"Thank you," he said. "I do feel a little better getting it all out."

"Of course." I smiled with a sudden idea. "Trove, can you take away these dirty plates and bring us some coffee and sweetdrops?"

The trove magic did as I asked, but Kas sighed with furrowed brows. "Sweetdrops," he said, as if they were the root of a great evil.

"I just thought you'd like a treat, after all you've been through. No good?"

"It's fine." His eyes dropped and wouldn't meet mine again. "Thank you."

There it was again. Whatever he was holding back was in his thoughts again. I reached across and took his hand in both of mine. "Kas," I said gently. "What is it? What didn't you tell me and Ady?" My heart beat faster. "You can tell me anything."

He took his hand away and stood, wincing when he put weight on his healing leg. "Nesrin, I..."

My heart sank at the clear guilt I read in his eyes, a shadow like storm clouds waiting to fall. I almost begged him not to go on.

He pushed his chair in and leaned heavily on its back. "I haven't been honest with you. Or with myself."

"What do you mean?"

"I'm not the man you think I am."

"Of course you are. You're the kindest—"

"But I'm not. After what happened with Ari all those years ago, I tried. I really did. I tried to dedicate my life to Hivathe. I studied, I prayed, I did everything required of me. But I've struggled to be beyond human temptations."

I leaned on the table with my elbows, holding his gaze. "That makes sense, Kas, as you are a human. What's bothering you?"

"Nesrin, since you left..." He looked into my eyes, down at his hands. "Honestly, since the day I met you..." He looked down and ruffled his hair with his hand. Then he looked back up to my eyes. "I wasn't up last night because I couldn't sleep. I was up because I was running away. I was running to you."

Warmth spread through my chest, and I pressed my lips together to keep from smiling at what was a difficult moment for him. Kas had been coming to *me*. "Is that what you needed to confess?"

He gazed at me for a few seconds more before coming around the table and kneeling by my chair. I turned toward him. Taking both of my hands in his, he looked at me the way he always did.

With his whole heart in his eyes. My heart pounded, and I was afraid to move lest I wake up and this be a dream.

"Nesrin, how I feel about you is against all my vows. After you left, I tried not to think about you, but I couldn't stop. You were the first thing I thought about in the morning, and the last thing before I slept. Except I couldn't sleep because you weren't beside me. And then yesterday morning, someone from the city brought us sweetdrops, and something broke in my chest." He cupped my face with one hand and rubbed my cheek with his thumb. "I belong with you. Not there. Not as a monk." He dropped his hand and sat back on his heels. "So, I waited until everyone was asleep, like a coward. I left everything behind but my journal." He pulled it from the pocket of his pants and dropped it on the floor beside him. "And I was running away.

"And just when I was making that faithless decision, Ramdar and my brothers were in a pit at the heart of the monastery, forsaking all their vows. Don't you see? All my life I've had my own pit in my heart. I never wanted to be in the order. I never wanted to make the vows I did, but I did. It's not like anyone held a knife to my throat while I spoke them. Nesrin, I've never told anyone this, but..." He clasped his hands to his chest. "I want my own life. A family, children. I love people too much to live away from them, and I lo—" He swallowed hard and searched my eyes. "Do you think that makes me an oath-breaker?"

I started to speak, but he raised his hand as if to block the words before they could come out. "And be honest. I don't deserve your kindness, or your pity."

"I'll always give you my honesty and kindness, but never my pity. My honest answer is that any vows you made to the order were under duress. Did they even wait for you to come of age? Did they force them on you when you were a child?"

He nodded. "I was thirteen."

"Kas, that's barbaric!" My fury at the order raged anew. "You'd only just learned the difference between right and wrong! You hadn't even begun to know your own body yet, or even what kind of person you wanted to be. Need I mention that it's far lower than the age of consent? Do you really think Hivathe wanted your vows that way?"

He breathed out heavily and shook his head, no.

"And while all of that matters, the plain truth is that the order's gone, Kas. Your vows are absolved, and you finally have the opportunity to choose your own path. Hivathe doesn't want anyone to go against their own heart."

"How can I know what she wants when I've been steeping in the order's lies for over half my life?"

It was heartbreaking how we'd both been trapped, both lost years of our lives to the whims or traditions of others. I wanted to set him free. Set us both free. But I couldn't open his cage or make his decisions for him, and I was dangerously close to kissing him.

Finally, I spoke. "You have to follow your own good heart, Kas. Only you can decide what you want for yourself. That's what Hivathe wants for all of us."

He knelt up again and took both of my hands in his, looking deeply into my eyes. "I nearly died in the monastery—more than once—but the only part of my life I've ever truly lived was the time I spent with you. I already know what my heart wants. It wants *you*, Nesrin, against all my vows. I want so much more than being your friend. So much more than being one of the men you let into your bed and send away."

I wanted that too, with all my heart. But was he in any shape to decide his future with a clear head? He'd lost so much today.

I laid my hand over his. "I won't be a source of shame or regret for you."

"You could never be either," he said, his eyes dark, his lips parted.

My heart pounded as I searched his eyes. Why shouldn't we act on our love? How could a loving union be wrong?

His eyes widened and he let go of my hands, standing as quickly as his injury would allow. "I'm so sorry, Nesrin. You don't feel the same. I'm such an idiot." He rubbed his beard and limped away toward the fireplace.

Selflessness be damned.

"Holy Mother of Wisdom, Kas." I pushed out from my chair and stomped up to him. "Do you really have no idea what I want? I'm not complicated." I took his face in my hands and stepped close, letting his familiar scent wash through me as I searched his eyes and rubbed my thumb against his beard. "I asked you to come home with me to stay because I'm in love with you."

His eyebrows rose, his whole face lightening in a near smile. "You're in love with me?"

I nodded. "Yes. And the only thing keeping me from making love to you right here and now is my worry that you've been through too much today. I don't want to do something you might regret, no matter how badly I want you, too."

He set his hands on my waist and leaned his face closer to mine. "I love you, too, Nesrin, and I want you for my own. I want to walk life's paths beside you. I want to share in your happiness and lessen your sorrows." He pressed his forehead against mine and slipped his hands to my back. "Every night, I want to fill your body with mine and learn all the ways I can bring you joy and pleasure, and I want to wake up every morning entangled in your arms." He took a deep breath and pulled his head back, searching my eyes. "I just want *you*."

"Are you sure?"

He licked his lips and eyed mine hungrily. "It's all I've ever wanted."

Warmth spread through me, and all my butterflies danced in sunlight. I tipped my face up to his. "Well, you have me." I murmured with a cheeky raise of my eyebrows. "What will you do with me?"

Smiling, he gently brushed a wisp of hair from my face and pressed his lips to mine. I wrapped my arms around his neck and gently sucked that delectable lower lip I'd been dreaming of—impeccably delicious—and then I went back for more. What he lacked in experience he made up for in natural talent and hunger, with his hands slipping down to my hips and his mouth quickly learning the dance. My eyes fluttered open to see the impassioned devotion on his face, and I ran my hands further back along his hard jawline, entangling my fingers in his loose curls and pressing my hips against his hardening.

He *mmmed* and melted into me, letting my tongue coach his and my hips set a rhythm. He tasted delicious, like an adventure and like coming home, all at once. I would take this as slow as he wanted...

He turned and pinned me against the wall with his hips, one hand on my ass as he gently ground his erection against me, and the other at the back of my head as if he was afraid I'd stop kissing him.

Fine by me.

Slipping my hands between us, I grabbed the fabric of his tunic and pushed his arms up with it. He let me remove it, and I ran my palms along the warm skin of his neck, his shoulders, his smooth back, the soft hair covering the muscles of his chest. I sucked kisses against his neck, and soft noises of pleasure slipped from his lips. My heart hammered, and desire built in all the sacred places of my body.

Kas's fervent affection lit a dark, empty place in my soul with a beatific belonging I hadn't even known I was missing. *This one.* No other would ever attract my heart and soul like this, like a moth to a flame. And gods, I want his fire to take me.

Our lips smacked as I pulled away from him and pushed him down onto my chaise. I straddled him and his eyes went dark and desirous. He leaned forward toward my mouth, but I held him back and held his gaze as I undid the hooks of my corset, one by one.

A little dazed, he watched my fingers with parted lips. My corset fell away, and I pulled my tunic off, baring my breasts to him. The heat of his exploring gaze made my skin prickle and my nipples pebble. I grabbed his face again, kissing him hard and rubbing the tips of my breasts softly against his bare chest. He groaned and kissed me hungrily, his hands roving to my back to crush me closer to him.

I instinctively thrust my hips forward to slot my hungry aching against his hardness. He groaned as I ground against him, slipping his hand to my bottom to pull me closer to his need. His other hand crept timidly up my stomach, gently stroking and grabbing at my skin, boldly inching upward. Not fast enough for me.

I slipped my tongue into his mouth and took his hand, guiding it to cup my breast, squeezing myself through it. He got bolder, claiming fervent kisses back, grasping both of my breasts, stroking my nipples, then slipping his hands back to cup my behind, pulling my writhing toward gently thrusting hips.

He stopped kissing me long enough to whisper devoutly, "Show me how to please you."

"Touch me, Kas, kiss me everywhere," I panted, pulling his face toward my neck. He rewarded me with soft licking kisses, and I tangled my fingers in the curls at the back of his neck. I arched my back and guided his mouth to my breast. "Kiss me here." He took instruction well, running his tongue around my nipple before his hot mouth latched onto my breast. A moan escaped my lips, and I pulled his head against me to make him keep sucking and teasing me with his tongue.

He thrust his hips up against me and I gasped. "I need you, Nesrin."

I stood and pulled him up with me toward my bed. On the way there, I undid my pants and let them drop to the floor.

"You're the most beautiful woman I've ever seen," he said passionately, grasping my face with both hands and kissing me hard.

I reached between us and undid the buttons of his pants and tugged them down. His considerable erection sprang hot and free against my wrist. I breathed sharply out, wanton desire filling me like a vessel and pooling heavier between my legs. "Kas, this has been in your pants the whole time?"

His dilated eyes crinkled. "The whole time."

I grasped his erection, and the smile fell from his face with a sharp gasp and then a moan as I gently slid my hand up and down his length. He captured my mouth with a hungrier kiss.

"You feel so good Kas," I murmured against his lips. "I want you to know what you're doing to me." I set my leg up on the low stool by my bed and guided his hand between my legs, dipping his fingers into my sacred place.

He whimpered and murmured my name against my neck as I taught his fingers to circle my bud. "Gently," I gasped as he did just that. His fingers slipped back and pushed inside me, and I cried out with the pleasure of it. "Do you feel how wet I am for you? I need you inside me, Kas."

I pushed him backwards and up onto the bed, stalking up his body as he watched me, his lips parted, his gaze soft and adoring, and his hands stroking at whatever skin he could reach. I ran my tongue across his stomach to the soft, vulnerable spot of his inner thigh where it met his torso, licking a warm kiss to his skin there, and he moaned. I ran my tongue up the full length of his erection, and he cried out, calling my name as I wrapped my mouth and hand around him for just a moment, then returning to kiss his lips.

His kisses wandered down my chest, and I stretched up, panting and winding my fingers through his curls, holding the back of his head to press my breast deeper into the caresses of his tongue, his teeth, his hot, sucking mouth. I was almost whole, almost blessed. I reached down and stroked him, and he shivered, softly called my name. I desperately wanted to satisfy the delicious, hungry aching I could no longer ignore.

I grasped his arousal and sank slowly down on him, inch by blessed inch, both of us breathless and moaning with the pleasure of how deeply, how completely, he filled me. I rode him gently at first, rolling my neck as I made slow, luxurious circles on him with my hips, the full length of him stroking me in the deepest places and setting my skin on fire.

He breathed hard, watching me with undisguised reverence and hunger, his ravenous hands stroking my body, his soft voice moaning in pleasure, his kisses blessing me. I felt beautiful, radiantly desirable like Hivathe herself.

And he was my Onsorbal, my holy, intimately devoted consort, equal in fire and passion. We were one, reunited and sublime, and our connection was transcendent.

I'd touched the others the way I'd been taught, but I made love to Kas with the full spectrum of love I had for him, the joy of belonging to each other. Limbs entangled, messy kisses, eager hands. I couldn't get close enough to him to bank this desire, this holy desire lit with soul-deep longing.

For as long as I could, I savored him, slowly, indulgently tormenting him and denying my all-consuming need to devour him whole and shatter us both. But when he sat up and captured my breast again in the sweet, hot, pinching torture of his mouth, thrusting his hips against me, I could wait no more, and we took on an ancient, undulating rhythm. My desperate need for completion built and built with every thrust, and then my body burst with waves of breaking bliss with his name on my lips.

"Oh gods, Nesrin," Kas cried out, his grinding lengthening the pure pleasure flooding my body. He lifted me bodily and laid me onto my back, his body between my legs, his thrusts delving even deeper and harder, wild and out of control in the most intoxicating way. "Oh gods, Nesrin, I *felt* you."

I lifted my hips to meet his bucking, so close to coming again when he began exclaiming soft *ohs* with every breath. He moaned louder, closing his eyes and crying out my name as he throbbed deep inside of me.

He panted against my neck, his heart a drum against mine. I had never felt anything so strong, so satisfying, a religious experience. I kept my body wrapped around him, unwilling to break the hot, thrilling place where our bodies were still joined. His skin against mine, the smell of him tangled up with me. I had experienced utter release, and yet I was still desirous of the hard planes of his lithe body against mine. We were one, and I was home.

This man. I pressed my forehead to his, and seeing his eyes wild with loving desire only made me want him more.

"Nes-*reen*," he murmured against my lips, his kisses no less fervent now. "My beautiful wild rose." His heart pounded against my chest, his sweat cooling on his skin.

"I love you," we both declared, and we laughed.

"I only just remembered how much my leg hurts."

I kissed his nose. "Then I vow to distract you over and over again through the night, in as many ways as we can imagine."

He sighed lustily at the thought, and he laid beside me. I buried my face in his neck, his pulse jumping against my nose, his arms around me. He planted a long kiss on the top of my head, and we talked about all the moments of our adventure when we knew we were falling in love, until sleep claimed us.

CHAPTER TWENTY-SEVEN

THE REUNION

A Veytian magpie flew into my room with the sun, its blue and white tail feathers fanned. It settled onto a perch near my desk and turned its black head to us.

Kyak-kyak-kyak!

Attached to its foot was a small scroll.

It took my entire personal sense of responsibility to disengage myself from Kas's warm, naked body to get out of bed. After slipping into my Kesna robe, I opened a little crystal jar to scoop out some pine nuts for the bird's trouble, dropping them into a shallow bronze bowl attached to the perch before I undid the message.

"Is that from Ady?" Kas asked. I glanced at him, fully naked in my bed, and I flooded with warmth. It nearly lured me back.

I dragged my eyes away from him to scan the short note.

"Yes. She wants us to meet her at the allied kingdoms' command post on the outskirts of the Vadic Plains." The magpie tip-tapped at his treat, contentedly unaware of the import of his message. "It's time."

After a quick breakfast, the trove helped me outfit Kas in sleek black fighting leathers, under which I made him wear fine chainmail. Once I had him as protected as I could make him, I let him pick his weapons and pulled a special sword from a wooden trunk against the wall.

"This is Ruination, the Scourge of Blades. Baney's mate." I pulled the sword from its sheath, its hilt sparkling with three oval rubies. "I call him Runey for short. I want you to carry him."

He took the sword from me, studying it. "I wish we didn't live in a world that required weapons."

I laid my hand against his cheek, and he kissed it. "And I love that about you. But you have to protect yourself. No one else on that battlefield will have a peaceful heart. Besides, Ady said dragons can ensorcel people with their magic. It's best to be prepared."

"*All* dragons can do that?" Kas asked warily, strapping the knives I'd given him to his leg braces and belt.

"Ady says they can, but she considers such behavior well beneath her."

"Of course she does," Kas grinned.

I stood back and admired my work, butterflies in my stomach. Warrior prince suited him quite well. Gone perhaps forever was the slight hunch with which he used to carry himself. Now he looked comfortable in his own skin.

"Do I look battle-ready?" he asked, bright eyes gazing at me with such love.

I pulled his face down to kiss him. "I'd happily go another round with you, any time."

"I'm at your service." He chuckled and kissed me again, his eyes darkening and his hands roving across my back and bottom.

I groaned, kissing him one more time...three more times. "It's not fair, but we're running late for the battle."

We headed out toward the position Ady indicated, Kas on Balembar and me on Starbuck, a chestnut stallion with a white mark like a star on his flank.

We traveled the cliff corridor of Araven along the gulf, the same one we traversed weeks ago. This time, we avoided the quicksand, but I stopped by the kavhavji vines, slipped on thick gloves, and clipped a short bit, stowing it and a leaf in a bronze vial.

"What's that for?" Kas asked.

"Seviiranth, I hope."

In the valley where Bocian sat against the Eldor River, the re-purposed Aravenian war tents flew flags of Nabul, Veytia, Opro-lodas, Opintol, the Mysterium Amanharate, Boekam, and other allies. As darkness fell, we handed our horses to groomsmen at the command post.

Inside, the tent was crowded almost to bursting with only a small opening in the center where Ady sat behind a map table flanked by lamps. Her head ducked low to fit, her voice commanded the attention of the nations' rulers and top generals. I hesitated just inside the door flap, not wanting to draw attention to myself, but Ady expected me. I squeezed Kas's hand before heading through the press of people.

Ady looked up, catching me in her dark gaze. "And here is my Knight, Nesrin, rightful Princess of Araven."

While I approached Ady, Kas stole along the outer perimeter of the tent's interior, not far behind an older Veytian man wearing dark kohl around his light eyes and a golden-shouldered cloak. Beside what could only be the velarch stood two younger men who looked so much like Kas. His brothers, no doubt.

Several tall men swathed in armor and weaponry turned from the table to look at me, among them Prince Javid and Prince-Con-sort Hirach, the Amanha, and at least three princes whose asses I'd kicked in the past year. My heart instantly went out to their families, to Queen Carusa, Javid's bride, the Amanhara and sweet Aira. We had to get everyone home safely.

Ady followed Kas with her black, glittering eyes, and her laugh pattered in my mind. *Sexy Eyes finally got laid, I presume?*

My cheeks heated. *Turns out it was quite easy to relieve his mind.*

She snickered quietly as one of the princes around the table held his hand out to me with a smile. "Princess Nesrin." Prince Forth shook my hand, bowing over it with his rugged fighter's body.

"You managed to get back home, then?" I smiled, actually glad to see him.

"No thanks to you!" He laughed, his merry blue eyes twinkling in the dim interior of the tent. He held up a hand. "But I won't hold it against you. It's good to see you out in the world, and we need your help. Lady Adydorrstea was about to share her plan to deal with the white dragon."

Ady lifted her head, eyeing the gathered men. "As I was saying, even your mightiest warriors are no match for Seviiranth. I'm a match for him, and he nearly killed me the last time we fought, when I helped trap him in the iron casket. He won't fall for the same trick twice, but we can trap him again."

"Why don't we just kill him?" Forth asked.

I had to admit I'd had the same thought.

Ady's condescending laughter filled the tent. "I'd like to see you try, little man. He's destroyed whole kingdoms on his own, and his magic is far darker and more powerful than even mine, but only because he's far older and nowhere near as honorable. He plans to make an entrance, I assure you. He won't reveal himself until your armies are in the thick of fighting. And when Seviiranth enters the fray, I'll engage him. But it will only be a distraction. The real battle will be won by the combined talents of my daughter, the Dread Dragon Calanddria; Knight Nesrin; our cleric; and the special force that will bring them inside the palace."

I suspected who the cleric was, and although my heart quailed at the thought of Kas joining us on a dangerous mission, my brain was stuck on Ady's mention of her daughter.

Ady had children?

"Our...cleric?" the Amanha asked, turning his head around to look for said man. "What help is a cleric on the field of battle, except to say prayers over the dead?"

"He won't be on the field of battle, my dear, or haven't you been listening?" Ady asked in her stately voice. "*Prince* Kasper of Veytia, please come forward."

All heads turned, but none as fast as Velarch Oh and his sons. Kas slipped through the crowd and approached the map table with his head high. My heart swelled with pride to see him step into the world as himself—no slouch, owning his birthright and his own power. His brothers called his name, pushed past others to embrace him. And even though his father didn't move, when he looked at Kas, his face beamed with relief and pride. Kas visibly relaxed as Ady continued.

"Prince Kasper is our cleric."

"Why do we need a cleric?" a woman in armor asked as Forth reached out and shook Kas's hand, introducing himself quietly.

"Can you speak ancient Drakonai?" Ady asked, her black eyes glittering. "Can any of you interpret runes from the Lost City of Ulsmati, or invoke the goddess Hivathe and have her heed your call?"

Kas said nothing, but at Hivathe's name, he paled and looked at me. With a pang I realized he was worried about how well Hivathe loved him after our recent amorous activities in the trove. I wanted to kiss his worries away.

"So, this special force just has to get Prince Kasper and Princess Nesrin into the palace?" Forth asked.

"Into the palace, and up to the highest battlement," Ady said. "My sources tell me Galter will *not* be on the battlefield himself, the perennial coward. So, the special force will serve a dual purpose: to kill Galter, and to bring Kasper and Nesrin to the tower without Seviiranth's knowledge. There, Calanddria will meet them, and together they'll strike a blow Seviiranth won't see coming. I hope," Ady added more quietly. "As I warned you, Seviiranth will use his powers of hallucination and living nightmares against the entire field of battle, so this special force needs to be the best your race has to offer. The fiercest warriors with the strongest minds and best of intentions. Otherwise, *none* of us will survive Seviiranth."

"I would fight beside Princess Nesrin any day," Forth said, his voice booming through the tent. "I volunteer for this force, if my father approves."

An older man, shorter than Forth but with the same eyes and shape of face, spoke. "You have my blessing, son."

"I knew I liked something about you, Prince Forth," Ady said, finally getting his name right on purpose. "We need one more lead and thirty as force protection."

"I'll go."

I turned toward the deep voice I hadn't heard in years but somehow recognized, speechless as the crowd parted around my brothers. My eldest brother, Talon, took my breath away. He'd grown into a replica of my father. And Pendor. He'd been a gangly teenager when I last saw him. They reached me, and the three of us just *looked* at each other.

So much that I'd pushed into the deepest places in my heart came back to me—my father's funeral, Galter beating Talon to within an inch of his life. Pendor, all of sixteen at the time, hugging me goodbye just before he helped smuggle Talon out of Araven. The hope in my mother's eyes when our ill-fated rescue began. Her wide eyes in the dark as her blood pooled on the ground, and my screams reverberating through the darkest, lowest passages of the palace, my arms pulled back painfully by traitor guards without faces. It all bubbled out of me in a sob, and I threw my arms around them. They hugged me tight.

Ady's voice rang out. "We'll disband now to let the family re-unite and to prepare for battle. But before we go..." She reached beside her and lifted a massive burlap bag, dropping it with a clank on top of the map table, which groaned under its weight. "This and other bags behind the tent contain armor from my trove. Its power isn't so much in physical protection, but in as much magic as I could imbue to offer you and your soldiers some defense against Seviiranth's deceitful magic. Spread it as far as you can among your soldiers, even if it's one greave per foot soldier. Breaking it apart won't decrease its efficacy. I have to leave for a while, but I'll return before the battle begins." She bowed and stalked out the back of the tent, and then the whole thing shuddered under the wind of her wings as she took to the sky.

Everyone filed out past my brothers and me. Kas walked out with his father's arm upon his shoulder and thronged by his brothers. He smiled and squeezed my hand as he passed, as though he couldn't help but touch me if we were near.

This small gesture between us wasn't lost on any of our family members. Kas's brothers whooped and pelted Kas with questions about me as they walked out, him laughing between them.

"So, you were the one who accompanied the velarch's son on his quest for the casket and rescued him from the wreckage of the monastery." Pendor asked when we were alone.

"We'd heard rumors." Talon shook his head, his hazel eyes dark. "You look so much like her," he added softly.

I put a hand on each of their cheeks. "You both look so much like Father, now that you're all grown up."

"Nesrin," Talon began, his voice wavering as he put his hands on my shoulders. "I'm *so sorry* we couldn't protect you. So sorry we failed you and didn't get you out. So sorry—"

I hugged him tightly, cutting him off. "I know you tried. Kas told me." I pulled Pendor into the hug too, tears rolling unchecked down my face. "You were so brave to bring our king to safety. I always wanted to tell you."

"We were so afraid you'd—"

"My apologies for interrupting, King Talon," a soldier said from the tent opening, "but the King of Boekam calls for you and Prince Pendor."

I smiled softly. "King Talon. I like it."

Talon chuckled and hugged me again while nodding to the man. "I hate that we're reuniting under these circumstances. But I'll see you soon for our adventure."

I hugged Pendor. "Take care of yourself. I didn't get you back just to lose you again"

"I'll be fine, Nes, don't worry!" He hugged me again, and they both walked away.

I found Kas sitting not far outside the tent beside his father and brothers in deep discussion around a campfire. He stood up when he saw me and held his hand out as I approached.

"Nesrin, this is my father, Velarch Oh, and my brothers, Princes Darior and Berem."

The brothers heartily greeted me and shook my hand then stepped back to defer to their father. I thought I would be cowed by meeting him, but this was the man who sent his young son against his will into a monastery. I held his gaze and my head high, daring him to disrespect me or Kas's decisions.

But the velarch stood and reached his hand to me too, clasping it in both of his and looking me directly in the eye. "Kasper tells me you're responsible for bringing him home safely from the quest and rescuing him from the wreckage of the monastery. Thank you. I am forever in your debt."

"Your Majesty, I would do it a thousand times over. And thank you, most sincerely, to you and your family for saving my life when I was held hostage by my uncle." I looked at Kas and smiled. "Your son's caring heart and intelligence are beyond measure."

The velarch looked between us, smiling knowingly as one of Kas's brothers elbowed him, winking. "I agree, Princess Nesrin. But I have to excuse myself to prepare for battle." He laid his hand on Kas's shoulder. "Kasper, I'm very proud of you. May Hivathe bless and guide you on your mission, and..." he paused, glancing at me, "on your new path." He embraced his son and walked away with Kas's brothers.

Kas slipped his arm around my waist, and we walked off toward an area of camp where fewer people were congregated.

"It seems like that went well?"

"Very well. He apologized to me for sending me to the monastery, not only for taking away my freedom, but also for exposing me to the evil there that, until just now, he thought had killed me." He grew quiet for a moment, but I could tell he had more to say.

"And?" I prompted.

"And I told him I wasn't going to be a monk anymore. I told him," he said, placing his hands on my waist and pulling me close, "that I have fallen hopelessly in love with a Knight of the Trove, and I plan to make my own way in the world with her at my side. If she'll have me."

I laughed, wrapping my arms around his neck and getting lost again in his bright eyes and the feel of him in my arms. "If she'll have you? You'll never get away from her, now. She's far too in love with you, too."

His only response was to kiss me deeply and hold me tighter. Tomorrow would bring only bloodshed and heartache. But tonight I had my lover all to myself, and I would take full advantage.

CHAPTER TWENTY-EIGHT

THE BATTLE OF VADIC PLAINS

Only a few hours later, I stood on a high, well-protected hill grimly overlooking Vadic Plains. The morning skies were unnaturally dark. Seviiranth's metallic, choking smoke hung low in the air and carried to us on the sparse wind. I pulled my scarf across my lower face and hooked it.

Behind me, Forth and Kas sparred, becoming friends. Down below, the opposing armies approached each other quietly on the field with a neutral ground still between them, and battle tension hung low over us all. From our lines, I picked out Pendor at the forefront of a huge contingent of Aravenians, and Rav, who'd arrived an hour ago with a fresh contingent of over a hundred soldiers.

My mouth was dry, and a headache threatened to bloom against my temples. Kas came up and wrapped his arms around my waist from behind, lending me courage with his steadfast presence. But my whole body was stiff with dread.

Although the numbers were evenly matched between the opposing forces, a pallor of fear lay heavy over the allied forces, and a cocky air of superiority bolstered Galter's. We could hear it in the taunts and laughs they threw across the break in the plains that echoed up even to us even at this distance. We all knew Seviiranth would enter the fray at some point, and he would certainly not be on our side.

"What are they waiting for?" I asked.

Forth stepped beside us, resetting his weaponry. "Everyone wants to be in prime position before the leaders sound the call to engage." He frowned, looking over the enemy's army. "He's got a mess of an army. Mostly mercenaries, from the look of it."

While the allied forces of the kingdoms of the south and east made a pied human landscape of a multitude of kingdom colors, flags, and armor that was somehow cohesive in their differences, the majority of Galter's soldiers wore stateless, mismatched armor and carried no flags, the exception being contingents in colors from Naitar, Terinor, and traitorous Aravenians.

I entwined my fingers into Kas's. "I hope he already paid them. Maybe they'll skip out before the battle starts."

"Why are the archers setting up there?" Kas asked.

I lost the thread of conversation as Forth and Talon patiently answered Kas's questions and looked past them to where Ady sat nearby, vigilantly scanning the skies. To the general dismay of the human leaders, she'd been adamant that she wouldn't enter the battle until Seviiranth appeared. She'd need all of her fire, magic, and energy to keep him occupied while our special force broke into the palace, and the last thing she wanted to do was fight humans.

She winked at me. *They seem to be forming a tight friendship.*

One side of my mouth quirked up. *It's nice, isn't it?*

Indeed. It may help Kas move into a lay life to have friends in it already.

The men shared a quiet laugh, about what I didn't know. And although I welcomed their kinship, the mission we were about to go on had my stomach in knots. We planned to enter the palace through the sewer where my mother had been murdered before my eyes. And nothing could prepare me for that.

Suddenly the opposing forces marched forward. Trumpets and shouts arose on the plain, and the two armies sprang into action, running toward each other at full speed. Forth crouched at the edge of the hill, as if he too wanted to be on that battlefield running toward glory or death. But I was glad he wasn't. I wished no one was. I wrapped my arms around Kas's waist and watched the fighting below.

If I hadn't watched my mother be murdered, this battle would have been the worst thing I'd ever seen. Even from our distance, the clanging of swords, the cracking of bones and slashing of flesh met my ears. Before long, the smell of the battlefield carnage reached me, too.

The next hour dragged by. The four of us and our force protection all paced and crouched, shouted and called each other's attention to different points of the battlefield—Pendor advancing there, Rav capturing an enemy catapult. But Ady sat still and watchful through it all, seemingly not focused on the battle, even though she tracked everything with her dark eyes. It was a hideous dance, each side gaining ground then losing it, pushing forward here, retreating or redirecting there. I constantly sought Pendor in the tumult, saying prayers that my brother would be spared.

But they were really doing it. The allied forces were slowly gaining ground, gaining weapons on the field. But did their progress matter at all? At the base of our hill, Rav led his contingent against a battalion in Naitar's colors. Even from this height I could see him laughing. Cocky. I hoped it wasn't the pride before the fall.

A massive white dragon burst out of the back halls of the palace, splintering the roof and shaking the earth. I fell to the ground with the others—the armies, everyone. And as Kas helped me to my feet, my eyes sought Seviiranth where he hovered, black and green feathers fluttering against his white scales.

Both armies were in disarray, still fighting, but most still getting to their feet. The white dragon landed on the plains, scattering Galter's forces in terror as he landed amid the carnage, roaring. A green mist clung around him, and it crept out toward the allied army.

Ady bristled beside me. She crouched like a massive black tiger about to tear her enemy apart.

"Ady, wait! How will we know when to go?" I asked her.

She grinned wickedly, her black eyes glittering. "On my word. And Nesrin." Her head leaned toward me, head feathers dancing. "My love and Hivathe's love goes with you. But be careful, and protect your consort at all costs."

My cheeks heated as all three men smiled at me. "My what?"

"Kas. He's your consort, isn't he?"

Thank the gods she didn't say *lover*. "We haven't put labels on it or anything. But yes?"

Ady grinned all her teeth at me and pounced into the sky.

Seviiranth was massive, easily five to ten feet taller than Ady. He moved his great head this way and that, hissing and taking stock of the armies arrayed against him, and his deadly green mist seeped more thickly across the ground toward the allies.

I rubbed the engravings on the enchanted vambrace I'd gotten from Ady's blessed armor. The four of us and our thirty protective soldiers got pieces of it, but not everyone had. Many outright refused to take something infused with dragon magic. But as Seviiranth's green enchantment drifted across the ground like an unwholesome fog, I wondered if they regretted it.

Hundreds of soldiers stopped in their tracks, shaking their heads or screaming, looking around like they didn't know where they were or what was happening. Some fought the air, some turned on their friends-in-arms. One took his own life, falling onto his sword. I turned away in horror.

The white dragon roared. I wasn't foolish enough to look directly into his eyes, but even peripherally I could see they were a pale, poisonous green, like the leaves of an ill plant about to die. He radiated evil and dread like a palpable energy in the air. I wrapped my arm into Kas's, trying to warm my cold fingers and weighted chest as I watched my beloved benefactor fly toward him.

Ady landed amid the chaos in the allied lines, and she sent a cloud of burgundy vapor through them, which cut but did not overpower Seviiranth's green.

He turned his great head and watched her land. "Adydorrstea." His deep voice, beguiling and mocking, made all the hairs on the back of my neck stand up. I clutched Kas tighter, and he clutched me back. It took all my willpower to keep my feet rooted, to not run away.

Ady merely smiled, her head high and her black eyes narrowed. She tilted her slender neck—seductively? And she spoke to Seviiranth in her wind chime voice. "Hello, lover,"

Kas's eyes met mine, reflected my surprise.

Seviiranth's laugh was even more terrifying than his roar.

"That can't be good," Forth said.

Kas gripped my hand tightly. "Is this the distraction?"

"Not yet. But *I'm* distracted," I muttered, all my senses tuned to the high-stakes drama unfolding before us.

"*Lover*," Seviiranth mocked. "Is that what we were, my dear Ady, so many eons ago? You seduced me, had my drakelings, and then helped trap me in that infernal iron casket."

Ady *tsked*. "You always were a smooth thing, but we both know that's not how things happened."

"To be honest, darling," Seviiranth said with no warmth in his voice, "I thought you died trying to defeat me. I *mourned* for you."

Ady blasted fire into the sky. "Do *not*," she roared, "*do not* cheapen my mourning with your lies. You tried to kill me and our children. I trusted you, Sev, implicitly. You signed the humans' treaty. You swore we'd keep to our principality and treat the humans with respect. But you turned on them. You turned on all of us, even your own drakelings."

"Talon, our cue's coming," I told him. "I can feel it." My brother and Forth pulled Kas and me into position, and our protective force closed around us. My heart raced, and my legs felt weak. I wanted to grab Kas's hand and make a run for it, away from the fighting.

But he grabbed mine first and whispered in my ear, "We're going to make it, love. I know it." We shared a frightened kiss as Seviiranth ranted.

"Humans are ephemeral wastes of skin. They come into the world pale and mewling like vermin, and they leave it desecrated and covered with their own filth. Who cares that I broke my word to humans? They live about as long and as well as flies. Watch! If you breathe on them wrong, they die." Seviiranth blew white fire sparked through with green onto a group of his own side's soldiers, burning them until nothing was left but charred bones and armor.

"Stop it," Ady commanded. "Only a soulless worm like you would take advantage of those weaker and smaller than you."

Get ready, Nesrin, Ady spoke to me. I parroted it to the others.

Just then a man in the enemy's ranks hollered and ran toward Ady with his sword out and at the head of a platoon. Even at this distance, I recognized Ashur. My hand tightened on my sword, and Kas's tightened on my waist. Ady turned toward the sound, bemused.

"Ah, Prince Ashur, so lovely to see you again," she purred. Before anyone could react, she stretched her slender neck out and crunched Ashur up in her mighty jaws, her teeth sinking into his flesh. Knocking his platoon aside with one swipe of her ferocious claws, she shot her sparking fire through Ashur's body in an inferno that ended with her spitting out his bones, then spitting again.

"Disgusting as your morals, Sev."

Seviiranth roared and blasted a flame at Ady so hot that even I could feel its heat. Both dragons pounced into the air, crashing into each other in a terrifying mangle of talons and teeth, screeching and fire, and both armies, which had largely stood rapt while Seviiranth and Ady spoke, burst into battle again.

Now!

"Go!" I yelled.

We ran down the hill inside our moving wall of soldiers. The first line peeled off as soon as we hit the plain. The second line wore thin within the next hundred feet. As I ran, I spared a fearful glance into the sky. The dragons were like cats fighting, growling, hissing, scratching, and biting, but a hundred times more frightening and spectacular. Over and over, Ady's burgundy flames met his white ones. Feathers drifted down onto the battlefield, black, green, burgundy, and white.

Nearly our entire protective force was lost or waylaid by the time we reached the lower palace walls, and the enemy started breaking their way through. I could barely spare a thought for Kas and the others fighting alongside me.

Talon and Forth reached the sewer gates first and, with our soldiers, took out the small force protecting them, creating a small area before the gates free of fighting. A horrible screeching echoed down from the air, and Ady and Seviiranth slammed down, rattling the ground under our feet in a graceless crash of bleeding limbs and torn wings.

Ady righted herself as she skidded across the battlefield, her talons digging furrows upon the earth. Her bright red blood dripped down her neck, and she crooked one of her wings at an unnatural angle.

"Ady!" I cried out, clinging to the gate I should have been running through.

Forth grabbed my arm. "There's no time." He tried to pull me away into the maw of the sewer.

"Let her be!" Kas shouted above the din, placing one hand on Forth and the other on me. He stood beside me in solidarity. "C'mon Ady," he breathed.

Seviiranth crowed a horrible, cacophonous shriek of victory, then...he melted. He melted, and in his place now stood a tall, powerfully built man with pale white skin, his long black hair streaked with white and green. He wore an elegant black suit that in no way concealed the powerful muscles rippling beneath. He smiled at Ady, and I felt his terrible beauty to my soul. He was magnificent and completely irredeemable.

I stared, open-mouthed. Dragons could become humans? My gaze zipped to Ady.

She reared up and flapped her wings. "No more foreplay, Sev? You never could last very long." She reared again, and as she came down, she melted too, until standing in her place was the most shockingly beautiful woman I had ever seen.

I gasped. Kas and Forth gasped. Where my friend and protector had been now stood a statuesque woman, well-muscled and proud. Her perfectly smooth skin was as black as her black-night scales, and her gloriously curly black hair was streaked with burgundy. She wore a dark burgundy leather corset and pants with black boots, and in her powerful hands were tightly wound, tri-bladed swords, their serpentine twists glinting in the fires that burned between her and Seviiranth.

"Gods you're gorgeous when you're angry." Seviiranth's voice was velvet, his deathly green eyes devouring her beauty. "I haven't had companionship for hundreds of years. What if we left these ants to their petty problems and made another set of drakelings?"

A cold, dangerous smile lit Ady's face. She was a force of nature, impossibly beautiful and unyielding. I stood staring at her in open-mouthed shock when the beating of multiple sets of dragon wings echoed down from the sky.

"Believe me," Ady said, her smile twisting, "the drakelings we had are *more* than enough to tear you into pieces smaller than your tiny dick."

Three dragons broke through the low, virulent clouds and formed a semicircle around Ady. As each of their claws touched land, what could only be her children transformed into stunning humans.

A green and black dragon became a gorgeous man with skin as black as Ady's and hair as white as the streaks in Seviiranth's. White tribal tattoos curled up his massive arms. The second, gold and burgundy, melted into a fiercely dazzling human with aurulent skin, burgundy hair edged with green, and shifting brown and yellow eyes as if they were made of fire.

The last to land was the most sublime. A black dragon with swirling white marks in her scales transformed into a stunning woman with hair black and iridescent as a raven's wings. In human form, her white swirls splashed across her brown skin in the same glorious swirls.

Forth let out a little sigh at the last dragon's shifting, and I tore my eyes away from the spectacle that had the attention of both armies to see sheer rapture on his face. I backhanded him on his chest, shaken from my own amazement. "Let's go."

We tore into the sewer tunnels, the scene of all my nightmares. Explosions shook the ground, and the piercing, screeching cacophony of Ady and her children fighting Seviiranth echoed against the walls. I ran with the others through the filthy waters, each step disturbing the malignant green fog hanging low to the ground. I ran until I hit the spot.

The very spot where my mother was murdered.

There was no marker, no indication that a woman, a queen beloved by all, especially her daughter, had died in the darkness there. I froze while the others formed a wall around me and fought the small force that ran at us from the next checkpoint. Kas fought beside me, spilling blood, protecting me with the weapons I'd given him.

But I couldn't move. Blood on the stone. Every time I blinked, I saw her. I saw the whole nightmare. Was it Seviiranth's mist or my own trauma? The sounds of fighting around me were muffled as if they were in another room altogether, and the edges of my vision tinged black and green. I shut my eyes against it.

"Nesrin!" Talon yelled. "We have to go! Come on!"

I heard him distantly through the fog in my head, but my body wouldn't move. More yelling. But with my eyes closed, the past and present merged together, and all I could see was my mother's face, her hands reaching for me in the dark.

"Nesrin," Kas said.

Two hands grasped my face. A loving kiss against my forehead.

I opened my eyes and saw him before me, his face close to mine, his eyes worried. I closed my eyes again, watching my mother in the darkness, watching her protracted suffering just to see her face one more time.

"Mama," I choked.

"Nesrin," Kas said again. His forehead pressed close to mine. "Nesrin, open your eyes."

"No," I shook my head. "She needs me. I can stop them." I felt my hands raise up on their own, my weapons poised.

Kas's lips pressed against mine. Hard. He wrapped his arms around me, and my arms went slack, my sword and dagger clanging against the stone. I opened my eyes and saw his face up to mine, eyes closed with passion as he kissed me. I blinked, and only darkness lay behind my eyelids. I kissed him back and pulled away, really seeing him.

"Not the time, lovebirds!" Forth yelled, finishing off a soldier with a sword.

I saw the world around me again. Forth and five of our force were behind us, guarding our backs, and Talon was ahead at a passage, six men at his side. I reclaimed Baney and my Andumaran dagger, nodded once at Kas, and we took off running toward Talon.

We fought our way through palace guards at each choke point in the maze of underground passages until the remaining pieces of our force protection were lost or had peeled back to watch our rear.

When we burst through the door to the bottom floor of the palace, I almost didn't recognize my once-home. My family's great hall had been neglected and defiled into disarray, its dirty floor cracked and missing tiles, all ornament gone, likely sold to finance Galter's wars. It didn't matter. The zinging, crashing noises of the dragons' fight outside the palace spurred me on.

The great hall was blessedly not well-guarded. We took down the three men we met, then my brother and I led the others up the wide staircase to the second floor, tearing down hallways and other staircases, up and up toward the highest battlement.

In an upper hallway, I paused to get my bearings with Kas, Talon, and Forth at my back. Nothing looked like it used to, and by Talon's confused expression, he too was having trouble reconciling memories with the palace we were in. Doors had been sealed over and new ones cut into the stone. A whole stairway that should've been *right there* was simply missing. And the green mist churned and swirled over everything, the torn rugs, the piles of refuse against the wall.

No one was here, but instinct made me slow to a stalking pace.

Footsteps and scraping metal behind me. I spun around. Galter and eight guards emerged from a side passage at the opposite end of the hall.

"Talon and Nesrin," he said, and my heart fell to my feet.

CHAPTER TWENTY-NINE

WE HAVE YOUR BACK

My legs trembled, and I froze back into the panic that had haunted my late childhood. Galter had barely changed. Still gaunt with dark circles under his eyes, though they had more lines. Still combing his greasy pale brown hair back flat against his white scalp, his eyes shaped like father's but without a soul. I could only stare at him, falling back into each moment of cruelty he and I shared: killing my mother. Driving an arrow through my calf while I called her name, reaching for her as she bled out on the filthy ground. He was the devil who defiled our statues of Hivathe and took concubines two and three times as young as himself. The monster who took away my childhood innocence without ever laying a hand on me, forcing me to watch special guests in his harem, making the ladies instruct me on how to please men so I would be worth more money when he sold me away.

Kas and the others arrayed themselves on either side of me, yet I still felt alone, a child again, fear-laced nausea roiling my gut. In a flash of dragon fire, Galter looked like the wolf that chased me in my nightmares. I shook my head, and in the corner of my eye, I saw Kas look at me. He placed his hand on my shoulder.

"Your reign of horrors is over, Galter," Talon said. "I'm here for my kingdom, and to make you pay for your crimes."

Talon spoke with such authority and controlled anger that with the green mist addling my mind, I had to blink twice to be sure it wasn't really my father come back from the grave to settle accounts with his brother.

Galter laughed, whirling his sword. "What a pathetic, motley group of so-called warriors you've assembled. A dandy prince, a monk who barely knows how to hold his sword, my dragon whore niece, and you. You couldn't stand up to me years ago, and you can't do it now." He tossed his head toward us. "Kill them."

Talon and Forth rushed Galter and his guards, waking me into action. I ran with them as Kas kept close beside me, and I sliced Baney across the belly of a guard. Galter slunk behind his men, his sword out, watchful but not brave enough to engage. I took a second man out while a third met his end on Kas's sword.

But the green-black mist pooled in my vision, and made me dizzy. I fought to stay above the pull of Seviiranth's magic. I engaged another guard, breaking his sword off with Baney, then my vision clouded.

I'm in the tunnels. My legs pump in the cold, filthy water that splashes me with every footfall. But still the howling beasts snap at my heels.

My vision cleared. The guard thrust at my gut with his broken-off sword, and I reflexively blocked it, barely in time. I hacked the sword out of his hand then dove Baney into his chest.

As I planted my foot into his gut to pull Baney out, my vision clouded again.

I'm falling, and the wolves converge on me, snarling and biting, rending my flesh with sharp teeth and wicked claws, howling their victory.

But no, I was still standing. I whirled around to see Talon and Forth fighting the two remaining guards. But they were slowing down, making unskilled thrusts and giving too much ground, crying out and protecting themselves as if they were suddenly afraid.

The biggest wolf tears his sharp teeth into my chest. His jaws tighten around my heart, and my body seizes. A bell rings from somewhere, and the wolf looks up, his maw dripping red with my blood. I spiral away into the spirit world with the other ghosts, and the bell rings again. It pulls me sharply back into my half-eaten body. I scream from excruciating pain, begging for death, scrambling for my own dagger to end it myself.

The bell resolves into a voice. *Nesrin, do not succumb.*

Lucid again—the screaming was mine. Ady's panicked voice chimed my name inside my head. I looked down at my chest, but my heart was still securely covered by armor and skin. No gaping wound. No guards were advancing on me. Talon and Forth were nearly through them. Kas?

Behind me. He was too near Galter, holding his hand to his head and screaming, like there was a monster in his brain he couldn't get out. He swung his sword wildly, unseeing. In my dragon-hallucinating brain, Galter's face shifted into a snarling wolf as he drove his dagger into Kas below his chainmail, and Kas crumpled to the ground.

Strong hands grabbed me from behind as I screamed, watching Kas's blood spill onto the floor. Too many footsteps behind me. Weapons clanged, and my sword was yanked from my hand as I screamed for him. My Kas.

A foot kicked to my gut threw me against the wall, and my head snapped back, pain sparking as it hit the wall. I collapsed beside Talon, and the now-shattered bottle of Ady's medicine I had stashed in my bandolier soaked through my clothes. My brother was curled up on the floor, unmoving and covered in his own blood and bruises. Just like that night so many years ago. So much like it. Was I living it for the first time or living it again?

"Talon!" I sobbed.

"He's alive, Nesrin." Forth's fingers were pressed to Talon's neck. His dirty blond hair, matted with his blood, stuck to his ruddy face, but his blue eyes were bright.

"He's alive," Forth repeated. "His pulse is strong."

But Kas—Kas wasn't moving.

I hiccupped back a sob and tried not to let my interest in him catch Galter's attention. He stood behind six fresh guards whose swords were pointed at us. But I couldn't stop staring to see if Kas's chest was moving. I couldn't tell with him lying in the mist, couldn't even see his face. He'd fallen with it turned away. My heart felt punctured, as if my barbed bolo was wrapped tight around it, and I was bleeding out. Like the palace was about to fall and crush me.

Forth laid a hand on my shoulder, his voice thick with pain. "I'm so sorry, Nesrin."

"No." I cut him off, still staring at Kas for a sign of life. I licked my swollen lip, increasing the metallic tang of my own blood in my mouth. He couldn't be gone. Not now. Not after all we fought through to be together.

"Couldn't take the dragon's magic, could you?" Galter's mocking voice cut through my nerves. But Forth and I didn't reply. All I could focus on was how to get to Kas, how to find a weakness I could take advantage of.

"Emperor Velius!" A man burst into the hallway from the stairs. Galter turned and conferred quietly with the man just as a thundering crash against the palace wall behind us showered stone dust down on us. Even the guards cringed.

One more crash like that. If I timed it right…I caught Forth's attention and gestured with my eyes to the wall that had shaken, then to the guards. He shook his head with wide eyes.

"I don't know what you hoped to accomplish," Galter said, dismissing his man and returning his attention to me. "But I'm glad you came. I gave up a long time ago trying to use you to my advantage, but once my dragon kills your dragons, I can sell you off to the highest bidder. Well, the next highest now that Ashur's met his end."

Talon stirred, groaning. I reached for him and helped him sit up, as if there was anything else I could do for him without Ady's medicine. He seemed alert now, despite the blood oozing from a gash on his head.

"You're not touching my sister," he growled. "And you're not keeping my throne."

Galter ignored him and spoke to me. "And you've delivered your brother to me. I'd wondered when he'd come skulking back."

"Why do you hate us so much?" I choked out. I couldn't bring myself to ask as a child, but I needed to know.

"My brother never should've had the throne. I told my father so, and he banned me from my own home. Just as I warned him, my brother was weak like our parents. Osric betrayed our ancestors, worshiping a weak *female* goddess, trying to keep peace with those who should be under our rule."

"Don't you dare say his name again," I hissed.

Galter smirked. "*Osric* raised weak children who'd be content, like him, to let the ignorant nations around them live in their own stupidity. They waste their resources when they should be given over for Aravenian use. Some of them don't even bother to learn our language, keeping worn-out traditions and worshiping a fictitious pantheon. They're like sheep who've gone astray. But I'll free them from their backwardness, their superstitious monasteries." He turned halfway around and looked down at Kas with contempt. "People who think I'm a monster clearly have never looked into the eyes of a priest before."

Ramdar. Where was he?

"I'm going to kill you," Talon said, "I'll kill you, and I'll enjoy it."

Galter laughed. "Ridiculous to make threats now. One word to my dragon, and you'll be throwing yourselves on your own swords."

A couple of men came up from the stairwell, and Galter gestured to Kas and the dead guards. "Take them down to the furnace."

Baney was against the opposite wall, past the armed men. But my sheer fury would get me there, and vengeance would be my shield. I shifted my feet flat to the floor, but Talon grabbed my arm, holding me back from what would surely have been my last action.

"Does that make you angry, little Nesrin?"

I could barely hear Galter over the roaring in my ears. My hands were fists as the men went to Kas. They lifted him, and halfway across the room, they dropped him. Kas flopped grotesquely, but gave no reaction.

The room spun, and my stomach lurched, hot tears down my face. Kas was gone. He'd been far too good for this world. It should've been me instead. Talon's arm went around my shoulder. Forth's hand landed on my other shoulder in solidarity as the men picked Kas's body up again and carried him down the stairs.

Kas was gone.

Talon and Forth pulled me to my feet, and the guards stepped forward, snapping Galter's attention back to us.

Forth glowered at him. "You can't have Nesrin, and we're not dying on the ground."

"No matter what happens to us," Talon said, "the true allies of Araven will never stop fighting you."

Their bravado seemed worthless. We had no weapons. We were outnumbered and injured. And Kas was dead. Nothing else mattered. All my hope and joy burned down to cinders and rebirthed into cold, virulent anger. I had nothing left to give the world but hell.

Another crash against the outer wall shook the palace like a tremor. I launched myself at the waists of the two guards before me. Shouting echoed beside me as Forth and Talon followed suit. And as I toppled the two guards with my momentum, I fumbled a dagger from the belt of the one on my right, slashing it across his throat. I barely registered his spurting blood as my hand arced to bury the knife in the chest of the guard on my left, who wasn't fast enough with his sword. I gutted him from chest to navel.

Before I could get to my feet, someone slammed into me from the side, knocking me to the ground. I cocked my dagger hand back to strike, but he held my arm.

"It's me!" Forth shouted in my ear, pulling me to my feet as Galter yanked his sword free from where I'd been seconds before. Five guards were dead on the ground, and the last one faltered under the punishing flurry of Talon's powerful fists.

Galter retreated toward the stairs, his advantage rapidly deteriorating. But Forth beat him to the stairwell, herding him back into the room where he took off toward another door. Forth landed two thrown knives—one in Galter's leg and one in his back. My uncle stumbled to the floor.

Talon reached Galter first, stepping on his wrist and wresting his sword away. Forth was on him in an instant, his sword under Galter's throat.

"What should we do with you?" Forth's menacing eyes were bright and determined, vigilantly watching his prey as I came up beside them.

"I'll slash your throat for what you did to us," Talon growled.

Forth shook his head. "The decision's yours, Your Majesty, but I think death's too good for him. He has to pay for his crimes."

I barely heard their words over the pounding of my heart in my ears. Even in defeat, Galter leered at me. Did he know he'd killed the man I loved? Poisoned my past and stole my future?

Talon's dark eyes studied Galter as he contemplated his fate. After a moment, he crossed the room and picked his sword up from our pile of confiscated weapons.

"Talon," Forth said warily. "This is your first decision as king. I want to disembowel him for what he did to your family, to everyone. But you have to ask yourself if that's the king you are. Who you want to be."

"Do it!" Galter cried, his face twisted with anger, eyes darting toward the stairs as if he hoped to buy time for salvation.

I walked to the landing and looked down. No one was coming to save him. Cold certainly came into my heart, and I smiled at my uncle.

He didn't like that. His frown shifted into mockery as he went back to egging my brother on. "You won't start your reign with my blood on your hands. You're too weak for that."

My hands no longer shook. I collected Baney and began to rearm myself with all my smaller weapons. Andumaran twisting sword in its special sheath. Every bandolier knife securely stowed. None of these tools of death had kept Kas safe. I hadn't kept him safe. Hadn't done my job. But I had one more job to do, and I sure as hell was going to get it done.

"It isn't weakness to choose mercy. I'm not like you, Galter." Talon spoke forcefully, but still his sword was out. He pressed it against our uncle's neck.

I joined my brother and my friend in their very important tableau before the Emperor of Araven.

Forth backed away. "I defer to the true House of Araven. Whatever you decide, I'll support you."

Talon's sword arm wavered, the struggle written on his face. I wasn't sure how I felt about Forth's advice. Talon had every right to take Galter's life. No one would fault him for it, and many would praise him. Were all the horrors Galter had put us through going through my brother's mind? And what would win out? Self-righteousness? Pity? Vengeance?

Talon shook his head. "He's not worth it." He pulled his sword back and sheathed it, backing away.

"I told you. Just a coward like your father," Galter spat.

Forth kept his eyes on Galter but placed his hand on Talon's shoulder. "For what it's worth, I think you're doing the right thing. Kings who forge their kingdom in blood live on borrowed time."

But that was bullshit. What about all the soldiers and guards we killed on the way to Galter? Their lives didn't matter? That was blood on Talon's hands. On all our hands. Some of them were Aravenians. What about all the people Galter had enslaved and killed? Why was it noble to spare only the life of the one man responsible for all those deaths?

No. I would not abide.

A warrior cry to Hivathe on my lips, I swung Baney straight through Galter's neck. The men jumped back, and as his head rolled, I plunged my sword so hard through his heart that I skewered him to the stone wall. And twisted it.

I pulled Baney back out and coolly tossed my braid behind my back. "I'm no king, and I don't give a shit what people think."

CHAPTER THIRTY

UNRAVELING

Talon and Forth gaped at me, looking between me and the beheaded asshole.

I wiped Galter's blood off my sword onto a ruined tapestry. Mother always hated it, anyway. My hands trembled, and my stomach lurched, but *he* was gone. I sheathed Baney and stepped back, furious, avenged, and cold.

His death would end the war. Well—it wouldn't stop Seviiranth. That monster had his own agenda, and now we didn't have Kas's expertise to save us. But it just might break apart Galter's army. All I'd have to do was hold his head aloft from the window, show his paid fighters their money well had run dry.

But I couldn't move. Couldn't think beyond my loss of Kas, my love and my life.

"Nesrin," Talon started gently. "I..."

A commotion on the stairs made us all whirl around, training our swords toward the unknown. A guard breached the stair landing, running from someone. He stopped short when he saw us, and the man chasing him ran him through from behind with a sword.

The guard toppled, revealing Kas behind him. Kas, very much alive and pulling his sword from the man's back with murder in his eyes.

I gasped, my heart thudding into life again. Kas whirled as three more guards burst onto the landing behind him. Forth reacted first, with Talon right behind him. The three of them made short work of their foes, then Kas turned to me.

I met his blue eyes, the certainty in them like a lighthouse in the fog. I ran and launched myself at him, jumping into his arms and wrapping my legs around his waist.

"*Ow-ow-ow!*" He caught me and put me down, holding me so tightly I could barely breathe.

"Gods, Kas, I thought you were dead," I sobbed.

He buried kisses in my neck. "I told you, my love, we're going to make it, with a little help from Ady's medicine." His eyes shifted toward Galter's body, and he gagged as he turned back to me. "Who finished him?"

"I did," I whispered, tears filling my vision. Would he think less of me for my brutal act? "I thought he killed you, and—"

"Oh, my love." He pulled me close and kissed my head. "You did what you had to do. That must've been so hard."

"It was *shockingly* easy. I'd do it again."

He pulled back and caught my eyes. "He had to be stopped. You did the right thing."

Forth's hands clapped both of our backs. "Well done, both of you, but we're still in a war, and you're needed on the battlement."

With great difficulty, I pulled free of Kas's arms. Footsteps clomped on the stairs below, and a dragon body collided with the wall of the palace, shivering the stones down to the foundation. Chunks of wall and wood crashed into the room, covering us with dust as Kas pulled me tight into him and shielded me from the wreckage.

In the unnatural quiet that followed, I looked past Kas to the hole in the wall in which a black and white dragon body was partially embedded, just for a moment, until she pushed off and flew back into the fray. Lightning struck just outside the hole, and I pulled away from Kas. Forth was right.

"Go on, Nes," Talon said to me. "We've got your back." He nodded at me, his eyes fierce and proud. Forth rose his sword in salute with a wink and a smile, then they both ran past us toward the stairs.

And I believed my brother. They did have my back.

"This way." I grabbed Kas's hand, and we ran up the last curving stairwell, pushing open the heavy wooden door to the highest battlement. The outside air was heavy with a metallic mix of dragons' smoke. One breath sent Kas and I into hacking coughs. I pulled my scarf across my face, and Kas buried his nose and mouth into the sleeve of his black tunic. We crouched low behind the merlons of the battlement, the discordant clamor of the fighting choking the air as thickly as the smoke.

"Now what?" Kas shouted above the din.

"We wait?"

I peered out through a crenel. The battles still raged on the ground and in the air beside us. Ady and her son were still in human form, casting spells at a still-human Seviiranth who held firm in a green protective halo of magic. Their hexes against him streaked across the field like black and gold lightning and moved the air like the hands of warring gods.

But Seviiranth's defenses deflected all but the most powerful spells. Ady threw a zigzagging strike that briefly penetrated his shell, but he crouched, gathered strength, and pushed it back out of his halo.

Ady's two airborne children dove at him with their talons out, but Seviiranth was too powerful and too quick. He threw an arm back as if in pain, but quickly cast it forward again, and with it shots of magic sent both assailants spiraling in different directions across the sky.

One of them barreled toward where Kas and I crouched behind the wall. We ducked just in time as her black and white body busted through the merlon above our heads, showering us with the wreckage. She slid across the stone as her talons clawed for purchase, then righted herself. The moment her eyes met mine, she turned her head and shrieked. Her fire drenched a brazier not twenty feet from us, and it went up like a bonfire.

Kas threw himself across me as the searing heat reached us, and when her roar quieted, I looked over his shoulder in time to see her shapeshift into the exceptionally beautiful woman with the white swirls on her skin. Calanddria. She moved like a jaguar in her sleek black suede corset and pants and carried a leather satchel slung over one bare shoulder.

"Finally!" Her soft voice, like the tinkling of narrow bells, was a spell in itself.

I stared at her, open-mouthed and unable to speak as she walked toward us past the brazier where her white fire burned with black sparks.

She pulled Seviiranth's iron casket from her satchel, presenting it to us. I started to fall into her mesmerizing grass-green eyes before I remembered Ady's warnings—never look into the eyes of an unfamiliar dragon.

"Mother says you need this." Calanddria crouched to place the casket into Kas's waiting hands, then she stood to go.

"Calanddria, wait!" I called, finally finding my voice. "What do we do with it?"

She smiled radiantly. "Put it in my fire and read the spells." She crouched low, then sprang into the air in a spin, shifting back into her dragon form and taking flight. She rejoined the fray with breathtaking ferocity.

Kas pulled me to my feet and toward the brazier. Waves of heat emanated from the white flames, and a black spark shot through it like lightning, bringing with it a punishing blast of cold. Kas stepped boldly toward it and tipped the casket carefully over the edge, shielding his body from the temperature extremes.

When the casket touched the flames, they crackled blue and green. He stepped back and took my hand in his. I shielded my eyes against the painful brightness, and within seconds, a stream of glowing letters, pictographs, and symbols shivered into existence and faded within the fire. Shivered in, then faded again in two revolutions, the same pattern repeating.

Kas watched them, squinting against the light, but said nothing.

"Can you read it?" I called out, barely able to hear my voice over the roaring wind that arose from nowhere and tore at my hair and clothes.

"It's three dead languages entwined. But..." His face crumpled. He shook his head, and his shoulders slumped.

I clutched his arm. "What's wrong?"

"We need someone else," he choked out. "She won't answer me."

"Who won't answer you?"

He released my hand and fell to his knees, tears slipping down his face. "Hivathe." The name only formed on his lips, the sound carried away on the wind. His shoulders hunched, and he buried his face in his hands.

I knelt beside him and put my face close to his, my arms around his neck.

He breathed raggedly. "The spell's an invocation to Hivathe. But I broke all my vows. After Ari...all the men I killed today. You and me."

I buried my face beside his ear. "Of course she will! She chose you every step of the way. She led you, protected you, brought you through so much to get to this moment. She loves you. Don't you see how much like her you are? Hivathe never *chooses* violence, but she's our fiercest protector, and you are mine. Today, you're all of ours. And Mother of Wisdom, Kas, She has a lover. Why can't you?" His lips quirked up a little. "You've done nothing to destroy Her faith in you. Don't lose your faith in Her."

His hands dropped, and his eyes met mine. "Do you really believe that?"

"I do." I smoothed a fluttering lock of hair from his face. "With all my heart."

He took my face in his hands and kissed me. For a moment nothing existed but his warm lips on mine, his devotion pulling me closer and closer into him.

Then he pulled away and smiled. Still kneeling, he gripped one of my hands in his and raised his other to the sky. His bright eyes were intent on the repeating sequence of the spell.

"*Drakkon prater sackiret Seviiranth ethravor Hivathe,*" he read. "*Drakkon prater sackiret Seviiranth ethravor Hivathe.*" He repeated it, shouting, glancing at me and nodding, encouraging me to join him.

I copied his gesture and chanted the ancient, entwined words as I heard him speak them, our voices carrying away with the rising wind. We spoke them again, and again, and our words grew louder with every repetition.

An unholy shriek arose from far below the tower, and a loud pop reverberated through my bones and cracked the stones of the castle. Kas and I lurched, nearly falling over, but we clung to each other and kept chanting. The screeching crescendoed until Seviiranth's human form tumbled swiftly up in the air past the battlement wall Calanddria had crashed through. Wrapped in blue and green lightning, his face contorted with wailing. Four dragons shot up like arrows, circling the tower.

Seviiranth writhed and twisted in an ever-increasing sphere of clouds and lightning. I blinked my right eye, trying to relieve the pain of the wind and heat, and I saw his human form. I blinked my left eye and saw only the great white dragon. With both eyes open, the illusion twisted my gut and made the world spin. Still,

I met Kas word for word, chanting through the sharp pain that threatened to split my head apart.

The two Seviiranths merged into one white dragon, and then the cloud of lightning struck inwardly, over and over, compressing him more with each barrage of strikes. His dragon maw contorted with shrieking, and his green eyes rolled in his head. But the vice-like grip of the cloud only increased as we chanted, diminishing him until he was no larger than a child's plaything. Then the world exploded.

Waves of sound blasted Kas and I backwards to the stones, ripping away our voices and shaking the palace to its very foundations. The world illuminated to white, and my ears rang to the point of pain.

I struggled up on my elbows, shielding my eyes against the sudden clear daylight. Kas and I pulled into each other as the four dragons touched down and shifted gracefully into their human forms. Ady rushed forward first, her exquisite human form all I could look at—my fierce benefactor. Her dark eyes, nearly the same as in dragon form, caught mine as she stalked the still, small figure of a green and white dragon on the ground, no larger than a squat toad.

"Where's Galter?" she asked, scooping the figure up carefully with both hands. Her voice in that stranger's body was a mystery, ringing differently in the air as when a familiar note on a lute is plucked on a harp.

"I killed him."

Ady winked at me. "That's my girl. Where's Ramdar?"

"We haven't seen him," Kas replied.

Ady hissed then turned to meet Calanddria, who'd rushed to the thinly smoking brazier and retrieved the open, empty iron casket, bringing it to her mother. Ady placed the reduced, inanimate Seviiranth inside.

"Wait!" I stumbled to my feet, digging the bronze vial with the piece of kavhavji vine out of a buttoned pocket. "I understand you have history with him, but...he's dangerous." I presented the vial to her. "And I hear maybe this can actually defeat him. For good."

Ady's brows wrinkled in a quickly-suppressed second of resigned pain. She nodded and lifted her hands, onto which slender golden gloves appeared as if woven by the air. "You were right to end Galter. Deferring great evil to another time only curses future generations. I will learn from your example, Nesrin."

Ady unscrewed the vial and pulled out the vine and leaf. She curled the vine tightly around Seviiranth, scratching the figure's skin with the sharp leaf in several places. Wherever the leaves scratched, dark stains of an inky, dark green spread across Seviiranth's white scales until he was wholly that color. Pieces of his body began to calve off until there was nothing left of him but heaps of blackened green dust.

Ady closed the casket, dissolving the gloves and the vial, and she ran a finger alongside the gap of the lid to seal it. "Now it is a different kind of casket," she said softly. She handed it to Calanddria and laid her hand on her shoulder. "You know what to do, my beautiful daughter."

Calanddria kissed her mother's cheek and shot into the sky, transforming instantly back into her dragon form and flying away opposite of the setting sun.

"Etrril, go with her," she said to her golden-skinned child with the eyes like flame, and they took off after Calanddria. "Rannatos, lend your magic to the healing tents." Her son with the tattoos and white hair nodded, leaping into the sky and into his dragon form as he banked and dove toward the ground. "Nesrin, where's Galter's body? I'll bring it down to help stop the fighting."

I explained its location. "But you might only need to bring the head."

She grinned, showing all her teeth. "I love a good tyrant be-heading. Excellent work, Nesrin. Kas, thank you. The moment I saw your sexy eyes, I knew your dragon heritage could activate the spells." She burst into the air, slipping into her dragon form and circling around the tower.

"Your what?" I said to Kas as he exclaimed, "My what?"

We stared at each other for a beat, mouths agape.

"You have dragon heritage?" I asked.

He shook his head with wide eyes. "She wasn't serious, was she?"

"Why is she like this?" That was a conversation we were *definitely* having at another time. But right now, the sound of the battlefield below had shifted and quieted some. Kas and I went to the edge of the battlement.

"I don't think they'll need much convincing to lay down their arms," Kas said, directing my attention with a pointed finger toward the west. "The mercenaries are already leaving in droves."

Sure enough, whole contingents of soldiers were deserting the battlefield. Large swaths laid down weapons, kneeling with their hands held high. But the fighting continued in small pockets around the red and black flags of the Naitarian host.

Ady circled to the front of the palace and landed near the thickest fighting, holding Galter's head aloft from her claws. "Galter Velius is dead!" she boomed in her loud dragon voice. "Killed by the hand of the true Princess of Araven, Nesrin, knight of my trove!"

"She didn't have to tell the whole world." I shrank into Kas, and he tucked his arm around me.

"She's proud of you. Your name should be legend."

But she wasn't finished. "And the white dragon was defeated," Ady continued, "by Princess Nesrin's lover, Prince Kasper of Veytia!"

I buried my face in Kas's chest and groaned while he chuckled and kissed the top of my head. "Maybe that'll cut down on the number of suitors who come looking for you."

"Gods, I hope so." I looked for the result of Ady's words and wasn't disappointed. Group by group, those still fighting laid down their arms and surrendered, even the Naitarians.

I wrapped my arms around Kas's middle. We were watching history unfold, a long, dark era come to an end. I'd lived over half my life under Galter's threats. Who was I in the world without his terror? How would we all move forward when it was so hard at this moment to even process that we *could*?

My head spun, thoughts drifting across the broken palace, the carnage on the ground, to Crokar and Drebia and all the places harmed by Galter's greed and blood lust.

Chanting began on the ground. I followed its source back to Prince Forth who stood on a crumbling palace wall: *Long live King Talon! Long live Princess Nesrin! Long live Prince Pendor.* The allied nations on the field soon picked up the cry, even some of the captive Aravenians. The crowds went blurry as my eyes filled with tears. All these people I didn't know were on our side. All these people came to set my family, my nation, and our world free.

I didn't know how we'd all move forward, but maybe it was enough to start believing that we could. And that we had each other's backs.

Kas kissed the top of my head, holding me tighter. We watched the horrors that Galter had wrought begin to unravel into peace.

CHAPTER THIRTY-ONE

EPILOGUE: SOMEONE AT THE GATE

Winter was colder than I remembered, probably because I missed sleeping beside Kas.

Reluctantly throwing off my heavy blankets, I gently scratched the white fluff under Pooka's neck and slid my feet into warm slippers. The magpie perch was sadly empty of both bird and letter. I thought for sure Kas would've written me back by now, especially after I sent him Forth's desperate-sounding letter about the rumor of another set of caskets. But then Kas's letters had been a little evasive lately.

A glance at the stained-glass window above my bed showed a white drift of snow sparkling in the late morning sun.

I pulled myself up and out of bed, not that there was much reason to. In fact, I seemed to be getting up later and later, especially as Kas kept putting off coming back. Those three nights he stayed in the trove after the Battle of Vadic Plains were the best of my life—relaxing, making love, and just existing together. But the past month and a half was wearing on me.

I stretched my back every which way and ran my finger along the clothing selections hanging in my closet, past the usual training and archiving tunics and pants to a comfortable dress I'd picked up in Kesna when Pendor and I attended Javid's wedding last month. It may not have differed much from my night clothes, but it *wasn't* night clothes. And it didn't matter what I wore, anyway. Kas wasn't coming back today.

He'd been delaying his return to me for a few weeks now, something always coming up. First it was the banquet his father threw in his honor, which to be fair he invited me to, but I'd already presented myself in Kesna for Javid's wedding and couldn't have made it in time, anyway. Then it was the dedication of the new temple, and after that it was the wedding of two former monks at which he was the best man. Another time it was Ady's son, Rannatos, holding him up, offering to meet with Kas and his family to discuss the dragon heritage none of them had known about and provide sparse information about the potential for magic everyone in the velarch's line had. Especially Kas, whose latent magic was responsible for trapping the white dragon.

These were all perfectly legitimate reasons not to come home. But besides the banquet, each time I'd offered to come to Veytia instead, Kas turned me down: he'd be coming back soon, so there was no reason for me to leave the trove.

His letters hadn't changed their loving and optimistic wording, full of "you are my sun" and "here's a picture I painted of you." I knew better than to think he wasn't being genuine with me, but in some ways, I felt like I was still standing on the battlements wondering what the future would hold.

I thought we both wanted to be together. I certainly wanted to. But what if he didn't anymore? I was too chicken shit to ask. Maybe he was just continuing to be "what you see is what you get" Kas, but his repeated delays begged the question, did he even want to come back?

I combed my hair at my vanity but didn't bother with a braid. At least it was clean, and I'd even let Ady talk me into painting my nails and toenails last night. I think she was trying to cheer me up, knowing how Kas's absence saddened me. But as I walked to the dining hall, I noticed she wasn't here this morning, either.

She was probably off with Rav and his first mate Dax again on a humanitarian mission to Crokar. Most of the time she forgot to tell me, and then a magpie would arrive with a hastily scrawled missive a few days into her absence.

At least I had the trove's kitchen magic to whip up my favorite—cinnamon rolls with icing. I'd discovered some romance novels in the corner of Ady's library, and they were keeping me company during my quiet mealtimes.

Of course I didn't expect Kas to drop all his important work in Veytia just because I missed him. The whole world had big and difficult tasks to do in repairing what Galter had damaged and rebuilding what he'd destroyed. Even I'd been busy helping Talon settle into a temporary house of government, helping him and Pendor find stewards and generals we could trust and trying to help those who'd been displaced.

But...didn't Kas miss me?

What if being a full Veytian prince was more exciting than he thought it would be? A beautiful young prince like himself surely had legions of stunning women fawning over him every day. Kas wouldn't be unfaithful, but would he forget how we made each other feel? Would his caring for me fade?

I pushed my roll away, half eaten. Once again, my appetite was lost in imagining some beautiful woman catching his eye. He was free from the monastery. Surely the last thing he wanted was to be trapped in a dragon's trove just for me. I wasn't even all that special.

But I would leave my trove for him. I really would uproot my life and move to Veytia just to be with him.

My heart thudded. I was going to Veytia. Right now.

I stood up, pushed my chair in, and strode purposely toward my chambers, but the front gate bell clanged. It still automatically aroused in me the worst feelings of irritation. Surely there wasn't a prince left in the twenty-seven nations of Mellora who didn't know I should be left in peace.

I growled and changed direction, stomping all the way to the front balcony where the bell was ringing *again*. Whoever was down there leaning on the doorbell was about to get a dragon-sized tongue-lashing from one very short, pissed-off human woman.

I grabbed a cloak off the hook at the base of the human stairs to the balcony and whirled it around my shoulders, not breaking my angry steps. Within moments, the frigid air hit me like a wall, dusting my hair and clothes with snowflakes.

I looked out over the edge and yelled. "I'M NOT—"

Ady sat on her haunches in the snow at the back of the clearing like an overgrown cat, a huge, black wing extended over Talon, Pendor, Kas's brother Berem, and a beautiful woman who could only be Kas's mother—all smiling at me. And on the ground in front of the gate was Kas.

My heart nearly jumped out of my chest. My Kas, with his brilliant smile, more beautiful than ever in a thick, black cloak, his long curls pulled back as he always did when we traveled. Riding atop Balembar, with his sparkling blue eyes fixed on me and a bright red bouquet of wild roses in his hand.

"Good afternoon," he said formally, his dear voice echoing through the clearing and making my eyes tear up. "My name is Prince Kasper of Veytia, and I come, with the blessings of both of our families, to ask for the hand of Princess Nesrin of Araven, Knight of the Trove."

I ran down from the pedestal, unlocked the gate, ran down the outer steps, yelling at the trove magic to let down the final set of metal steps that would bring me straight to him.

"Kas!" Slippers and all, I ran out into the snow to find him dismounted, standing in a fine black suit that accentuated his tall, lean body in all the best ways. We practically collided as I jumped up into his arms and wrapped my legs around his waist through the slits of my skirt. He laughed, spinning me around, stopping only to kiss me.

But then he set me on my feet and took a step back, holding my hands in his. "Nesrin, you set me free. You brought joy to my life when I didn't have any. Your love has been a compass needle pointing me toward the home of my heart, my purpose, and my faith. I told you on our first night together that I wanted to walk life's paths by your side, to wake up every morning entangled in your arms, and be there for you in your happiness and sorrow." He pulled a tiny wooden box from inside a pocket in his cloak and dropped to one knee. "I want to do all that and more as your husband."

He opened the box and revealed a delicate golden ring of twisting wild rose vines with an emerald set in the middle. "Nesrin, will you be my wife, my partner in all things?"

I wiped my face and dropped to my knees in the snow, just to be nearer to him. "Yes," I said into those bright eyes. "Yes Kas, nothing on this earth would make me happier."

He slipped the ring on my finger and kissed me as Ady crowed and shot fire into the sky and our families cheered. They surrounded us in hugs and exclamations, and before I could barely meet Kas's mother properly, Ady whooshed into human form and pushed her way in front of me.

"Nesrin," she said, her eyes sliding to Kas. "I have been informed that I've been remiss in showing you affection, so please accept this arm-encircling as a long-overdue sign of my abiding love for you." Ady pulled me into her embrace. *I told him emeralds are your favorite. And thank the Goddess you said yes, or that poor man would never have recovered.*

I laughed, my arms around the neck of my beautiful, fierce guardian. *You did wonderfully, as always.*

And I was right about Sexy Eyes.

I never doubted you for a minute.

All lies. Nevertheless, I appreciate you saying so.

She pulled away with a dazzling smile and shifted back into her dragon form. With a swipe of her formidable foreclaw, the trove magic brought trunks from a wagon I hadn't seen at the back of the clearing sailing over our heads and up over the balcony into the trove. She called on our family members to follow her, and they all began climbing the set of steps I'd run down just a few moments before.

Kas wrapped his cloak around me and lifted me into his arms, my legs around his waist. "I missed you so much," he said, his blue eyes twinkling in the bright daylight as he studied my face.

I adjusted a curl that had fallen into his beautiful eyes. "I missed you too. What took you so long to come home, and why didn't you write me? I was starting to worry you'd forgotten about me."

His eyebrows rose. "Forget about you? Every day was torture, waiting for our families' schedules to align, waiting on your ring—that jeweler was happy to be rid of me checking on him twenty times a day. I didn't write much because I was worried I'd tell you *everything*, and I didn't want to ruin the surprise."

"I was definitely surprised." I tossed my head toward the trove. "How long are we having guests?"

"Just tonight. And then we should probably get on the road to help Forth as soon as possible, right? He doesn't sound like himself, and I'm a little worried about him. But also, the sooner we go, the sooner we can come home."

I bit my lip. "About that...where do you see us making our home?"

"The trove, I assumed. Honestly, Nesrin, wherever you are is my home." He buried his face against my neck, his mouth warm against my pulse, his kisses there making my toes curl.

"You know," I murmured, "they're all experiencing a dragon's trove for the first time. They won't miss us for an hour."

"Or two," he agreed, kissing me.

"Or three. You're staying here with me tonight too, aren't you?"

His eyebrows raised. "Nesrin, my love, I'm staying with you forever."

Did you enjoy *The Knight of the Trove*? Check out this witchy scifi romance novel, also by Holly Rose:

Hurtling away from Earth is the worst time to learn that your ship's being held together with duct tape and spells, but astroengineer Gemma Abadie is a witch with a bigger problem—and no, it's not the whole-Earth evacuation thing. It's her dangerous, hidden magic she's planning to have removed when she reaches humanity's new planet. But she didn't count on steaming up the engine room of the dilapidated space hotel with witchy Beck Breaux, who believes Gemma's his meant-to-be.

Want a free ebook? Get the prequel chapter to *Until the Stars Fall*, "Two Days to Liftoff," when you sign up for my newsletter! Scan the QR code below to get started.

About Holly Rose

Holly Rose is the author of *Until the Stars Fall* (Book 1 in the Interstellar Witches series) and *The Knight of the Trove* (Book 1 of The Knights of Mellora series). She lives in Louisiana with her husband, two sons, and two cats, Loki and Olivia Newton John. She eats too much cheese fries, loves stargazing, and writes books about people falling in love.

For the latest information about my books, find me online.

https://linktr.ee/writerhollyrose

Thank you for reading!

★ ★ ★ ★ ★

I hope you enjoyed
The Knight of the Trove. Please
consider leaving a review on social
media, Goodreads, and/or your
preferred retailer to help others
find my books!

COMING IN 2025

THE KNIGHTS OF MELLORA
2

THE PRINCE
OF THE
OUTSIDERS

Prince Forth is plagued by nightmares in which he's a creature of decay and darkness with an appetite for violent murder. To prove to himself he's not a monster, he heads north to where his dreams take place to reimprison the beast he's convinced has been unbound.

Still mourning her sister's brutal slaying, Princess Knight Sorcha initially distrusts the outsider prince, but soon the two are bound by a love neither of their families will approve of. Obligated to take her sister's place as heir, Sorcha must work with Forth to unite the squabbling provinces and stop the savage beast roaming her kingdom before its bloodthirsty legions extinguish the living world.

ACKNOWLEDGEMENTS

This book would not have been possible without my Sarah rooting for me and this book since day one. She goes first because she tells me that *The Knight of the Trove* is her favorite of my books, and she has been an unending source of encouragement, silliness, and friendship. May you have an eternal supply of purse/pocket cheese, napping on the beach vacations, goblin cave retreats, and winning lottery tickets.

Thank you to Brett, Luke, and Jack for your constant encouragement, even when I swear, yet again, that I mean it this time and I'm done writing. You know I'm not, and you kindly never call me on it. I love you all so much. My sweet boys, never give up on your dreams.

Thank you to Schoener A., Schoener M., Joe, Carl, Cole, Lee, Wes, Ryan, and Barbara, who always believe in and support me. Thank you for asking about my writing, showing up to my signings, helping monetarily when I need it the most, and in general making my indie career possible. I love you all!

Special thanks to Kalla, one of my staunchest supporters and dearest friends; to Kahlan, who I know has read this book several times and never fails to shine her sunshiney encouragement on me; to Marina who has been with several revisions of several books and is always there for me; to Darcy whose feedback and friendship mean more than I can say; to Olivia who always so kindly builds me up and makes me feel like I'm kicking ass (when the secret is I'm barely keeping my head above water); to Skyla for all your support and kindness; and to all the HQties who have supported me in my bookish and life endeavors. I love you all so much!

Thank you, my dearest Owls for taking me into your fine, funny, irreverent, and loving nest. I can't express how much I appreciate your friendship, fellowship, and special charts (you know which ones). Y'all are absolutely delightful, and I love you.

And finally, thanks to the Newk's Eatery (which ain't dere no more) and Burgersmith near where I used to work for your hospitality, multifarious cheese distribution systems, and Diet Coke. The first draft of this book was mostly written in 30-minute sprints on my lunch break and on weekend mornings with unlimited McDonald's Diet Coke (and it always tastes best there).

STAR SIREN PRESS